Susan Shwartz was born on New Year's Eve, 1949, in Ohio in the American Midwest. She became interested in fantasy and science fiction when she was seven years old, and a cousin gave her Edith Hamilton's *Mythology*; her father, who grew up on *Planet Stories*, subsequently introduced her to Robert Heinlein, Andre Norton and Isaac Asimov's books at about the time that Alan Shepard went up in his suborbital flight – and she has been hooked ever since.

She was educated in Massachusetts, at Mount Holyoke College. During that time she spent two summers on exchange, living in Trinity College, Oxford, in a programme sponsored by the University of Massachusetts. She studied Shakespeare, paleography and medieval romance. She went on to take a Ph.D. at Harvard University, and was a specialist in Arthurian romance.

For three years she taught at Ithaca College, in upstate New York. Then, wanting a business career and to be closer to the New York publishing scene, she moved to New York City. After switching jobs too many times, she went to work at BEA Associates, an investment firm for which she manages electronic mail, a few other databases, personnel functions, and much of the in-house communications. She daily courts overwork with a heavy writing schedule, too. She has written a good deal of non-fiction for major US papers, and is also active on the circuit of fantasy and SF conventions.

Susan Shwartz has written a mass of short stories (many of which have been mentioned in the Nebula Preliminary Ballot), numerous articles and essays (including an essay on 'Women in Science Fiction' for the *New York Times Book Review* and an article on Jean Auel for *Vogue*), and several science fiction novels, including *White Wing* with Shariann Lewitt, writing as 'Gordon Kendall'.

Byzantium's Crown is the first book in a trilogy. The subsequent books, *The Woman of Flowers* and *Queen's Blade*, will also be published in Pan.

Susan Shwartz

Byzantium's Crown

Volume One in the
Heirs to Byzantium
trilogy

Pan Original
Pan Books London and Sydney

First published in Great Britain 1987 by
Pan Books Ltd, Cavaye Place, London SW10 9PG
9 8 7 6 5 4 3 2 1
© Susan Shwartz 1987
ISBN 0 330 29789 9
Photoset by Rowland Phototypesetting Ltd,
Bury St Edmunds, Suffolk
Printed in Great Britain by
Richard Clay Ltd, Bungay, Suffolk

Acknowledgements

I am deeply indebted to Jean Lorrah and Judith Segal for long hours of anguished plotting. I must also thank Lohr Miller, of Zachary, Louisiana, tactician and military historian, Andre Norton for her enthusiastic encouragement, and the late Tim Daniels and Gillian FitzGerald for technical discussions and story conferences. A special thanks goes to John Irvine, Shariann Lewitt, and friends.

I would also like to express my gratitude to the Thomas J. Watson Library of the Metropolitan Museum of Fine Arts in New York City, for its research facilities.

A note on sources: many of the rituals described in this book are adapted from *The Egyptian Book of the Dead*, transliterated and transcribed by E. A. Wallis Budge (Dover, 1967), and R. T. Rundle Clark's *Myth and Symbol in Ancient Egypt* (Thames and Hudson, 1978). H. R. Ellis Davidson's *The Viking Road to Byzantium* (Allen & Unwin, 1976) helped with the Varangians. And, of course, the poems of William Butler Yeats and Charles Williams have always made Byzantium glow with a magic light for me. Though Lionel Casson's *The Ancient Mariners* (Macmillan, 1959) and Ian Heath's *Byzantine Armies 886–1118* (Osprey, 1979) were my guides, I am the only person responsible for strayings – even in an alternative time-line in which magic works – from historical semi-accuracy.

That is no country for old men. The young
In one another's arms, birds in the trees
– Those dying generations – at their song.
The salmon-falls, the mackerel-crowded seas,
Fish, flesh, or fowl, commend all summer long
Whatever is begotten, born, and dies.
Caught in that sensual music all neglect
Monuments of unageing intellect.

An aged man is but a paltry thing,
A tattered coat upon a stick, unless
Soul clap its hands and sing, and louder sing
For every tatter in its mortal dress,
Nor is there singing school but studying
Monuments of its own magnificence;
And therefore I have sailed the seas and come
To the holy city of Byzantium.

William Butler Yeats
'Sailing to Byzantium'

Chapter One

Night rioters had set half the trees that bordered the Golden Horn ablaze. Their reflections burned in the dark water. Muffling himself in his hooded cloak, Marric slipped up from the harbour and glided from shadow to shadow. The burning trees turned the defensive walls of Byzantium, its port stews, and the façades of its temples and great houses, into eerie hell.

Hardly a prince's homecoming, he thought. *There should be guards turned out on the quay, waiting with a horse bridled in pearls to bring me to the palace.* But Alexa, Marric's sister, had sent for him in secret, so he had returned stealthily from Cherson, the rebellious Crimean province to which his father's orders had banished him.

He had no escort. His closest companions had mostly been the younger officers who were too closely watched to join him on this venture. He had not bothered to woo their superiors, preferring to ride free on the plains, wild as the Huns who relished his fits of bravery and temper, to winning the experienced generals' favour or pacifying the rebellious province. What he really would have liked was to ride to World's End, like his ancestor Alexander. But he had realized that his father, the Emperor, would never permit that.

Before he moved on, Marric glanced about. Though he wore a plain uniform, he carried himself with the arrogance of the imperial line. Alexa had always compared him to the dusky jungle cats that the imperial beastmasters had never let the imperial heirs caress. But they had been balked of little else. Far too little, reproved the white-robed Osiris priests, who were always reproving him. 'Heads of beasts and men's bodies,' his favourite tutor, a witty cynic, had jeered to console him. 'Use your reason, Prince.' Applying reason to the state-religion of his line, Marric had learned to be sceptical of all but scepticism itself. How the shaven-skulls had frowned!

He sniffed the air, his senses as keen as those of the great cats. Jealously, he surveyed his city. It was too greatly changed.

Shouts echoed against the massive walls of the great buildings and down the twisted streets. Here, in the lower city, the air was heavy with the smells of smoke, of rancid food, and the more pungent reeks of feral cats and more feral people. A file of fair-haired men passed, hands prudently near their axes: the northern fighters who served the Emperors as a personal guard. 'Miklagard', they called the great city Antony and divine Cleopatra had fortified. Home. Joy to be back made the flaming tree to Marric's right dance in a rainbow haze as his eyes filled.

Ever since the Emperor Alexander had departed beyond the Horizon, Marric had not seen his home. His father . . . last time Marric had seen him, they had quarrelled again.

'Almost thirty, and with less sense than a recruit!' Alexander had shouted. 'I grant you've the skills of a free-captain, but you've got to learn that there's more to a prince than leading armies – and not leading them well.'

'I've never lost a battle!' Marric knew he was as fine a strategist as he was a soldier, but his father's criticism stung. Alexander had a serenity Marric knew he lacked.

'Nor won a conquered people's hearts. Go and learn how. Cherson will school you. Or kill you.'

He saw the Consort Irene look triumphant at the sentence of banishment: the more chance for her son, Ctesiphon, especially if Marric died in Cherson.

The province had tried to kill him and, gods knew, come close enough. Gradually it came to obey him as the lion does its trainer, as long as hand, voice and courage hold firm. Just as he began to take pride in this achievement, he had had word of his father's death. His sister's messenger said that Irene had been out of the city when Alexander died. Other informants hinted darker things. But unless the priests' mumblings were right, Marric's father would never see how his son had turned out.

Like his father and the Macedonian who had begun their line, half man and half god, Marric's name was Alexander. And it was also Antony, after the cosmocrator who had defeated the Roman Octavian at Actium and built the imperial city as a link between East and West. But Marric was what he called himself. He had taken the name from an ancestor who had travelled to Byzantium

10

from the West. Unlike Alexander or Antony, no one knew much of the first Marric, so no one would reproach him with his ancestor's steadfastness . . . especially the priests.

'Irene!' Some imbecile bellowed a paean to the usurper. Other drunken voices took it up, and the streets rang with shouts. 'Irene! Hail, Empress!'

Marric's lips skinned back from his teeth. Call Irene an empress? She was a usurper, had never been much more than a Syrian consort jumped up to wife – a woman of scant royalty and scanter character. It was Marric who should rule in Byzantium, with his sister Alexa, in the old ways of the Pharaohs.

'Irene!' Three more men roistered by. Each wore a strip of cloth tied round his arm. So Irene had been bribing the charioteers again, had she? Judging from appearances, the Hippodrome riots had got worse. Irene's tactics might make herself acceptable to the mob. Glut them with wine and winning horses, and they would howl her name until their throats closed. Was that all there was to it? Spies said no. But he had no proof.

A body lay in the gutter. As Marric approached, a figure slipped away into an alley. Moonlight glinted off the stained dagger the assassin clutched in a mittened paw. The man was quite dead. Great bloodstains rusted the fine dalmatic from which all the gems had been slashed. Beneath the bloodstains was the richness of murex dye. About the corpse's arm was still twisted a strip of blue cloth. Blue, for the aristocratic faction who wagered fortunes on the chariots, and never really trusted Alexander's upstart second wife. So that feud was heating up, too?

Avoiding the too-well-lit Mese, Byzantium's great central avenue, Marric moved down a sidestreet. He spared a glance for the Arch of Antony. Beyond it lay the palace and the twin temples of Isis and Osiris. Beyond them was the necropolis. *Forgive me, my father, for neglecting your tomb. When I rule as Horus-on-Earth, it shall not lack for offerings.*

He could still hear his father's voice. 'You fancy yourself an Achilles. But let me tell you, my son, Achilles would have made a poor king!'

A shadow whipped across his path into a gateway.

'Ho!' Two men ran towards him, cursing and shouting. 'You there!' They carried their yard-long swords unsheathed.

'You! Have you seen a greyrobe lurking hereabouts?'

'One of the accursed Druids,' explained the second, an evil-visaged man with the elaborate diction of a drunk. 'We ought to kennel them all or send them back into the damned Mists that spawned them.'

Like the Varangian mercenaries, the Druids came from the West. Many in the Empire, which worshipped Isis and Osiris and their imperial manifestations on earth, regarded Druids as spies. But Marric's father had always let them live unmolested, deeming them harmless fortune-tellers who eked out a living by snaring coppers from foolish adolescents. That odd tolerance was the only softness his father had ever shown. He had been, Marric remembered with pride and sorrow, all Hellene, as proud of his rationality as he had been of his titles: Horus, Pharaoh, Emperor. He had made the precarious compromise between faith and reason. Marric, relentlessly secular, could not fit himself into the same mould.

Upon a time, his father had told him, the title Horus had enabled the Emperors to summon up powers. But in these latter years the rites which turned an emperor into semi-divine priest–king had fallen into abeyance. *And just as well. Father would never have trusted me with such secrets, and he'd have been right.* For Marric, power was a matter of armies, weapons and plotting, not the sonorous murmurs of priests in bare cells. They knew nothing of real life, life on the knife's edge. Much as Marric had hated Cherson, the danger had exhilarated him. Twice he had nearly been murdered like his two predecessors. Once a friend had saved him, once a courtesan.

Intent on their Druid-hunt, the soldiers ran on ahead.

'I know you're there,' Marric called to the shadows. 'Come out, or I'll shout for the Watch.'

What could a grey-robed, decrepit old fraud do to him anyway?

The Druid slipped from the battered doorway of a shrine. Above the entry-way a fish – two crudely joined semicircles – had been scratched in the stucco. Another of the mystery cults with which the lower city seethed. Judging from that sign, the old spy had been skulking under the shelter of a cult most hostile to all the others. Marric shrugged disdainfully. Barbarian priests were even less acceptable to him than the priests of Osiris. They were less clean.

The Druid's hood fell back. He was an old man. Unlike the priests of the Great Temple, who went shaven-skulled as they had since the Mysteries had been revealed at Heliopolis, he had long hair and a longer beard. But his eyes were as keen as those of the High Priest himself, and as critical. Marric was used to such criticism.

'May the Goddess light your way,' the Druid began, courteously enough.

'Save it!' Marric snapped. More guardsmen half-ran, half-lurched down the street. Several turned towards the Temple of Min. Its gate swung wide and Marric's nose tingled from the scents of incense and musk. Min's worship would definitely distract those men, but their fellows would not miss Marric or the Druid.

'Get back.' He didn't wait to see himself obeyed, but strode forward, one hand on his swordhilt.

'What are you men doing here?' He had had the tone of command since he was a boy.

'Chasing Druids, sir,' one man answered. His companion muttered, 'Who is this man, anyhow? Don't tell him a damn thing.'

'On such a night, and with the Greens winning?' Marric asked. He deliberately roughened his own speech to approximate the men's common accents. Then he laughed easily, sensually. 'Your friends had the right idea. They headed straight for the Temple of Min.'

From his earliest days in military training, Marric had had a gift for anticipating events. Now he fixed his will and his hopes on the Temple of Min, where bright torches seemed to make the erotic paintings daubed on the walls dance suggestively.

The temple's gate opened again. A woman ran out. She caromed off one of the soldiers into Marric's arms. In the lurid shadows of the burning trees, Marric saw her painted eyes and nipples. She was one of Min's sacred prostitutes – and his rescuer.

He laughed again and kissed her, tasting wine and the heaviness of opium as his lips parted hers. Unbidden, his senses stirred, and he bent her body back until she staggered and clung to him for support. His hand cupped her breast, smoothed with oil of myrrh, and for a weak moment Marric burned to abandon the Druid, to forget all missions, and compel this woman to fulfil what her mouth and hands promised. Then he freed himself. He had already made promises to two women: to Irene, a promise of retribution; to Alexa, his loyalty.

'I'm changing your game,' he told the soldiers. 'Catch!' He spun the woman towards them. Ironically, he bowed to her as she wound her arms sinuously about the waist of the nearest soldier. 'I am sure these soldiers will . . . amuse you. Unless, of course, they prefer Druid-hunts—' another laugh, knife-edged to slash at their male pride, completed his statement. What half-drunken guard – or what prince – would not choose to rut rather than pursue an elusive old Druid? And if Alexa had not summoned him . . .

After the group staggered past, Marric beckoned the Druid out of hiding.

'If you want to live . . .'

'I would be on the next ship for the Isles of the Mists,' the Druid agreed. 'But where the Goddess' will is concerned, what is my life? So I remain here. By her will, it seems I owe you a debt. So listen to me, *Prince*—'

Marric grasped the man's robe at the throat. A ropy veined hand restrained him. Marric raised his eyebrows: people had claimed that the Druids were strong.

'Look you.' He turned, and Marric turned with him. 'Beware the port.'

He raised hands over a scummy puddle in the alley. Were there accomplices lurking hereabouts? Marric doubted it, following the Druid as if this were foreordained.

The Druid's lips moved in an invocation to the Goddess who Marric had always called Isis. Intrigued, he bent forward to watch; conjury had always amused him. Surely he saw figures forming in the oil on the water.

'By the Hawk!' The priests of Osiris required extensive prepa-rations before they scried, but this shabby barbarian performed

14

his magic in the streets. Clear images were indeed forming: a man and a woman fighting, light erupting from her form; a body falling, another man, bleeding from many wounds, swinging a blade, then falling near a ship.

A prowling cat wailed in the background, and Marric's dark hair roughened with fear. Was the woman who fell Alexa? Ever since their mother had departed beyond the Horizon so shortly after Alexa's birth, his father had kept the imperial heirs close at his side. With Alexander dead, there were few people Marric trusted, and only one whom he loved beyond all measure. Even as a child, he had been so devoted to Alexa that her servants had called him the imperial nurse. Alexa – the thought of his sister-queen waiting for him – had sustained him in his exile. When he gained the throne from Irene, Alexa would share the Empire with him as Isis – sister, wife and mother of the next heir.

'Is that your sister, Prince?' the Druid chuckled. 'Love is like fire. It nourishes or burns. Take care that yours, and hers, are of the right kind.'

All right, so the Druid recognized him. All these tricksters had craft, Aillel, a Varangian he had taken a fancy to in childhood, had told him. But Marric resented his loose talk about Alexa.

'The gods rot you!' He raised a lean fist, and the Druid chuckled again.

'I show you but a possible future, and you would wreak the very vengeance on me that you denied those soldiers?'

Thwarted by the fearless old man, Marric stepped back. Actually, there had been no real insult given. Except for the vision. But the Druid would hardly babble that all over the stews. He glanced down at the puddle again. Tiny figures still struggled within the water. Now, guards were dragging the wounded man to lie across a horse. They rode towards a building that looked like a prison. It was all illusion. Marric brought his foot down on the puddle. He would not believe it.

'Prince, Prince, you scorn my warning because you are un-tested.'

Untested? What could the Druid know of the strain, the discipline and the pain Marric had suffered. The last strategos of

Cherson had been murdered by his own guard. The one before him had died, screaming, in a flux unlike any his physicians had ever seen. And the assassination attempt on Marric before Alexander's death had left him debating whether to invoke stark justice on the troops, or simply leave half the province's nobles without heirs. He had done neither, dimly aware that such choices represented an irrevocable step from law into tyranny.

And then the news had come of his father's death, Irene's seizure of the regency, and Alexa's summons. Marric's grief had been fresh and silent; his fears for Byzantium, left to Irene's slender, beringed hands, grew overwhelming. He had dallied far too long here, wasting time Alexa might need. She might be thinking him captured now . . . *just like the prince in the vision*.

Marric heard himself breathing harshly. Though he had never trembled before army or assassin, now he shook before a man thrice his age, an old man whose neck might be snapped by a single blow – assuming he allowed it to fall. Perhaps the Druid was referring to the great tests of centuries ago, in the days of the Pharaohs. But the gifts of healing, of power over fire, of summoning the Elder Gods, had fallen from Marric's line. Emperors were no longer initiates into the Mysteries, able to command divine powers . . . assuming they ever had been.

What I could do with such powers, Marric thought. *Gods* . . . His mouth twisted sardonically. After Alexander thought he was a god, he ran mad and died. No one was fit to be trusted with such gifts.

'You have your life,' Marric spoke at last. 'Leave me before I regret the gift.'

'My life is not yours to give, but the Goddess'. Let her bless you, Prince Marric.' The Druid raised a hand, sketched a sign which glowed blue-white in the fetid night air, and vanished down the dark street.

Marric shook his head. One sun-bronzed hand went to his throat where an amulet lay under the uniform he wore. No Osiris priest had ever read Marric that swiftly. Even they, he remembered, claimed to respect the Druids as supremely gifted prophets. If only half the stories were true, no wonder Druids wandered free in Byzantium.

This one knew too much. Marric toyed with hunting him down and silencing him. He smiled mirthlessly. How would he find him? Had the Druid even needed Marric's protection? He could easily believe that the old man had used it merely to deliver his warning.

Surely there had been a moment when the Druid could have killed Marric. He could still betray him. But something about the old man commanded his reluctant trust. He had no hope, now, but to be rash. He started off towards the palace again. Rats and the lights of burning trees danced together. Whores, beggars and guards reeled past, and Marric eluded them all.

Now he could smell the fragrances of the stalls of the perfumers by the palace walls. Here the streets widened and were kept immaculate. Up ahead loomed the portico of the Temple of Isis. Across from it was the Temple of Osiris, her husband and god-brother. Marric began to hear the music of fountains from within the walls.

Ahead was the gate. The Watch changed and soldiers marched back and forth. Marric was tempted to try to overhear the password. If only he had had more time, months even! He'd have ridden into Byzantium at the head of an army thirsting for Irene's blood.

There was no point in might-have-beens, Marric decided. Away from the state entrances, around the back, were trees he might climb, as he had done when making his first forbidden explorations into the city. Once again he would slip quietly into his home.

With his man's height and strength, the trees were easier to climb than he remembered. A leap brought him from the branches on to the wall, then down into the gardens. The moon shivered in the water of a flower-bordered pool. Marric nodded thanks to it, then set off towards the women's quarters.

In the shadows of the exquisite garden, behind a great fountain, Marric stood outside Alexa's suite. Its furnishings were rich: gilded, sleek-lined ebony, the backs of chairs and couches coiling up in smooth spirals, the feet clawed. Almost-sheer draperies, brought from the Silk Routes over deserts and mountains, blew back, revealing the girl who stood in the centre of the room as if she were on a stage.

Alexa's profile was as pale and cool as that of Isis portrayed on the mosaic she gazed at. Goddess and Princess shared a beauty that seemed fragile, and a pride that was anything but that. Except for Marric's sunburn and more prominent modelling of brow and jawline, Alexa's face resembled his. But where he was tall, she was tiny and very slight, the simple white robe she wore outlining her body as it fluttered in the night breeze. Her long dark hair, so much straighter and finer than his, flowed loose, bound only by a thin circlet of gemmed lotuses.

Her lips moved in a silent prayer to Isis, and to Osiris, who stood in his jewelled wrappings next to his Queen. But the patrons of Empire, as if ignoring the plight of their descendants, stared out into infinity.

'Goddess, grant it.' Alexa's voice drifted out to Marric. He started towards her from the shadows. Had she prayed for him? She turned and drew a filmy scarf about her slender shoulders, gazing out over the garden as if watching for someone. From her lips came a trilling sound.

Marric grinned. So the little vixen had remembered their old signals! He whistled softly and his sister's face lit with joy. They had never shared with anyone else the codes that had enabled them to dodge their tutors. Connivance started early in Byzantium. Marric stepped into the room and pushed his helmet from close-cropped, crisply waving hair.

Even though Alexa had been expecting him, she drew back at his sudden entrance. Her hand reached for a dagger with an emerald-set hilt, and she drew herself up to face him. *Fast reactions*, he noted with approval. *Good girl*.

He threw off his dark, coarse cloak.

'By our father who rules in glory, sister, it's truly me.' There was an unfamiliar tightening in his chest. He wanted to whoop, to pick Alexa up and whirl her about as he had done before that one loathed and soon-departed pedagogue had remarked that royal children should not behave so indecorously. Though he had reproved them but once, the memory of his disdain had inhibited them both thereafter. They had dosed him with senna for it and vowed never to forget.

'Marric?' Alexa held out a hand which shook. The poor little one, to have lived in such fear under Irene's rule! Then her green eyes blazed with recognition and joy, and she ran forward to throw herself into Marric's arms.

'Brother!' Her voice was shrill, and it broke. Though she had to stand on her toes to reach, she had her arms about his neck.

'Softly, little one,' Marric said, laughing a little shakily. 'Here now, sweetheart, rest easy, 'Lexa. Remember, I'm wearing armour; you'll bruise yourself.'

But Alexa burrowed closer into his embrace, no imperial princess now, but a young girl too-long forced into battle-readiness. Marric could feel her shivers in his own flesh. He wrapped his cape about her and made the soothing noises that he dimly remembered his mother using on a nightmare-ridden princeling. So short a time they had all been together! His mother's face was like Alexa's, yet more serene, with a strength that had enabled Antonia to conceal for too long her weakness after Alexa's birth. Even the priests could not help her. Her husband had never recovered from her death. First cousins, they had been brought up together from childhood as brother and sister: right hand and left of the same body. And then Alexander had married Irene. Granted, he did it only to secure peace from a brawling Syrian branch of the imperial family, but Marric, who adored his mother's memory, could not forget that the priests had not saved her, nor could he forgive his father.

Irene's son . . . had there ever been a time when Ctesiphon had cared for Marric and Alexa, when they had wanted to love him? What Marric remembered most clearly was the day Ctesiphon had jeered at Marric's outlandish western name.

'It's a barbarian name. Maybe you're not of divine Alexander's blood at all!'

'Father says it's a hero's name, the name of a warrior come out of the West. What do you know about the West, you greasy Levantine?'

'He's just saying that. Mother says that I'm the true Prince. One day I'll rule as Horus-on-Earth.'

'That's a filthy lie!'

Marric had knocked him down and Alexa had kicked him. Before their pedagogues could separate them, Ctesiphon had leapt at Marric, a woman's jewelled dagger in his hand. So, at age ten, Marric had had his first battle-scar from a brother's hand.

Alexa, her body relaxed in his cloak and protective hold, turned in Marric's arms. One fingertip traced the thin line, faint after twenty years, in the deep tan of Marric's neck.

'He still hates you,' she said. 'I didn't want to bring you into danger, but I had to see you, talk with you . . . *she* . . . Irene . . .'

'Come, is this how a princess acts? This is my home, not the camps of the Kutrigur Huns: *those* are dangerous. Did you know that in Cherson the last two governors before me were murdered? So I'm not afraid here. Besides, Alexa, you know that your fate is also mine. Whatever we face, we face together.' His words had a fine ring to them, and he meant every one. Once he was emperor, he would finally make his father proud of him.

Alexa nodded, freed herself, and walked over to a graceful table. She poured him wine from a flagon that lay half-buried in snow. 'Do you still like honey-cakes?' No trace of her earlier fear showed now. At least Irene had not been able to turn Alexa into a timid fawn, or her creature. The time Ctesiphon had attacked, Alexa had been the first to dab at the bleeding scratch with cloth torn from her own tunic. It had been precious cotton brought all the way from Hind, but that hadn't bothered her. She had been sick afterwards. Alexander had called her reactions hysterical courage, and spoken to her gravely of self-command.

As Alexa handed Marric the goblet, he saw a dancer's grace, the counterpart of his own warrior's training, in her movements. Brother and sister, sword and dagger. They would be well-matched in their dream of Empire.

Marric poured the libation for the gods, then saluted his sister more enthusiastically before he drank.

'Clever work, sister mine, getting that message to me. Not even my spies on Irene's spies found it out. How did you manage?'

Alexa drank and smiled. Colour flowed back into her face. 'Let us keep that as my secret, brother.'

20

More and more Marric approved of this sister of his. 'Has Irene told you anything of her plans?'

To his surprise, Alexa nodded her head, Yes. 'She watches me, Marric, and I hate it! You know what her eyes are like – deep green, slow poison. They drink your will.' Alexa dropped her head briefly, then forced herself to meet Marric's eyes again. 'And I have heard her speak *words . . .*'

Such study had always fascinated Alexa. Marric could believe that she might feel that Irene's delving into lost powers made her more dangerous.

'She uses Ctesiphon to make my life a continual misery. Ever since the harvest failed they both have been hinting that he and I should appear together in the temples and bless the Empire.'

That was Marric's privilege as rightful Emperor. He hissed with anger. 'The bastard presumes! I am father's eldest son, born in the porphyry chamber while Irene was little more than a concubine. *Our* mother, not Ctesiphon's, was the true Isis.'

'I told him, "Brother, Marric is your elder and my full sibling, Alexander's lawful heir," but he laughed and warned me that Cherson was full of strange fevers. I was afraid that he might . . .'

'I prefer Huns to that kind of game,' Marric said slowly. He had resented exile. Now he saw the sense in his father's decision.

Had Alexander known his second wife's capacity for betrayal? Pray Osiris, Ptah, and all the other gods, that he had never guessed how Irene had caressed his elder son with her eyes. Marric had been in his early twenties then, with a reputation that fully justified her interest, even were he not the royal heir. But perhaps Alexander had known: why else would he send Marric away and die without sending him a word? Or had he feared that Irene would seduce his son only to kill him?

'I think,' mused Alexa, 'that only the fact that Irene has no daughter has kept me alive this long. She needs a daughter . . . now she schemes for a marriage between herself and the Reaver-jarl of Jomsborg . . .'

'The city is dying!' Marric interrupted. 'I saw. It needs its proper rules right now. When I came up here the guards were

21

drunk and there were corpses in the gutter. That never happened when Father ruled. Alexa, have you told me everything? I don't think so.'

'I haven't,' she whispered. 'Ctesiphon sees what you do. That is why he presses for me to appear in the temples. I think, too, if the harvests continue to fail, that I might have to . . . for the Empire's well-being.' Then she burst out, 'Don't look at me! It's *my* realm, too! Father raised me to put it first. Do you think you're the only one who wants power?' Then she covered her face with both hands. He could barely hear her next words.

'And there's more, too. He leeches!' Alexa cried in a low, passionate voice. 'Since he came of age he has lounged about me until I fail to invent ways of dismissing him. Or Irene summons me and there he is, standing too close, touching me while she smiles. They watch me as if I were a crippled bird and they a cat!'

Marric slammed a fist down on the curved arm of his chair. Under level brows, his dark eyes flashed. Alexa and the Empire were his! 'If he apes Osiris, then let him look to his dam for an Isis!'

Alexa gasped. Her hand moved in a sign to avert punishment for blasphemy from Marric. That was where they were unlike. Marric's father had complained that Marric paid the priests too little attention; but the priestesses of Isis had cautioned the Emperor that Alexa's interest in ritual seemed overstrong. Magic – Marric remembered the Druid's vision and made a sign of his own.

'Do you remember that Aillel told us that in some lands brother with sister is a sin? And Ctesiphon is your half-brother—'

'He sickens me!' Alexa poured more wine and gulped it. 'Marric, *you* are the rightful Emperor, and that is the way of things. Before I let him touch me I will draw a blade across my face or swallow fire!'

'No need,' he soothed her. 'By the gods, 'Lexa, he sickens me, too. He always has. What do you suggest?'

Alexa gestured to the mosaic on her chamber wall. Wrought there was the story of how the line of Old Rome had united with that of Alexander's Egypt after Antony and divine Cleopatra's victory over the pretender Octavian had won them an Empire. A stoop-shouldered, pock-marked Octavian knelt and offered up his blade to the divine pair. Behind him stood a priest and a physician, waiting with the poison that was stark imperial mercy to the defeated foe. Had he won . . . a Roman world: what a solemn bore that would have been. Like the Marcellini, those walking solemnities his father had bade him learn from.

'I have collected gold, gems, horses – purchased under other names. I have even arranged passage with—' she laughed and seemed only a young girl, not a princess or a conspirator. 'Do you remember a Northerner who styles himself Bearmaster?'

'By the Hawk! Audun!' Marric exclaimed. 'I knew him when I was a lad.'

'Shortly after Father died he brought you a bear cub, did Audun. White, of course. Irene coveted it, but—' Alexa's laugh was malicious, 'when she stroked it, it scratched her. She ordered it killed and Audun was furious. He never came back here until a few weeks ago, when I bespoke passage from him. Like Cleopatra, we'll flee the palace and return with an army!'

'To Tmutorakan in Cherson?' Marric considered the idea. Perhaps his army there would follow him. Or the Huns and Northerners might help him gain his throne. He rose and paced panther-fashion across the room. Alexa had planned carefully. Surely Ellac and Uldin, sworn to him by exchanges of hospitality and gifts, could be trusted – assuming you could trust Huns at all. And the Bearmaster – Audun had never been a party to intrigue . . . at least, not before this. Alexa's plan would do.

Then Marric stiffened. As the silver door opposite the garden whispered open, his hand went to his dagger. But a middle-aged woman, stout, decorously clad as befitted a palace servant, entered: Alexa's old nurse.

'Be careful, Princess. Ctesiphon is coming!'

Chapter Two

Alexa flushed, her initial surprise and fear turning swiftly to anger. 'I dreaded this. Ctesiphon's been trying to get his courage up to force himself on me so I stand dishonoured unless I submit to an evil marriage.'

'You have me with you, sister. Can you flee now?'

'I'm ready.'

'Well done.' Marric might have been a general approving an under-officer. Alexa was so strange, yet so familiar. If the nurse hadn't been in the room, he would have kissed her. Of course he must spirit her away; she was too precious to risk. For himself, he would prefer to stay and fight. He had been silent and stealthy for too long: every nerve in his body strained towards release either in passion or in blood.

Alexa was ordering her nurse to fetch simple, warm clothing and then to disappear. Outside her suite came the measured step of one very sure of his path, and surer still that no one would dare hinder him from a long-anticipated scheme of pleasure. Marric and Alexa looked at one another. Then Alexa nodded almost ceremonially, as if opening the Games. *Let it begin*.

She moved a chair to face the door and seated herself. Chin raised, eyes distant, Alexa looked as regal as if she wore the moon-crown of Isis and held audience for mere mortals.

'That's my girl!' Marric padded noiselessly to the door and flattened himself against the wall. He drew his scabbarded dagger from his belt and tapped its heavy pommel against his hand with satisfaction.

Alexa flung off her scarf so that it drifted behind her. She drew her shoulders back, revealing the fine lines of her body more fully. Only the pulse that fluttered rapidly at her throat betrayed her tension: after so long a wait, to finally face battle!

The door swung open and Ctesiphon swaggered in.

'All alone, sister mine?' he asked. His eyes roved down her body. 'Contemplating the God and Goddess? Shall we do that together – or, better yet, unite to become gods ourselves?'

Ctesiphon had the cockiness of a spoiled adolescent and the arrogance of a man, Marric decided. Irene's idolatrous love for her son had marred the weakling further. Marric signalled Alexa to rise and walk towards their half-brother. He wore purple-dyed silk sewn with pearls. A collar of rubies and mooonstones circled his thin shoulders and thinner neck in imitation of the ancient style of the Pharaohs. A dagger, too richly encrusted with gems to be of much use, hung from his girdle. He was dark-haired like his elder half-brother and -sister, but there the resemblance ended. Ctesiphon lacked Alexa's tensile strength or Marric's toughness. Marric was tanned from field-duty, Ctesiphon was as pale as Alexa – a courtier-prince, but never an emperor. Weakness betrayed itself in the thick-lipped petulance of Irene's treacherous, sensual son. Marric wanted to slash the gloating expectation from his face with his own gaudy dagger.

Enticingly, Alexa moved towards him.

'It grows late, my brother. Too late for idle visits. You do me no good by coming here when I am alone.'

'But Alexa, it is only good that I would do you!' Ctesiphon declared fulsomely. He reached out to embrace her, fingers curving greedily toward her breast.

As Alexa tensed in revulsion, Marric moved forward silently on the balls of his feet. He struck Ctesiphon on the side of the head with the satisfactory bronze pommel of his dagger.

The princeling fell forward into Alexa's arms. Taking his weight, she staggered. Then, with a disgusted little sniff, she let him fall on to the marble floor.

'Do you think you killed him?'

'Fratricide stinks to the gods – even with such a brother. He will escape with a sore skull, though he may be so sick he might wish for death.' He had seen enough death in Tmutorakan, his capital, not to relish causing it unnecessarily.

Prince and Princess smiled at each other. Marric swept up Alexa's scarf to bind the unconscious man. Ctesiphon groaned and struggled against the bonds. Louder he groaned and Alexa started to gag him.

'We cannot expect that Irene will send no one to check on her precious son's . . . wooing,' she said. 'So, at least part of the way we must take him with us. Let his mother think he has borne me off somewhere secret.' She attempted to laugh knowingly, but as her hands touched Ctesiphon's face, they trembled. Marric took over the task of gagging him.

When the nurse entered with clothing, Alexa kissed her cheek. 'Isis guard you,' she whispered. 'I've provided for you. Now, run!' She pulled a heavy garment over her white robe.

'We take him with us?' Marric preferred to travel light. 'How did you suggest we manage?'

'Like royal Cleopatra again, brother.' Alexa indicated a rug nearby. 'Here. Wrap this cloak about you and you look the perfect merchant. A rug-merchant, who brought this rug to the palace and will now take it away in a tidy roll . . . with our beloved brother wrapped in its centre.'

The excitement had stimulated her. Now she seemed a different woman from the fragile girl who had stammered out her fears in her brother's arms. Her eyes, enlarged by kohl, gleamed.

What an empress she will make! Marric exulted. He rolled Ctesiphon in the carpet.

'Ha! He reeks of perfume,' Marric commented. 'We'll have Audun stop at the first port so he can unload this cargo and air out his ship.' He unsheathed his dagger and cut a hole in the rug above the unconscious Prince's face.

'It is a pity to ruin that rug,' Alexa remarked. 'You take great care for his life.'

'He shares our father's blood.'

'Does he?' Alexa shrugged.

Marric clasped the cloak she handed him with a bronze brooch. The old Druid had been wrong after all. Alexa was the best shield-companion a man could wish, his brother had fallen into his hand like an ornamental fish to a cat's paw. All the oil-borne visions had been ravings.

An orderly march of feet brought him up sharply. He swept up his sword.

'Only the Watch, brother.'

The guards marched down the hall. Just when they had begun to breathe more slowly, a clash of boots on the paved floor warned them that several men had broken away from the main force and were heading towards their room.

'Set take her!' Marric swore. 'Does Irene set watchdogs over her precious son even when he tries to rape a princess?'

'I think she fears I might kill him otherwise.'

'You may indeed have to kill someone. Unless, of course, you have guards in your pay.' He tossed her a dagger.

'I told them to await us outside!' For the first time, Alexa looked dismayed.

'Then we're on our own.' Marric drew blade, kissing its hilt in salute first to Alexa, then to the gods in the mosaic. 'For luck!' he cried softly. Did some radiance come from the figures as if blessing their heirs? Marric shook his head. Heated by the anticipation of a battle, he was imagining things.

Alexa took Marric's old place behind the door.

'I hear about three men,' Marric said. 'If I despatch the first two, can you take out the third?'

'I must!' The footsteps and jingle of harness grew louder. Now subdued laughter filtered through the door, rude jokes coupling Alexa and Ctesiphon. Marric nodded reassuringly and saw his sister grip her dagger more firmly. He doused the lights and waited.

The door edged open.

'Prince Ctesiphon?'

'It's dark. Perhaps he's abed with the little lady. I wish him joy, taming that one.'

'He wouldn't welcome interruptions.'

'We have our orders. Plague on it, it's dark here. Strike a light!'

As one man struck flint, the hindmost shut the door. Marric lunged at them, his sword slashing out a lethal pattern. Alexa launched herself on to the third guard's back. He fell under her slight weight and shrewd throat-slash almost immediately.

As Marric fought the other men, she watched for an opening and darted in to hamstring the second man so Marric could kill him quickly.

'Now, fast!' Hoisting the unconscious Ctesiphon on his shoulder, he gestured Alexa before him out into the garden.

27

Behind him, the delicate curtains bellied into the room where
dead men lay, and dabbled in the blood on the marble floor.

As Alexa had arranged, there were horses waiting outside the
gardens. Unfortunately, guards also hovered nearby.

'Mount and ride,' Marric panted. Ctesiphon and the rug
were no light burden to a running man. As Marric threw the rug
across a packsaddle, Ctesiphon began to kick and shout. Even
through the gag he made himself heard. The guards started forward.

'Have to check that, sir.' One started to unstrap the rug.

Set take them, were Alexa's men drunk? Where were they?

'Ride!' Marric slapped Alexa's horse. It galloped down towards
the harbour. Two mounted men rode out from the shadows after
her.

Marric leapt for his own horse. Kicking one of the guards
brutally in the face, he made his horse rear, and laughed as the
other men leapt free of the dancing, lethal hooves.

'Hold!' someone shouted behind him.

'Hai!' Marric yelled and grabbed the reins of his packhorse,
digging spurs into his mount's flanks. As his enemies ringed him,
he drew sword to fend them off, holding both horses' reins in his
left hand.

'I am Marric . . .' he gasped ' . . . rightful Emperor . . . in my
father's name . . . stand off!'

One man hesitated then moved in beside him. When another
guard pressed the attack, the newcomer struck him down.

'You've killed a comrade, soldier, but saved a prince – and the
prince is grateful. Ride with me!' The man's face lit at Marric's
words.

There were barriers at the gates. Irene's security was formi-
dable, but they rode the watchers down and pounded along the
road to the harbour where Audun Bearmaster waited.

Why was Audun their ally? Marric wondered. So he had
brought Marric a white cub. Like Alexander, Audun had always
spoken of a proper order to things. Slight enough reason for
risking his life and those of his men, if that was what drove him
to ally with what might easily be a losing faction. Certainly Audun

was rich: no reward that Alexa could offer would move him. But Marric had no time to ponder. He rode on even faster.

Now he could see the charred stubs of what had been tall trees. Some trunks still glowed red. They had passed them, riding faster and faster as passers-by screamed and dodged. Marric used the flat of his blade to beat his horse into greater speed.

'Look behind you!' cried the man who had joined him.

Several of Alexa's men ranged themselves behind Marric, preparing to secure his escape with their lives. That was only good service, Marric thought. Still, he hesitated, unwilling to let them throw their lives away. Just as he opened his mouth to shout at them to flee, Alexa rode back. Her hood had fallen from her hair, which streamed behind her like night clouds in a high wind. She drew her knife and rode towards the packhorse.

'Get away!' Marric screamed at her.

'We need time, brother,' she gasped, and sawed fiercely at the ropes binding the rug and Ctesiphon to the horse. 'We'll buy it this way.'

Irene's men rode nearer. Alexa waited, clearly calculating her moment. When her enemies could no longer rein their horses aside, she pushed the rug off the packsaddle into their path. Even through the uproar, Ctesiphon's death agony reached their ears.

'*Now* we ride!' Alexa screamed, and kicked her flagging mount.

Marric spurred even with her. Bile suddenly flooded his mouth; he spat it to one side. Another damned senseless killing: Alexa was too naïve in her death-dealing for his liking.

'Why?' They careened into a sidestreet. Loiterers ducked into the nearest taverna as they headed for the harbour. 'I thought we had agreed . . .'

'Let Irene hurt!' Alexa cried. She glared at Marric. Her face was very white in the moonlight; her teeth, biting her lip as she concentrated on keeping her seat, were even whiter and very vicious. 'You hate her, too. And he was *her* blood, not ours, never ours . . .' she gasped.

When they reached the harbour, Alexa half-tumbled, half-swung down. Marric dismounted only a second later and caught her against him, holding her as he might a lover or an enemy. 'Never, never go against my orders again, my sister.'

'*Your* orders? Am I not Isis-on-Earth?'

'*My* Isis, not a vicious little cutthroat!'

'I'm glad he's dead. I wish I could slay Irene, watch horses stamp on her, blot her out . . .'

Marric shook her hard, then slapped her. Cold, unforgiving rage flared in her eyes. With a hawklike scream, Alexa drew her dagger and went for Marric. Her other hand moved in a strange, deft pass. It was unlike any knife-fight counter-move he had ever seen. He had been wrong. Alexa was no naïve killer, and she hadn't been content merely to dabble in half-forgotten rituals. Like Irene, she had sought more, and been corrupted by it. If only he'd known that earlier!

Not wishing to hurt her or be stabbed, Marric had all he could do to hold her off. And the soldiers were gaining on them.

More shouts, and on all sides, hoofbeats. Over all of them boomed a great, furry, accented voice. 'Lady, lady! To her, my brothers!'

Then there were guards, there were more and more soldiers, a whole troop attacking at once. Alexa turned, abandoning her rage at her brother in the face of this greater danger. They fought back-to-back until the swirl of battle separated them. Then she dropped her dagger and raised both hands. Light rose from them. She chanted, and Marric shuddered at her words. So magic did remain in their line, but weakened so that it turned from blessing into taint. Marric would have traded all he had to be spared that knowledge, or knowing that Alexa had succumbed – or sensing the attraction that her magic held for him.

But too many men assailed them. Too many. One by one, Alexa's servants fell, even as the voice from the dock shouted orders he could not understand, over and over. More feet pounded in from a different direction. Marric saw Varangians and started to give up hope. Irene would have had their formal oaths by now. He swirled his cloak at one man's eyes to blind him, dodged his axe, and cut him down.

His arm was tiring; the next engagement would most likely be his last. Blood flowed down his arm, down his side and legs from tiny wounds. They were not serious in themselves, but they drained his strength even as their pain sharpened his senses. The wind had never been so fresh, the salt tang smelled so sweet, or the moon shone so brightly, a sharp, perfect sickle in the heavens, reflected in the water. Marric's city, his world. He loved it fiercely.

Then Alexa shrieked and the light about her was quenched. Hacking down the man he fought, Marric started towards her. She lay on the ground surrounded by soldiers and roughly clad strangers.

Marric saw himself, covered with blood, reflected in the water. *The Druid!* he thought, and screamed in pain, rage and despair. Just let him hold his dead in his arms or die avenging her. He leapt across a dying Varangian. Where was she? And to think he had struck her! Fighting on with insane strength, Marric reached the place where Alexa had lain. The men backed off, preparing to rush him in a group.

Her body was gone.

With a final snarl, Marric turned at bay. The grief-maddened strength flowed out of him with his blood, and he was moving slowly, so very slowly. He whirled to face a danger to his left. But as he turned, a swordhilt smashed down on his skull.

Marric's world exploded in flaming agony. He spun, astounded. He had not thought that anything remained after death. Why hadn't the priests warned him that one reached the Horizon through a world of smouldering trees, screaming men, and devouring pain?

Alexa, wait! he thought into the darkness.

Chapter Three

Someone was moaning. Who? The soldier who had defended him? Marric must go to him. He struggled out of safe unconsciousness into the blind darkness of a filthy cell. Sweat, mould and carrion made him gag, and the sounds of whomever it was who could not control his suffering like a man added to his misery. Then he discovered that he was the one moaning. Shame scalded him, rousing him fully.

With awareness came the beginnings of fear. Marric lay in total darkness. Had that blow on the skull blinded him? He thrashed his legs and jack-knifed his body until his face scraped the dank stone of the cell wall. One arm was stretched stiffly above his head, secured by a wrist-shackle and a chain too short to let him lie at ease. His arm felt as if molten lead had been poured down from his wrist to his armpit, stinging in every separate wound. He tugged at the chain weakly. If the iron were in as bad a condition as this place smelled, perhaps he could snap it. But he was too weak and could not see what he was doing. To be trapped away from the light . . . to be unable to see! In panic, Marric squeezed his eyes shut until lights burst like flaming naphtha behind his lids. Did blinded men ever forget what light was like? He forced his eyes open, the bravest thing he had ever dared. Gradually, shadow separated itself from shadow. Part of the wooden door to his cell glowed with rot. The grisly light revealed to Marric the curve of a stone wall, the low arch of the ceiling, and splotches of filth on a floor littered with musty straw. Dark blood stained his body. They had taken most of his clothing, and he shivered.

Again he tried his chains. This time fire leapt out of the links. A bondspell! He would have to believe anything now. Whining a bit from the magic fire's pain, Marric abandoned his attempts on the shackle. The fire of the bondspell faded and he lay again in the dark.

From the way his wounds felt, no one had tended him. He was giddy with fever. Then he blacked out for a time and woke disorientated. There was . . . yes . . . there had to be a reason why he awoke in chains . . . yes! Had the rebels trapped him shamefully in the Governor's residence? Back in Byzantium the wits would make epigrams: the Prince whom banquets, not battles, conquered. Then he remembered again. Marric lay pent in a dungeon of Byzantium, deep-delved and so foul that he would have challenged any man who claimed it existed to prove in blood that he did not lie.

Memory flooded over him like blood from a slit throat. He struggled against a keen of anguish. Why amuse any guard who might be eavesdropping roundabout? Tears made the shadows shimmer and Marric forced himself not to sob. Alexa, Alexa! Why had they ever fought over Ctesiphon? They would have been free if only they had not fought. His life or death wasn't worth even one of her eyelashes. Alexa was gone, and it did not matter that she had loosed Ctesiphon to fall into the path of the soldiers' horses, or that she had laughed as he died. It did not matter that she had drawn steel on Marric himself, or that she was no stranger to magics best left untouched. None of that mattered against his memory of seeing her fall.

Dead. Alexa was dead. Marric let his chin fall into the mouldering straw of his pallet. And he was Irene's prisoner. Could he starve himself, or would the fever in his wounds suffice to kill him? Despair made him even weaker.

Maybe it had all been a cheat after all. Alexander had been a good man, but he was not a priest. He had been unfortunate, too, in his sons: Ctesiphon who was no man; Marric who was no priest and no emperor. The line was unhealthy; best it die out. So, when Irene killed Marric she would end the entire line of Antony, of Alexander, of the Pharaohs themselves. Marric's amendment had come too late and been denied. But it was the Empire which would pay for his negligence.

After years of bargains with the gods or yawning through rituals, Marric found himself praying passionately to Osiris – may he turn his face toward his son! – that he could retain some measure of integrity. Prayer had never come with such force or simplicity.

If the fever didn't kill him, perhaps he could struggle against his chains until the bondspell's agony stopped his heart. Death would come soon. He lay back, eyes lolling in his head. Then he saw the Darkness, like a cloud of ebony smoke, hovering beneath the room's low arch. It was too crude to possess a recognizable shape.

'Come out!' he croaked. By Horus, was all the city corrupted by foul magic? Or had Irene simply left him a guard to turn his very hopelessness into worse torture? The blackness drew nearer, sending out tendrils that promised him . . . he could draw them into himself, go free . . . just accept it, bow to it, give himself up.

'I will not surrender,' he muttered. 'Begone.' He stared at the black blot as if it were a human enemy he could face down. Then he had a sense of power offered to him. There would be blood to slake his grief, if only . . . no, he would not be bought either.

If it were Marric's fate to die, so he would. But he could at least die cleanly, not at the power of some demon-thing. Having made that decision, Marric fell into exhausted sleep.

A screech of outraged, resisting metal woke him. Shadows reeled as men thrust in first a torch and then their heads and shoulders. Marric forced himself not to cower. Regardless of what misbegotten sorceries Irene used, she could only command his death, not his self-betrayal.

'On your feet, Prince!'

'He's lazy, or drunk. Can't move without his slaves to stir him up.'

'Or his catamites. Maybe he likes to play rough, Demetrius. Hoist him up.'

Both guards laughed. Alexander would have sent such offal to labour in the mines, not in the city's prisons. How could such places have existed during his father's reign?

Perhaps they had been kept for the vilest of felons, men who violated their mothers, deliberate parricides, traitors – breathing carrion. But now Irene had cast a prince into them.

As the guards, still jesting foully and manhandling Marric, forced him on to his feet and bound his arms behind his back, he summoned all his remaining strength. He would not threaten. He would not fall. He would not plead. He would deny them the chance to kick and jeer at him. They forced an iron bar between his arms to brace them, and it grated painfully against the untreated slashes on his arms and sides. He did not cry out. And he would not stagger when they brought him before Irene.

That was where they were taking him. He was as sure of that as of his own heartbreak. Perhaps the sight of him would enrage her so that she would order him killed.

34

A shove at the base of Marric's spine forced him into the passage where torches smoked. Orange light and violent shadows made it spin about him. There were no windows down here. Water trickled over the walls. Even the immense beams which prevented this den from crashing down on the rats and human refuse that scrabbled about in it were moist and phosphorescent, sagging with rot.

Let Marric walk the dark passage, he thought through the haze of fever, and at the end of it would stand a throne of wood, gleaming in decay, surrounded by a nimbus of evil light. There, guarded by jackals, decked in jewellery looted from a hundred tombs, secure in powers he dared not think of, Irene would queen it over the dead.

That was not Empire. The true Empire lay in the sunlight where the Golden Horn gleamed and the blue water flowed cleanly beneath the keels of great ships. Marric couldn't have loved it half as much as it deserved. But he would try to remember it as he died.

The prison corridor wound and twisted upward. One of the guards counted passageways under his breath. Doors like rotten teeth studded the walls. From behind one of them puffed the nauseating sweetness of something left too long unburied.

If there were only water – Marric longed to wash the vileness of this place from him. Finally, a last black door loomed up. Iron studs formed an unsightly pattern in its heavy crossbeams. One man thumped on it with the butt of his spear. Slowly, the door opened.

More jailers were waiting on the far side. As they passed through, Marric paused for a moment, even though they struck him. Set deep into arched embrasures were narrow windows. Sunlight poured down. Though the light hurt, Marric stared at it avidly. *Hail unto thee, oh Ra, in thy rising* . . . the old prayer ran through his mind. He turned to examine the three new guards, slouching in heavy armour, brutal of face. One croaked something.

'What's that?' shouted the one who seemed to be in charge. 'Can't understand you!'

The man had gobbled his words because his palate was deeply cleft.

The third man spoke not at all, but set his massive shoulders to the door and shoved. As the door screeched and grated shut, he of the harelip grunted a protest. The other man did not notice. *Deaf*, Marric thought, *and the harelip is as good as mute. Isis preserve us all, where does Irene find – or make – such men?*

'Move, Princeling!' barked their master.

Marric moved. He remembered the day he had leapt from his warhorse to mount one of the fierce little ponies that the Huns cherished more than anything but their sons and their shamans. Ellac and Uldin were adopting him. They rode, they feasted, and then they rode again, exulting in the feel of the wind against their faces. He had raced Ellac over the plains toward the Euxine. Then they had turned back to greet their men. Had he savoured his freedom enough?

The small procession passed door after door. Now the doors were of silver. Somehow they had travelled underground to the palace. There had been times when Marric had strode through such doors dressed in gilded armour with an honour guard at his back. *Princeling. It was a role I played. I never really had any power* . . .

As Marric passed, forced towards the Hall of Audiences, men grounded their spear-butts. *They mock me.*

The hall was long and wide, a richness of stone wrought into the likeness of a garden. On the walls were mosaics of flowers so fair that Isis might have plucked them to wear in her hair.

And at the end of the hall, enthroned in splendour, sat Irene.

Light flickered around Irene as she sat between rows of her favourites. Her dark eyes, beneath arched, imperious brows, lifted to regard her victims.

The usurping Empress wore the robes of Isis-on-Earth, silks brought from beyond Hamadan and Nishapur, heavily woven with silver and sewn with gems of the moon: pearls, corals and moonstones. Rubies studded the collar that overlay her robe, fluted in the archaic style of the Two Lands. At her ears hung

36

enormous pearls; on her dark hair gleamed the crown of Isis, a disc of lucent silver that flashed in the light. A great crimson cloak lay draped over her throne.

Marric's guards prodded him in the back then pushed him down in the full, over-elaborate prostration on which Irene, a lady jealous of her dignities, had always insisted. Before they could keep him there, Marric rose to his knees.

His eyes locked with hers, a glance that sent hatred down the length of the hall, robbing it of some of its beauty. A breeze from the great windows carried the incongruous freshness of roses.

The men cursed. One began to bend Marric's stiff neck for him.

'Kiss earth, Prince,' the man muttered. Before he could stop himself, Marric spat a few words he had learned from the Huns. The man backhanded him and blood trickled from his split lip.

'Stop that.'

Irene stood. She raised her hands. Marric saw that she held in them a twisted glitter of opals, rubies and moonstones – the splendid collar that Ctesiphon had affected the night of his death. The goldwork was mangled from the hooves that had tramped Irene's son to death.

Can I make her angry enough so she will kill me quickly? As Irene approached him, Marric launched himself up from his knees at her. Perhaps one of the courtiers would stab him.

Fever had left him too weak to fight. A soldier hurled him off-balance. Marric fell heavily, unable to rise for the minutes it pleased Irene to make a leisurely circle about him. No one laughed.

'Prince Marric,' she mused in that heavy accent that had always reminded him of a camp follower from Aleppo. 'You come before me in disarray. I am surprised.'

He heard her approach more closely and tensed his belly muscles for the kick that must surely come.

'Are you surprised that I appear before you at all? I assure you, I do not do so of my own free will.' From where had he gained that new, measured dignity? He sounded like his father. Well, it would probably pass before the end.

37

'Raise him,' Irene ordered. After he had been dragged back on to his feet, she spoke again.

'This meeting has cost me much.' She displayed the ruined collar.

'I wish it had cost you your life.'

He had been foolish to say that, he realized instantly. Nails raked his cheek. He smelled the perfume she wore – musky and too sweet. At least Alexa had seen to it that Ctesiphon would not live to rule as his mother's puppet. Had Irene truly loved her son, or only the power he might buy her?

'You murdered Horus-on-Earth!'

'My father was Horus-on-Earth. You betray him,' Marric replied. 'He acknowledged your whelp, that much is true. But how do we know he wasn't the get of some charioteer – or a slave?' *Or some demon.* Marric tensed, awaiting the scream of rage, the blow that never fell. He heard the mutterings of Irene's courtiers and raked them with his eyes. *Traitors, all of you.*

'So, now what do you do . . . Isis? You have no Consort and yet you must have one. Will you take the Reaver-jarl of Jomsborg to your bed? The Empire will never accept him.'

'You remain . . .'

'I?' Marric spat bloody froth on the tiles and bit back the retort that he would rather be a eunuch; such could be made all too easily, and he preferred to die a whole man.

'I can give you power,' Irene said. 'Look!'

Red light burned at her fingertips.

'You tasted my power in your cell, did you not? The power to bend, to control emotion, to rule for ever –'

'Powers of Set,' Marric whispered. 'Why?'

'To confirm my rule, Marric. To keep it and enjoy it for a thousand years. Why rule for just one lifetime?' She stepped closer to him and ran her hand down his bare chest. Marric stood motionless.

Irene raised his chin in fastidious, disdainful fingertips. He had no choice but to look at her. Even at arm's length he could smell the oils with which she anointed herself.

How could this woman be his stepmother? How old was she?

38

Irene looked as if she had not aged a single day since Alexander had installed her as a minor wife. Marric was almost grateful for the pain that kept him from responding to the promises of the senses: voice, glistening eyes, the lush figure hinted at by her robes. Irene's nostrils quivered with suppressed eagerness. She had always been a woman of strong passions; the strongest of them was for power.

'I need a Consort who will do *my* will.'

'Steal the consecrated bull from the priests of Mithras,' Marric suggested. 'That might service you adequately.'

'Enough! I offer you co-rule and you spurn it. But you do not delude me, Marric; you want power. You simply need time to consider my offer – time and a place to think it over.'

Little time he'd have if she sent him back to that dungeon. Fever would kill him in days. But better fever than that black cloud. Sooner or later it would find the weakness in his soul that Alexander had seen, and then Marric would be damned as well as lost. Like Alexa. *My poor child, my dear one,* he thought.

Still, if Irene needed him she would neither kill him nor torture him. *Weak, corruptible.* Marric hated himself for the surge of hope that he felt.

'No. Not the pit again,' she mused. 'Hard work, yes, to make you appreciate the future you would toss away. You have called me low, vile things; you shall yourself be low and vile – a slave, sold with a bad character. In a year or two I may send for you, to see if you have reconsidered. If you still abuse me then, there are always the Silk Routes. Few slaves return from them.' She paused, amused, sated. 'No word, my poor Marric?'

Despair warred with a rage for vengeance that shook him almost to ecstasy. He mastered it. Pride was all he had left.

'Better let the Empire die than let you corrupt it.'

Irene gestured. A richly dressed man approached, prostrated himself, and awaited orders.

'Antinous, are your merchant ships ready to sail?'

'At your command, divine lady.'

'Good. Take this rebel fool and be sure he sails aboard your next ship. Alexandria or Antioch: just let me know which. I will

39

not have him sold to the quarries or into ship's service, however. Let him wish for death, if he will. I want him alive.'

Marric had steeled himself to endure death and disgrace unconquered. Slavery? His legs almost buckled beneath him. Even a slave, he had been taught, had his own human dignity. But philosophy was one thing, the slaveblock quite another. Even with his new-found poise, Marric had far better die than risk being spirit-broken. He tried to hurl himself on to an outheld spear. The spearshaft, rawhide around a metal core, slammed against the side of his head. The hall burst around him into splintered light and chaotic shouting. Over it all, he heard Irene's sweet, contented laughter.

'Take him away,' she said. Soldiers hustled him out. The last Marric saw of the throne that should have been his was Irene sitting and brooding, her sharp-nailed fingers caressing Ctesiphon's necklet.

Chapter Four

Marric heaved himself over on to his side. Someone pushed him sharply back and jerked away.

'The jackal eat your soul! Do you think it's rose petals you're lolling on?'

His head ached, and would ache worse before long from the stink of close-packed men and human filth. Someone had been sick recently, and nearby; the brine could not disguise the stink of vomit.

Brine? With a groan Marric returned to the senses he had abandoned in order to drift in and out of his body – the way mages of long-ago Chaldea had been said to do. In what seemed like another life he had thrown silver to the singers of such tales. The deck rocked beneath him. He was on board one of Antinous' merchantmen, bound – as Irene had gloated – for the slaveblock. And then what? Irene had said she did not care whether he were sold at Antioch or Alexandria, but sold he would be.

Twice on the way to the ship Marric had tried to kill himself, once by hurling himself at the armed guards, a second time as his captors forced him out of the palace along the back ways where the road bordered the high walls. Marric had almost burst his heart trying to break free long enough to toss himself down on to the rocks or into the uncaring blue of the harbour below.

He dashed a hand across split lips and discovered that he was chained again. The heavy metal of his wrist shackles gleamed in the light which filtered through the grilled hatch. He stared fascinated at his bonds. Did these alone make a slave of a prince?

Cautiously, this time, he shifted position and felt movement on either side of him. He levered himself up. His neck hurt. The smith who had fitted him with his collar had not been gentle, and Marric had fought. He remembered the harbour smithy as a vision of hell.

His mind and body had been too strong, so he was spared nothing of the long, ignominious progress down to the docks with the slaves – *the other slaves* – nor the painful crowding as they waited to be collared: not one hammer blow of the whole degrading process. Now he was marked as property: anyone's prize, should he escape. That was almost worse than the possibility that someone might have recognized him among the coffle of slaves.

'The Prince, in chains!' they might cry. He would have been helpless to hide his shame and the disgrace to his blood. His rebellion – no, he must not think of it as rebellion – his just attempt to assume his father's crown had failed. It had been premature, a desperate action. And as he had walked in chains they pushed at him till he blacked out. Then they threw salt-water on him till he woke, then waited so he could spare them the trouble of lugging him on board. 'Be thankful you weren't whipped,' one man told him. Marric fantasized ways of killing him, shrugged, then regretted the gesture.

He had had one look at the ship – gaudy – hulled and bearing the bright device that proclaimed that Antinous was a wealthy man, and likely to become wealthier before long. Square-rigged like most merchant vessels, it had a fighting turret and leather shields to protect the oarsmen in battle: good rowers were valuable property, more so than slaves. Threatened with naphtha or drowning, the slaves on their way to market might have to row for their miserable lives, too.

'So you're awake now, are you?' asked the man next to Marric. His chains were secured to the same rusty ring that Marric's were. 'For a while there I thought we might have one less to crowd this hulk.'

Now Marric became aware of the rhythmic splash of oars and the surge of the ship through the water, the bright sea he had always loved. It had brought his ancestors world dominion.

The last time I sailed, he recalled, *I stood on deck in fine armour and . . . clean clothes, with the captain asking my will.*

'I . . . live,' Marric said. 'The gods grant that I do not continue to live for long.' Burdened with the collar, his neck bent before he knew it, and he buried his head in scraped hands.

The man laid a hand on his shoulder. 'Your chain is too tight. They didn't trust you when they brought you on board. Said you were vicious.'

'They sell the vicious ones on the frontier,' another slave cackled ghoulishly. 'The Berbers kill them . . . or the Huns. Depends on where they're sold.' The man's accent was so thick Marric could barely understand him.

'Never mind,' said Marric's chain-mate. 'We're all bound for hell on earth one way or other, so we may as well resign ourselves to face it. Dignity becomes even a slave.'

That was no gutter-speaker. Marric turned sharply to look at him and paid for it with intense, nauseating dizziness. His companion was pale. Below their harsh bracelets, his hands were uncallused: the hands of a scholar, perhaps, or a minor civil servant.

'By Osiris in Glory,' Marric began, 'what brings *you* here?' The other slaves growled.

'Do not ask such questions of slaves, stranger,' said the man. 'But I will tell you. Why did I, Nicephorus, wind up in the hull of a slaveship, bound for Alexandria or wherever? I was a scholar whose debts – and bad luck in my choice of creditors – reduced me to this. The men I owed had friends at court.' He spat and made a sign of derision. 'When drought killed the harvest I had counted on to save me, fool that I was, they had my lands seized. To pay – well, I had a choice: myself to the block or my . . . oh gods, my wife or my children. To save them, I chose this.'

Marric bowed his head in respect.

'But you, stranger. Surely your voice is not the babble of the streets, nor that of barbarians.'

'No,' said Marric. 'No. I was a soldier, and, like you, I ran afoul of the court.'

'As they say, those who live by the sword shall perish by it.'

'Stow it!'

'What does that mean?' The slaves packed in nearby grumbled.

Marric hoped that this man, Nicephorus, whose voice was the first comfort he had found in days, would not now preach some cult whose asceticism maddened its disciples. But wasn't his proverb true? Warriors died in combat. Had Marric fallen in battle, he would have no complaint to make. Indeed, he had fought to the utmost of his strength.

'You worship the sign of the Fish?' he asked reluctantly.

'Nay, not I. I serve Isis and Osiris, but I seek wisdom wherever it may be found, in slums or in scrolls. Once I owned many scrolls, but now it looks as if it's slums that will teach me.'

How could this Nicephorus be so damned resigned? Was he a coward? Marric studied the man – scholar-slight and pale, unused to physical hardship. Unless some rich family wanted a pedagogue, he probably wouldn't last out the month. And he would never again see the family for which he had sacrificed himself. Yet he spoke calmly, kindly, to another man.

'Why?' Marric husked. The hatch up above his head slammed shut and he had to strain to see Nicephorus in the dark.

'Light,' Nicephorus murmured. A pallid light gleamed between them. A brave little man and stronger than he looked if he could summon magic even in chains. Strange: Nicephorus' light did not revolt Marric the way Irene's red flames or poor Alexa's magic had.

'You are no ordinary scholar,' he said.

'I have sat at the feet of the traders from the Country of Gold beyond the Silk Routes,' Nicephorus said, 'and I have spoken with the Druids. All agree. Beyond this life lies many another, and we live them out to atone for our misdeeds. One seeks in this life to be worthy that one may be even worthier in the next – or escape the Wheel entirely to guide others along the Way. I believe – yes, I do truly believe,' he tested the words with satisfaction, 'that no one lives or suffers in vain. Who knows? Perhaps in another life I did that for which this one is only fit recompense.'

A Druid had warned Marric of failure. Now, this weak-eyed philosopher threw the greyrobe's words back at him in the hold of a slaveship. The whole thing was absurd. Marric laughed. As if pleased at the sudden surge of spirit, Nicephorus laughed too.

'Ye mind when old One-eye started to cackle?' a voice interrupted. 'He didn't stop for hours. They came and knocked him on the head. Then there was a splash, and he'd gone to feed the fish, had One-eye. Careful, stranger, that ye do not follow him.'

'That's laughter, not madness,' Nicephorus said. For some reason he had appointed himself Marric's protector. That idea set him chuckling again even as it warmed him. He would need time to recover, time to think, and the little man could provide that.

With grisly eagerness the other slave pointed out empty spaces in the chains. That man had died of fever, another had gone mad and leapt overboard while they were adjusting his chains.

'Terrible,' Nicephorus said. He looked at Marric with those eyes that gained added strength from their shortsightedness. Marric started to disagree. It was no shame for a warrior to fall on his sword. Once you were dead, you stayed dead. Rebirth was a fable, the Cynic had taught him. But he had been wrong about other things: why not this?

'Suicide violates the order your Druids teach, does it?' he asked.

'Not my Druids, and no order of theirs. Merely that which *is*. Life is too precious to be tossed away like rotten oranges.'

'Enough of your talk, little man!' yelled a voice out of the shadows. 'And douse that damned witchlight! Where's order when the lands starve and no rain falls? My crops went too, and then I had nothing but my body to pay my debts with! And now no gods rule us. When the Emperor, Osiris bless him, ruled, the rains came at their appointed time. Not like now . . .'

An appalled hush settled on the slaves. The man paused, then continued more softly, 'Them as rules do not understand the way of the land. Isis and Osiris it is for the Empire, and no other way. When the law be broke, the land be barren.'

'What of Alexander's heirs?' asked Nicephorus.

'What of the Prince?' another slave whispered as softly as if he feared that men with whips would come and silence them. The slaves leaned forward, expectant. As if, Marric thought, they fed their souls on such tales. But why not? Stories, hyssop and barley bread, a little oil, perhaps: that was all the food they had for soul or for body.

'A wild lad, he was. Too wild. But, even so, he was the rightful prince. So Irene sent 'im away – out to the frontier where the slant-eyes run loose. A man could die fast out there. Have ye heard how the Huns feed? Say a Hun takes a good long ride, he rides, see, with raw meat beneath his saddle, so when he's hungry, it's all soft-like . . .'

Two chains down, a man retched. Marric closed his ears.

'Perhaps he might have grown into a true ruler,' Nicephorus said softly. '"Cometh Horus upon the water of his father. He dwelleth in decay. The gods have given him the crown which maketh him to live for millions of years." What do you think of that?' he asked Marric. Then suddenly, sharply, he added, 'Comrade, you've not given me your name.'

'M . . . call me Mor,' said Marric. He would not allow his name to be spoken here, disgraced as it was. Nicephorus disturbed him. He spoke such cultivated Greek and he quoted the rituals of the Two Lands. Had he been too wise? Was that why Irene's creatures had had him sold?

'A dark name, friend,' said Nicephorus.

'Aye.'

'Now, Mor, you were a soldier.' Nicephorus peered at Marric with those large, light eyes that saw far too much. 'What of the Prince?'

'Even the greatest warrior may be slain by a hurled rock or poisoned wine,' Marric said bitterly. 'Or betrayed by a woman . . .' *not to think of Alexa's body, the blood staining her garments – NO!* 'I believe that they are . . . both dead.'

'Then the Empire is weakened, perhaps lost,' Nicephorus said. 'They say among the Aescir, "one land, one lord". In the Misty Isles the land's welfare is allied to its queen's life.'

If Nicephorus suspected that Mor was actually Marric, would he betray him? If the land's life was bound up with the life of its ruler, dared Marric choose death and leave it unprotected? He was only flawed; Irene had fallen utterly.

Nicephorus' words had penetrated to some reach of his spirit that was still proud, still prince. He would have to live.

Marric withdrew into his thoughts until the hatches were flung open and men with brutal voices flung down food. Getting a share of the musty bread and foul water suddenly became more important than empires. A burly man with teeth missing snatched at Nicephorus' share of the food. Marric shoved him away.

'Try that again and you'll lose the rest of your teeth,' he said. 'Do they do that often?' he asked Nicephorus, between bites of bread. With the decision to live taken, he ate ravenously.

'Not so often I cannot endure . . . Mor,' the scholar said. 'But more often than I like. Thank you.' The bread was coarse and filled with husks. Both men fell silent, eating with the respect slaves must have for any food when they are hungry enough.

Marric finished first. 'It will not happen again,' he promised. Slaves they might be, but they were men, not gutter-rats to tear at one another for scraps. And he meant to see that they all remembered it.

For days the merchantman cut its way through the Middle Sea. Whether the trips were harsh or easy Marric could not tell, having never been aboard a slaveship before. He spent hours recalling his last voyage across the Euxine. Consciously he tried to relive each hour of his governorship. He had subdued the mutinous city guards; he had negotiated an end to raids by Ellac and Uldin, the bandy-legged khagans of the Huns, and had won their respect along with the truce. They had given him steppe ponies, their harness encrusted with cabochon rubies the size of Marric's thumbnail. Sometimes he could all but see them.

Then Nicephorus would speak and hale him back to a present in which imperial Prince Marric, fastidiously clean, dwindled into the filthy, scarred slave, Mor who hunched in the foul gloom of below-deck and fought like a gaunt wolf for scant rations.

The two men became an unlikely team. Nicephorus' patience shielded Marric from despair; Marric's strength, aided by a reputation for brawling, kept the other slaves from stealing their food. Oh, they liked Nicephorus well enough, Marric supposed, but hunger was hunger and Nico was the smallest. For each man, hearing the other's cultivated Greek was the only pleasure he had left.

Nicephorus had been telling Marric about Druids.

'I knew a man of the Isles once,' Marric recalled. 'Name of Aillel. He had copper hair, bright as the sun on polished armour, and I always thought how strange it was that there might be two—'

'Two what?'

'Incarnations of Horus. My—' *my father*, he had almost said, but stopped in time, 'my friend . . . and the Emperor, may he dwell in glory. He used to carry me, did Aillel, on his back . . .'

'I won't ask you where you met such a man, brother Mor,' Nicephorus said. 'After all, there is no "where" for slaves.'

Marric's eyes flashed rebellion.

'Mor . . . who speaks the pure tongue and has a warrior's pride. There is much more to you, my friend, than – gods above help us, what's that?'

Above them feet pounded on the planking of the deck. Shouted orders sent more feet running. Marric imagined how the great square-rigged sail would belly out as the ship steered before the wind. A thin shaft of sunlight filtered down to the slaves. Judging from this angle, noon was long past. *We were fed when the sun was high*, Marric thought. *That light is golden. One more day survived . . . almost.*

With a jolt, the ship's oars cut the water and its speed increased. 'What *is* it?'

Marric had crouched so silently, so intent on what must be

happening on deck, that he hadn't answered his friend's question.

'Oars,' he said. 'The pilot – yes, I hear him now – has just ordered the skins of vinegar to be brought up on deck. Do you hear that? Now they're lashing the leather shields into place.'

The other men watched the hatch, their eyes too bright in bearded, shrunken faces. Marric nodded at Nicephorus.

'We're going to fight!' a tall man howled. 'Osiris help us!'

The other slaves took up the lament until the hatch slid aside and sailors lashed them into subdued mutterings. For a precious moment Marric could smell clean air, laden with salt and pungent with vinegar.

After the hatch slammed, he breathed deeply to ward off claustrophobia. 'Just hope that hatch isn't secured.'

'Sea fire?' Nicephorus murmured.

'There used to be a swarm of pirates on Crete. Antonius IV cleaned them out, but they're back. They'll have dromonds, good as anything in the Fleet. With bronze rams. My guess is they'll try to take us amidships and ram us.'

'Wouldn't they want the ship's cargo? Why fire us?'

'All the Empire's ships carry sea fire. The captain assumes that if he uses it, the pirates will retaliate. The pirates think the same way, so there's usually a race to see who uses it first. We slaves thus have the enviable choice of death by fire or death by water.'

Each fibre of Marric's body quivered in sympathy with the oarsmen. He found himself straining forward as if his own battered strength could help the ship outrun the pirates.

There came a lurch. Several men fell heavily, swearing in pain and anger as the ship came about.

'We're too heavy to outrun them,' Marric said. 'The captain turns to fight.'

Pirates – by now his orderly would be helping him into his armour, he would be leaving his cabin to supervise the sailors as they drenched the leather shields and sheets with the vinegar that just might protect them against the naphtha, quicklime and saltpeter that consumed all that they touched. The Empire guarded few secrets more jealously than that of sea fire, yet the pirates had learned it. *They* called it Greek fire.

On deck, soldiers dragged up catapults and adjusted the tube which would spray flaming death upon the enemy fleet. Scrapes and shouts rose from the prow, then were silenced. The ship waited.

'Ever since the Empire retook Alexandria,' Marric whispered to Nicephorus, 'the Arabs have been wild for revenge, even the outlaws among them. Quiet!' he shouted at the other slaves. 'Meet your gods, if you have any, with some dignity!'

A hiss of water, thumps of missiles launched from catapults, and shouts warned them that they were under attack. Nicephorus reached for Marric's hand. 'In a better life,' said the smaller man. They braced for impact.

With a shriek of rending wood, the pirate dromond sheared through the oarbanks and smashed into the hull opposite Marric and Nicephorus. Men were torn apart by the resistless bronze ram; blood and salt water frothed into the breached ship. The living slaves were flung into grisly embrace with the dying and the dead.

Marric lashed out with his chained arm. He had to get free! Again! The impact of the ram had loosened the bolts; he felt his bonds weaken. Once more. The ship lurched and shuddered. Some of the planks were splintering beneath him.

'Help me with this thing!' he shouted at Nicephorus. They both tore at it. At the next try the bolt pulled free. Marric dangled a length of chain. If he could once get on deck, what a fine, lethal weapon it would make.

The ship settled as more water poured into it. Soon this entire hold would be awash. Taking ships was always a two-part contest. First came the race: who could sail faster and more skilfully to make the other ship stand and fight. After the ship had been rammed came the second part of the contest. Could the pirates seize its cargo before it sank? If so, the slaves might be permitted to live out their wretched lives for at least a little longer.

Marric eyed the slaves.

'Think they're worth it?' he asked Nicephorus.

'Yes, yes!' Now Nicephorus was fighting his own chains. Marric helped him. As he started to climb on deck, he realized that his friend had stayed behind to help the others.

'Listen!' Marric screamed. 'You can't do it like that, you

whoresons. I want every one of you to pull at once, damn you, PULL!'

Nicephorus gave them the light to see what they were doing. Then Marric was up the ladder and hurling his shoulder against the hatch. He emerged into what looked like the rape of a smithy by a slaughterhouse. Ships blazed in the blue sea, and men shouted as they fought. A sailor cloaked in flame reeled shrieking past Marric and pitched overboard. All the water of the Middle Sea would not douse that fire. Marric fell flat on the deck and crawled over to a dead marine. Fouled as his sword and helmet were with blood, Marric took them. Nicephorus came up behind and he tossed him the dead man's dagger.

'Guard my back,' Marric ordered, and leapt into the fight.

Which side to join? The slavers? In all probability they were Irene's creatures: he owed them nothing. The pirates, then? His family's hatred of the raiders who challenged the Empire blazed up in him. A target for Greeks and Arabs alike, Marric fought only to survive.

His freedom had been stolen, his throne usurped, his sister slain, himself tortured. His rage erupted into the pure fury that the Varangians called berserkergang. It felt wonderful! He was free, at least for as long as the battle and his life lasted. Wounds reddened on his body. He watched a curved dagger bite along one arm but, miraculously, he felt nothing except a determination to kill the man who had pierced his guard. He did. He swung his chain around and brought it crashing down on a man who slashed at him from below. The chain ripped half the pirate's face away.

But, step by step, the pirates were backing him up towards the ship's forecastle.

'Look out!' Nicephorus shouted. A light exploded about him, blinding several fighters. Four more jumped Marric. He brought up his sword in time to impale one. The dying man's weight tore the sword from his hand. He swore as he had the night Alexa fell, longing for her magic – regardless of its consequences – to aid him. To his battle-maddened senses, it felt like forever until the Arabs brought him down still alive. He shrank from the blow he expected to heart or throat, but forced himself to lie unmoving.

I die in battle. That is more grace than I expected.

Marric lifted his chin proudly and looked out over his own death. Sunset and burning ships cast a bloodglow over the sea and the sweaty, intent faces of his captors. Screams and splashes told him that others were disposing of slaves and sailors too badly wounded to be worth healing for the block.

He pressed his fists against the deck. 'Get on with it,' he muttered. A gleaming blade hissed back over one man's head in a fast, deadly arc, swept forward—

'Hold!' a voice ordered from the forecastle. 'Bring him here.'

Marric's captors hauled him unceremoniously to the pirate captain's feet, and let him fall.

Chapter Five

Marric shut his eyes, then opened them again. He tried to study the lateen rigging of the pirate dromonds as calmly as if they performed naval manoeuvres in his honour. He would try anything to cover his fear that he might beg to be allowed to go on living. The sinking ship's deck had dropped almost to the waterline. The pirates were busy transferring cargo on to their own vessels. Slaves, among them Nicephorus, were being herded over the side. One man fell into the water and was fished out with curses and blows: he was too valuable to be allowed to drown.

When he had himself firmly in control, he permitted himself to look at the pirate leader. Ironically, the man saluted him. Marric touched his hand to lips and heart with equal irony and added greetings in Arabic.

'You fought well,' the captain observed, one hand on the nephrite handle of his scimitar.

Marric folded his arms on his chest. He did not want to provoke the Arabs who eyed him so suspiciously, too close to their leader

for their liking. The evening wind chilled Marric's bare body, but
he mastered his shivers as his sweat cooled. A cut he had not
noticed before dripped down his side. The rest of his wounds
began to ache.

'How does such a fighter become goods for market?' asked the
captain.

'I was unlucky.' Now that the sun was down, the water looked
dark and cold. Most of the burning spars had already sunk.

'Unlucky!' The Arab roared with laughter.

Marric stood motionless. Imperial Cleopatra's first husband,
he remembered, had been captured by pirates, but he had managed to turn them into his own private bodyguard until he was
ransomed. Of course, he had vowed to hang them all. They had
laughed at him, too. But the next year he had led a fleet against
them and hanged as many as he caught.

'Is there someone to ransom you?'

Irene would give gold to know that her plans for Marric had
miscarried, and more gold to have him back in her grasp. At
least this attack had enabled Marric to escape her.

'No one,' said Marric. 'Unless, of course you appeal to the
Consort. But I fear the Fleet might burn your ships to the
waterline before you reached the Horn.' He braced himself for
the blow that might pay off his insolence. It never came.

'Then, fighting man, I offer you a choice. A warrior's choice.
Swear loyalty to me – and to the jihad! – and you will share with
us, rise in the ranks,' he offered. 'Or you can rejoin . . . your
fellow slaves.' His voice lashed Marric contemptuously with that
suggestion. 'Or return home free.'

His gesture showed Marric what that meant: over the side and
into the water to drown.

So, honourable death still lay within his reach? He had only
to dive overboard and swim until he sank. No one would stop
him. Or he could live as a slave. If he took oath to demons, he
could join the pirates. But how? Even if the Empire were ruled
by a usurper, Marric could not ally with its enemies. And if it
were beneath Horus-on-Earth to ally with pirates, then the
honourable death they offered was no honour at all. This very
dawn Marric had prayed to his gods and to his father, Alexander,

who ruled as Osiris beyond the Horizon, for freedom. Never had he dreamed that the path of honour lay in renouncing it.

The ship wallowed heavily now. 'Will you wait until the ship sinks?' asked the Arab. He made no move to leave, either, unwilling to be bested by a wounded slave. Letting himself sink with the ship was only suicide by default, Marric thought.

'I will take my place again among the slaves.'

'The *other* slaves.' The pirate stressed the word.

'Yes. I will rejoin the other slaves.' Marric felt only a great weariness.

'That is your loss. Akbar, Auda, take him and bind him!'

The two men hustled Marric off the ship. He clung to whatever dignity he had left and to a fragile hope that as long as he lived, he could hope to escape and, at least, take vengeance for himself and his sister. But the blood was flowing from his wounds, and he felt as heartsick as if he fought a losing battle and then knelt beneath the yoke of his worst enemy.

Seawater stung in Marric's wounds. His skin felt too tight from fever. Despite the heat of below-decks, the water on his skin made him start to shiver again. Nicephorus tried to steady him and offer him drink.

'Easy, Mor. Come back to us.' Marric heard chanting, thought he saw soft lights. He slept fitfully after that. In his dreams he fled from black clouds, from an accusing figure who wore a crown and stood in judgement above a dead girl. Then he saw a face that drew him – and opened his eyes.

The gloom of the hold hurt to look at. A face, pale and fine-featured, but not the face he dreamt of, hovered over him.

'Nico . . .'

'Quiet, Mor.' The scholar eased Marric's head against his shoulder. To Marric's surprise, when he smoothed his hair back, none of the slaves hooted.

'How long . . .'

'Two days, I think. Fine scholar I am, losing track of the time.'

'On board the . . . other ship, there . . . that man had fever . . . and they flung him over.' Marric's tongue was thick.

'Yes. The Greeks drowned him. But these pirates have decided that you will fetch a good price, should you live. So they have given you the chance to try – and all the water you need.' The arm steadying Marric tightened. Not for a moment did he believe Nicephorus about the water.

'No . . . need now.'

'You are still weak. But at least, praise Isis, you no longer rave.'

'What . . . ?' Oh gods, what had he betrayed?

'Mor, you enlivened our days and our nights here by claiming all kinds of outrageous things.' Nicephorus laughed tolerantly. 'Even after your voice gave out, you still whispered! Be at peace: who ever listens to a wounded man's ravings? And among these, who has the will to care?'

Marric looked at Nicephorous, then at the other slaves. Most were apathetic or asleep. A few watched him with the rough-and-ready sympathy unfortunates sometimes have for people in an even worse plight. Nicephorus was right. Truly, none of them cared. He could have claimed to be Osiris in Glory (and perhaps he had), and no one would have listened. That was a humbling development. Just as well: the Arabs would have murdered a prince of Byzantium. Marric sighed and sank back in Nicephorus' arms.

'I . . . my thanks,' he began. 'And anything I can ever . . .'

'Be well,' said Nicephorus. 'Just be well. The rest is in the hands of the gods. If you do not pay me, you will pay another. And if not in this life, then in some other. Now, Mor, rest quiet.'

But Marric had one last question before he surrendered to the true, healing sleep which his body craved. 'Where are we bound?'

'Still Alexandria.'

Marric bit back the laughter that might have hurled him into madness. Bound for the city of Alexander, first Horus-on-Earth of Marric's line, and he would arrive in chains.

The waters of the Delta cast the ferocious sunlight back at the slaves. They squinted, and shuffled unsteadily off the dromond on to the dock and towards the holding pens.

No one asked in this part of Alexandria whether a ship was

Arab or imperial. What mattered were goods to sell and the gold to buy them.

Marric tried to shield his eyes. His upraised arms tightened the other slaves' chains and they swore at him. The slash of a whip distracted him from the pain of the glare. His feet shrank from the wharf's heat, then scuffed in hot, soft dust.

Tears ran down Nicephorus' contorted face as he grimaced at the light. It was doubly painful, after the darkness of the slave-hold, to his weakened eyes. Nevertheless, he gazed eagerly about.

'So much gone,' he mourned. 'I'd hoped to see the Pharos, but of course we were below-decks. And the Library – a sad day for the Empire when the pirates sacked the city. Oh, Antony Philadelphus could rebuild the lighthouse and the causeway, but all that learning gone . . . I would have given my eyes to have it untouched.'

'And how should you study then?' Marric asked. 'The last Emperor promised to have it restored but—'

'Like all else. Libraries are not as important as better ships, faster horses for the Hippodrome, flashier trappings and finer weapons for the Tagmata regiments . . . and for Irene herself . . .'

'Silence!'

The lash curled about Nicephorus' shoulders but did not cut too deeply. The Arabs clearly wanted their wares undamaged, to attract better prices. But Marric, now: his healing scars would only give him the appearance of fierce strength: useful should someone want a bodyguard or a fighter, an interesting challenge for a master who wanted to try his hand at slave-breaking.

Alexandria's harbour was almost bare of grain barges. The water level was low, and beggars hunching against the old ware-houses looked even thinner and more ragged than normal.

Alexandria had been tossed from allegiance to allegiance so many times that it seemed to be neither Arab nor Byzantine. Had it any loyalties at all? Marric sensed in Alexander's city the same aura of loss, corruption and sinister pleasures that had disquieted him the night of his disastrous return to Byzantium. Languorous, Alexandria might be, but it sheltered a secret excitement. Marric felt his blood begin to stir, but he marched forward, eyes on the whip.

Several times he nearly felt it on his back for turning to stare at the harbour. His ancestress, Cleopatra, might have stopped right there, he imagined, when she came to Antony dressed as the Goddess.

Nicephorus, too, kept turning to look at the city. Finally, they were shoved along twisted streets shadowed by overhanging houses, their plaster cracking and their narrow windows barred. From time to time the file of slaves had to give place to a troop of cataphracts, who thundered down the crowded streets with total unconcern for the dust their horses kicked up – or the people those horses kicked.

In the apostases, the warehouses where pottery, wine, and cheeses were stored, Arabs jostled Hellenes. No one thought it strange, least of all the native Egyptians, poorest of the city-dwellers. They had already outlasted pharaohs, caliphs and emperors. Imperial Alexandria had sunk to the level of a thieves' market.

'The Temple of Osiris,' Nicephorus jerked his chin at a huge and imposing building. 'A great one, they say, though a greater yet lies down the Nile at Heliopolis.'

The City of the Sun! Long ago Heliopolis' priests had taught his ancestors to revere Horus, Isis and Osiris in the undying lands, and to use their powers well. What powers? Marric thought bitterly. *He* had none – or had he?

Chains, fall from me, he commanded silently. Then he chuckled. Power might exist . . . did. He had had stern proof of it. It was a pity he didn't possess it, or was it? He might abuse it, too.

'You laugh, Mor?' Nicephorus asked. 'By Horus, you give me courage. I hope we are sold together.' The scholar reached out to touch his taller friend's shoulder. Then, as a man gestured threateningly with his whipstock, he shrank back.

A warmth, very different from fever or the merciless sun, filled Marric. As a prince he had tended to have associates, servants, officers. But no friends. Especially not for him, because of the daily treacheries in his life. But here was friendship, given him for the man he was, not for any imperial favours. Or did Nicephorus, with that Sight of his, know who Marric really was?

It hardly mattered either way.

Overseers and hired swords herded the coffle into a warehouse where the factor entered into loud, anguished bargaining. Finally, the slavedealers allowed the slaves to be fed and watered like the rest of the livestock. One man tossed Marric a flask of cloudy oil. He worked it in thoroughly, easing the aching stripes and wounds on his body. It would also serve to make his body gleam so he would draw a higher price, perhaps from some wealthy lady bored with too many long, idle afternoons. But he could not cavil: to be clean, fed, and out of the foul slavehold and savage streets were blessings for which slaves quickly learned to thank the gods.

Marric watched them lead Nicephorus to the block and thought he might be sick. He had seen death, had not shrunk from causing it, but this casual sale of a friend, reducing the scholar, the magician, the all-but-brother to sinew and muscle – if he retched here, they would beat him. He almost didn't care.

And since when, Marric, did you get so sensitive about slaves? You've owned enough of them, a voice commented inside his skull.

Since I became one. He grinned mirthlessly and forced himself to watch the transaction as if it meant little to him.

The bidding rose high. Professional counters translated prices in ingots, dirhans, even gold armlets, into their worth in imperial solidi. Nicephorus' skills as a scribe found a ready market.

Finally, the bidding narrowed to two people: a priest, and a freedman who was obviously the major-domo of some villa. The priest had his skull shaven and wore only a kalasiris of fine, pleated linen in the archaic fashion. But his eyes caught, and held, first Nicephorus' gaze, then Marric's. He raised the major-domo's bid, then looked back at Marric.

'Can he handle accounts?' shouted another bidder from the crowd.

'You! Can you figure?' the auctioneer asked Nicephorus. He

nodded. Despite the resignation he professed, he looked afraid. The new bidder topped the priest's offer.

The priest's eyes seemed to expand, engulfing Marric's consciousness. Under their commanding gaze, Marric felt simultaneously lighter and more aware. And then he *became* the priest, who seemed outwardly only to examine a sturdy slave:

So that is the missing Prince, thought the priest of Osiris.

Marric was stunned. He had known people were said to speak mind-to-mind, but had never believed it.

Tall, shoulders muscled from racing his chariot and reining in horses. Definitely a warrior: harsh-tempered, stubbornly loyal, angry at the world and at himself. Those scars are healing well . . . Holds his head high, with the very falcon's pride. Is he a ruler yet, fit to be consecrated? The High Priest ordered that he be tested.

The priest glanced aside and Marric knew he had been examined, judged and dismissed. Though that was no more than he expected, crushed hopes made him strike back. *I am Marric, Alexander's son!* he shouted inside his mind until his eyes ached. *I am Emperor, Horus-on-Earth! Listen to me, priest! By your loyalty to my father, aid his son. I am master here!*

Priests . . . you could never make sense of them, like that old shavenpoll back in Byzantium. He had thought, though, that you could trust them. Now it seemed as if even the High Priest knew of his plight and spurned him. He would never have believed that Irene could prevail with that one: his father had trusted him with his soul.

This priest stared at Marric. *Master of no man, least of yourself. And thus, a slave.*

He broke the contact. When the auctioneer appealed to him for a higher bid on Nicephorus, he shook his head and he and his entourage swept from the market.

Nicephorus was knocked down to the major-domo. A pity for Nico: he might have liked temple service. Then Marric clenched his fists, fighting the twin follies of cursing a priest or hurling himself after one. A push at the small of his back sent him stumbling on to the block. He breathed deeply to control his rage. Sick disgust rose like bile in his mouth. The auctioneer saw this and praised his chest expansion.

Set take you, I'm not a warhorse! Marric turned on the man, murder in his eyes. The audience gasped. Men with spears pointed them at him.

'Spirited,' the auctioneer recovered his ready patter of encouragement to the crowd, 'but, high-tempered as he is, he is biddable. Watch this, my masters!'

Holding Marric's eyes with his own, the way Marric had trained horses, he slapped his face. Marric's head jerked to one side and his eyes dimmed with shame.

Master of no man, least of yourself.

It wasn't just his line that was unsound. He himself was disastrously flawed and Alexander had known it. His father had taught Marric that the priests of Osiris never did anything by chance, so Marric's enslavement must be ordained as surely as the Nile's next flood. Even if he escaped, though, Alexa was dead.

Marric fixed his eyes above the heads of the dealers, owners, agents and passers-by who stared at him. A big man hurled an overripe fruit at him and it spattered over his face and chest. Marric started forward. As the spearsmen raised their weapons, he froze – but only barely.

'Did I not tell you?' the man said to the major-domo who had bought Nicephorus. His voice had a piercing quality that Marric could not shut out.

'The slave is dangerous.'

'Of course he's dangerous. That's the challenge. But he could be broken, moulded by a better man. Ahhh, Strymon, just let me work him over during the summer and you'll have a slave-guard worth twice as much as he'll go for now. We could resell him.' He grinned and poked the major-domo, an austere freedman, in the ribs.

'What d'ye say, Strymon? The mistress gets pleased by the profits and maybe she splits it with us. Or maybe you and that new scribe juggle—'

Strymon raised a hand, increasing his bid for Marric.

'—juggle the accounts and she never—'

Again Strymon's hand went up.

'—guesses. And if he doesn't take to . . . training, why then, he isn't going for that much more than a field worker. Even after the sea-crossing, look at the muscles on him.'

'Do I hear another bid? You, sir? You, my lady?' A leer from the auctioneer set the audience laughing raucously. 'No? Your loss then, on those long, dull evenings. Going once . . . going twice . . .'

Strymon raised his hand again. No one matched his bid.

'Sold!'

'Sutekh,' Strymon told the bigger man, 'I'm buying him not for your reasons, but because we can get good labour out of him – that is, we will be able to, assuming you're half the overseer you claim to be. But when you school this one, take care. Lose our mistress her investment again and, Maat witness, I'll have you on that block yourself to pay her back. Am I quite understood? Do you want me to repeat it more slowly?'

Sutekh, the overseer, nodded, though his blockish face reddened under its shenti, and the muscles straining his coarse tunic swelled as he fought down anger at the threat. He glared over at Marric, and Marric realized that he had been sold for the price of a good cavalry remount into a household where the overseer already resented him.

Chapter Six

Marric trudged with the other newly acquired outdoor slaves towards their barracks. The household for which he had been purchased was no great one. While the main villa seemed substantial enough, its looks might have been improved by a new wash of paint on the outer walls. The outbuildings showed that the owners and Strymon (now riding in a wagon with the more valuable indoor slaves) took decent care of the estate's livestock, animal and human.

Probably a regimental officer garrisoned in Alexandria had decided to retire here, and had taken land outside the city walls, fronting Lake Mareotis. Sensible of him, Marric thought. The man's descendants had obviously shared his good sense by tending the land, buying more, and adding a new wing to the original house. As a general, Marric would have prized such an officer.

Master of no man, least of yourself. The Osiris priest's rebuke came continually to mind. Would Marric indeed have valued such a man?

The overseer, Sutekh, stalked past the line of slaves and pointed to the barracks with the whip he seemed to use as a badge of office. Given the number of men crowding into it, the long room was as clean as might be expected. Marric had seen soldiers housed in worse quarters, and had shared them. But sun beating down on the lake, and the breathless heat of the day, would make the place not just stuffy, but suffocating. Doors and windows might let a breeze in at night, but the windows were set so high that Marric didn't think they would do much good. Not even brimstone would cleanse the place of the reek of too many bodies.

He turned quickly from the thin pallet beneath one of the windows and glanced about. Surely a household of this size provided bathing facilities for its slaves.

Deliberately, Sutekh stepped into his path. Though the overseer was shorter than Marric, he was far stockier. He had the body development of a man who had overtrained solely to win at wrestling rather than to achieve the all-round coordination of the charioteer, which was the Byzantine ideal. Sutekh's powerful arms and chest would make him a nasty adversary. Marric examined him. The skull under the reddish headcloth would be quite as hard as the jaw which the man thrust out.

'Looking for a bath, are you?' Sutekh anticipated Marric's question with more shrewdness than he had expected. He laughed, as if Marric had told him a ribald tale. 'There, slave!'

He pointed lakeward with his whip.

'Just don't let the crocodiles eat you. Around here, slaves who are too clean don't live long. But any time that you *have* time,

61

go right ahead and risk a bath. Just don't expect me to come with a spear to pry you out of the crocs' jaws.'

Marric turned away. He would watch the more experienced slaves and do as they did. Most of them seemed to avoid Sutekh. They stepped out of his path and looked down whenever his eyes swept over them.

At nightfall the slaves were fed: bread, onions, and thin, sour beer. Marric had eaten worse on campaign. He would simply have to think of this as one more battle to win.

In the days and weeks that followed, Marric found his resolve to survive and escape sorely tested. None of his barracksmates were the sort of men he was used to. Whenever he had walked among soldiers they had been rough, cheerfully obscene, and wily, with the craft of men who know that if they survive this campaign they will have money in their purses and the thanks of their officer. Here, most of his companions were spirit-broken fellahin. There were a few exotics from the Upper Cataracts, sold into slavery down in the Delta for reasons Marric never learned. There was even one Northerner – one of the Gepidae, Marric thought – who grunted incomprehensible hostilities at any attempt to speak to him. Like the others, he seemed only to understand the whip.

As scribe and account-slave, Nicephorus was kept within the house. Marric missed his serenity, his quiet faith that there was a purpose to the scant food, the hard labour in someone else's fields, and the daily, odious sight of Sutekh stalking in front of the sweating labour gangs, whip at the ready.

Once, the major-domo had sent Nicephorus out into the yard to fetch a slave to move some heavy chests.

'You!' Sutekh had bellowed at Marric. 'The bather! Clean yourself so you do not pollute the house.'

The day had been so hot that the big crocodiles basking on the dried mud of the shore would probably be too torpid to move fast. At least Marric hoped so. He dived into the water, savouring the short minutes it caressed his dried-out skin, then stood dripping before the overseer and Nicephorus. Too quickly the sun dried him, and he followed his friend towards the house.

'How does it go, Mor?'

'I live.'

'You are thinner.' Nicephorus' concern made Marric feel more human than he had since he was sold. He was thinner, lean and muscled as he had never been despite his life as a field officer. 'But still you endure—'

'All for a purpose?' Marric's mockery was gentle.

'Aye, whether or not you want to believe me. I but wish—' A man in a clean grey robe glided by, almost as if he were trying to avoid being seen. Marric stopped short. A Druid? In Alexandria? The greyrobe glanced at Marric, and Nicephorus urged him on.

'Nico,' he said. 'That man. Surely he is—'

'This way,' Nicephorus interrupted. 'The Lady Heptephras has decided that certain chests and heavy tables must be moved – immediately – and they are beyond the strength of the house staff.'

Nicephorus led the way down a corridor towards the mistress' suite. The founder of the house had built in the Egyptian fashion, with the women's quarters in the secluded inner court, the coolest part of the villa. Some mediocre wall-paintings adorned the hall. Rough tesserae of simple mosaics alternating with stonework provided cool footing.

'Does Sutekh trouble you, Mor?'

'Not beyond what I can stand – yet.' From the moment of Marric's purchase, he had had an enemy in the overseer with the ill-omened name, and he had hated him in return. Hatred – except of Irene – was a new lesson for Marric. Few men had ever dared to show him anything but smiles, however forced, and he had always managed to transfer men he disliked out of his sight. But standing silent under abuse, taking orders – alien though they were to him – taught him more control daily.

Sutekh had the power of any freedman over slaves. More than that, he was the overseer. He relished his power and exploited it. Marric would not have tolerated such a man in the army training recruits. Sensing this, Sutekh seemed to find Marric, who carried himself soldier-straight, a challenge far more satisfying than the easily cowed fellahin or the brutish Northerner.

As Marric and Nicephorus entered the room, Lady Heptephras

looked up. Nicephorus bowed to her. She gestured with pretty, plump fingers at the tables and chests she wished moved, then glided out into the court where a rippling fountain in a lotus-strewn pool provided a haven for which Marric might almost have traded his next day's meals. He stood blinking in the shadows until his eyes adjusted to the room's dimness.

All he could see of the woman who came up to Nicephorus was a shape in white. She looked young, and her grace awakened memories that could only break a slave's heart. That last night Alexa, too, had worn a white gown—

'Nico,' the newcomer said, her voice soft but with overtones of humour, 'my lady has told me where your companion must place the new chests.'

'This is Mor,' Nicephorus nodded at Marric. 'He will move them . . . once and for all, I hope.'

The woman laughed softly. 'So do I, but I doubt it. Mor, thank you for your help.'

'It is my pleasure to serve you.' The old, courtly words slipped from him. The woman stepped closer, her eyes flashing in surprise to Nicephorus.

'I told you of this one, Stephana. He kept the men on the ship from stealing my rations.' Clearly Nicephorus liked and trusted this woman, who must be the lady's personal attendant. 'He fights like a pirate and speaks . . . like a prince.'

Now that Marric could see better he noticed that the woman wore the delicate, silvered collar of a pampered body-slave. She was quite pale, a sign that she kept within the shaded courtyard, and her white dress was very clean, draped gracefully over a slender frame. But the most arresting thing about the woman – had Nicephorus called her Stephana? – was her hair, which was wound in a heavy coil. Once it had been a soft brown. Now it was heavily silvered, and it caught what light there was in the room, twisting it into an ornament. Stephana meant 'the crowned one' and, indeed, she walked with light shining on her hair like a diadem.

Stephana met Marric's eyes with the same measurement that the Osiris priest had shown in the market. Marric felt the same stirring of awareness he had felt then, but it subsided as ripples subside in a pool after the lotus has fallen from its stalk into the water. Stephana's eyes were the blue of just such a flower. Dreamer's eyes, like Nico's, eyes that saw too deeply, held too much power. As if suddenly aware of his thoughts, she looked away.

'Stephana?' Outside Heptephras clapped her hands. The slave-woman hastened to attend her.

'A friend?' Marric asked Nicephorus before he lifted a sandal-wood chest to its new place.

'Nothing like that. She is a wise, very gentle girl,' Nicephorus said, 'and one who has endured a great deal.' In a much lower voice, he added, 'And she is an adept . . .' He broke off as Stephana, this time accompanied by her mistress, came back into the room. Before the lady was appeased, Marric had to move first the sandalwood chest, and then the others, three times.

After that, Marric had little chance to speak with his friend, although he saw him quite often. It was almost as if Nicephorus were watching out for him. He saw Stephana only once. She rarely ventured into the slave-quarters, which was prudent of her. And he never again saw the Druid, though he looked for him, nor felt some curious power probe his thoughts.

Druids. By Osiris, did they rove the Empire as they wished? They never came to court; they would not have been welcome. Should Irene meet them— here he broke off his thoughts, welcoming even the gruelling field labour as release from the familiar anguish of his failed coup. Thinking of Irene was dangerous. It filled him with rage for which he had no release but folly.

He had been fool enough for a lifetime already.

But what were Druids doing in Alexandria? Marric had a brief, mad vision of grey-robed sages studying in a rebuilt library – assuming they would be allowed inside. The way Nico avoided mentioning the man after they had seen him made Marric wonder if people throughout the Empire did not protect them. Such people – hadn't Nicephorus called them 'adepts'? – had a way of seeking one another out. Look how Nico had recognized the maid Stephana.

Why could they control magic when he, a prince, could not?

Master of no man, least of all yourself. The priest's rebuke still stung.

Would such control make his slavery any more bearable? He laughed without mirth.

'What are you laughing at, slave? Need more work?' Sutekh came up behind him.

Day by day he pressed Marric towards a confrontation that would only mean disaster. He tried to show that he meant no challenge, yet his very presence, enslaved and yet unconquered, was in itself a challenge: silent defiance of a man used to beating the spirit out of those under his orders.

And ultimately it was just such men who were Marric's undoing.

As the year turned towards high summer, the days grew hotter and hotter. Sunlight battered the water as a blacksmith pounds iron. The ground scorched even the slaves' toughened feet. The dust of the walks roiled and drifted like boiling water. In the house-cisterns the water-level sank. Not even moonrise brought any coolness to the slave-barracks.

Marric had never thought of himself as squeamish, but he found the combination of slavery and imprisonment in that hovel utterly unbearable. The foulness of so many penned-in bodies cost him sleep until, one day, he could scarcely rise after the noon break. And, as Sutekh told him, he was lucky to be let off with a light beating from a rod: the overseer wanted him healthy. The next time, however, he promised he would use his whip. Sutekh had woven lead weights in with the leather thongs. That whip was a man-killer.

Then Marric discovered that the barracks door might be slipped from within. So long as no one caught him, he could slip out at night and sleep under the stars. He didn't think of escape. He had no place to run and no plans made. Since the other men slept like mummies from the instant that their bodies hit their pallets, he was safe enough. The nights of unbroken sleep in clean air strengthened Marric, and there were no more beatings.

One night, blessed and unexpected rain had settled the dust. Marric slipped out to wash. He had become passionately concerned with cleanliness, as if he could somehow wash off his own

66

slavehood. As it dripped on the overhang of the barracks, the rain soothed him. Marric dreamt that he lay in his tent, troops camped in safe, orderly rows about him . . . or that he rested comfortably in the palace . . . secure in his father's care, a boy again.

A blow shattered Marric's dreams and enraged him. Who dared kick the imperial heir? Then he remembered where he was, and that angered him more. He reached out and caught the bare, callused foot as it kicked at him again. He twisted it and brought down the hulking Gepid. He fell half on top of him, half into the mud of the courtyard.

The Gepid bellowed and raised a fist the size of a club. Marric dodged and rolled away. The blow splashed down into the mud. With another wordless shout, the man hurled himself at Marric again. This time, he had gained his feet. He crouched in a fighter's stance, his eyes alert to his enemy's movements. Years and place fell away; he stood once more with his agemates in the fighting ring, awaiting the armsmaster's command, '*Palë*! Fight!'

But this time Marric dared not close and wrestle with the man. His heavy arms could crush the life out of him. Marric must use speed and guile, the weapons that the heavier, more stupid Gepid lacked. He darted in under the man's defences and punched, then danced away. As the barbarian lunged forward, Marric brought joined fists up into his belly and followed that blow with a chop to the Gepid's neck that almost broke his hand.

The barbarian reeled and crashed against some empty cases before he fell. The boxes toppled down upon him. Amazingly, he picked himself up and started towards Marric again.

By now all the slaves had left the barracks to watch the fight. They formed a ring about the two fighters and screamed jeers and encouragement indiscriminately.

Bruises and blood stained the bodies of both fighters.

'Mor!'

Marric turned for one second too long. The big Gepid's fist sent him sprawling. A yell went up, as if a wolf-pack watched two members fight for rule, and one had fallen. The bright dawn sky whirled and roared about his head, and Marric clung to consciousness. Again and again someone shouted his name. Nicephorus? He had no place here. Where was the voice coming from?

Watch out!

As the Gepid hurled himself at Marric again, he took the mental warning, brought up both feet, and pitted them in the man's belly. When he thrust back, the barbarian crashed down. Then Marric was on him, kneeling on his chest, raining down blow after blow until his knuckles split and bled.

Sutekh hauled Marric off his victim and shook him. Marric dashed a hand across his stained face and spat blood. Though the Gepid lay unconscious at his feet, he felt no triumph. For an instant, Marric met Nicephorus' gaze. He jerked his head for Nico to get away, but he refused.

'Quite the hero!' the overseer commented, his voice deceptively quiet. He bent over the senseless man.

'The savage isn't dead, but he'll be useless around here now. Might as well get rid of him. Hero, you need to be taught a lesson. So do all you other slaves. Fighting around here – as long as you win, it's all right by me. But losers – losers deserve to lose everything. So now you'll just pick up this carrion, hero, and throw it to the crocodiles.'

Marric stared at Sutekh, appalled. He would have killed the Gepid to save his own life. The death didn't bother him; meeting the overseer's eyes did. All their long-suppressed hatred suddenly kindled.

Marric turned on his heel and walked off.

'I gave you an order, slave.' Sutekh grabbed Marric's shoulder.

He could not swear to the pirates. He could not obey now, could not serve as Sutekh's private butcher-assassin. So the choice had returned to what it was in Byzantium: live foul or die clean. Well, he might as well be thorough about it. He chose his words with care, and with the insolence he thought he had abandoned. If they were his last, he was going to enjoy them.

'Shove your order, you *fellah*!'

The blow that toppled him was no surprise. Neither was the agony of Sutekh's pet whip. The only thing that surprised Marric was the appalling length of time between blows.

'All right, you bastards, watch this!' the overseer shouted.

Each time he struck, Marric felt as if Greek fire consumed his back. He choked back vomit and scrabbled in the dust, searching for something, anything to hold on to. *I will not scream*, he vowed.

'Set curse you, lay off!' The command drowned out the torrent in his ears. Strymon's voice? 'I warned you, Sutekh!'

A torrent of explanations followed. 'He made Mor mad—'

'—kicked him—'

'The overseer ordered him to throw the big one in the lake—'

'Beat him, he did, in fair fight.'

'—toss him to the lizards—'

'I warned you, Sutekh! If you've killed that man—' the major-domo repeated his rebuke. Marric braced himself for a blow that never came.

'Mor, Mor, come back now. It's over.' Marric flinched under Nicephorus' hands. Nico must have seen the quarrel and fetched Strymon to save Marric's life. If you could call this life. Marric was floating above his pain, above this battered body. There seemed a vast distance between him and the bloodstained, trampled ground where agitated slaves milled about.

Pain ground into his body from a new source, drawing his attention by its unexpectedness.

'By all the gods, Mor, you shall not die!' Nicephorus' voice took on an edge, a power Marric would have sworn the little man lacked. 'By your blood, by your unfinished tasks, I call you back!'

And back Marric came, entering a body so torn by metal and leather that even drawing breath forced a moan from him.

'Osiris' death, you men, don't turn him onto his back!' Strymon snapped. 'You two, lift him. Gently. Gently now. Take him to the old shed by the stables. I'll have medicines—'

Wasn't Marric valuable property? Strymon ought to take care of him.

'Steady, brother.' Nicephorus was helping the others lift Marric onto a crude stretcher. The movement forced a cry from him. Tears of pain ran over his face, and Nicephorus wiped them tenderly away.

'The priest,' Marric moaned. 'He knew, he knew . . . Father, *why?* Oh gods, I hurt, Nico . . . don't let me scream . . .'

Mercifully Nicephorus reached out and pressed a spot behind Marric's ear.

Chapter Seven

Marric lay in a shed that smelled comfortingly of horses. He watched with drowsy pleasure the sunlight squeezing through the cracks in the walls. The day was dying and he was dying with it.

As the sunlight faded to the violet afterglow, the pain faded, too. Marric had observed this numbing many times after battles. First the pain lessened. Then consciousness dimmed, and death – when it came – was peaceful. How many men had he seen die thus?

NO! All Marric's youth, strength, his desire to make his father proud, rose up to fight the numbness. He longed for the earlier torment; at least it meant he was still alive and fighting. With that, pain surged up in him like a fire on which fresh fuel has been heaped, and he moaned.

'Steady, Mor.'

Strymon had let Nicephorus sit by him. His friend's voice was hoarse, as if he had been talking for a long, long time. Marric could not answer. And now the numbness was coming back.

'Send for Taran.'

'You don't give me orders, Nicephorus.'

'Then, Master Strymon, you lose a valuable slave.' Marric heard footsteps and the sound of a door shutting. Nicephorus must have won his point. Marric began to drift again. Why had he feared the numbness? There were more footsteps. He brushed them out of his thoughts.

'I reset the wards,' said a woman's voice. 'Strymon won't be back. He doesn't want to know what we do.'

'I think he's dying,' Nicephorus told whomever had come in. 'Can you bring him back?'

'Perhaps.' The voice that answered was older and it possessed an accent that teased at Marric's fading consciousness. What did it remind him of? There was no reason to remember now. Marric let his eyes drop open. The shed was very dark.

Abruptly his pain ceased and Marric's spirit detached from the battered flesh he had always called 'himself'. His attention, then his spirit, followed the waning light to the horizon. The squalid little shed in which his body lay surrounded by strangers was left behind. Now the evening star drew Marric's attention: beautiful, welcoming. Was this magic? Was it for him? It could do no harm to admit he found it beautiful. Nicephorus said he was dying. He drifted closer.

And suddenly he was driving towards it in a chariot pulled by two winged horses, one black and fiery, the other white and docile. Distance and time fell away; his chariot and horses seemed to travel inside a gigantic pearl. The chariot vanished and Marric stood upright. Curious, he tried to touch the wall of the pearl, but found no surface. Even his feet moved without actually touching anything he could think of as 'ground'.

An enormous hawk came flying towards him, its feathers jewel-bright, its hunting call somehow more poignant in this strange air. The hawk dropped lower to stare at him. Its eyes were not those of an ordinary raptor. They contained an intelligence so keen that Marric dropped his own gaze, abashed.

An incantation he had learned when he was young trembled on his lips. It might have been made for just such a time when he wandered out of body into a realm of pure spirit in which he confronted the hawk that was his House's patron.

'I have come before thee in truth,' Marric told it. 'I have not done evil to mankind, nor have I harmed animals, nor committed falsehood in the place of truth. I have not known evil nor have I acted wickedly. I have not caused misery, nor affliction, nor have I done what is abominable to the gods.'

He did not think he was dead . . . not yet. But he found the words painted on so many tombs the only fit way of explaining himself. He trembled, lest the hawk speak and call him a liar.

The hawk turned and flew back the way it had come. One wing dipped, and Marric obeyed its silent command to follow.

'May the shining ones who live upon right and truth, without deceit, who abominate wickedness, destroy my evil. Blot ye out my offences. May they destroy all evil belonging to me. Grant that I may enter these halls—'

With a flap of its wings, the hawk sped on ahead to hover above the heads of those who now faced him. Marric fell silent, awed.

Before him stood two pillars that towered upward forever without a visible base or capital. Light splintered between them, then solidified into two forms: a man, his body bound in gravebands, and a woman who wore the moon's disc on her shining brow. In her hands she held an opalescent bowl. To the left and the right of the figures gleamed a shadowy court, lights in colours Marric had never before seen glowing above their heads, reflected in the white radiance of the pair enthroned between the pillars.

As he had never imagined he would do, Marric prostrated himself before them.

'Rise.'

It was blasphemous to stand in that pair's presence, but it was worse blasphemy to disobey them. Marric visualized his spirit-form standing upright and found himself again on his feet. That voice! He gazed at the man. The man's eyes were as infinitely wise as the hawk's, but far more compassionate, sad with knowledge and with loss. Beneath that unremitting gaze Marric knew himself understood, forgiven and well-beloved, now and forever.

'Father?'

'My true son.' Only the fact that the man wore the mummy's wrappings prevented him from reaching out to embrace Marric.

'You are so weary,' said the woman, and she had his mother's voice.

'So foolish, are you not, to grieve at what is only a short parting,' said the woman. 'And you have so much to do, so much to learn.' Her voice rebuked but did not blame him. That had always been Antonia's way.

72

'It is as I was told,' the man said. 'He is no adept. Still, even without being fully aware, he seeks.'

Light blossomed over Marric's head. Surely he must say something to this pair. But what would not sound pitifully inadequate?

'What would you ask of us, son?'

Peace. Release. Your blessing. Marric could have asked for any of them. Instead, words from the rituals burst from him. 'May I renew myself, may I become strong. Grant that I may come forth and that I may obtain power.'

The eyes of the man and woman studied him, then softened into such love that Marric shook from its intensity. He felt himself slipping from their presence and could have wept at the bereavement, save that he knew how necessary it was . . . for now. Again he was driving the winged chariot. This time he felt rushing wind, speed, vertigo as the horses plunged back from the place towards the world. He tried to remember his exaltation, his sense of calm power. The dark horse reared, attempting to take the chariot on a mad dash through the tranquil night sky. He was Marric. He was master. The magic would not hurt him. He sought to believe that as he restrained the horse. He had all but mastered it when something horned and hideous leapt up from beneath its hooves. The horse screamed and bolted. Marric hid his eyes. The thing had had his face.

He cried out and felt himself tossed from the chariot. Then he was falling, falling . . . a voice was hailing him back to a world of pain and the body he had abandoned.

He lay on his belly, the scratchiness of blanket and pallet protecting him from the dried mud of the floor. That pair who were mother and father to him – they were gone. And the beast with his face guarded their threshold. Loss gnawed at him, and he sobbed.

The voice that had called Marric from the place was chanting over him now. He felt his entire body tingle. His hands, propping his chin, seemed to glow. Then the chanting stopped.

'Rest. You have wandered all night.'

Marric tried to rise, to rush into the departing night to seek that place once more. A fragile hand forced him down, then lifted a wet cloth from his back. The touch felt as if crocodiles of fire gnawed at him. He wept, biting his arm for a more manageable pain lest he shame himself by screaming. Perhaps the numbness would return and he could escape. This time he would not come back.

New fire lashed across his back. One of those hands, slender and very sure, which tended him had touched him shrewdly, restoring his awareness of his own body.

'Afraid to die, yet unwilling to live: is that it? Awake, coward, and take up your life once again.'

Coward? Rage flowed through him, uniting his body and spirit once more.

'You call me a coward? Had I my strength, I would kill you for saying that.'

'Do you think I have not wished for death?' the voice answered. 'Every time I was sold, or taken again, I prayed for it. If the gods will it, you may yet be my death.' That was the maidservant's voice, wasn't it? What was her name? Stephana. Why would Nicephorus' friend taunt him?

'Mor is no coward,' Nico said.

'Not if he can fight. But you forget, Nico,' Stephana's voice was cool. 'Cowardice is what I know about. My life is a misery because I was a coward in my last. The more shame to me! Doubtless this man will stray on the path, but as I have strength and will to help him, he will not die a coward.'

'Will he die?'

'Now now,' said the third voice, the accented one. The man walked toward Marric and he saw a grey robe.

'Taran?'

'Remember, Mor, you saw a Druid within the villa? Taran is my teacher and my friend. Trust him. And brother, stay with us.'

'You must get hold of me and take care that I do not run away from you.'

'If you can quote Plato, you're not dying,' Nicephorus said. His tired face lit and relief quivered in his voice. He shifted positions, irresolute.

'If you have duties, Nico, you should return to them before we are both missed.'

74

'Leaving you unprotected?'

Stephana laughed. 'Taran and I have this place warded. And in any case, Strymon has locked Sutekh up until his hot head cools. But even if Sutekh were a-prowl for me, I would stay here. I am not afraid now.' Her voice held an exultation Marric could not fathom.

'Then I rejoice for you.' Nicephorus bent over and touched Marric's hand. 'Rest, Mor.'

He and the Druid left. Marric turned his head and looked at the woman whose reproof had shamed him into taking up his life again. Her silvered hair, escaping from its thick coils, drifted around her face. From time to time she brushed at it with delicate, thin-fingered hands, too workworn for beauty. Now her eyes were almost the same blue as the shadows of strain and doubt that the fight to keep life within Marric had hollowed out.

Biting his lips against pain, he reached out to touch her hand.

'I did not mean that I would kill you. I regret my harsh words, lady.' Marric used the words and tones with which he might have addressed a woman of the palace.

'Lady?' Stephana laughed, a rippling music that made Marric think of a breeze upon his forehead. 'I invited your anger, Mor, to draw you back to life.'

'I would not wish to be angry at you, lady,' he brought the words out carefully.

'Stephana, please. Not lady. I am but a seamstress, a broidress, a dresser of hair—'

'And a healer, a mistress of power. My friend calls you an adept.'

Gentle fingers pressed against his lips.

'Both you and Nico talk too much.' Marric kissed her fingers. They trembled, then jerked away as if his lips were hot coals. There was near-panic in her eyes which did not accord with her earlier words. But she regained her former calm quickly and relegated Marric to the role of invalid.

'You are fevered. Last night you almost died. Now drink this and sleep.'

She gave him a potion heavy with syrup of poppies. Where had she found that to lavish it upon a slave? Marric gulped at it until it was gone. He was desperately thirsty. He murmured thanks up at the tired face within its halo of soft hair.

'I am here, Mor, if you need me.'

As Stephana took the cup from him, the light fell on her and turned her into a creature all white and shining. Marric tried to tell her how she looked, but the effort was beyond him.

Stephana laid a hand on his head. He imagined he felt strength flow into him from her fingers. The last women to touch him had been Alexa and Irene, both enraged, both abusing powers they could not control and should never have summoned. Stephana was so different. Her touch healed and blessed him.

Chapter Eight

Beyond the wall of Marric's shed, horses stamped and whinnied. Slaves brought them fodder, forked through their stalls, and curried them. Marric's labour gang would have been at work since dawn, but the light slanting across the floor showed that the morning was already well-advanced. Marric tried to raise himself and stifled a gasp at the pains which jolted across his back.

Strymon had had him brought here to die, but his friends had helped him back to life. Now his task was simple: heal and wait. Marric took comfort from the pair he remembered seeing. They had all but told him he had something worth waiting for.

Carefully Marric settled back on his belly. If Taran had defended this shed, he was safe enough. A Druid's prophecy had brought him here. Magic had kept him alive and consoled him. It was not the Druid's fault – or Nico's or Stephana's – that he himself was not fit to be trusted with it.

Marric sighed and rested his cheek on his arm where blue marks still showed from where he had bitten his own flesh to keep from crying out. Whatever salves Taran and Stephana had used on his lacerated back seemed to work. He hurt, but he was no longer devoured by agony.

Had they fed the Gepid to the crocodiles after all? Marric wondered. He shuddered. And Sutekh himself: had Strymon punished him, or would the overseer still swagger about brandishing that whip of his? There would come a day of reckoning, that Marric promised himself.

The warped door creaked open as a boy edged in with a tray. Nicephorus followed. Before kneeling beside Marric, he closed his eyes, gestured at something, and muttered. Closing the wards?

'How does my back look?' Marric asked.

'Like raw meat, if you must know, but it will heal cleanly. Stephana says you are to eat all of this. No, don't move!' The boy brought the tray nearer, and Nicephorus raised Marric's head.

All that day Marric drifted in and out of sleep. Around dusk, the door opened, startling him. A flash of white skirt told him that his new visitor was Stephana. Marric smiled up at her.

'Mor? Wake and drink.'

Though he was still half asleep, he drank. When he had finished, she washed his face. Her touch was cool and deft. The broth had smelled better than it tasted, but he had forced himself to drink all of it, lest Stephana call him a coward for refusing the food that would help him heal.

Now she opened the phials she had brought. The cleanly fragrances of nard and valerian filled the room. 'I must work these into your back,' she warned him. 'You know you must not struggle, or the wounds will reopen.'

Marric braced himself. As she anointed his back, Stephana talked to distract him.

'Nicephorus has been busy today,' she said. 'This morning he took your story to Lady Heptephras. While she was still weeping, he asked if I might tend you.' Stephana laughed, telling him that she would have nursed him in any case. 'The Gepid has been sold. Strymon was all for selling Sutekh, too, but . . . then he considered how efficient he is. It is a shame.' Her voice quivered for so brief an instant that Marric thought he had imagined it. 'When you recover, you will not return to that barracks. You are to work inside – light work until your strength fully returns. Perhaps, as a door-guard—'

Marric chuckled. So he was to be promoted, was he? Stephana hushed him with a touch, then continued. 'Mor, you must avoid Sutekh. As long as you stay within the house, he cannot harm you. But if you go outside . . .'

Marric yawned. *I wish that Sutekh were crocodiles' meat,* he thought contentedly, and slept.

As Marric's fever abated and his strength returned, he began to wonder when his inexorable nurses would ever let him stand and move around. They were being over-indulgent. If this were Cherson's frontier, he would have had to fight in this condition. His allies, the Kutrigur Huns, rode with worse wounds and counted it of little importance.

Marric lay listening to the shaduf labouring to pump water into the fields from the canals. This year the floods had come late and not risen as they should have.

Running feet approached. The door slammed open. Marric leapt into a defensive crouch, the blanket that was his only covering falling down along his hips. The gouges on his back and sides ached, but no trickle of warm blood told him that the scabs had broken open.

Stephana stood with her back to the door. She was breathing hard and her face was distraught. She clutched her medicines to her breast with both hands.

'I won't be afraid. I'm not . . . I'm not!' her voice trembled on the knife-edge of hysteria. Three times she attempted to reset the wards, then dropped her hands in despair.

'Only fools never fear,' said Marric. 'What happened, Stephana?' She sank down on her knees and he reached out to her.

'You're trembling,' he said. 'Here, before you drop those jars, give them to me.' He pried the unguents out of her fingers.

Stephana's eyes were wild with fear and with a remembered revulsion. One hand inched upward to her mouth; Marric caught the other one. When she jerked away he began to understand.

Her light garment fell from one shoulder to her waist, exposing flesh reddened and scratched from breast to throat, as if someone had tried to tear her clothes from her and had clutched her breast so hard as to leave finger-marks on her skin.

'Who hurt you?' Marric asked in a soft growl. From the way she held her head low and shook it – did she fear for *him*? Or was she ashamed? Only Sutekh, the overseer, would be rash enough to lay violent hands on the mistress' favourite maid.

'How else . . . did he harm you?' Marric made his voice gentle.

'He . . . no, not this time. This time I got away.' Stephana's voice was dull with humiliation. She brought up her hand to rub at the scratches on her body.

Marric reached for the ointments. 'Come here, Stephana. We'll use some of these on you.' As he inched closer, he sensed that she feared nearness to him, and bent to draw his blanket over his loins.

'You helped me. Let me help you,' he urged. He unstoppered a glass tube with one hand. With the other, he pried gently but relentlessly at her fingers.

Why had her magic not spared her this? Anger blazed up in him and Stephana winced away, moaning at her own helplessness.

Though she had fought Sutekh bravely, now, as reaction to the struggle began, she had no more fight left in her. Marric laid his arm around her shoulders. He only wanted to draw her close and comfort her before he tended her scratches, but she went rigid.

'Steady now,' he murmured. 'You saved my life. Do you really think I would try to rape you?'

What was it about this woman that tore so at his heart? Some invisible cord seemed to draw them together. The sight of her panic, her fear of him and of his touch, made him ache. What a terrible life for a gentle woman: most nights a different master or stranger, and most of them brutal. 'I'm not afraid,' she had declared so proudly. But she did fear, now, and Marric wanted to help her.

He laid a hand on her shoulder again and tipped her face up with his other hand. 'I am going to smear some of this balm on those scratches,' he said.

'I don't need it.'

He shook his head at her.

'Enough talk on the subject. This way I will not worry that you go untended. Come closer.' Marric remembered what an old army surgeon had once told him: *better tend a wagonload of wounded men than one battered woman.*

'Look, you can put your hand on top of mine if you don't trust me – and to make sure I do this right,' he added. 'Come, Stephana. Who is being the coward now?'

She let her head droop. Marric reached for linen, wet it, and began to dab delicately at her shoulder near her throat. Nails had bitten into her flesh and raked downward. As Marric worked, Stephana's unsteady breathing, still too much like sobs, fanned his temple. He thought he would more quickly forgive the overseer for his own beating than for abusing Stephana. Damn the man, he had enjoyed it. Now for the nard. Marric took a generous fingerful and began to work it in. Stephana's skin was very soft. It warmed as the salve sank in. Though her hand hovered protectively close to his own, she relaxed somewhat.

But Marric's injuries were healing, and his body let him know it. Rose scent clung to Stephana's hair, makng him dizzy. His breathing grew more rapid. He tried to keep the motion of his fingers, smoothing down her shoulder to her breast, steady as he worked in the ointment. He tried to think he was dressing the wounds of, say, a common soldier, but the contact was too intimate. Accidentally, his finger brushed her nipple, and it hardened. For a heartbeat they both held motionless.

Stephana gasped. Her hand closed over his and pushed it away. It would be dishonest to ask, *Have I hurt you?* just so he could replace his hand and caress her. For this time his touch would indeed be a caress, not an expression of concern. Even as Marric wondered how she would feel in his arms, he realized that he would never force even the slightest touch upon her. How could he destroy any faint trust she might hold for him? But Isis, Isis, he wanted her.

Very slowly and very carefully, he moved away.

'Knot up your gown,' he said, and turned to the food she had brought him. He was very hungry.

'Your back heals,' Stephana said after a long pause. 'Does this hurt?' She ran her fingers tentatively across the welts. 'Not much? Good.' In some places Sutekh's lash had wrapped about Marric's sides. She traced these lines too. Marric drew back, unable to tolerate a healer's touch he found so unexpectedly erotic.

'I see,' she whispered.

'Do you?'

'You're the one who doesn't see, Mor. You never have. You still think like a man whose will is his own, not a slave.'

'I am a man, not a slave.'

When Marric had been a prince, a governor, even a junior officer, he had always found women: high-born ones, his for an easy chase; slaves, his for a casual summons. And they had all seemed eager, had seemed to take equal pleasure in the sport. Had any of those women had to battle with fears like Stephana's? Had he ever forced a slave? He was bitterly ashamed that he couldn't remember clearly.

Slavery was far worse for a woman than for any prince, for any man at all. With that agonizing sensitivity of hers, Stephana faced added humiliations. Marric wanted her, but her life had been so painful that he wondered if she could ever respond to anyone.

She scrambled her jars, plates and linen together, and fled. Marric did not know if she would ever come back.

'You will be scarred,' Taran the Druid told Marric after inspecting his back.

'Do you think I care about that? I was a soldier. But—' the question escaped before he could stop it. 'What can I do?'

'About Stephana?' asked the Druid. His eyes met Marric's and a familiar roiling in his soul warned him that Taran looked into his thoughts. This time, however, instead of rebelling or recoiling from the touch, Marric held firm.

'So you sense that your life is joined to hers?' Taran asked. 'I think you are right. But . . . I imagine, Mor, that you are not the sort of man to whom things of the spirit come easily.'

There had been that Place of Light. Even the glimpse of it that he'd had had changed him. But for the rest of it, no, the things of the spirit came hard.

'However long on the Wheel it has taken you to come this far, I begin to understand you. I know you.

'Stephana knows you, too. You see, she is not just an adept and a student, she is a seeress, and far advanced in her tale of lives. She has foreseen that if she makes no grievous errors in this life, she will be freed to take the next step along the Way. Now she must atone for one thing and one thing only in all her past lives before she wins release: cowardice caused her to betray a friend. It was a slave's act, and she has been reborn as a slave to atone for it. So, in this life she knows that she must battle fear, and aid someone who needs her. That person, too, is ordained for her.'

Marric gestured impatiently.

'But you want more of her than prophecy or her quick wits. You want *her*. That terrifies her still further. She has suspected, you see, that you are the one who will demand courage of her. Mor . . .' the Druid let Marric see, from the tone of his voice, that he knew his true identity. 'Not an easy man to help, are you?'

I don't want this. I don't want to be responsible for a slavewoman or for a sorceress. What happens when I escape?

Yet the remembrance of how soft her skin was made his fingers tremble with desire to stroke it.

'I would not harm her. How could I? Sutekh had hurt her. I only meant to care for her as she had done for me. Yet the instant I touched her—' he remembered his desire for her. Then he drew the last thing, the unbearable memory, out. 'She said once that I would be her death.'

'Adepts do not fear death, my son. Not as you do. Violation, humiliation: these are the things that Stephana fears.' Taran waved a hand and turned aside. When he spoke again, it was in a deliberately inconsequential tone.

'You're well enough now to do light work. I will have Nicephorus tell Strymon.'

'Is Nico also a seer?'

'Just a scholar with some small power. Nicephorus is too

committed to individuals to be greatly adept. He fears for them and fights with all his heart to protect those he loves. He fought bravely for your life.'

'What are they – Nico, Stephana – to you?'

'My pupils, now. In another life perhaps they were my teachers, and I repay them now. Later they may be guides to other spirits, as will I.'

'And I?'

'You know well what you are and why we are drawn to help you. The land withers.'

'The water sinks . . . I saw . . . in the city, fights, hunger . . . they hunt Druids . . .'

'Just so. The land fails when deprived of its proper leadership. One day I must tell you of my homeland in the Isles of the Mists.'

'A man I once knew came from there.'

'Aillel, who joined the Varangian Guard? He was a prince among us.'

Marric no longer bothered to wonder how Taran knew Aillel's name. 'I met a Druid in Byzantium and he – what do you call it? – he scried for me. Warned me. Are you warning me, too?'

Taran glanced aside. The sky was reddening before a fierce dawn. 'I see danger for both of us if I do not leave now. But let Stephana fight her own battles. Little as she may trust herself, she has enough courage for the task.'

Taran slipped out of the shed. A faint tingling, followed by a sense of vacancy, a way laid open, told Marric that the wards that had been protecting him were removed. He was free to take up his own life again.

Chapter Nine

The morning star dimmed in the sky. With a sudden flash of green at the horizon, dawn drove the last soft traces of violet night before it. Marric gazed east, narrowing his eyes as the red sun smouldered in the shrunken lake. The canal that began at the Nile and ran many miles to Alexandria carried less water, too. The water-levels in the house-cisterns had sunk still further, and the fresh, living mud that had made Egypt the granary of Empire was very thin this year.

All the slaves feared the great crocodiles which were ravenous and torpid by turns. They were going to get hungrier still. But Marric had no intention of remaining a slave long enough to see.

As the food ran out, soon the poorest and the oldest in Alexandria would begin to starve. The babes at their mothers' breasts would thrive for a time, then die quickly. People would knife others at first for a loaf of bread and, later, for even a chunk of a loaf. Disease would scythe through the crowded Old City.

Out here the slaves would not starve; still, the prospect of hunger, of – give the things their proper names – famine and plague in Alexandria made Marric feel helpless and guilty. By rights he was the land's steward, as Horus had been when gods still walked the earth. If the Empire starved, it was his fault. Hellenes, his dynasty called themselves. Still, this land was dear to their hearts.

Sun, water and land quivered in the early morning quiet. Even a slave might find the sight peaceful. The sun felt good on Marric's healing back and chest. Now he felt strong enough to try to escape.

A shadow, stunningly dark in the brilliant light, startled him. With the pitcher on her head supported by an upraised, slender arm, Stephana looked to a casual glance like any one of a hundred women carrying water, but Marric would always know her. Something in her bearing, a blend of assurance and fragile grace, delighted him. The light made her gleam. She raised a hand to shade her eyes.

Once he escaped, he would never see her again.

He shut that thought from his mind. Why was Stephana out here? Usually she did not venture far from the inner courts, as he well understood. From what he had seen, and what Nicephorus had let fall, it was no wonder that her hair had silvered when she was little more than a girl. But no maid: the secluded innocence of maids had been utterly foreign to her ever since slavers had snatched her in childhood from her seacoast home. Since then, Taran and Nicephorus had been the first men who had perceived her as more than a pair of hands or a convenient female body. Then Marric, wanting to comfort her, had had to touch her too intimately and destroy whatever trust she might have come to have for him, too.

She might not trust him now, but Marric was sure of one thing. Standing alone at the water's edge, she was too vulnerable to attack from slaves or crocodiles. He moved slowly towards her.

She had her back to him. Lifting the pitcher from her head, she knelt and filled it. With the care of a priestess performing a solemn ritual, she poured the water back. The place where she had emptied her pitcher lay unnaturally calm, reddened from the soil and the sun that simple folk said quickened the earth to produce frogs. Stephana stared rapt at the smooth water.

Her low cry broke the morning's peace. The pitcher fell unnoticed from her hands and shattered. A shard of the unglazed pottery rolled into the water and broke the spell she had laid upon it. As if released, Stephana leapt to her feet and turned, ready to flee.

She had been only a child who liked to stare out over the winedark Aegean, imagining, as children did, that she could see pictures in its surging waves. Then, as the child grew towards womanhood, she *could* see. What she saw terrified her. She ran from the visions straight into the cruel actuality of a slaver's hold.

How could Marric sense her terror so clearly? If he ran after her now, she would panic. So he doubled back to cross her path. As she came up beside him, he caught her in his arms. For an instant she struggled against him, reliving the old nightmare of kidnapping and enslavement.

'It's Mor, Stephana. Mor. What troubles you?'

'Did you see it too?'

'See what?'

'In the water, Mor. Ships, pirates, oh, Isis, and they had

terrible curved swords . . . horses jumping over broken walls . . . burning . . .'

Men with curved swords . . . pirates or Berbers attacking overland? Had Stephana seen an attack on Alexandria?

'This land is guarded,' Marric tried to reassure her. 'Foot soldiers. The City Guard itself. And the great houses have their own trained men.' Stephana's silvered hair was very soft against his mouth.

Light danced in its tangled strands as she shook her head vehemently. 'Not so, Mor! What if the guards are withdrawn?'

'Where do the soldiers go, Stephana?' Her fear compelled him to believe, little as he liked it, and he stared at the lake as if he could see troop transports assembling.

'She . . . she cannot hold what she has seized. Mother Goddess, help!'

Exhausted by her vision and the violent backlash from it, Stephana slumped. Marric supported her, welcoming the slight weight of her body against him.

Why would troops be withdrawn from Alexandria, which was the gateway to the Nile. There could be only one reason: Byzantium itself was in danger. Had Irene recalled—

'You would really choose *this* as a meeting-place?' Sutekh's voice was heavy with sarcasm. In his weeks of house-duty Marric had forgotten how much he hated it. The way Stephana shuddered made him hate it worse.

Marric turned so that he stood between her and the overseer. Now she was out of the man's reach. Up by the house, people were stirring. The labour gangs trudged off to the fields. Marric had a sudden vision of nailmarks on Stephana's body, another vision of Sutekh striding across the fields, brandishing his whip at labouring slaves.

'Run back swiftly, Stephana. I'll keep you safe.' He released her and she darted up to the gates. When Sutekh would have stopped her, Marric stepped forward with his arm outstretched to block him.

'Walk carefully, hero. What I did to you once, I can do again. Want another lesson to add to the ones you already wear on your back?'

'Find a willing woman!'

Sutekh's fist drove out, but Marric was prepared. He caught the man's wrist and twisted it, a grip that would have brought a smaller man writhing down on his knees. They faced off, almost as close as brothers embracing after a long parting. Each struggled to upset the other. Finally, Marric threw the overseer off-balance just slightly.

Drawn by the struggle, the crocodiles were crawling out of the water. Marric glanced at Sutekh's whip, coiled at his belt. If he could only wrest it away . . .

But Stephana, who hated violence, was safely beyond Sutekh's reach. She had tried to tell Marric of a vision of war throughout the Empire. That was more important than a personal grudge. Emperors had no right to personal grudges. Let the man live, then.

'You have your duties, as I have mine,' he said quickly. 'Perhaps your labour gangs will escape while you tend to me. Or do I go tell Strymon that once again you're adding slave-murder and rape to your tasks?'

Marric turned his back on the overseer and walked towards the house. At any moment the whip would curl agonizingly about his tender shoulders. If Sutekh struck him now, Marric was afraid he would fight until one of them died.

Master of no man, least of all yourself.

If Marric couldn't master himself, how could he hope to win his rightful place? Sutekh was unimportant.

'You'll pay, slave!' the overseer shouted at him. 'By my name, you'll pay!'

Decently attired in a plain tunic, Marric searched the house for Nicephorus. As always, he ignored the slaves who scuttled along the sides of the corridors as he strode boldly down their centres. In the accounts room he found Nico.

'Nicephorus?'

His friend laid down tablets and scrolls. He turned to face Marric, who leaned against the lintel. Then, as he saw that Strymon was also in the room, he straightened politely.

'Why this disturbance, Mor?' Strymon asked.

The man was old and shrewd; Marric thought fast. 'I walked by the lakeshore this morning . . . master. I observed how low the waterline is. This year's crops will be meagre. Perhaps I could suggest that the house buy supplies now – for use and possible resale. Prices will rise . . .'

Nicephorus stared at Marric. Well, let him. How could he explain in front of Strymon that Stephana's vision had disturbed him – or even that she had had a vision? Neither could he say that a trip to Alexandria gave him the ideal chance to escape alone. Even Nico would slow him, and he had to get back to Byzantium.

'How is this your concern?' asked Strymon.

'I have been a soldier, master,' Marric gave him part of the truth. 'An army is only as good as its source of supply.'

Strymon rubbed his chin, rose from his stool, and opened a bound volume of grain records.

'Well thought of. Even if we do not need the grain we can, as you said, Mor, resell it. Excellent. In fact, you might reap a reward yourself for your forethought. Nicephorus, you will take the wagon into the city to market today.'

Marric looked earnestly at Nicephorus. *Ask for my help.*

'I'll need someone to carry the sacks,' Nicephorus said. 'How about Mor here?'

Strymon stared narrowly at Marric, who forced himself to assume an expression of earnest docility, eagerness for an outing and a future reward. And he thought courtiers had been servile! Finally, Strymon unlocked a chest and tossed a purse at Nicephorus. 'Mor,' he said, 'you will consider yourself under Nicephorus' instructions. Watch that you do not strain yourself; I understand that you are only recently returned to duties.'

Marric bowed his head just deeply enough. With luck, this would be the last time he would have to bow to any man.

'May we leave now?' asked Nicephorus. 'The noon sun will be like hammer on anvil.'

They walked side by side down the corridors, Marric moderating his long, impatient stride to the shorter man's pace. From a side room Stephana emerged. She parted her lips as if to speak, then turned away. Marric forced himself not to look back at her.

*   *   *

Nicephorus wiped his eyes which streamed from the dust on the road into Alexandria. 'Grain,' he said in disgust. 'What devil in your skull made you drag us both out of the house on a hot day?' He glanced up at the huge sun.

'Strymon agreed,' said Marric. He shook the reins. 'You've seen the water levels. And the wharf rats are thin. It's only prudent to fill the storehouses.'

'And you're just the prudent soldier, are you? Surprising that you haven't turned your warrior's training towards escape. I had expected you to be long gone by now.'

'With this collar on me or a raw back?' Marric laughed shortly.

'You are healed now.'

Marric shrugged. 'Not all sickness is of the body.'

Nicephorus looked over at him: a slight, indoor man with weak eyes. Marric might topple him from the wagon into the ditch, might kill him for the silver he carried. Nevertheless, he sat relaxed, unconcerned.

He laid a hand on Marric's arm. 'I cannot go home. I am as well served here as anywhere.'

'But if you were a freedman—'

'Who among us is truly free? You, Mor? Since the moment they tossed you into the hold beside me, you've been like a wing-clipped hawk. Doubtless I will contrive to protect myself after you—'

Marric drove on in silence. He was ashamed. What if he did take Nicephorus with him? The scholar had been tough enough to survive the crossing. And he was shrewd, or he would have died in the fight with the pirates. But, brave as he might be, he hadn't the instincts of a fighter born and trained. If he thought remaining a slave might help his family, he would refuse to leave, and Marric would have to abandon him.

When I rule, I will restore you to your home, Marric promised him silently.

'Tell me, Mor,' Nicephorus asked after a long silence, 'did you see Stephana this morning?'

'Saw her, yes, and prevented Sutekh from doing more than that. Why do you ask?'

89

'Something distressed her badly – besides Sutekh. I thought you might know.'

Now the truth could come out. Nicephorus must suspect that Stephana had had a vision that propelled Marric into action.

'She said she had a vision,' he began cautiously.

'Then she did.'

'As you say. She saw guards withdrawn from the city, soldiers summoned from this entire region to the capital.'

'Do you believe her?' Nicephorus asked.

'I believe in my observations. She is worth observing, too.'

Nicephorus laughed pleasantly. High above his head a bird circled in wide, lazy swings, scanning for prey. 'Always the soldier, Mor. You felt you ought not to trust, so you invented this errand as a way of arranging a reconnaissance.'

Marric let the reins fall and looked at his friend. He grinned in a way he had not done for a long time.

'So look about and content yourself, brother.'

The bird dived, a burning gold arrow's flight in the sky. With a shrill cry of triumph it stooped upon its prey.

I shall miss you, Nico. And Stephana too. But if I took you with me, what help would you be? A party of two men and a woman, especially a woman with that hair of hers, would be suicidally conspicuous. *She is lovely, gentle, but she fears my touch, and I am leaving here. Why think of her at all?*

He slapped the reins against his sleepy oxen and they plodded on. Ahead gleamed the faint silver ribbon of the Delta waters and the city walls loomed up before them.

Marric identified the market, swollen with people, in which he had been sold. Again it was a blaze of colour, a tumult of 'come, buy!' – beasts lowing, children crying, and smells that assaulted the nose like a blow. Above the market circled a spark of gold.

Sun poured down upon battered awnings, weakening them even further, when Marric and Nicephorus entered the tidal rush of shoppers.

'Way, make way!'

A horseman shoved a lance against people who crowded from all the demes of the city into this narrow place. They flattened against the wall where an eye had been painted. A troop of peltasts followed the rider. That was not the first such troop Marric had seen. With so many men shipping out, he could slip away, take service on a boat, and cross the Middle Sea to Byzantium.

Sullenly the people waited until the soldiers passed, then poured back into the marketplace. They were thinner and more ragged than Marric liked to see. He glanced at the stalls. Unless he counted wrong, there were more stalls of old wares – rugs, furniture, cheap jewellery – than stalls with cheeses or bread. Samian wine was selling at a price Marric considered outrageous; the other prices matched it. No one shopping here could afford such prices long. Frequently, bargaining broke off prematurely in a spate of insults. To Marric's left, a thin man harangued a seller of cheeses from Chios. Even staples like dried peas were in short supply.

'The granaries?' a ragged boy answered Nicephorus' request for directions. 'That way, near the harbour. Little enough they'll give you unless you have ready coin. The factors cry bad crops and raise the prices day by day.'

These market urchins were an uncertain lot – doubtful of parentage, of morals, of their next meal. Marric had never looked at one longer than to make sure of his aim with a coin. Unlike Marric now, the boy had his freedom; but he was scrawny and ill-cared for, while Marric went decently clad and fed. Famine was harder on the free poor than on slaves.

'The grain-sellers cannot charge so much that I will not repay you for your help,' Nico told the lad. Marric saw the glint of silver.

'You'll have every mangy brat in the bazaar down upon us,' he warned.

'The boy is starving, Mor. As a father myself, could I do less for any child?'

'Thanks, master!' The boy was off, leaping boxes, cannonning into a donkey tethered against a building.

'Not so fast, gutter rat!' shouted a merchant. She was a thin, harsh-faced hag with one eye. As the boy's hip struck her stall, pots toppled loose from their careful stacks. Three broke on the ground. The woman set up an outraged howl, her hands lifting the green-glazed fragments to show passers-by how she was abused.

A man stuck out his foot. The boy sprawled over it. His fist opened and the coin spun out of his hand. He flung himself after it, hating to abandon his assurance of a day's food. But others had seen the money too.

'My good silver!' screamed the potter. 'See, he steals my coin! Catch him!'

A howl went up and people started after the boy.

'He'll lose his hand for that lie. And I gave him the coin,' Nicephorus muttered. 'I *gave* it to him!' he shouted at the mob. He started to climb down from the wagon.

Marric started to haul him back, then thought better. Now, while Nico could honestly say he was distracted, he could get free. And blame wouldn't fall on his friend – at least not too much. Just a moment longer. The crowd would part Nicephorus from him and he would run free.

The boy too darted for freedom. Someone else tripped him. This time he fell against a stall, overturning it into some nearby crates. Splintering wood added to the uproar. Over all the noise rose the boy's agonized shriek. 'My leg . . . my leg!'

Nicephorus – a white tunic flashing among drabber clothes – pushed into the thick of the mob and shouldered people aside with a strength born of anger. 'I gave him the coin, I gave it him,' he repeated, as stubborn as he was rash. He hurled another coin at the potter. 'Go away! Maat curse you for a liar, but get out of here!'

He flung himself down beside the boy, forgetting grain, wagon, Mor, the purse hidden in his breast, because of a brat that reminded him of his own lost family. Marric slipped down from the wagon. *Goodbye, my brother.*

He heard a new clamour: the jangle of harness, the clatter of hooves and the yells of a crowd trapped before armed troopers.

A band of cataphracts rode through the market. Right in the path of the oncoming riders, Nicephorus, unseeing and uncaring, knelt and tried to shift the injured child free of a weight far beyond his strength.

Chapter Ten

Marric swore. The market was in chaos, he had a god-given chance to escape, and Nicephorus had to go and endanger himself for some bastard beggar-brat!

In that last battle on the steppes, a man had leapt forward and died with a spear through him. It had been meant for Marric. Wasn't this a battle too? WASN'T IT?

For an instant, Marric hated himself, Nicephorus, and all misbegotten bazaar urchins. Then Nico looked up. As he saw the oncoming troops, his face tightened with fear. His lips moved – *summoning magic*? But then he shook his head and bent over his hopeless task of freeing the injured boy.

Damn you, Nicephorus, save yourself!

Marric hurled himself through the crowd. He was glad to see the hag who had accused the boy go sprawling into the muck. Dust and outrage soon stifled her. He glanced at the rubble that covered the child, seized a long board, and wedged it into the heap.

'When I tell you, Nico, pull him free.'

With supreme disregard for the people they should have protected, the troops rode at a canter through the marketplace. Surely most of them would be able to rein in. But even a few horses could trample them to death – as Ctesiphon had died. His death-screams had sounded even through the gag they had put on him.

Marric strained against his improvised lever. A hot trickle down his back warned him that the fragile new skin had broken in at least one place. Both Nicephorus and the boy held still. The child bit one fist to keep from crying out. Marric was curiously touched by that gesture.

'Good lad,' he heard himself say with surprise. 'Steady now. Brace yourself!'

Nicephorus took the boy into his arms, hiding his face from the plunging horses.

'Now!' Marric exerted his full strength. Boxes and stall toppled.

As the first horseman reined his screaming mount aside, Nicephorus pulled the child free, then laid him flat to inspect his leg.

'Just as I thought,' he said. 'Broken.' He reached for a long, straight stick. 'Mor?'

'Crocodiles eat your livers! Your damned brat almost cost me my horse!'

'We're from Lady Heptephras' villa,' Nicephorus spoke fast. 'Master, the boy directed me to the granaries and I gave him a coin. I couldn't let him be trampled for helping me.'

Bent almost double, Marric still leaned against a stall. He breathed in great gulps and his tunic was stained with sweat and fresh blood. Nicephorus sat him down then tore strips from his own tunic to bind the boy's leg to the improvised splint.

'Lady Heptephras' slaves, eh? I have kin-ties there myself. I should check on your story.' He turned from Nicephorus to Marric.

'Set take you, man! Did you know you could have been trampled?' the captain shouted.

Marric lowered his head, silenced by exhaustion and a vast frustration. If he were a proper ruler, he would let others suffer in his place, preserving himself for his realm.

I could not, Marric told himself. His father had not been ruthless, or even exceptionally harsh; he had not needed to be.

The officer stood over Marric. He wore a klibanion of lamellar scales, but had left off his helmet and greaves because of the heat. Freshly blazoned on his gear was the insignia of a commander of fifty. He was very young for the rank. Had he purchased it?

'Did you hear me, slave?'

A cuff brought Marric's attention back from the circling, brilliant mote in the sky.

'I heard you,' Marric said dully. There was a shriek of victory. The mote dropped towards him and took shape as a great golden hawk.

'By all the gods!' cried the young officer. 'What's that?'

The hawk perched near Marric's hand. It belled once and commanded his full attention. Behind him, onlookers gasped and made signs against magic. Some fumbled after amulets.

'Give the man room to breathe! What if that bird turns on

him?' That was Nicephorus. But he didn't believe the bird would strike, even if the soldiers did. One man swung a spear, clearing a space between the hawk and the crowd.

I know you, Marric thought at the hawk. His eyes were fixed to its fierce, steady gaze. *The night I almost died, I saw you.* He was flawed, imperfect. Why had the hawk chosen now to come to him?

He stretched out a fist to the bird so that it could walk up his arm and perch on his shoulder. Its savage talons barely pricked his skin.

Tell me.

The bird mantled its great wings, then flew over Marric's head. With a shriek it climbed higher in the sky, heading for the portico of the Temple of Osiris.

Well, I did ask for a sign, Marric thought wryly. *Shall I go to that self-righteous priest and ask for help? Might as well sell sand in the Sinai.*

The shaven-skull had refused to buy Marric out before. And yet . . . the priest had fathomed his mind. And the hawk was Horus, his proper guide.

Like the priest, it had forbidden him to escape. Why? Interesting: beneath all his carefully nurtured scepticism lay a core of belief, after all. Whether he wished to or not, he would have to walk the path the hawk chose for him.

'What was that?' the officer asked again. He grew restless.

'That,' Marric answered, 'was a hawk. Why it landed here, only Horus knows.' It galled him to call this stripling 'master', though he would have to. 'The hawk guides us well. Master, the lad is injured. There will be doctors at that temple, so I will bear him there, by your leave.'

'A local healer might do better,' suggested the officer.

'If you permit, sir, I think it better for Mor to follow the hawk,' said Nicephorus. 'But, sir, if my fellow takes the boy to the temple, I am left to buy and load my household's grain alone. If you are kin to the mistress, can you aid me?'

Go, he wished Marric silently. *Before he thinks of a reason to forbid you.*

'This will hurt, lad,' said Marric, 'so I'll make it quick.' He lifted the boy so swiftly that he had time for only one sharp outcry.

'Be a soldier,' Marric urged him. 'Like the master there in his fine armour. Would you greet the priests with tears?'

The lad had not enough muscle to match his gangling limbs. Marric wondered if he ever would. *This is my son*, he thought, moved by the lad's trust. He forgot that the child had cost him a chance to escape.

The boy let his head loll against Marric's chest, confiding himself utterly to a stranger.

The temple's main gate was shut, but a sidegate used by temple servants in their daily errands was open. Marric climbed the slight rise to the gate and entered. Above him, the hawk screamed.

Priests, novices, scribes and servants stood astonished. *A bloody man and a battered boy. When will they call the Watch?*

'He broke his leg in the market,' explained Marric. 'Can a healer examine him?'

'That way.' An acolyte pointed.

As Marric walked toward the physician's quarters, a low-voiced chant and the rattle of a sistrum sounded from the sanctuary. In the clean little cell he laid the boy down. 'Rest now. And, as I told you, be a soldier. This good doctor must set your leg and that will hurt. But unless he sets it, you will be like one of the bazaar cripples, fit only to beg.'

'That's all I can do now,' the boy answered sullenly.

'Not so. Right now I am a slave, but that doesn't mean it's all I am – or will ever be.'

The boy's eyes widened. He had not connected Marric with slavery. 'I will leave you here. Be well,' Marric wished him.

'But man, you're hurt too!' protested the healer.

'Some old cuts opened,' Marric said absently. 'I will heal.'

He had to escape the sight of the boy, for whom he could do nothing more. That was the worst of slavery: he had nothing to give. And when he had not been enslaved, had had the power to give, he had not done so.The punishment was just. Since he had not given before, now he could not defend Stephana, provide this child with a future, return Nicephorus to his home—. There must be a pattern, he thought, in which all these losses added up

– not just the largess of a prince rescuing one or two souls from the gutter.

'He has no home,' Marric told the healer. 'He is a strong lad. If you could put him to some use—?'

'So many of these children need homes. Rest assured: a lad who comes to us under the hawk's wings will be cared for.'

'My thanks, master.' Marric did not begrudge the physician the title. He walked down the corridor towards the gate. His back hurt and he was very tired. He would have to return and help load the grain. The stonework made the hall delightfully cool, but even this unexpected comfort enervated him.

Now what? he asked the hawk silently. *You didn't bring me here simply to aid a beggar, did you?*

Ahead of him lay the inner courtyard. Incense drifted through it in grey spirals. Marric turned aside and drew close to listen to the chant he had heard earlier. Ahead of him lay the shrine, the place that represented the Horizon, a place on the earth but not of it. Tiny against the great inscribed pillars was the Semty, or Celebrant. He wore a leopard skin draped over his back. Facing him was the Holder of the Rolls.

Before the altar lay a statue of Osiris made out of linen. The Semty poured water upon it and chanted:

'I am the plant of life
which comes forth from Osiris,
which grows upon the ribs of Osiris,
which allows the people to live.'

The figure was beginning already to send forth green shoots.

'I live as corn,' responded the Holder of the Rolls. 'The love of me is in the sky, on earth, on the water and in the fields.'

'Isis is content for her son, Horus,' chanted the Semty.

'She is jubilant in him, her Horus, her god.

'I am life appearing from Osiris—'

Light flared. Coils of sweet incense smoke flattened as the hawk flew into the shrine. Again it screamed and mantled its wings. Then it was aloft, flying back to Marric.

He had heard these rites many times as a very young prince standing beside his father. Now they – and the hawk's gaze –

compelled him forward, his hands outstretched to take into them an empire and a power he had always longed for but never dared think he might fully possess. When the Semty noticed the bloody figure at the door to the shrine, he came forward.

The priest from the slavemarket! Marric's opened cuts stung where his tunic stuck to them. He glared at the man.

'Did you think I would die because you refused to help me?'

'Not if you were fit to live.'

'Master of no man, least of all myself, you called me.' Marric padded closer to the priest, looming over him. It would be so easy . . . one swift blow to avenge the name he had received, to make the priest share at least part of his suffering. Marric breathed deeply. 'I have often thought of your words.'

'And, I daresay, hated me for them.'

'Aye.'

'Well enough. Have you mastered yourself yet? Judging from the blood on you, not very well. Pray come with me, Prince.'

The title seemed unfamiliar to Marric. So did the priest's courteous gesture that Marric precede him from the shrine to his quarters. There, he compelled Marric to remove his tunic and sit while he himself examined him. 'Well enough, except for the bleeding,' he said finally. 'Tell me what has befallen you.'

That was an order. As the priest anointed Marric's back and sides with oil and cleaned the open wounds with fiery palm spirit, Marric spoke. He felt less anger than he would have thought possible: only grief at the deaths along the way.

'And now,' he concluded, 'the armies withdraw from Alexandria, leaving this city defenceless. Let the Berbers test it once, and all the Delta will fall before them.'

'Dress yourself, Prince,' said the priest. 'Who had the tending of you? This Druid you mentioned, or the slavewoman.'

'Taran and Stephana both.'

'You want them given their proper respect, do you, and called by their right names? What do you call yourself now? Alexander, after your father?'

'Marric. And recently, Mor the slave.'

'Marric. The name of a warrior from the Isles of the Mists. Fighting man: it describes you.'

Marric bowed his head. Fighting man he might be, but he had not killed the Gepid, had not fought Sutekh, had not fled to the wars at the cost of a friend's life.

'You learn. But you are tempted; your first thought is always a fight. Look at today. I know you planned to escape.' The priest looked up. His eyes were gelid, an icy grey that drew attention from his lean face with its shaven poll and hollowed temples to the power of his spirit.

'I am under obedience, but still I can tell you that if you had run, you would have been utterly defeated. Captured, killed – and what of your Empire then? Or the boy you brought in, or your friends?'

'What becomes of them in any case?' Marric made his question a challenge. A goblet stood at his hand and he drank: not wine, but barley water with something else added. 'I did not escape. And you refuse to buy me free.' Marric sighed heavily. Whatever was in that drink made him think very clearly, and he wasn't sure he cared for the clarity of his reasoning. 'I must free myself before I free anyone else, I know. What then? Shall I involve my friends in my own dangers?'

'You might let them choose.'

'I won't let them choose death!' Stephana's voice the night he almost died, *Doubtless you will be the death of me, but not, I think, right now*, rang in his ears. Already she was very close to release from a brutal life, from the Wheel itself. Could Marric take the burden of shortening her time upon himself?

'Already you are too much involved in their lives to cut free.'

Marric sprang up. There was no room for him to pace. He wanted to leave, but he sensed that to walk out of the priest's quarters now would deprive him forever of desperately needed information.

The priest stood too. Marric thought he had somehow displeased him. *So it is over. Even before I could ask for help, I ruined this chance, too.*

But the priest had gone to the door only to summon an attendant. Shortly afterwards the acolyte ushered Taran the Druid into the room.

'You never wondered how I knew so much about you?'

Marric shrugged. There was no point in attempting to learn how priests – or Druids – knew anything.

'Are the Druids your spies?'

'Hardly,' Taran said. 'But the Goddess has many faces. In the land where I studied, she is Modron. You of the East call her Isis. But she is the same Goddess. The God? He, too, has many faces. And their servants work together . . . Prince.'

'Then help me serve them, too. My city is falling. Irene cannot hold it.' He realized why these men were watching him so closely. Certainly the Empire needed an intermediary between gods and land, but it needed the right one. 'I can protect the land; she cannot.'

'Can you?' asked Taran. 'Are you sure? When I first worked with you, you lay near death. Stephana had to call you a coward to keep life within you at all. And then you threatened to kill her. And now, look at you . . . protector! – covered with blood again.'

'I was helping save a child.' Marric felt oddly apologetic. 'It was Nico's idea. Else I might have run free.' All his longing went into that last word. What was free, though? If Marric were truly free, he'd be riding the borders now with his sworn men, or towards World's End.

Taran stood beside Marric. His face went gentle in a way that that of the priest of Osiris could not.

'You will be free, Prince. But not yet, and not alone. Your life is bound up not just with thrones and armies, but with individuals. Imhotep here concurs.'

'You may come back,' said Imhotep, 'when you understand fully that you must accept your fate without rebelling. When you are fit.'

Testing, testing, always testing – like that bleached crow ruling the Temple in Byzantium.

'You say I am not fit,' accused Marric, 'but when I lay imprisoned, Irene sent a – a thing, like a black cloud, to make me despair. She tainted my sister's mind with evil magics. Now she would use them to poison the whole Empire. Am I less fit than she – or have you another claimant for Empire?'

'You cannot survive a fight with her yet,' Imhotep said. 'She would consume you as flame consumes chaff. Initiation into the Mysteries would help, but you are impatient, too impatient to present yourself for training and submit yourself to our disciplines. And you are afraid.'

Marric's eyes flashed. Then his head sank.

'There are many paths to freedom, Prince. You must discover your own. When you do, return to me. I shall not turn you away.'

The Empire was rotting at his feet and all the priests could find to do was lecture him. Marric thought he would strike them if he remained a moment longer.

'All I do is hear reasons why I must remain a slave. I am my city's rightful heir, so I should guard it. What else I might want, that does not matter. And I accept that. I try to do my best. But you speak to me only of unworthiness.' To his shame, his voice went ragged, but it did not fail him . . . not quite. 'I am not an initiate, nor – as you point out – am I likely to be. I am only Mor, the slave, who will be beaten if he does not return to help Nico with the wagon. Excuse me, *my masters*. I will leave you to your wise talk. It is too high for slaves.'

He found Nicephorus waiting outside the temple with a loaded wagon and an empty purse. Relief lay ill concealed on his face. At his side, tapping fingers impatiently on his swordhilt, was the young cavalry officer. *Watching your kinswoman's property, are you?*

'You took your time, Mor,' the captain said. 'One of my troopers had to do slave's labour. Hurry. The gates will close soon.'

Marric nodded and fell back into the character of Mor: strong and sullen. 'The boy would not be comforted. When he consented, finally, to being tended, I asked the healer to bind my shoulder. Then I left.'

He mounted the wagon and took the reins. The officer moved his horse alongside.

'My widowed aunt sends slaves into the city who tell me that they buy grain against a famine of which no one has spoken. Even before I do, they know of the movement of armies. I'm coming with you.'

He brought four troopers and their tetrarch with him. At least he had not brought his entire force! But now Marric would not be able to escape for as long as the men stayed at the villa.

The drive back was long and quiet. Mist laid the dust to rest. The moon had begun to cut its way, a gleaming sickle, through the field of stars. A breeze from the river soothed Marric's eyes but did not cleanse him of his resentment.

The quiet night made the cavalry officer talkative. He was like so many junior officers under Marric's command. Named Djehutimes in the old language, he had recently adopted the Hellenic form of the name: Thutmosis. Once again Hellene and Egyptian blended together. It would be a shame if the Berbers destroyed that once and for all. Thutmosis – the Pentekontarch Thutmosis, Marric cautioned himself – was still talking. He had never been to Byzantium. He had heard that it was magnificent and that the last emperor's consort ruled now. No one knew what had become of the Prince. Of course, it was noised about that he had died in Cherson, the turbulent province he had governed too laxly. Thutmosis would have ruled differently.

He had heard that the Prince had governed Cherson so ill that the Huns who dwelt there on imperial sufferance had grown so arrogant that they had moved their camps to the western edge of the Euxine, scarcely a day's ride from the city.

Archers firing from the wall as the infantry retreats. Now comes the sortie. The horns sound and the Tagmata ride out, even their horses heavily armoured. But the Huns' ponies and light-armoured archers will skewer them. Byzantine troops had speed, but the steppe archers would feather them long before they could bring their twelve-foot kontoi *into play. Against bows, lances were useless.*

Gods, Marric prayed. *Holy gods, save my city.*

Behind the walls the citizens would panic. Some would flee to boats, some to villas. The Guard would stand firm; they valued honour and would die to a man to protect the ruler. But Irene? Marric would wager that if the city fell she would escape, treasure-laden, into Syria where her family would shelter her.

My Byzantium in flames.

'I asked, "are you ill, Mor?"' Thutmosis' voice was sharp.

'No, I thank you, master. I but thought of the wars.'

'Do you wish to serve under me? You are strong and, from the look of you, a fighter. I could use an orderly.'

'That will be as the mistress commands.'

'Aye . . . that is the way of it.' Clearly, Thutmosis had all but forgotten.

That might be a way back to power: start as orderly to this young man, manoeuvre him, subtly guide him . . . Marric let the reins slacken on the oxen's backs. He would be only as powerful as his tool, however, and Thutmosis – more callow than Marric could ever remember being – did not strike him as a sure road to power.

Slave-thinking. Manipulate the master and rise. But Horus, he was desperate enough to snatch at any offer of escape.

After Marric drove the wagon into the yard, he helped the outdoor slaves at their work. Suddenly, the endless routine of heavy labour struck him as an escape from his thoughts.

Chapter Eleven

When Strymon sent a slave to roust Marric out of the tiny cubicle he had made his own (he was constantly grateful that his reputation made it unnecessary to fight to keep it), he suspected that Lady Heptephras had summoned him on account of Thutmosis.

A doting aunt: so she was willing not only to house her spruce young kinsman and his troops, make him an allowance (Marric knew the signs), but also to lose a slave? Marric pulled on his clean tunic and followed the child down the hall. As always, he looked away from the mosaics – inferior work. It was a shame that Alexandria could afford no better. But the polycandelon

103

which lit the so-called art was handsome and – as he knew well – brilliantly polished.

Heptephras' reception room was more Egyptian than Greek. A few pieces of claw-carved and gilded furniture were elegantly arranged in the airy room which opened onto the lotus courtyard. Beyond the bubbling fountain there stretched a view of the low villa walls. Beyond them the crescent moon was reflected in Lake Mareotis. The crocodiles were silent.

Thutmosis sat at his ease. His armour had been replaced by cool white linen. Stephana hovered discreetly near her mistress, assuring them both that the rainbow-tinted wine ewers were filled. A fine frost dulled the glassware's subtle interplay of colour and misted the matching goblets. Burning cressets cast shadows in the corner which danced as Stephana moved about the room. As she finished her tasks and went to stand quietly in the shadows, the play of light on her hair subsided. When Marric entered the room, she met his eyes, then quickly glanced away.

The lady of the house and her nephew were deep in talk.

'Why must you leave home now?'

'The Empress needs all loyal men to defend the Empire against invaders. The Huns and, from down the rivers, the men of Jomsborg—'

'Don't speak of them!' Heptephras threw up her soft hands. She drank and set her goblet down too near the edge of the delicate table, where faience animals rollicked. Stephana stepped forward and steadied the glass, then retreated once more.

'Lady, they must be spoken of,' Thutmosis declared. With the assurance of a man new to command, he began to reassure his aunt.

Marric's eyes sought out Stephana. Her prophecies had warned them all of the danger which lay before Alexandria. How rare she was! Even in the twilight the woman seemed to draw light to herself, wisps of silver hair gleaming like dew-sprinkled cobwebs about her. Her eyes were as large, blue and unreadable as those of the cat which lounged at Heptephras' feet. As if sharing its mistress' agitation, it stretched and leapt elegantly away, its tail quivering as it headed for the garden. Stephana turned to follow it, but her mistress forestalled her with an upraised hand.

104

'I do not wish to speak of such things. What will become of us here on the Delta?'

'Certain regiments of the Guard will be kept in reserve.'

It would be a skeleton army, Marric thought, too weak to defend the city against raiders.

'And the grain prices,' Heptephras was worrying on. 'Only today Strymon asked leave to send slaves into town to purchase grain.'

'That was Mor's idea,' Strymon spoke. Until that moment Marric hadn't realized that he was in the room.

'Mor,' said Heptephras. 'The one you transferred into house service after a fight, is it?'

'Aye, lady. He awaits your attention.'

Marric stepped forward and bowed. Thutmosis motioned him closer.

'Why did you fight?'

'A barbarian kicked me, lady. I kicked back harder.'

'And then?'

'The overseer wanted the slave thrown into the lake as an example to other brawlers,' said Strymon. 'Mor refused. Very properly. After he survived a beating for disobedience – which I must say was overly severe – I assigned him work indoors.'

Heptephras shrank back a trifle. Thutmosis seemed pleased.

'A fighter and a man who thinks. I like that. Tell me, Mor, have you considered my plan to take you to Byzantium with me?'

'I will warrant you, young sir, he has been a soldier,' Strymon put in.

'I can see. Well, man?'

'There are times when . . . it is best that a man escape his past,' Marric began obliquely. He might be noticed, captured – and then he had another thought. Who would notice one orderly among the thousands in an army? He must seize this chance!

'If he has been a soldier,' Lady Heptephras interrupted, 'then I want him here to protect this house. One orderly more or less will not matter to the Empress—'

'Every man matters! As a subject of Her Imperial Majesty, you are asked to part with but one slave . . .'

'Some day,' Heptephras replied calmly, 'this estate will be

105

yours. I have no other heirs. How much can I give you now without wasting your inheritance? Let this . . . this man Mor stay here and defend it.'

Idealism and shrewdness warred in the young man's face. He looked into his goblet as if an answer lay there, swirled its contents in the glass, and drank them off. He clearly understood his aunt well enough to know when he was defeated.

Thutmosis saluted her with the empty goblet and waved away a refill.

'What say you, Mor?'

'My will is my owner's,' Marric answered. The words came too easily. He had heard slaves say them all his life, but until this moment he had never realized how bitter they were.

'A pity. Guard my aunt well.'

And your inheritance too?

Stephana moved forward to refill Thutmosis' cup. He drank half and held the goblet up again. When she would have withdrawn, leaving the wine near him, he caught her wrist.

'At first I could not tell if this one was young or old,' he remarked to his aunt. Clearly, Stephana was a useful change of subject. 'It is her hair: see, it is all silvered. Come into the light, pretty one.' He pulled her forward and almost upset her across his lap. 'Have you owned this girl long, Aunt?'

'Since last floodtime,' Heptephras said. 'You have not seen her before, have you? Perhaps you should visit me more often?' She laughed at him, watching indulgently as he raised Stephana's chin in his fingers. Stephana shuddered and Marric clenched his fists.

'Do you like her? If you do, it is such a simple thing to assign her to you for your stay . . .'

Stephana's eyes filled. Marric felt her own effort not to break reflected in his helpless rage. She was just a slave, to be traded and humiliated by a mistress who was kindly in her own way, but who regretted having to deny a favoured nephew his request.

Stephana's eyes met Marric's imploringly. He realized that she feared for him, feared that he would unleash the rash temper that already meant he would walk scarred of back for the rest of his days.

– Not for me, Mor. No more anger. No violence. –

Marric formed his own emotions into a message he hoped Stephana would understand: grief for her humiliation, acceptance of her. *– I wish I might spare you this. –* A tear rolled down her cheek and touched Thutmosis' fingers. He wiped it away as Marric would gladly have done. Then he rose and kissed her on the mouth.

'I thank you, my aunt, but, Isis! she's a melancholy little thing and far too thin. Smile, can you not, girl?'

'I can now, lord,' whispered Stephana. 'Thank you. Thank you.'

'You may go, child,' said Heptephras, and Stephana fled.

Sweet Isis, she thanked that lout for letting her alone! Marric thought his heart would burst. The lights in the room swung in rainbow shimmers and something within him snapped . . .

Marric saw all the people in the room, the pretty frivolous room itself, with a clarity he had never before known. They treated him like a beast of burden with an uncertain disposition, regarded Stephana as a physical convenience, that was true. But in the far greater order, under the Eye of Horus, they belonged to him. Heptephras and her fears, Thutmosis and his misplaced ardours, Strymon and his accounts: they were his responsibility as surely as he wore their collar. He felt a sudden protective warmth. It burnt away his anger as fire combats fire. Gods grant he could protect them, then he could watch over Stephana, too. If only he could have kissed her as that young fool had, he would persuade her to abandon all her fears.

When Strymon dismissed him a little later, he stumbled back down the corridor in a daze of revelation and worry. His responsibilities were greater than he had dreamed. It seemed Empire was a thing of the spirit as well as the land; and he had never known.

He flung himself down on his pallet, glad of the thin door that helped protect him from the multitude of self-betrayals that wore out a slave's life. His back no longer hurt. Even the exertion of his work and the humiliation of that scene with Heptephras had left him restless rather than exhausted.

If he could not pace off some of his restlessness, he would go mad. He rose and looked out. There was no one in the corridor, no sound, even in the kitchen building where sometimes the upper servants gathered for a late meal or to prepare refreshments for wakeful guests.

Kicking his reed sandals off, Marric padded along the dusty floor towards the courtyard. The fountain, the pool, the fresh green things would refresh his spirit. They were worth a risk. Then he laughed shortly. Had the lady not said he was to guard her?

No lights gleamed within the women's courts. Lady Heptephras must have taken her fears with her to an early bed. Moving soundlessly, Marric entered the garden. He remembered another time, another garden on to which a bright room opened like a stage, when Alexa had helped him play out the scene that had brought her to death and himself to slavery. The man he had been – how would he regard the Marric he was now?

Today, in the market, for example. Perhaps a real emperor would have let the boy die. *And Nico too?* History was full of men dying for their emperors. He himself had had men die for him. Doubtless, he would again. But as he walked under the trees, grateful for the fresh green smell and the moonlit glimpse of large blossoms, he began to understand. Marric-that-was might have sacrificed the individual for a larger goal, like that young Thutmosis who so blithely terrified his aunt with his talk of stripping Alexandria's garrisons. Marric, though: he was unable to sacrifice anyone he cared for . . . if he could prevent it. Even a slave's life had meaning.

Seeing that Marric had to live a slave's life, that was just as well.

He brushed aside a low-hanging branch and came out in front of the pool. There, on the stone curb, a silver pitcher at her side, sat Stephana. At least she had not been packed off to Thutmosis' bed! Marric felt sudden gratitude for that and counted it another weakness.

He paused, unwilling to intrude on her visions. She might have been a moonsilvered statue, so quietly she sat. The wind cast a cloud over the moon and rippled the pool.

Stephana dashed her hand across the surface of the water and began to rise. Sadness showed in the very slump of her delicate shoulders. She turned and saw him. One hand went to her mouth in alarm.

'Don't tell me I should not be here,' he said, holding up one hand. 'I know it well. But you, too: you do not rest.'

'I am too tired to think clearly or rest,' said Stephana. 'I had to spend ages with Lady Heptephras, soothing her. Each time I thought perhaps to get away, she fancied some new terror and I could not leave her.'

'You are wearing yourself out and' – Marric decided to be frank – 'today has been a horror for you.'

He came forward to join her.

'Did you have another vision just now?' he asked, low-voiced.

'I can see nothing beyond what I told you this morning!' Stephana whispered, looking into the pool. 'Berbers riding in and bloodstains polluting the water. We will be defenceless when the regiments leave.'

'Not so,' Marric said.

'You are but one man, Mor. You can refuse to kill one slave or to rescue another. You can protect me, as you did this morning. But what good is one man against an army?'

'You were the one who called me a coward,' Marric reminded her. Though Stephana had had the courage to go on living with a quiet dignity that commanded his admiration, she was closer tonight to breaking than he had ever seen her. Her voice trembled and her hands shook. The least he could do was to help her renew her courage – if only to go on living as a slave.

'So I did.' She chuckled a little. 'I wish . . . I do wish you could leave here with Thutmosis. You don't belong here, and Sutekh hates you. You know that if he gets a chance he will kill you.'

'What if I killed him?'

'Why did you have to come here?' The words burst from her and her eyes flamed the blue of a burning candle's heart.

'Slaves don't choose who buys them. I would have sworn this morning that you were glad I was here.'

The fight went out of her. 'I was. But then . . . this evening, you heard how I was tossed like a guest-gift to the captain. I think . . . Isis, I hated for that to happen before you. I was ashamed. No, not that . . . I try not to hate, but I wanted to scream at Heptephras and ask her how she could treat another woman so.'

As he had longed to do, Marric reached out and gathered Stephana into his arms. 'You, ashamed? Because you have been forced to submit to what you would never consent? I wanted to kill them both for belittling you.'

Stephana turned her head so it rested on Marric's shoulder. He could not see her face. 'Heptephras is not harsh, and not unkindly,' she said drearily. 'Not usually. And, so long as I hide within the house, I am safe, if slavewomen are ever safe. But Thutmosis is her heir.' She gulped, then laughed a little wildly. 'He is young, at least, and clean: I have survived worse.'

As she attempted to pull away, Marric loosed his hold but did not totally release her. 'Is that all you can hope for? To be used and then ignored until, finally, you achieve whatever quest you are fated for?'

'I have trained myself, Mor, not to weep over what cannot be helped. You were right to call me a coward. My life punishes me for it.'

'You've more courage than any general. Let yourself rest, Stephana; don't pull away from me. You know I won't hurt you. You can be at peace.'

She tore free and stood up. 'Don't you see? I am *not* at peace! Until you came here I had courage to endure till my life's end. Then I saw you and I knew that if I had lived my life for some purpose, that purpose faced me. Nico—' she sobbed once, then stopped herself. 'Nico was kind to me. He didn't want you to die. So perhaps that was it, I thought: saving your life.'

She walked away to stand across the pool from him. 'I hoped that I could heal you and you would run away. You didn't. And then, when you treated me gently . . .'

That one night she had run to him, her shoulder and breast scored by Sutekh's nails. He had comforted her until his touch had become a caress.

'You touched me, yes. I was afraid. I knew then that you didn't want just my help: you wanted *me*. Me – to be for you what I have been compelled to be for so many men.'

'You want me to escape. But if I did, how could I leave you here? Taran says our lives are bound up together.'

'Tonight,' Stephana turned her face away again, 'I looked into the water to read . . . your future. I tried to see mine, too, but there were only fragments.'

Holding her with his gaze, Marric sat beside her on the basin's edge and reached out a hand. 'Look again. Please.'

'How can I tell now if what I see is true – or what I want to see?'

Marric tightened his arms around her. Now her head rested against his heart. He rocked her, hoping that her body would relax against him.

'Then I will tell you what *I* see at this very moment. Look in the water, Stephana. Do you see what I do? My vision takes no special magic. Do you see the man and woman sitting beside a pool? Look how well she fits in his arms.

'Look again. In a moment, the man will raise her face – as I am doing now – and look into her eyes. Then he will kiss her.' Marric brushed her lips gently with his.

When his mouth freed hers, Stephana's hands fluttered. He took them up, cradling them against his chest.

'You disturb my peace,' she whispered.

'I don't call what you had peace.' He stroked her face. 'You were resigned to joylessness. Stephana, do you really wish I had left you?'

He had not wanted this bond with her, but now it overwhelmed him. He saw his face reflected in her eyes, saw pain in it, and hid from the sight by kissing her deeply. His hands stroked her back until all resistance went out of her.

'Oh gods,' she whispered. Then her arms went around him and she embraced him with the urgency he had hoped to kindle. But her hand, kneading along his shoulder, rubbed an open slash, and he winced.

'Mor, Mor, I hurt you!'

Marric laughed. Now he knew how to proceed with her. 'We have been harshly treated, Stephana. So now we must be gentle

111

with one another. There's no pain now.' He rested his head between her neck and shoulder, delighted to feel her hand stroke up the back of his neck and tangle in his hair.

'Don't think it's simply gratitude, or that now I've my health back I simply want a woman, any woman. Do you think you don't trouble my thoughts as I do yours?'

'No. Oh no.' She was stricken by that, yet still her hands stroked his back and, very carefully, his shoulders.

'But yes. We escape together, if we escape at all.' He pressed his lips against the pulse that beat in her throat, smelling the rose scent he loved. 'Stay with me, be with me, Stephana, my rose. I need you. Isis, witness how I need and cherish you . . .'

How much he meant it shook him. One-handed, he plucked the pins from her hair and let it fall about them both, enclosing them in sweet-scented waves. He buried his head between her breasts, cupped them in his hands, and felt her tremble. Then he raised his head to look at their bodies reflected in the water.

'You see, Stephana? The woman in the water, how she responds?' Again he kissed her before he stood up and raised her to stand beside him.

'You can still draw back. But won't you come with me now?'

Stephana's eyes were enormous. They never left his. Her lips, reddened from his kisses, said 'Yes' without sound.

Marric propped himself on one elbow, watching the setting moon's light tangle in Stephana's hair. He put out a gentle hand and brushed it away from her face and breast. Even as she slept, she smiled at his touch. Her face held such joy that Marric wanted to weep.

As she stood before him in his tiny room, she had not been afraid, even though she knew only the painful invasion of her flesh that slavery had made her submit to. After loosening her belt, then her long chiton, Marric had run his hand along the sweet curve of her side until she had pressed against him for warmth. Only then had he lowered her on to his bed and knelt beside it to pull off his clothing. He would need all his tenderness, all his memories of joy, to heal her.

'I wish we had a better bed,' he had murmured against her

112

lips. He remembered some room or other he had shared with a lover once, sleek taffetas on the bed, cool against bare, heated skin. Or perhaps they might have rose-scented oils that he could rub into his lover's soft skin, wine in an exquisite goblet they would share, or veils to drift over her. How would that pale body, marred only by a thin scar on her side, looked wrapped in blue gauze?

'I would like to drape you in pearls,' Marric whispered. He kissed her ear and heard her laugh, a carefree, joyous sound.

For a long time she had lain still, as if gauging her own response to his touch. Finally she met his ardor with her own. Her astonished joy – *how could I have forgotten this?* – leapt through him at the moment of her ecstasy. As her breathing slowed, she had slid a hand between their bodies to try to touch where they were still united. The gentle questing reawakened his desire. And this time she moved eagerly beneath him.

'My rose, my heart's dearest,' he had called her, and meant it.

Now, her legs still entwined with his, Stephana lay sleeping against his side. Marric caressed her. The moonlight had silvered her body; that he touched soft flesh, and not precious metal, came as an intoxicating surprise. He traced a flower on her breast, centring it around her nipple, and then kissed it. Her flesh hardened under his lips and tongue, and she gasped, waking into passion once more. She raised her hands to stroke his face, reading his eyes as she had read the visions in the pool. What did she see?

When she spoke, Marric knew that he had betrayed himself to her entirely in the act of love.

'Marric,' Stephana whispered. 'Marric. My Prince.'

Marric took her hands and pinned them above her head. His body held hers beneath him.

'Where did you learn that name?' he asked.

Stephana arched her back and brushed his mouth in a fleeting kiss. She tested his grip and apparently decided not to struggle. 'Knowledge came to me with our union; I suspected before. You called me your heart. How could I fail to know? Even as a slave, you act the prince. So I know you now, Marric. Does it change anything?'

She lay completely vulnerable to him, trusting him completely. Even if he had to, how could Marric bear to kill that new-born trust?

'You hold my life in your hands,' Marric said. Delicately he kissed the hollow of her throat, right below the fine wire of her collar. 'And I am well content to have it so.'

Her glance slid to the tiny window, then back to him. The sky was lighter.

'Then love me,' Stephana said. 'We have so little time left.'

Chapter Twelve

Thutmosis departed in a cloud of dust, leaving behind advice to Heptephras that Marric would never have considered in his own house: arm the slaves. If raiders came, Thutmosis wanted them to protect his aunt and his inheritance with their lives. But arming slaves was profoundly dangerous; periodically the Empire quaked at tales of slaves rebelling and massacring their owners, or roving as bandits. Granted, house and field slaves with swords in their hands were not as fearsome as trained fighters. Many, in fact, would probably prove too broken in spirit to learn to hold a sword.

Why was Marric objecting, anyway? Arming the slaves might mean that he could find a chance to strike out for his freedom and that of his friends. For the villa slaves, Thutmosis' advice meant additional hours of work to master hacked-up shields and blunted blades. It left them aching and exhausted. For Marric, too, arms practice was sheer misery. He might have dreamed of having a sword in hand once again, but the one he was issued was poorly balanced. He had wanted to fight against equals, not hold back his hand practising with someone less skilled than a twelve-year-old boy, especially with Sutekh looking on suspiciously. The familiar habits of hand and eye meant that Marric had to force himself to lunge clumsily, to use his shield like a tyro and expose his midsection, otherwise the overseer might fear him and contrive his removal. He knew Marric had been a soldier: best let him think he had been an incompetent.

So, with the submissive manner he had learned all too swiftly, Marric shared the slaves' tongue-lashings. At the end of each practice he turned in his weapon under Sutekh's baleful scrutiny. For the rest, he avoided the man as if his life depended on it, as, in fact, it did.

Even life as a slave was precious to him now because of his deepening love for Stephana. Many times she would slip from the inner courts to lie by his side. For those short hours, he could hear himself called by his true name and feel himself to be a man and a lover, not portable property. But gradually even Stephana's love contributed to Marric's growing depression.

One night he sat in his cubicle stropping a worn-out blade that he had managed to steal. Cast-off blades were melted down but never tossed away for fear some slave would do precisely as Marric had done. The whetstone scraped harshly in his ears. Though it set his nerves on edge (while failing to put an edge on the blade), he kept scraping away stubbornly.

He heard footsteps and tensed. As Stephana came in, he relaxed. He had no time to hide his booty but, in any case, he trusted her completely. Concern widened her eyes as she saw what he had been doing.

'If they catch you with that . . .' she warned.

'At least now I have a weapon to protect you with.'

'I don't need that kind of protection.'

Marric dropped the blade and took her roughly into his arms.

'They'll punish you if they find you with it,' she whispered against his mouth.

'I am being punished by just living already. How do *you* stand it, my heart? Today Heptephras found me in the garden. I was looking for you. Yes, I know I should not have gone there. "What are you doing here?" she asked me. Do you know, Stephana, I actually felt guilt? So I lied. I said I thought one of the tiles that bordered the lotus pool had seemed loose. She praised me for that, then told me to fix it later. I was ready to kiss her feet or caper before her because I'd *been let off*.'

Marric's voice rose and he pounded one hand against his pallet.

'It's not bad enough to be sold as a slave. Now I feel myself becoming one. What will be left of me, Stephana? I don't know how much longer I can keep going . . .'

Stephana held him close and would have spoken.

'The worst of it is that I cannot ease your way, cannot safeguard you as I would wish. Oh, I would give you joy . . .'

'You do, you do.'

'But I cannot help you, cannot get you free!' He buried his face against her hair, kissing it, and then her eyes and lips.

'For whatever reason, Marric, that's not our fate now.'

'Isis!' The Goddess' name came out almost as a sob. 'Once I was a man, not a slave.'

'You still are, beloved,' Stephana assured him.

'What will be left of me? A slave master and a slave Empire. You heard: Irene cannot hold it safely.'

Somehow (Marric loved her the more for it) in those hours they stole together, Stephana found a way to let him feel like a man, a lover, and even a prince again. She would lie in his arms, head pillowed on his chest, whispering reassurances until they both slept. Sometimes she carried warnings to him.

'I have heard that Sutekh watches you at practice more carefully than he does all the other slaves combined. Can you be more awkward?'

'More awkward than I am already?' Marric laughed without joy. 'One day, one of us will kill the other.'

'There is already too much death in the world!' Stephana cried softly. 'And much of it by your own hand. Have you forgotten already, my love?'

'What makes you think I would be the one to die?'

'If you kill him, you will be executed. Then what will become of—'

'What will become of us in any case? Say I submit. Say that gradually I become used to the collar. Then, one day, perhaps, when your belly swells with my child—'

'Isis grant!' Stephana laid her hand over his as he stroked her, lingering over where a child might lie some day.

'Do you think I want our child to live as a slave?' Marric held her so tightly that she cried out. 'Since Heptephras favours you, she might let us be paired together, mated like prize animals. Perhaps we would grow smug in our privileges, like some slaves I have seen. And that is the most we can hope for.'

Stephana stroked his brow with her hands. He remembered now that she had done that when he was weak with fever. 'You were not meant to die a slave, Marric.'

'How can I be sure? Stephana, I cannot trust myself. I told you about Alexa. Even if I got free, what sort of . . .'

She raised herself on one elbow and looked into his eyes. 'Trust my visions, Marric. Trust me.'

'Forgive me,' he muttered.

'Forgive you? For helping me come alive? Marric, I need you so.'

He fell into sleep holding her and knowing that his love for her bound him here more strongly than the collar that marked him as a slave.

For the fifth time Marric beat down the stableman's awkward guard. The man's entire left side lay open to a lethal blow. Marric thwacked him hard with the flat of his blade.

'Keep your arm up, damn you!' he shouted and stepped closer to tug it into position himself. Then he repositioned the man's oval shield. The Egyptian would never make a fighter.

'Hold it steady,' he ordered, then bore down on his arm to see if he would be obeyed. Of course the man let the shield droop. So did his sword, an antique spatha that was far above the man's weight. Already demoralized, the stableman lost his balance as Marric pulled at him and sprawled on to the practice ground.

Marric gave him a hand up. 'Try again, and thank the gods that you face me, not a Berber.'

'A Berber?'

Why would anyone have told the man whom he might be fighting? Arms practice was simply one more incomprehensibility to the slaves. Perhaps Mor the slave wouldn't have been able to piece the story together either; Marric, schooled in the niceties of power struggles, found intrigue the breath of life. Stephana had prophesied only that a raid would come from the East. The Emir there was pushing the Berbers out.

'You! You're here to practise, not lounge about like a lovesick girl,' Sutekh snapped at him. *His* blade looked like fine army issue. 'You heard me. Jump to it!'

'He's winded,' Marric said. 'I'll take him on again when he catches his breath.' For a moment Marric forgot that Sutekh was the hateful overseer whom he wanted to kill. He saw him instead as a drillmaster, necessarily harsh in a harsh job.

'Who conducts these drills, slave?' Sutekh shouted. 'You or me? I say you fight – right now!'

Marric glanced about the practice area. All the other men were sparring and hacking more or less incompetently at one another. Slightly defiant, he folded his arms on his chest and looked meaningfully at Sutekh's blade.

'Perhaps your memory fails you, slave. Shall I beat it back into you?'

'With that sword, or your whip?' A vein pounded in Marric's temple: at last, at last.

'Come on then, hero,' said the overseer. He swung his whip about to clear room for them and motioned Marric forward.

'Let's see how you do against a real man.'

From the corner of his eye, he saw a flash of white, saw several more following, and knew that Lady Heptephras was obeying her own share of Thutmosis' instructions by sending the indoor slaves to do outdoor work while the men practised. A filled jar poised against her arm, Stephana watched dismayed while Marric and the overseer faced off. Marric nodded reassurance at her, then pointed with his chin: *get away, get out of Sutekh's line of sight*.

'Come on, Mor! I thought you were our fire-eater.'

Stephana disappeared and Marric drew breath again. She was out of sight now, safe, in case he – he had no intention of losing this fight. Perhaps he could even make Sutekh's death look like an accident. But it had been long, too long since he rode with his army or met a real fighter blade to blade. If slavery had made

118

him doubt he was a man, could he be sure he was still a warrior?

As he had learned in recruits' training, Marric brought his weapon up in salute. The other man simply raised his sword and grinned.

'Pretty, pretty. Let's see if you know anything else.'

The other slaves gathered around. Once, Marric had watched a pack of dogs circling its leader and the scrappy, younger challenger. The pack would help the stronger dog by hamstringing its rival, then tearing out the loser's throat. Marric had broken up that fight. What about the slaves, though? Remembering Marric's fight with the Gepid, would they curry favour with Sutekh by tripping him up?

He dared not think of that, or of anything but the movements of the overseer circling him, waiting for an opening. He was a big man, but not a clever man. Marric could take him.

And then what?

Ya illaha Allah!

Warcries shrilled out as Berbers dropped over the wall into the courtyard. Leaving their horses behind, they had crept up on the household. Doubtless they planned to take villa after villa until they cleared a path to the very harbour of Alexandria itself. After that first shriek, they fought in silence.

Marric ducked under Sutekh's guard and gestured with his sword at the astounded slaves. 'Get them!' he shouted. Horus grant that they fight like men, not property heedless of who owns it. He started forward alone and was immediately engaged by a Berber. Marric countered automatically, and remembered that parrying a curved blade was different from parrying a straight sword – especially given the fine steel the Berbers used. Behind him, he heard the screams that told him how quickly some of the other men in the courtyard had forgotten.

'Keep your distance!' he shouted. 'Get out the *kontoi*!'

The yard boiled into the confusion of a battlefield where screams, shouts, and the stinks of sweat and blood always robbed men of most of their senses. The household, by sheer weight of numbers, might repel the attackers . . . Marric spitted one man, yanked his blade free, and pushed forward.

The field worker next to him shrieked. Blood gouted from his face and off the curved blade that had sliced half of it away. Another man took his place.

'Nico, get back!' Nicephorus had grabbed one of the *kontoi* and wielded it to deadly advantage.

'Not me, brother,' said the scholar. 'The safest place to be is at your side!' The Berbers fell back before him. As Nicephorus' arm tired, he dropped the lance and caught up a sword. His size made him nimble.

Marric laughed. All the indignities, the whippings, the enforced docility fell away from him in a shower of blood. Let Sutekh bellow: he could see that the slaves were following Marric's lead.

Again Marric shouted and gestured for the slaves to charge. They obeyed, some waving swords, others forcing the raiders back against the retaining walls with the long spears until the only Berbers left in the yard were dead or dying, their blood mingling with the blood of slaves in the thick dust.

Ready to pursue the Berbers, Marric leapt at the wall. Nicephorus grabbed his arm. Marric caught himself before he struck him.

'You can't,' Nicephorus gasped. 'Over there . . . regroup.'

So the scholar was also a strategist? Marric breathed deeply to calm himself. A gash on one arm and scratches along his side began to sting.

'The city . . .' he gasped.

'Safe, for now.'

'No!' Marric's eyes kindled. Now, while the household was confused, while people were still sorting out the living from the dead and wounded . . . or the slaves who had broken and hidden, now the gods had granted them all a chance to escape. When you find your own way, come back, Imhotep the priest had said. Well, he had found it. Nicephorus was beside him. Stephana, he hoped, was still hiding in the stables.

'What are you, Mor?' the scholar breathed. 'Or who?'

'Don't call me Mor.' Marric spoke fast. 'The name is Marric – as if you didn't know!'

They ran for the stables. Marric slapped two houseslaves on the shoulders as he passed. 'Mount guard,' he ordered. Most of the men had simply collapsed on the ground among the wounded and the dead. They were too weary even to wipe their blades or feel pride in their victory.

There were horses and harness in the stable. Strymon might as well blame their loss on the Berbers. Marric was saddling a horse, whose sleek limbs and arched neck promised speed and unimpaired stamina, when he heard an evil chuckle behind him.

'So the hero is simply a slave who would be a runaway. I think I like this, Mor. I like this much better than gutting you in a practice bout.'

Marric's hands undid the saddle girth. One heave, and Sutekh would have the saddle in his face.

'Don't try it. Turn around. I want to see your face as you die. *Move!*'

The swordpoint jabbed his back. Reluctantly, Marric turned. Just when he thought that the gods had finally turned their eyes towards him – this was how it ended? Then he remembered the dagger he had honed and that he carried as a final weapon in his loincloth. Marric eyed the overseer narrowly. Could he dodge, draw, and come up under the big man's guard before Sutekh drove his point home? Marric calculated feverishly. Nicephorus must have gone to ground. Perhaps he would appear to distract Sutekh just long enough.

'Don't *you* move.'

Stephana's voice was even softer than usual, and it quivered. But the grip of her hands on the shaft of the bloodstained *kontos* did not shake, and her glance was relentless blue fire. Now it was her turn to give the orders.

Her enemy turned and laughed. 'You always did keep at arm's distance from me, didn't you, girl? As if you was made of silver. Well, that's over now. Your . . . friend here is an escaping slave and a thief. And you? You're an accomplice. You know what you can expect –' a pause and a suggestive laugh – 'but there's no reason for you to die if—'

Sutekh moved nearer to Stephana. She brought the lance up sharply towards his chest. Horror warred with determination in her face. Certainly she could kill the man, but then what? Stephana was too near release from the Wheel, and far too precious to Marric to have bloodstains on her hands.

Still Sutekh moved towards her. He had misjudged her utterly, taking her reluctance to kill for cowardice. Grinning, assured of his prey, Sutekh reached out to grasp Stephana's lance.

Light exploded from it, and Sutekh brought his hands up to his face.

Marric leapt at him, dagger ready. He drove the knife home beneath Sutekh's ribs. His death shriek became a gurgle as blood filled his lungs. Then he collapsed. Marric pushed the overseer's body away, then straightened up to face Stephana. Would the sight of death revolt her? Would he?'

'I would have killed him for you,' Stephana whispered.

'I thank you once more for my life.' Marric reached out and broke the slender collar she wore from her neck. He hurled it aside. The soft metal rang as it hit the stable walls and disappeared.

'Do we run now?'

'Once we find Nicephorus. Nico?'

'Here, Mor. What should we call you now? When I saw Stephana move in, I figured that the two of you could settle with Sutekh while I finished up with the horses.'

Nicephorus' calculations were riskier than Marric liked.

'We should hide the body,' Stephana pointed out. 'And this.' She buried the lance in fodder. Nicephorus began to tug bales down over the overseer's body.

Rubbing her throat where the collar had rested, Stephana studied Marric and Nicephorus. 'We will need clothes, medicines,' she paused and an expression of distaste crossed her face. 'Money. And Lady Heptephras trusts me.'

'Shall I go instead?' Nicephorus asked.

'You can't.' Stephana vanished before he could protest.

Clean rags hung from a nail, and Marric used them to bandage his friend's injuries.

'Just as well we were not severely hurt, my Prince—'

'Marric. Or Mor, if you feel more at ease with that name.'

'Where do we go next?'

Now that was a problem. Out in the swamps were Berbers, angrier now and more desperate since they had lost their first fight. They were too dangerous to be encountered by two wounded, tired men and a woman with hair the colour of silvered wood. And the roads were patrolled. If the officers saw two men wearing slave-collars—

Taking hammer and chisel, Marric pried off Nicephorus' collar. 'Now,' he ordered, 'don't let your hand slip unless you want to commit regicide before I'm even crowned.'

Nicephorus laughed too long at the feeble joke and bent to his work. 'To think that we have been slaves together.'

'We are slaves no longer, brother.'

When his collar was off, Marric flung the thing into the pile of bales that hid Sutekh's body. The time when any other man was Marric's master was long gone.

Nicephorus held out the sword with which Sutekh had planned to slay Marric. The Prince belted it on. Freedom, headier than any vintage from the imperial cellars, began to pound along his veins.

'Nico, do you or Stephana know where the Druid lives? Best we lie up until nightfall, then head for the city.'

'I also know where Taran lives.' The unexpected voice spun them both around.

'Strymon!' Nicephorus cried. Former slave and major-domo stared at one another.

'Aye.'

'How long have you listened here?'

'Long enough. I came into the stables to check for wounded. Instead, I witnessed a fight. An execution, I might say. Being too old to be warlike, I hid.'

'Don't stop me now,' Marric said. Even to his own ears, his words sounded more like a plea than a command. 'I don't want to kill you—'

'But you would. Or Nicephorus would. Even Stephana, whom I used to think shivered at the sight of a bird flying across her shadow.'

'I was not seen,' said Stephana. She came in with her arms laden. 'I took no more than we will . . .' she broke off, and looked beseechingly at the major-domo. 'I only took what we would need. Strymon, please, if you saw that fight and overheard, then you know that Mor – that Prince Marric must go free.'

Incongruously the old man laughed. 'It's like a tale told in the taverns! If this were a ballad, I would applaud the singer.'

'And so?' asked Nicephorus.

'This much I understand. There was a battle. Our . . . brave overseer was gravely wounded. He crept here to die. In the confusion, one of the most rebellious slaves robbed the house and fled. He took with him his friend and his woman. In times like these, such things often happen.'

'You understand discretion, too,' said Stephana. 'Isis' blessings be upon you, Strymon.' She walked towards him and kissed his cheek. 'Thank you. I shall never forget you.'

'If you are to reach Taran's before sunset, you must ride quickly, child.'

Marric led his horse outside. He lifted Stephana into the saddle, then mounted himself.

'Can you ride?' he asked Nicephorus.

'Ride? I could fly!'

Stephana laughed and Marric tightened his arms about her. Nicephorus mounted and they pounded out of the gates, away from slavery and into an uncertain future.

Chapter Thirteen

As soon as they cleared the villa's gates and reached the twist in the road that protected them from watchful eyes, Marric turned off the road and stopped. He waved Nicephorus in closer.

'If we keep to the road, catching us will be like feeding a tame crocodile,' he said. 'Stephana, you may trust Strymon's good heart; myself, I think it's been too long devoted to good book-keeping. Nico, can you find Taran's place by yourself?'

'Certainly. I have slipped out to see him by night.'

'And yet you always returned.' Marric was astounded.

'Didn't you come back after you took that boy to the healers? I knew there was something I had to do here. I never guessed that it was to help a prince regain his father's diadem.' He laughed ironically.

Stephana leaned forward. 'Nico, ride now! They're less likely to see us if we split up.'

'You have not seen the city under Irene,' Nicephorus told her. 'I stay with my Prince.'

Hoofbeats made both men reach for their swords.

'Who's that?'

'Does it matter?' Stephana cried softly. 'Into the swamp!'

In the marshes, insects hummed and fluttered about, making them glad of the hooded cloaks Stephana had plundered, dark ones blending well with their surrounds. Whispered directions allowed Marric to make steady progress through the treacherous land.

'This is the long way round,' Stephana said. 'We'll have to take the rest of it in the dark.'

'Nico,' Marric ordered, 'get moving. You can tell Taran to expect us.' At least Nicephorus would get through safely.

Stephana laughed. 'The Berbers could search the area until the next flood and still never find Taran unless he wanted to be found.'

Nicephorus nodded and was gone. His horse's footfalls died away. It galled Marric that Nico and Stephana shared knowledge of which he understood almost nothing. But, after all, they were initiates into the Mysteries of which Imhotep had hinted. Marric had been hearing of some ritual or other most of his life, but he had not believed what little he had heard. Upon a time, he had been taught this much: that his ancestors had ruled as more than men. Now the Great Horus name that each emperor still assumed was useful only for inscribing on triumphal arches and obelisks, or for curses. Marric had long ago decided he could dispense both with the symbolism and with any power that might linger about it. It was just possible that he had been mistaken.

'You were,' Stephana answered, though Marric hadn't thought he had spoken. 'Once, the ruler possessed the gods' powers to pass through fire and water, to read hearts, to fathom minds and to bind men to his cause.'

Marric's arms tightened about his lover as if to bind her to him. She was a seeress and he believed in her powers: why not wish for powers of his own? *What would I do with them? Become another Irene? Even Alexander chose to use only his secular powers.*

'Softly,' he said. 'Sound travels in the damp.'

'Head south, Marric.' Now the sun was a brazen disc that smouldered to extinction at the horizon. The horse picked its way along the driest path.

'Are we far from Taran's?'

'That way.' They rode on for a few minutes. 'Now, left,' Stephana whispered. 'Taran couldn't tell you about this place before because, as long as you're uninitiate, you remain vulnerable—'

'How much risk do I place you in now?'

'We have no other choice.' Stephana, despite the dangers ahead, laughed. As Strymon said, this whole situation – escape from slavery, hiding from Berbers – seemed like some tale of Digenis the Borderer. The dangers seemed unreal, the creations of a singer's harp.

'Power to pass through fire and water,' Marric mused. 'To read hearts and minds. To bind men. My father had such a power, yet I have never heard—'

'Really, what could you hear until you were ready?' Stephana asked. 'Do you know the children's game "What I tell you three times is true"? Have you ever just learned of a thing and then, the whole day long, heard of nothing else? It's just so with initiation.'

'Imhotep – the priest of Osiris in the city – said I was not ready.'

'Ah, but you will be. You will be. Already, can you not detect truth in a man – or the lie? Did you not bind Nicephorus to you, even when you were almost dead? And what about me?'

Marric might have kissed her if he had not been intent on their path. Time was precious. Full night would render the marshes

126

treacherous. Already the red and yellow flowering plants had dulled to grey, and the rhythmic chirp of swampdwellers had intensified.

'Have I bound you?' he asked. 'Then I am content. My heart, I am prince of a line that cannot continue, even if it deserved survival. There were only two of us in direct descent. And Alexa is dead. We had employed the Bearmaster from the north to aid us, but we could not even help ourselves.'

'Is the Bearmaster a great lord?'

'An Aescir, one of the men of the Ash,' Marric said. 'He brings white bears to rulers. The bears never harm him. He calls them his children though—' he chuckled, then obeyed Stephana's instructions to turn at the hummock – 'a cub did scratch Irene.'

'He wields power,' Stephana decided. 'The King rules beasts as well as men and land. He *is* the land. Why else do you think you turned from the power you already had to risk your life to gain Empire?'

'Alexa summoned me.'

'She could have escaped alone, Marric. No. My love, you seek the throne not because it belongs to you, but because you belong to it. You are still a slave, Marric, slave to the Empire. What will you do?'

Anger at being taunted, even in Stephana's familiar, beloved voice, flared briefly, then died away. 'I will thank the gods for such bondage.' As they rode, he thought about it. 'My allies among the Kutrigur once offered the chance to ride the borders . . . I refused, but until now never knew why. And I'd have liked to travel to World's End . . .'

The sun blazed one last time as it sank, and the pools they rode past were reddened, as bloody as the day itself had been. The horse's hooves made sucking sounds in the mud.

'I'd best lead him,' Marric said. He started to dismount. Stephana kept her arms about his waist, holding him for a moment longer.

'I am sorry if the truth angered you,' she said, 'but if you accept that you belong to the Empire, then you must understand . . .'

'What I understand right now is that these lands are totally impassable after dark. Unless, of course, you have cat's eyes as well as the powers of prophecy.' He kissed her lightly to end the conversation. Her lips tasted of salt.

'Marric, you cannot return to Byzantium without some idea of what you face. Promise me you'll let me scry for you tonight. Promise.'

It would be the most intimate involvement he had ever had with magic; he wasn't certain that even for Stephana – yet she had asked it of him, she who asked nothing. What was the worst that she could say? Reluctantly, Marric nodded. Taking the horse's reins, he walked forward.

The horse's head bumped Marric's shoulder, and he froze at a sudden noise. He had been right. That was the sound of harness, the squelch and clatter of horses picking their way through the swamp. He heard a suppressed oath, but couldn't make out the words to know if they were Greek, Egyptian or Arabic. He drew his sword and set his back against the horse.

'Get down and hide,' he hissed at Stephana, who refused to move.

Closer and closer the noises came. Then they passed, as if whatever force lay out there regrouped for an attack. A troop against one tired man. Let Stephana hide and he would send the horse out to distract them. If he had time, he would join her.

The troop rode back in their direction.

'Get down!' Damn it, had terror paralyzed her? She had been brave enough facing down Sutekh. He reached up to assist her, but she pushed his hand away.

'Watch the mist,' Stephana said, and gestured. From her parted lips came a trilling sound. Shadows thickened on the ground. The evening mist rose and encircled Marric, wreathing about curved blades and the metal of warriors' trapping. He saw the Berbers' eyes, fierce, bright, and filled with bloodlust as they rode straight at him.

'No,' he whispered. He shut his eyes against what would be his own death if he could not fight it. This was illusion, illusion cast by Stephana, and therefore beneficent. It would not harm him.

He opened his eyes, saw her nod approval gravely. She moved

128

her hands and glanced about as a general might survey the site of a battle. The mist thickened still further. Now it rose as a wall between themselves and the Berbers who trespassed into the Druid's realm.

Clashes of swords against shields and armour, screams of battle and of death agonies, the snapping of wood, and the confused shrill whinnies of panicking horses, ripped the night. What were they fighting?

'The mist shows them enemies drawn from within themselves. Stand firm; this cannot last much longer.'

How could Marric ever have thought her frail? As an adept she held powers that left him shuddering. And yet, if he possessed them, if he dared draw them into his land like a sword or sceptre, what might he not do?

Echoes of the fight, intensified by the dank, standing water, rose, then died away. Someone staggered near them. There was a whimpered plea, a splash, and a slithering sound. The voices of the swampdwellers rose again. Marric dashed chill sweat from his face and turned to look at Stephana.

'Don't move yet,' she ordered softly. Ahead of Marric the mist still rose from the hummocks he skirted with such care. 'There is a glamour over the house. Taran and—' she paused, her head lifting as if she sniffed the air, 'Nicephorus, I think, set the wards. They cannot maintain them while helping us. So we will go to them.'

She slid from the saddle and came up beside Marric. 'This fog is not of my doing,' she said. 'I will guide you through it. Taran calls this *druidechta*, Druid's fog. But I can pierce it.' She grasped his arm.

'Be careful,' he couldn't help warning her. Yet he was the one grateful to fling an arm about her shoulders as they walked. Adrift in this magic-spawned fog, Marric feared that had he been left to himself, he would have lost his way and strayed into some bog or other before morning. But Stephana moved as surely as if she were guided.

She is, he thought. A priestess: and she had been willing to kill for him, had saved them both in the swamp . . . yet had suffered life as a slave. It was a paradox Marric could not resolve.

Suddenly the mists parted. Wrapped in shadow stood a tiny cabin. Outside it, sitting in concentration that amounted to trance were Taran and Nicephorus.

'I think,' Stephana murmured, 'that if you had tried, you might have seen through the glamour yourself. After all—'

You are the Prince. 'Being a prince is more than leading armies,' his father had always said. Though he felt disloyal in thinking it, perhaps being a prince was more than his father knew, too. He seemed to be heir to ancient magics as well as to his Empire.

'The next time, I shall try,' Marric promised, despite the dryness in his mouth.

But I am no priest! He had said that so often it had to be true, didn't it? Another paradox.

But the paradoxes made him confront the Druid with a smile on his face. Taran rose, approached, and with complete, ceremonial deliberation, made the deep bow due to Marric as Emperor.

Mor, rebellious and brutalized, shrank back. Then the pain of the last months faded, and Mor was encompassed by Marric. He was the Prince again. Graciousness revived in him with that, and he inclined his head, acknowledging Taran's homage. He felt almost dizzy from the immense change his months of slavery and the transition into freedom had made in his thinking.

He looked at Stephana, too, with these new eyes. She would not be, could not be Empress, or even Consort. But there would be a place, an honoured place, very close to him, for the woman who had healed him after he had renounced his life. Stephana would never be hailed as Isis, Mother of Empire, but she was his heart and she had given the Empire new life.

Slave-seeress, scholar, Druid and fugitive prince – against Irene and the wounded strength of the throne. Had there ever been a less likely conspiracy?

'Did you kill your enemy?' Taran asked. Now that Marric was himself again, Sutekh's death no longer seemed of overmastering importance. He had simply been a savage man whom the Prince had killed in the same way that a farmer destroys the cur who has bitten his wife.

'My enemy sits on my father's throne.'

Taran smiled. 'Come within. I can give you safe rest.'

Why were they all willing to help him? From the first moment of his slavery, Nicephorus had been ally and friend. Stephana was – she was his, he thought. And now Taran risked his precarious security to help a foreign prince.

Your line has the power to bind hearts, Stephana had said. Marric's heart filled with love and grief for the risks his friends accepted for his sake. He drew Stephana close and extended a hand to Taran.

'I have not been the prince, or even the man, you would have me be,' he said hoarsely, 'but thank you.' They followed Taran inside. 'I did not seek this,' Marric said. 'It simply happened—'

'As do all things when you place your feet on the Way. Had you forced your way on to the throne you might – you would have ruled well, but never would you have been more than a warrior-king: ambitious, dealing the justice of a lion to its pride. Well enough. But from having been nothing, you have earned the chance to become much more.'

In this very swamp, Marric recalled, Isis and Horus had fled from Set and been sheltered.

'I am not an initiate priest,' Marric told him, 'nor likely to be one.'

'So you always say,' Taran replied. 'But now, when you have just escaped, is no time to talk of such matters. Be seated.'

Several stools ringed a low table. Marric sank down on to one, aware for the first time of how weary he was. Nicephorus waited until he was seated, then sat too. Leaving the last stool for the Druid, Stephana drew a mat forward and sat at Marric's feet, leaning back against his legs. She reached up to take his hand and cradle it against her cheek. The caress reassured him, in this humble place that seemed to hint at mysteries too high for anyone but templedwellers.

'The last time I saw you,' Taran said, 'you had been fighting too. In any case, you were wounded. You must take better care.'

'Be assured,' said Marric, 'I take no unnecessary risks now.' Never again would he fight as he had in the provinces, when he had ridden the steppes, or as he had when he fought the pirates or the Gepid, strictly for relief from thought and purpose. What

131

was the matter with him? Everything Taran said seemed to prick his conscience. He tightened his clasp on Stephana's hand.

'I must return to Alexandria,' Marric told the Druid after they had all washed and eaten. Mellow light and cinnamon-scented incense rose from braziers placed in the corners of the hut. They were of beautifully wrought metal and looked like gifts from the Osiris temple.

'Indeed you must. But how? I will find out. While you rest, I shall ask.'

There were no horses here, save for the ones Marric and Nicephorus had ridden. Taran kept no servant and would not, in any case, have risked one by sending him forth into treacherous swamps prowled by soldiers and defeated Berbers. And though there were doves and other birds, some with splinted wings, hanging in cages from the rafters, he had no carrier-birds.

'Curious, Prince?' Taran's face gleamed in the lamplight and the moonlight which shone through the hut's one window. 'While the rest of you sleep, I too shall appear to rest. But I shall be travelling out of body to Imhotep, my friend, and we shall confer. A way will be found.'

'Stephana told me that I must look ahead to see—'

'What you face? Aye, that you must.' He rose from his stool and went to a battered chest. Kneeling before it, he opened it and lifted out an object swathed in clean linen. Carefully, he removed the wrappings from a silver bowl, thin and blackened with age. This he placed on the table before Stephana.

She rose, sat on Taran's stool, and drew the bowl towards her. Nicephorus filled a ewer with clean water and placed it, along with a phial of oil, within her reach.

Stephana poured water into the bowl, then moved it so that the moonlight shining through the window lay mirrored in the water. Unlike its blackened outer surface, the bowl's interior gleamed silver. It shone even more brightly as the moonlight pooled in the gently rippling water. For a moment Stephana sat with her slender hands cupping the bowl. Light flowed from it around her hands and up her arms, caught and tangled in her flowing hair, and touched her face with an austere serenity that made each man present catch his breath.

Was this the same woman who had trembled at his touch? She seemed more priestess or goddess than woman now.

Stephana breathed on the water, then delicately worked the stopper from the phial and let a few drops of oil fall into the bright water. The shrill cry of a creature in mortal terror and the triumphant shriek of a nighthawk stooping on its prey rent the air, but no one moved.

'The Hawk strikes,' Stephana whispered. 'Yes. We shall see the Hawk tonight . . . and whatever else the Goddess wills us to see.' She raised her face from the bowl to the moonlight. Now, it seemed a palpable thing, a path of silver connecting the hut with the realm of the Goddess.

As she extended both hands over the water the light grew so intense that her hands gleamed pink where it touched them. 'Hail, O great Mother, Who art called Lady of Earth, Water and Sky. Nourish us by field and river. Enlighten us by the radiance of Thy face. We, Thy children, praise Thee, and we invoke Thee by the power with which Thou endowest me. If it be Thy will, grant us sight!'

'So may it be!' Nicephorus and Taran responded. To his shock, Marric realized he had joined in.

The moonlight, which turned Stephana into a breathing representation of the Goddess, died away. Only her hands still shone. She parted them. Now the water's glow faded into evanescent haze. She bent to stare into the bowl. The oil swirled in the water, if the substance in the bowl could still be called water. Now shapes coiled and smoked in its depths, faded out, and reformed.

'Prince, what would you seek?' She was a priestess addressing a royal supplicant now.

'My future,' said Marric. 'I go to regain the throne of my fathers and my mothers from her who has stolen it and who sucks the life and health from the Empire I was born to serve. Show me what I must know.'

'Give me your hands.'

Marric placed his hands over Stephana's.

'Watch, Prince.'

As Marric sat, scarcely daring to breathe, the golden oil in the still water swirled:

133

Ships – high-prowed and clinker-built – sailing down the rivers, across the Euxine towards Byzantium, beaching to unload warriors with a grudge against the Empire.

Irene, haughty in draped chlamys of a purple so bright that it was almost crimson, bringing jewelled fists up in anger: 'When we fired the tents, did we not teach the barbarians our power? Perhaps they need a sharper lesson.' Flame lances from her fingers and ignites the map. 'Well, the Tagmata will give them one.' About her stir men with braided hair, sworn to her by oaths of service, but linked to the Aescir with ties of blood.

Audun Bearmaster, gesturing furiously, his white bears moaning in sympathy, turns on his heel with the briefest of bows, stalking from the court back to his camp. 'I could not move her because she would not permit me to speak,' he tells his men.

Opposite the city cluster felt yurts, the travelling homes of the Kutrigur hordes. Their horses, hardy and steppe-bred, smaller than the massive chargers of the klibanophoroi, *graze in the fields outside the walls. Within the largest tent, seated on a heap of furs, are Ellac and Uldin, khagans of the hordes, and their brothers by fosterage. With them is the shaman who casts the scapular bones of divination.*

'I made my treaty with Marric, the son of the khagan of the city. He is a man and a warrior. Where is he? Gone, says this little Queen of weak power and less truth. Had Marric wanted to ride free, we offered him the freedom of the steppes. My faith is to the man, not to his city.'

Marric groaned. 'No! You have it wrong. The *city* is what is important; you made peace with it! Friend, they will slaughter you; don't do this—'

'Silence!' ordered Stephana.

'Caravans I will permit,' said Uldin, 'but not an invading army. Let this feeble Queen and her clumsy troopers ride at me, and my sons will fill them with arrows.'

Marric saw that Stephana's face still bore that divine calm. But the contrast between moonlight and darkness – moonlight on the bowl, darkness elsewhere – was less distinct, more akin to the separation between normal light and shadow. She was tiring, yet he must know more.

For a third time the oil swirled in the bowl:

A tall, familiar form – himself! – grasped an enraged woman in a cloak clasped across her breasts by hands stained with red light. Alexa.

Marric remembered how she had loosed Ctesiphon to die under their pursuers' horses and saw the whole, sickening story replayed with merciless clarity in the water:

Alexa struggled with Irene's men, her sharp dagger dripping blood on her robes, screaming defiance as she tried to summon Power even against her brother. A guard's blade slashed her side and she was falling—

Why could Marric not weep for the blow that ended his House?

Even as Marric fell unconscious, men charged down from a ship on to the docks.

Why should Stephana exhaust herself merely to show Marric his own wilfulness? He should never have let her scry for him: this was too close a contact with magic for his comfort. He raised a hand to break her trance, but then the water showed still another scene.

And then came the rush of the Bearmaster's men over the side of their vessel, overpowering the cataphracts who surrounded Alexa, then lifting her gently and returning to their ship.

The Bearmaster bent over a pallet on which Alexa lay. The sheet covering her rose and fell as she breathed.

Alexa was alive! Marric exulted. He would have hidden his face in his hands save that Stephana still clasped them. Her own hands had gone very cold, but the visions were not yet over.

Alexa, wearing the dress of an Aescir noblewoman, walking on the riverbank as the Bearmaster's men compelled their ship upriver over the rapids . . . Alexa, riding at Audun's side in a green land, her face peaceful . . . staring out to sea, no aura of evil about her now . . .

The film of oil on the water was thinner, darker now. More and more feebly it swirled. Stephana's hands shook.

'One last thing,' Marric begged. 'Let me see my sister as she is now!'

Stephana drew a shuddering breath and bent over the bowl.

135

Alexa's dark hair was brushed back into long braids bound with gold. She wore green, girdled with metal leaves, and she stood between a man and woman, no, a king and queen. Both were tall and golden-haired, crowned with simple circlets. Alexa parted her lips as if to speak to Marric and—

And the vision guttered out. The oil in the water caught fire and burned for a brief instant. Smoke rose from what was now only a bowl of water stained with ashes. Light and life had fled from it. Stephana's hands jerked and the bowl turned over. She lurched sideways and Marric came round the table to kneel at her side. He was glad to bury his face against her hair and hide his tears.

He wanted to shout, to laugh, to weep, or to swing Stephana high into the air. Alexa was alive and safe in the Isles of the Mists. The brother and sister who ruled there would protect her against the time he could come to claim her. Alexa would reign as Isis yet!

Stephana raised her head. 'Your sister, my love? Indeed, I am glad she lives; you grieved so. But are you—'

He kissed her words to silence.

'Once more you give life and hope back to me, Stephana. What manner of woman are you?'

'Yours,' she said faintly. 'Yours . . . and the Goddess'.'

Marric bowed his head over hers. *Goddess, don't let me fail her as I failed Alexa.* He carried Stephana to the mats that Taran unrolled and covered her with her cloak and his own.

Nicephorus brought water again. 'I have reset the wards. Now Taran can speak with Imhotep.' He put out one hand and smoothed back Stephana's hair. She opened her eyes and smiled at him, then rested her cheek on her hand and slept.

Nicephorus glanced over at Marric.

'Nico, I swear by all the gods that Stephana will never want for anything as long as she lives!' Did Nicephorus think that Marric could ever abandon her, sister or not? 'Least of all,' he continued, his voice shaking, 'for my love.'

Nicephorus patted his shoulder. 'Rest, Mor. We face a long road in the morning.'

Could Marric love two women? Apparently he did. Joy filled him.

Carefully, so as not to disturb Stephana, Marric settled in next to her. Nico was right: they had a long road ahead of them. At the end of it lay an empire to win, a queen to regain, and all the rest of their lives to celebrate their victories.

Chapter Fourteen

Prince Marric leaned back against the railing of the merchanter *Pride of Isis* and tried to force himself to inner stillness. It wasn't easy; he doubted it ever would be. Once again he had a new identity – Alexandros the merchant, sailing with a party of priests to Byzantium with one of the all-too-infrequent grain convoys. Behind them, across open water, lay Alexandria. By avoiding the usual night harbours, the captain and convoy hoped to escape pirates.

For the moment he was safe, and Stephana and Nico with him. He might as well stop scanning the horizon for pirates.

That night, in Taran's cabin, Stephana had restored his hopes. And Taran had travelled out of body to speak with Imhotep. Returning to himself at dawn, he told Marric that the Osiris priest had foreseen no more difficulties with Berber raiding parties. They were cut off, the only route of escape lying through the Necropolis west of Alexandria. And the tomb guardians – not all of them possessing bodies or human form – would punish those who profaned them. Marric, agreed the priest, had found his own path to freedom. Let him come to the temple with his friends.

'You come with us,' Marric urged Taran. The Druid had refused.

'I am eyes and ears for my Order here. Would *you* abandon your post?'

Long ago, in what felt like another life, Marric had done just that to try to take up the Empire he thought he owned – and which owned him. Now, he shook his head.

'It is hardly the same—'

'Because I am old and bear no weapons? Prince Marric, innocent of war as you think I am, if I had not wished your coming here safely, you would be wandering the swamps. Please believe me—' his glance left Marric and lighted on Stephana, who still slept, exhausted, 'I am in less danger than any of you.'

At twilight, Stephana had led them through the fog again. Nicephorus, tied to his horse, maintained the glamour that let them approach Alexandria invisible to guard, traveller or thief.

By midnight they arrived outside the south wall. Stephana headed for a small concealed entrance. After he forced it open, Marric found a long underground passageway of dressed limestone that led to the temple itself. Imhotep awaited them. He nodded and hurried them inside. No one else saw them – and thus could not be blamed. As the passage wound on beneath the city, it pressed in on Marric. Half way to the temple, by Imhotep's reckoning, his torch flickered out.

'Do you wish me to summon light?' Stephana asked. Echoes hissed and grumbled here.

'Light has never shone here.' They continued in darkness.

As Marric began to wonder if being lost in a tomb could be more unnerving than this – and what if they *were* lost beneath the maze of streets – the passage opened into the brightly lit inner precinct of the temple. None of the priests and scribes there stopped to wonder at their superior's shepherding a bandaged man with the bearing of a general, a woman with silvered hair, and a slighter man who might have been one of themselves, were it not for his look of hard usage.

They were assigned quarters where they found supplies and garments suitable for a sea voyage.

When Marric had left Tmutorakan for his capital, at Alexa's summons, he had had no doubts of his fitness to rule. Now, turning over the contents of the sea chests, he felt unsure of his strength. Could he reconcile Huns, Aescir, and the Empire? And then there was Irene. He had sense enough to fear her powers, and no idea of how to fight them.

As Marric finished donning the breeches and full tunic of a prosperous merchant, Imhotep entered.

'Do you think I can do it?' Marric asked without preface.

'Can you not try and go on living?' The priest's irony reassured Marric more than any assurances. 'There are dangers, and you know them now. But you are not without allies. We in Alexandria will alert our brothers and sisters in Byzantium. They will harbour you while you make your plans.'

'I have to thank you—'

For the first time in their acquaintance, Imhotep smiled. Then his face changed and Marric laughed. He knew that expression from the days before he entered training: priest reproving him for his temper.

'You are going to warn me against rashness again, aren't you?'

'Only a rash man would attempt what you do. I will give thanks for your rashness each day of my life. But I do wish to remind you of one thing. Prince, you are on the Wheel. For all that you do, there comes payment. There will always be payment, either in this life or another. Be careful you do nothing that will make you pay more than you can bear.'

Marric would have questioned him further, but Imhotep held up his hand, forbidding questions. Marric remembered that gesture, too.

'Come now and join your companions.'

The long tunic of a scholar made Nicephorus look younger, yet more dignified, than Marric thought he could. But Stephana – she was the wonder. Over her blue tunic she wore a rich dalmatic with embroidered key-trim at hem and knee. A semicircular cloak in a darker blue lay over her arm. The gold brooch that would fasten it gleamed with a sapphire. She bore herself like the great lady a kinder fate would have let her be. Marric grinned and she whirled before him, delighted by his admiration. Seizing his hands, she led him to a seat.

'In seven days, a grain convoy will embark for Byzantium,' Imhotep told them. 'Until then – well, no one objects to worthy, pious citizens who take quarters in Rhakotis, by the temple, and spend their days in prayer.'

'Is that safe?'

'Rhakotis is the oldest part of the city. Those who live here are Egyptians of the old stock, loyal to the temple and to me. Of course, I could send the lady to the temple of Isis Pharia: the island is well-secured—'

'Let me stay here!' Stephana interrupted. 'If I am to help him —' she broke off and laughed. Marric had never heard her sound so carefree.

'I assume your plans are the best possible under these conditions,' said Marric. 'We will stay together.'

'No one will know where to seek us,' said Nicephorus.

'Not on this level of being,' said the priest. 'I caution you against venturing out on any other. By now Irene knows that the Prince has eluded her. She has creatures who will search the astral planes for Marric. If they find him—'

'*I* cannot travel as Taran did,' Marric objected.

'Not that you perceive, though it lies within you – and your companions' gifts quicken your own. But since you cannot yet defend or conceal yourself, you must be protected.'

Marric started to object to that term, but Stephana broke in.

'You protected me, love. When I would have lived out my life joyless, you forbade it. Let me thank you by doing this.'

'If you wish to protect me, love,' Marric smiled into her eyes, heedless of their companions, 'we left your lance behind.'

'I am not joking,' said Stephana. She turned to Imhotep. 'Do not even think of separating us. Who can guard him better, night and day, than I?'

The priest inclined his head in respect. 'I cannot withstand fate. Be it as you will, child.'

The wind blew Marric's cloak about his tall form. He smiled reminiscently. Now, on board *Pride of Isis*, he played the part of a well-to-do merchant. Stephana posed as his wife. As far as Marric's feelings were concerned, that was no imposture. Day after day – even while learning the disciplines of breathing and thought which Imhotep put him through – Marric had watched his lover flower. Even Antonia, his mother, could not have borne herself with more grace.

But Stephana could not escape her past. Some evenings Marric found her seated before a candle flame, seeking calm with the patience adepts had. At other times, nightmares made her toss and moan. After he woke and comforted her, and before she could sleep again, she would perform rituals of protection. The air would shimmer with blue light. And even after that, when she was exhausted, she would lie and shiver in his arms.

What was she, anyway? Marric had known women who made a profession of beauty and turned pleasure into high art. He had known women who were royal, whose birth and strength of will equalled his. Why, then, did he love this woman whose great arched eyelids and slender bones made her look fey, a woman who had spent part of her life in misery and another part – equally arduous – in esoteric study he couldn't even understand? Power had cost her cruelly, but it did not deprive her of her essential shrewdness. Marric trusted her judgement, as he hoped one day to trust his Empress – assuming Alexa was learning the same harsh lessons slavery and despair had taught him. But Stephana . . . she had courage and humour, a great capacity to take joy in even the smallest gift. She would have made a fine empress.

Stephana's maid, muffled in a heavy cloak, approached Marric. Her very intonations a copy of her lady's, she repeated a message: Did my lord intend to fast *all* day?

Now Marric remembered. Not all gifts gave Stephana pleasure. Daphne had been one such.

In Alexandria, Imhotep had opened the treasuries to Marric. 'You are Horus. Take what you need. All we have comes from you and is held in trust for you.'

With that money Marric was even able to purchase the gifts with which he would bribe Irene's servants. His own needs, like Nicephorus', were simple: one attendant would serve them both. And they had him: the urchin Marric brought to the temple was pleased to leave Alexandria, but he would stay with the ship.

Marric assumed that Stephana would need a serving-girl and that she would require what any other lady needed in a maid:

health, strength, pleasantness, skill in fine sewing, hairdressing and, perhaps, music. Stephana's own skills, in short. It would be an interesting challenge to please her. Seeing Daphne in the market, Marric decided she satisfied the requirements and did not even bother to bargain for her. He tossed a pouch to the dealer, sent a temple servant to procure her a decent gown, and told her to dress and follow him.

He had presented her with some anticipation to Stephana. 'This is Daphne,' he told her. 'She will serve you well – won't you, child?'

'Yes, please, lady,' the girl stammered. She watched Stephana with eyes almost blank with fear, and she shrank away from Marric. *Had the girl really thought he wanted a concubine? She was scarcely thirteen!*

'Daphne, did my lord explain we have a long way to go? Will you come with us?' Stephana asked.

'Will I?' Daphne fell on her knees and burst into babyish, astounded tears. Stephana took the girl's head between her hands while Marric started to leave the room in embarrassment. It was not going properly. He could rely on Stephana to calm the child down.

When Stephana's fingers brushed Daphne's collar, no thicker than the one Marric had broken from about her own throat, she went rigid. Stroking Daphne's curly hair, she looked up.

'Marric!' she called. Her voice was indignant and reproachful. 'You *bought* this girl and simply would give her to me? Oh, Marric!' Pain shimmered in her eyes.

Stephana had needed a maid; he had provided her with one. That seemed simple enough, didn't it?

'She is unfree,' said Stephana. 'A slave. As were we, my lord, as were we.'

Daphne would be well treated, Marric started to say. Seeing that she would serve Stephana, how not?

'How could you forget?' Stephana asked. Tears spilled down her face. Before Marric could reach her, Daphne flung both arms about Stephana's waist and they were consoling one another. As Stephana promised that no one would ever hurt her, and Daphne protested that she would be happy to belong to her, Marric stood astounded. Then Stephana explained how sorry she was and – embarrassingly – how her lord had simply forgotten her hatred of slavery. Daphne glanced at him, so much taller than she, terrifyingly male, as if – *What does she think? That I would rape a child?* That was what had happened to Stephana. He could understand it now: the older women awaiting sale, seeing him, envious of the child, determined to terrify her.

Ashamed of his forgetfulness, Marric walked over to the weeping women and raised Daphne. A pretty, healthy girl, she had light-brown hair which curled freely down her back, a high complexion made pinker by tears, and amber eyes.

'I did forget one thing,' he said. He was aware that Stephana watched him closely. He snapped the girl's collar between strong fingers. 'Be free, Daphne. I will register it tomorrow. But please, serve my lady well. She is worthy of all you can give her.'

He would never be sure how he found himself embracing his lover and her serving-maid, or why his eyes stung.

Now, standing on the deck with Daphne watching him, Marric recalled himself to the present. Daphne was waiting for an answer. He smiled at her absently and she flushed. 'I'm not going to fast any longer at all,' he said. 'I'll come now.' Nodding to the sailors and the ship's captain, he went below.

Quarters on a merchanter were spacious, far better than anything he would have on a warship, and there was no comparison to his last voyage in the hold of a slaver. Remembering slaveships had sobered them all for the first three days of their voyage.

On Stephana's lap lay one of the ship's cats. Lean, scarred, a real veteran, the cat spurned all the crew and passengers except for Stephana. Marric had requested that it not bring her rats and not sleep with them; he had scratches from enforcing that rule. Now, Stephana stroked the cat while Marric watched her and coveted that touch for himself.

When she saw Marric, she slipped to her feet. The cat glared balefully at him, then leapt past and skittered around the corner towards the hold.

'You adjust well to the sea,' he observed.

Stephana laced her arm through his and drew him to join Nicephorus.

'I'm coast-bred, Marric, and not a fragile lady: I am used to much less than we enjoy here. This is luxury.'

'I have been telling Stephana,' said Nicephorus, 'that one never steps in the same river twice . . . or the same sea. One day, you are a slave, the next, a prince's lady, wearing silks. How do you maintain equilibrium in the midst of all this flux, Stephana, my dear?'

Stephana went suddenly tense. 'Just for now,' she said, 'I float with it. Just for now, for the time we are in transition. I want to pretend, just for now, that we are . . . free of the Wheel. Let me, please, Nico.' Her voice became sad and earnest. 'I want to be simply a woman, not a seeress. For just this little time, is that so dreadful?'

'Have you seen danger?'

'Let it be, Nico.'

Marric never envied his friend his place in Stephana's confidence, his sharing of her secrets of power. But now, for the first time, he wished that he understood better what they meant. The priests had taught him a few tricks of meditation: Marric still used their teachings to compose himself for sleep.

More useful were other kinds of knowledge: friendship, for example. Nicephorus' friendship had survived his discovery of Marric's identity; and Marric, freed from plotting, struggling to survive, and – just for now – danger, could relax and enjoy a new luxury: unfeigned friendship.

'Have done with your dreary metaphysics,' he teased Nicephorus. 'Drink up, now, that's a good fellow. The day is fine and you skulk here, babbling about your precious Heraclitus. Save your gloom for sleepless nights.'

'When he has no one to share it,' Stephana cut in acidly. She rested her hand briefly on Marric's shoulder. Looking at her, who would not have thought her a carefully reared Byzantine maid of good family?

Daphne served them all and disappeared to allow them privacy. She had become devoted to Stephana. When the meal was over, Nicephorus rose and stretched, then went up on deck.

144

'I never really had such a friend before,' Marric said.

'Your sister?'

'I entered training so early,' Marric explained, 'that we never were really close once we were out of babyhood. Besides, I think that even during our childhoods we knew that what mattered was the Empire, not our own lives. We always knew—'

'Has Nico turned you melancholy?' Stephana asked. 'I wish he had not.' She slid her arms about Marric's neck and kissed him, while lingeringly her hands rubbed the tension out of his arms and shoulders. Rose fragrance, mingled with the scent of the sea, teased at his senses. Marric pulled her close.

'You make me dizzy,' she said.

'Not the wine?'

'You. You're so alive,' she said, and ran her hands up his back. 'Even when we bound your spirit within your flesh because we feared you might die in the night—'

'I returned from the place of my own will.'

'Your gift is for life, Marric. Remember that. Love, if I died tomorrow, I would still bless you for having shared it with me. I had given up—'

'You don't have to think of it.' Marric wanted to promise her extravagant gifts – love, honour, safety, wealth – for her whole life. She asked only a brief time of peace.

He kissed her, letting his hands rove over her slender body for the sheer delight of her response. Footsteps approached and they released each other with a start.

'I think you had best come on deck,' called Nicephorus.

'What's wrong?' Marric asked. Stephana snatched up a cloak and followed the men outside.

The convoy was tacking into defensive position. The fleet was making good headway; the winds favoured them. But fortune, it seemed, did not. Coming towards them – too many to evade or to fight – were dromonds, clearly armed for war: the banners flying from their masts were green and charged with the crescent moon.

Chapter Fifteen

'Pirates again,' Nicephorus said grimly.

'Not pirates this time,' Marric answered. 'The Emir's fleet. Gods, does the whole world hate the Empire?'

If I died tomorrow, Stephana had said. She might die today, and Nicephorus with her; and it would be his fault.

'Get below,' he told her. At least he could spare her the sight of battle. 'Send the boy for my—' He was Alexandros the merchant, not a warrior; he had no place among the ship's fighters. Slamming a fist on to the deckrail in frustration, Marric observed just where the Arab fleet would intercept the convoy.

'War or not,' Stephana pointed out, 'they will surely want the grain, and grainships carry passengers who can pay ransom. I foresaw a knife's edge for us; now we balance on it.'

'Imhotep would ransom us,' Nicephorus said.

'It's jihad,' Marric reminded him bleakly. 'The Emir would not deal with the Temple. Stephana, you remember that dagger I gave you? Get it. Promise you will not let them take you, beloved.'

She whispered the promise. With a rustle of skirt and cloak she was gone.

'I swear to you, Nicephorus, I will not be sold again.'

The captain, navigator and commander of marines clustered by the helm, and Marric longed to join them. 'If we sacrificed three ships to engage them, we could make a run for it,' he calculated.

'Hard on the ships that were chosen,' Nicephorus observed. 'Would you start your reign with a massacre?'

'What if we used sea fire before they could?' Marric asked. Sea fire would give the convoy a chance to defeat the larger fleet, but there were too many risks in this business already! Was it another test? Marric dared not fight, yet by training, birth and inclination, he was not only a fighter but the rightful leader here.

'A test,' Marric muttered. 'These powers Imhotep gabbles on about . . .' The acceptance he had learned in the temple dropped from him, and he cursed captious priests, the Wheel of Fate they nagged about, and the Arab fleet that some malignant chance made their instrument.

The wind was freshening, tossing a light spume up on the waves. Far to the west lay the crumpled shadows of storm clouds. Phlebas, the *Pride of Isis*' captain, already had the ship on a northeastward heading, trying to widen the distance between the convoy and the Emir's fleet. But even if Phlebas added oars to sails and burst the hearts of all the rowers with exertion, the heavy laden grainship could never outrun the enemy dromonds.

'Clear the decks!' Phlebas roared out orders while the marines prepared their defences. Twice Marric moved to let them set up the catapults.

Then the priests came up on deck, and Phlebas did not dare protest. Merikare, one of the senior priests, approached Marric. 'You are a general,' he said in an undertone. 'What do you see here?'

'Trouble,' Marric said. 'Phlebas cannot outrun them. Sooner or later he'll have to turn and fight. And we're overmatched.'

Was it for this I trusted you? he wanted to ask the priest.

Merikare gazed at the horizon where the stormclouds loomed. He licked a finger to test the wind's direction. 'Still thinking only of men and battles. There are other ways of fighting . . .' The priest eyed Marric narrowly, and the Prince braced himself for the next words. 'There is another way to vanquish such a fleet.'

'How? If we lose this battle, the whole Empire loses. Not for myself . . . no, though I want to live. I am the shepherd of Empire and the flail of its enemies. But I must get home to take up my power. And there is another thing. Once I lay in slavers' hands and swore to rid myself of them. I'll die rather than be sold again.'

Merikare glanced out. 'The distance between the ships is widening.'

'They're coming about. Once they do, they'll close fast. See, now they begin to turn. Priest, if you know a thing to do, I suggest you do it now. Or go and pray.'

The ship's seventy marines ran by, skins of vinegar ready to pour over the thick leather shields that were so inadequate protection against sea fire. The catapults stood ready at the ship's prow.

'Clouds,' said Merikare. 'Nun, god of lightning, and Tefnut, goddess of rain, might aid us in this desert of tossing water. And the Elder Gods might help us to destroy our enemies . . .'

'Then call them.'

'They would not answer me. But you are the son of Osiris. They might heed you.'

Silence fell between them and lengthened.

Marric stepped back, alarmed. He had seen how the adepts through whom the gods spoke were drained by the rituals once they had been abandoned to their humanity again. 'I have no powers.'

'You have the potential. Open yourself as a channel for power. Let it flow through you. If it does not teach you how to entreat the Elder Gods, we are all lost.'

Marric bowed his head, more to hide his face than to collect his thoughts. He clenched his fists to hide the trembling of his hands. So it had finally come to just what he feared: the priests would use him, claim him for their own. Pray Horus he would not be a weapon to snap in their hands. Another priest handed a cup to Marric, who drank and tasted the heavy sweetness of some unknown drug. He felt his limbs go numb. His mind became more keen, and he perceived the ship and the people on board as desperate nets of energy, appetites to go on living. He saw the Arab fleet as a scarlet hunger, a fire he ached to put out. Involuntarily his arms raised and his hands spread out in rejection. He was Horus-on-Earth and he would forbid the ships to approach.

They would be within bow-shot soon. He should step back, he thought idly. But the drug removed his fear of a lucky arrow. He was not a target; he was a weapon.

Behind him, sistrums rattled and the priests began to chant. 'Summon for me the All-Seeing Eye, with Shu, Tefnut, Nun, Geb, and all the fathers and mothers who lay with Re in the primaeval water.'

'Let Nun himself come with all his court.'

'Ancient gods, hear us.'

'Behold, mankind, which comes from you, has achieved against you. Let your water be poured out.'

'Let the flood devour them.'

'Let the opener of the skies approach and grant life to his people.'

'Let the powers come, let the gods send water to aid their people.'

As the chanting grew more feverish, Marric's spirit struggled within his body. His flesh was inadequate to contain the energies the priests summoned, and he shuddered convulsively. Would the priests kill him? He felt an instant of wild fear. The power hurt as it flooded into the channels it wished to use in him. He had no escape except outward, out of the mere flesh. And then his spirit lifted from his body and looked back at it – tall, sea-tanned, but paling under the strain of the powers coursing through it. His spirit took the shape of a giant hawk which screamed with rage and swooped down to attack. Arrows, and then sea fire, burned against its golden plumage. The hawk landed on the flagship's rigging. Flames spurted up around its pinions. Again and again the hawk darted from ship to ship, and the burning followed it.

It looked down upon its dazzling reflection in the tossing sea, mantled its wings, and screamed defiance at the Emir's ships. Then it returned to the body it had abandoned.

As if from a great distance, Marric could hear Phlebas and the other ships' captains shouting orders, tacking, increasing the stretch of open water that lay between their ships and their astounded enemies.

Once again Marric was buffeted by the force of the priests' wills, the carefully constructed mnemonics of their chants. He raised his arms, letting the power evoked by the ritual swell through him in a rising tide. It was easier this time. Light crackled from his fingertips towards a darkening sky.

As the priests began a final invocation to the gods of lightning and waste places, that power erupted. Lightning danced from Marric's fingers to the skies. It hurt like Sutekh's whip.

Now wind and wave were stilled, stunned by the unexpected thunder and lightning. The priests fell silent, too. Yet the demand of their wills still beat down upon Marric. He could feel his body tingling from the lightnings' aftershocks.

This is too much power. What more do they want?

In a spasm of panic, he struggled to break free, but sensed that that would be fatal. Was it for this that his father had ruled? This, for which he had bled in the dungeons and Delta marshes – to die because he feared to use the weapons at hand? The power coursed through him again, burning because he fought it. If he did not stop fighting and work with it, it would consume him.

Coward! He remembered Stephana's accusation. She was waiting below and he knew that she would not hesitate to use her dagger as she had promised. The lightning crackled and lashed him again. How long could he take this punishment?

'Ha-k ir-i!' The incredibly ancient words of Osiris, trapped in his own death, ripped from his throat and chest like a spear pulled from a cloven heart. 'Come down to me!' Come save me, heal the land, make an ending.

From the clear sky flooded Nun, the primaeval ocean.

Walls of rain toppled, and the *Pride of Isis*' decks ran with water like the Nile at floodtime.

Waterspouts punched through the decks of three dromonds, and ropes, spars and bodies whirled with them between sea and sky. Several other ships foundered, leaving only one to keel over. Its sails filled with water, and, very slowly, it sank. Then a great whirlpool emerged from the face of the sea and sucked up, first the refuse, then the rain which that last anguished scream of Marric's had drawn from the sky. Even in destruction, the Elder Gods were cleanly.

The Horizon itself shimmered and seemed to open.

'Father!' Marric gasped. He staggered and almost fell. Awe filled him and he tightened his grasp on the rail, on consciousness itself. He could not lose his senses now! A golden bird, greater and brighter than his own hawk-sigil, circled above the merchant ship and perched on the topmast. It cast a healing, warming light, and the water pooling on the decks dried up. Marric felt restored. If he died in the next minute – and he still feared that he might – he would die of exaltation, not exhaustion.

Though the priests' arms were upholding him, Marric knew he would not fall. He released himself and stood clear. The air was sweet, as if it had newly been created. He took a few experimental steps. How strange the deck felt under his feet, yet he had walked it many times. The ship rolled and he compensated for the motion automatically. What a wonder he was! He was aware of his body as a gift from the gods who had preserved it to do their will.

Sun shone in his eyes, drew tears down his face. He turned and faced the priests.

Followed by the others, Merikare kissed ground before Marric in a form that had been old when Pithom and Ramses were still being built and Byzantium itself not yet thought of. He lifted a hand, permitting them to rise. Yes, they might have used him. But now he was their master. He felt only a vast surprise. So this was what priesthood felt like. It was too much power for any man, let alone an emperor. He did not think he would dare it again.

Phlebas and his officers were hastening over to him and he gathered his wits quickly.

'In truth, merchant, who are you?'

'Alexander *is* my name,' Marric told him huskily. 'Among others. As you value your life, captain, do not press me for more.'

Too many people, too much awe thrust at him from the people on deck. It made him feel very lonely. Even Nicephorus – a magician himself – had drawn a little apart from Marric. Empire, he thought, was isolation enough without this further barrier. *I cannot bear this.*

Marric held out his hand to the scholar.

'Help me,' he whispered. 'Get me away before I fall.'

As Nicephorus supported him away, Marric turned back once to look over the sea. The phoenix had flown back to the Horizon. It was bare of everything except a great rainbow that arched over half the sky.

Chapter Sixteen

On the last day of the voyage, Marric and his companions stood at the ship's prow. Crew and officers hung back, allowing them the best vantage point. In the long, restful days since the battle at sea, they had come to recognize that the merchant who travelled on priests' business was no mere merchant – and that they owed him their lives.

This grain convoy might provide Marric with the germ of the military support he would need to take his throne. If the ships' crews spread rumours, in the bazaars and tavernas of Byzantium, of a new, supernaturally gifted war leader, and the soldiers told of a battle in which only enemies perished, Marric would also have access to the Mangana, Byzantium's military district. And it was near, very conveniently near, the imperial palace.

Marric strained his eyes for a first glimpse of his city. Water . . . clouds . . . there! At the outermost range of his vision, white and golden against the blue of the water and the paler blue of the sky, shone his home. It seemed so small from this distance that a god could hold it like a jewelled toy in the palm of his hand.

Surely no other city was so beautiful. The silhouette of gleaming roofs was utterly familiar and utterly dear to him, calling him with an urgency he had no desire to resist. Tears blurred his sight of it. *Osiris, protect the city; Horus, hover over it with your wings; Isis, make it flourish.*

His friends allowed him privacy to calm himself, then they joined him at the rail. Nicephorus scanned the roofs for landmarks. Stephana grasped both men's arms and laughed, watching their joy. They interrupted one another, pointing out things they recognized. It was all new to her; Marric would delight in showing her the city, if only he might. But once they docked they would have to return to tension, to weaving intricate plots that must enfold an entire empire.

'The triple walls,' Marric pointed at the city's defences. 'Do you see that second tower? It marks the Golden Gate, the one that emperors and victorious generals enter by, and – what's that?' He shook free of his friends and leaned out as far as he dared. Below the great walls clustered what looked like an invading army.

'It's the Huns,' said Marric. 'The Kutrigur, the Utrigur, even the minor clans. Just as you prophesied, Stephana.'

She nodded matter-of-factly.

A small boat came about and a pilot climbed up on deck.

'I need to know what news this man brings,' Marric decided. He joined Phlebas and heard the pilot conclude. . . . 'On account of the Aescir ships, the Horn has been barred to non-military traffic. Her Imperial Majesty has ordered the chain drawn across the Horn. I'll guide you in to Eleutherium.'

'We come just in time,' Stephana murmured.

'Pray Isis.' Now that Marric saw what looked like the entire world ranged against the Empire, he feared as he had never feared since he faced Irene's guards and expected death – at the best. His jaw clenched. Irene's guards and Irene's magic! They were the same, to his mind. They would prevent himself and Alexa from reaching Audun's ship; they would try to take them.

Stephana laid a hand on his arm, gentling him.

Audun! If the Bearmaster had joined the Aescir, perhaps Marric could reason with him.

'She must be half mad,' Nicephorus said. 'The city appears tranquil enough.'

'The Huns and Aescir bide their time. Sooner or later someone will run out of patience. And Irene has an arsenal of dark powers –'

'Did you not summon the Elder Gods?' Stephana asked. 'You return, as I told you, just in time.'

As the *Pride of Isis* docked, Marric pulled the hood of his light cloak down over his eyes. Doubtless the rumours were that he campaigned on the frontier, or had died of a fever, or ran renegade – some convenient fiction, probably the last. Rumours . . . before he started his own whispers in this city of whispers, he must listen quietly to all that he could.

Near the dock hovered at least three entire files of soldiers. Their weapons looked too well worn for Marric's liking. So

Irene's security was so tightly drawn that guards would check incoming ships, even grain ships, for contraband? He leaned forward, drinking in the sights of the port.

A party of priests arrived. Probably the High Priest had sent his brothers an escort.

Then, lurching under the whips of overseers, a coffle of slaves was herded on board a nearby ship. Many of the slaves were wounded. All were too well muscled to be anything but fighting men condemned to the collar and the block.

Clearing his throat to alert Marric, Phlebas the captain came up beside him. 'The Empress sent a regiment against demonstrators in the Hippodrome recently. When it refused to butcher them, she ordered it decimated.' He paused. 'My . . . Alexandros . . . you know you have only to command me – or the rest of the convoy.'

Seventy fighters on board each ship. Turned loose with a story or two, doubtless they would bring Marric even more followers.

'Would you serve me?' Marric asked. 'For now, simply be my eyes and ears. And wait for my call.' This was not the time for the Fleet to herald his return. First he must speak with the priests and persuade the patricians and civil servants to support him, for his father's sake, or because they hated Irene, or, perhaps, because they thought he might have the makings of an emperor. And he had to speak to his former allies, now assembled outside the city walls.

'But you will employ us,' Phlebas insisted.

'My word upon it.' Marric suddenly thought of something. 'Could an accident, let us say, hold that ship in harbour?' He pointed at the slaver being loaded with the betrayed regiment.

'Such accidents are frequent.'

He would need the men that ship held, veterans of a crack imperial regiment. Emperors had been catapulted to the purple before by adroit manipulation of malcontents, soldiers and slaves. *I can win them and hold them. Do you see this, Father?*

'I can be reached by a messenger to the temple of Osiris,' Marric told Phlebas in a whisper, and clasped his arm. Just in time, the man prevented himself from making the full bow due his Emperor.

The priests of Osiris had provided a litter for Stephana and horses for the men; no one of rank walked the filthy lower streets willingly. Beggars on the wharf cried out to the priests. As they disembarked, the harbour guards drove the beggars away with the flats of their swords. Marric winced and mounted.

Feigning difficulty with his stirrup, he bent and listened to an altercation between Phlebas and the prefect.

So taxes had been raised. Irene had developed the practice of confiscating the goods even of suspect nobles and criminals. Merikare strolled over to listen. Had she moved against the temples yet? Judging from how Merikare overawed the prefect of the harbour, Marric thought not. So the temples would afford him protection – for a time, at least.

The priests conducted them to a house they claimed was safely held. Built of stone, two floors high, it was far enough away from the Mese to be obscure. With thick walls and narrow windows that appeared to turn in on themselves, it was the sort of place a man might pass every day for years without noticing. The men serving in it were soldiers who accepted the guise of slaves in devout service to the gods. Marric would give a good deal to know how the priests inspired that sort of loyalty.

Within the house Marric found more luxury than he had known since his days in Tmutorakan: cool, well-lit rooms opened on to an arcade that enclosed a small, exquisite garden. In its centre was a fountain more beautiful than any he had seen outside the palace.

Marric was surprised when Nicephorus refused to have his family notified of his safe return. Ariadne would be safer this way, he said.

They sat in this new-found comfort drinking chilled wine and listening to Theophilus, a thin, intense priest whom the Temple had sent to brief them.

'Irene woos and threatens the people according to her whims,' said the priest. 'One day, she looses soldiers on them in the Hippodrome. The very next, she declares that she will revive the festivals of the dying and reviving god.'

'The old Dionysia?' Nicephorus asked. 'How does the Temple regard that, Theophilus?'

155

'The god has a thousand forms. Regardless of the names we use, our prayers – assuming they are sincere – rise to the same power.'

'She is losing control,' Stephana said unexpectedly. 'She seems to act at random and tries one thing after another. Now, the Dionysia . . .'

It had not been celebrated in almost fifteen years. Marric could remember the last one. But it might be of use. Like the games in the Hippodrome, such a sacred festival could be manipulated by ambitious people. But Marric's hand closed on what was of more use to him: the roll of names that Theophilus had entrusted to him, names of officers known to uphold the old Warriors' Oath, civil servants discreetly critical of Irene's heavy taxes, some nobles.

For now, Marric would concentrate on the officers stationed in the city. Chief among them was Caius Marcellinus, a man whose house was so ancient that it proudly used Roman rather than Byzantine names. Marcellinus was domestikos, or commander, of the Scholae, the decorative but highly competent regiment in which Marric himself had started out. Marric remembered him, somewhat ruefully, as a strict disciplinarian who had despaired of the imperial Prince – or who would have, if he hadn't decided that that was disloyal. For Marric's father's sake, perhaps he would hear him out.

Meetings with other key officials could be arranged, Theophilus assured Marric, in the safe house, or the temple, or even the cautious silence of the military compound.

Tired, Stephana withdrew. Shortly afterwards by her orders, (Marric assumed) more food was brought in.

'I can imagine her deciding that we mustn't plot unfed,' said Nicephorus. 'Ariadne would do the same thing. No: she is safer where she is. Let it be, Mor.'

Marric ate then, unaware of what foods were placed before him, or even of the sunset reflected in the waters of the Golden Horn. Hours later, Nicephorus disappeared. Lamps flickered as their oil burnt low, and still Marric spoke with the priest.

All the temples – from the great ones of Isis and Osiris by the palace, down to the smallest shrines – would know of Marric's return, Theophilus promised. The only ones to be left out would be those cults hostile to any god but their own and, of course, the dark adepts. They had, in any case, already isolated themselves.

While grateful for the priests' assistance, indebted to them for life itself, Marric would have preferred less contact with magic and more with the warriors he knew how to move. Then he thought of his friends . . . Stephana was as much a priestess as any templedweller, but her magic didn't distress him. Nor did Nicephorus'.

'In case Irene's dark adepts seek you out, Prince, this house is warded,' Theophilus told Marric. He was reassured.

When he finally left, Marric walked out into the tiny garden and dashed water from the fountain over his face. Above him, the night sky paled; the violet glimmerings of a fair dawn quivered between sea and sky. He stretched. Suddenly moved, he turned the gesture into an invocation of the gods, brief thanksgiving for his success thus far. The wind caressed his face.

Climbing to the roof terrace, Marric gazed out over his city. Soon it would re-erupt into its raucous daily routines: for now, it slept. Gradually, torches began to flicker as workers started out towards their tasks. Out in the harbour, ships' sails bellied in the wind. All Byzantium stirred beneath Marric's loving gaze, like a child faintly aware that its father watches over it in its sleep, wondering what it will become and swearing to help make it grow strong.

The rising sun touched Marric's brow. His excitement draining from him, he yawned.

I will heal you, he promised the sleeping city. He might be strong enough now. Two years ago he would never have believed that, given the choice, he might pick slavery over honourable death in battle, patience over conflict. Marric-that-was could never have become a channel for the gods' power. It was well that he was gone.

Theophilus had been impressed with that story of how the Elder Gods came at Marric's call. 'An adept-emperor, working as a conscious focus of power,' he said, 'would restore the Empire to heights it has not enjoyed for centuries.'

They would take my humanity from me, Marric thought. He remembered the pain of the burning as the Elder Gods used him and waterspouts crushed the Arab ships. Irene had such power and was corrupted by it. Their line was old, old. Perhaps, as such dynasties tended to be, it was unsound.

Maybe Alexander, Marric's father, had feared the wrong things.

But if initiation meant life and health for the Empire, Marric would have to consider it. Which, damn it all, the priests were counting on. He would think about it later. Now his head ached and his hands shook as they usually did after all-night strategy sessions.

He went looking for Stephana. She would heal him. He found her asleep in the sort of silken, quiet refuge he had longed to share with her since their first night together. How many Stephanas, gentle like her, slaves such as she had been, had died, or fought despair with their generous hearts to comfort others in pain? He could not help them. Not yet. He had freed Daphne, certainly. But freeing one girl was not enough. He would never be able to do enough.

With grief, he thought of that line of chained soldiers. Each of them was a Marric unjustly doomed to the slavery which only Stephana's love had changed from living death.

He pulled off tunic and hose. Time was when he planned with his staff all night and then fought the next day. But this was a much harder campaign than any of his others.

Marric lay down beside Stephana. Her lips parted as if she spoke in her dreams. Her face shone in the dawn light like an icon of the Goddess. Beneath her heavy lashes and high, arched eyelids, her gaze shifted as if the vistas she saw in her dreams altered moment by moment.

What do you see, beloved? Stephana's visions manifested themselves where and when they would: they were merciless. For a brief moment, Marric resented the power that used Stephana so harshly. Then, he bent to kiss her. She smiled and murmured against his lips like any other woman with no magic beyond that of her love. Her touch sent peace flowing into Marric. He rested his cheek against her hair and closed his eyes.

Chapter Seventeen

Riding towards the gate which pierced the city's defensive walls, Marric practised the breathing exercises he had learned in the temple of Osiris. Draw breath through the nostrils and down the body, they said. Imagine different coloured lights at head, throat, chest, loins and feet. He could almost see them. Make them glow and let that glow serve as a protection.

He would need such protection when he reached the gate. If guards loyal to Irene were on duty, he was finished. If he passed beyond the walls safely, he would face the Huns with only the barest formality of an armed escort. And he wasn't risking just himself. Stephana and Nicephorus rode with him. Their skills made them really too valuable to risk, yet Marric could not do without them.

His party looked simply like a senior officer accompanied by ten horsemen, their dekarch and two civilians. One of the civilians was a woman choosing, somewhat unconventionally, to ride rather than be conveyed in a litter; the second was small and slight. It seemed a small result for weeks of scheming, of persuading and coordinating nobles, soldiers and foreign-born auxiliaries.

Caius Marcellinus, the regimental commander, had been frank with Marric. 'Prince,' he had saluted him. 'One look tells me that you are Alexander's son – may he dwell in glory beyond the Horizon. But the gods help me: if I am taken as a traitor, my grandfather, my wife, my children – Irene will kill them all. I never thought to say this, but my family – I must place them before . . .'

Marric shut his eyes in pain. Marcellinus misinterpreted the gesture.

'I am no coward!' he snarled, smacking his fist down on the table that separated him from Marric. The goblets on it danced.

'Of course you're not a coward!' Marric's fist banged down beside Marcellinus'. 'Who ever heard of a Marcellinus turning coward? And, aside from my father's blood,' he added with a sly grin, 'you have no real reason to trust me. I may be just as unstable as Irene.'

There had been the time during Marric's arms training that he had painted a number of obscene slogans on the senior officers' horses. Marcellinus, because he was in charge of the cadets, shared their punishment. He had not been amused. Now, the general looked up, a surprising plea for understanding in his eyes.

'I know, man,' Marric said. 'I've a few I'd hate to lose myself. And you're one of them. Look, Marcellinus, I honour you. I had the choice between dying and wearing a slave's collar to keep alive, and I chose the collar because that way I might get a chance to keep on fighting. I don't think that makes me a coward any more than your doubts make you one. Stop this!' He had never given Marcellinus as direct an order before.

The general caught Marric's hand in both of his and kissed it, then dropped it quickly.

'You heard what happened to Antinous, didn't you? Some *cargo*' – he stressed the word – 'went awry, and Irene had him put to silence.'

Marric grimaced. While he held no love for the man whose ship had carried him into slavery, Antinous had been well born. He deserved, at least, the dignity of a swift death.

'The priests can deliver you the old nobility, Prince. But the Tagmata regiments: you will need their support.' Marcellinus was thinking fast. 'By all the gods, this much I can do for you right now. Irene hasn't reviewed the troops in months, and the mercenaries are wondering when they'll be paid. There have been many newcomers – imperials, mind you, none of these barbarians from the outer themes – but they're not likely to be under her eye. Give me a week, Prince, and I can have names, duty rosters—'

If Marcellinus' information failed, if a hostile officer watched at the gate, Marric could expect that phosphorescent cell again, far below ground, and the lash of Irene's scarlet flames on his body.

He glanced behind him and reined in his horse, waiting for his companions to catch up. It was unsafe to ride alone here. Even at this early hour a rabble of beggars, some mutilated in war, others beneath a beggarmaster's knife, squatted in the streets. The morning mists made riders, beggars and passers-by look like figures out of a dream that he longed to wake from. At any point, for the worth of horse and armour, such people might turn on him.

'Alms, alms, great lady, for the mother's sake!' Urged on by their ragged mother, a hag with no teeth and a bulging belly, children shrilled up at Stephana and clustered around her horse. It shied, but, even as Marric spurred towards her, she had the beast firmly under control. Marric guided his horse with his knees and grasped her mount's bridle.

'Let the lady pass!' he cried. 'Come on,' he urged in a lower voice, 'let's get out of here.'

Stephana had opened a tiny purse and was scattering small coins.

'Here, sir,' said one of Marric's escort. 'Let me lead her horse for you. We haven't time for this.'

'We haven't time for anything else!' Stephana cried. 'Look at these people. Oh, Mor, how could I leave them without—'

Mor.

'Later,' Marric promised. When he was Emperor, Stephana might do all the charities she wished. He would bless her for it. But they must get past the gate before the watch changed.

'Please go,' she implored the children. They were risking their lives by clinging to her horse. 'You will be hurt.' Her voice shook with pity; her entreaty succeeded where the officers' commands failed.

The horses minced clear of the beggars. Marric waved his party on, urging speed. At least this episode showed him how his companions would react to Huns. Undoubtedly, Nicephorus would observe them; the soldiers would follow orders; and Stephana – the Huns would probably want to adopt her. She had the gift of winning hearts and courage enough to lead armies. He glanced over at her. Her deep-blue cloak had fallen back, and the dawnlight touched the silver in her hair with fire.

Looming up before them was one of the three gates they had

to pass. Its towers rose a hundred feet above their heads, and slingers stood ready upon them.

Their horses' hooves echoed as they rode underneath an arch which was more like a tunnel. Here, the innermost wall was almost twenty-five feet thick. Torches in iron holders set into the dressed stone cast smokey light. At the end of the tunnel stood soldiers.

Varangians! Marric steadied his breathing. He had always suffered from battle jitters. Aillel, his first teacher, had said that they would make him a better soldier. He had been a Varangian, too.

Marric thought of the guards he had spoken with in the Mangana.

'Never in our years of serving Miklagard have we betrayed our oaths,' one officer had said. 'We will not begin now.'

'Then you will not betray me, either,' Marric had said.

As the Varangian lifted his axe, Marric had tensed. But he laid it over a map of the city which was spread out on the table in the Mangana.

'You are of the blood of Miklagard, too. We will no more betray you to Irene than we will betray her to you. She rules as Empress—'

'And pays you—'

'Well enough—'

'What if she pays you in the blood of kinsmen?' Marric had asked. 'The Bearmaster lodges outside the city. What will you do if he sends the Aescir against you?'

The Varangian had stroked his axe, as if checking for rust. 'We are soldiers; so are our brothers. The Bearmaster and the jarls – they understand.'

'All I ask is to be your messenger,' Marric had told them. 'Since your oath binds you, do not aid me. But by the white bear of Hropt himself, do not hinder me. Just allow me safe passage.'

These Varangians closed in at the gate and escorted Marric's party silently along the winding road. At the second gate archers leaned from the tower. They held their fire. Above the archers' heads Marric saw the blunt muzzles of engines which could spray fire down on any invaders who penetrated this far. Not even Irene's magic could hurt worse than that burning.

Outside the second gate, the Varangians left them. Between it and the outermost gate lay a bridge over a wide, deep moat. Beyond that lay a no man's land between the city and the enemy camps. Marric touched heels to his horse's flanks. How like Irene to let him get this far and, just as he scented success, have him hauled back.

Stephana rode up beside him and laid a hand on his. *I should not have let her come*, Marric thought, then dismissed his fear. Among the Huns, shamans accompanied warriors. If Marric brought his own seeress, he demonstrated respect for the Huns' customs.

The dekarch of Marric's guard rode to her side. Marric sensed his disgust at the thought of having to detach one of his men to send a timid woman – for so he thought her – back to her soft nest.

'I can ride alone,' Stephana told the man. 'I would speak with you,' she whispered to Marric. Her blue eyes were uncharacteristically bleak.

Loving the intimacy of the contact, even if it were magical, Marric steadied himself to speak mind-to-mind.

– My love has only to ask. –

Feelings of love and reassurance. *– Marric, the captain at the last gate. Look closely. –*

A shadow waited at the end of the tunnel, beckoning to them. Marric narrowed his eyes and wished for the vision of the Hawk.

'Snuff the torches.'

The gloom allowed him to see more clearly. *The man was – by Horus, it was Thutmosis, the young Alexandrian captain!*

As an outsider, he had probably only been told that, by the general's orders, a party must be permitted beyond the walls. Once outside the city, their welfare was out of his jurisdiction. What if he knew that three in the party were his aunt's former slaves? The man was young and zealous. Which way would his loyalties go? He had entered Irene's service with all the zest of a man choosing his first mistress.

Thutmosis' voice echoed in the passage. 'What do you?'

A scrape and glint of metal revealed that he had drawn his sword.

– *Can you delude him?* – Marric asked Stephana. He had a vivid recollection of standing as a focus of power on a ship's deck.

Stephana paused. Her small teeth gnawed at her underlip. She looked like a lady hesitating over embroidery silks: this purple thread or that one to work in next to the gold? Marric suppressed a smile.

'Take my reins,' she whispered to the dekarch. She needed her hands free to work a spell.

'Go on ahead,' Marric ordered the soldiers. 'Lie, and lie fast: the lady has lost a stirrup, broken her reins . . .'

– *Nut, hover over us with your veils; Isis, protect us; Horus, spread your wings to cover us* – Marric heard Stephana's invocation and joined his will to hers. He knew how this drained her. Now strength flowed from him, too, but he barely heeded it. As long as they could maintain this level of concentration, Stephana could convince Thutmosis of what she wished. Confidently, Marric rode out into the light.

The young Alexandrian stared narrowly at them. With his enhanced clarity of perception, Marric touched Thutmosis' thoughts.

A general . . . soldiers . . . two squalid magicians . . . Marric smiled as he caught Thutmosis' mental pictures: Marric himself scarred down brow and cheek, Stephana and Nicephorus wizened and unkempt. Silent laughter inside his head meant Stephana shared his amusement.

The Alexandrian looked far older than he had that time he rode beside Marric's ox cart. Then he had been eager, cocksure. Now, perplexity lurked within his shadowed eyes. So imperial service hadn't been what he had dreamt? He had come here, all high hopes and polished armour, to find his new regiment a welter of plots and to learn that the city of his ardent imaginings festered under Irene's rule. Marric had heard beggars, too tired of life to be careful, call her the Red Empress. *What a disillusionment for the lad*, Marric thought.

In his own way, Thutmosis had been kind to Mor, and he had

not taken Stephana to his bed. On impulse, Marric bent towards him. 'Would you hear our mission, Captain?'

Nicephorus' indrawn breath showed that he thought Marric had gone too far. But Marric remembered what Taran had said about his power – assuming he could use it – to stir men's minds and hearts.

'For the good of the Empire, Captain, would you share our mission?'

Thutmosis kindled briefly. Then he sighed and sagged back into his role as watch-officer like a much older man. 'Should I be questioned, I can merely say, 'By my orders, I allowed a party to pass beyond the walls.' If I know more, I disclose more. Sir, I best share your mission by knowing nothing.' He drew closer to Marric. 'But if it is for the Empire's weal, the gods ride with you.'

A scream from above drew their eyes. A great hawk flew overhead. Marric's face heated. The glamour which disguised him and his friends faded as the hawk called.

Thutmosis gazed at him, then up at the hawk. Was he remembering an Alexandrian market and a slave named Mor, or the portraits of imperial Prince Marric displayed in the city (assuming Irene had not ordered them torn down)? Then the officer was on his knees.

'You!' he gasped.

A shout brought Marric's head up. All they needed now was a crowd. He spoke rapidly.

'Let us through quickly, Captain. They can call it a trick of the light. You know better. Now!'

'Open the gate!' Thutmosis shouted.

Marric signalled and they pounded outside, across the bridge and out into the barren land that protected Byzantium from the camps of the Huns.

The city walls were a narrow line far to the rear when Marric signalled a halt. Standing dark against the horizon ahead of them was a party of Huns mounted on their fast steppe ponies. The dekarch and his men drew in beside him.

To most Byzantine soldiers, Huns were two-legged brutes who, mounted on four-legged brutes, became like centaurs, but lacked their wisdom. The dekarch probably believed the stories about how Huns ate their meat raw, never bathed, and totally lacked culture or humour. Marric had guested in their felt tents. He liked Huns far more than he liked many courtiers.

'What now, lord?' the dekarch asked.

'They see us. So we wait.' Marric's tone was curt as he assumed the manners that would impress the khagans of the hordes. He must seem khagan of khagans, not a supplicant. Riding out here light-armed, accompanied only by a young seeress, a scholar, and just enough of an escort to make him look respectable, displayed the arrogance that Uldin of the Kutrigur, or Ellac of the Golden Horde, would respect.

He rode forward a few steps. 'Stay behind me,' he told the soldiers. Nicephorus and Stephana moved up so that the three of them rode knee-to-knee.

Now the Huns rode towards them. Their blue-dyed horsetail standards fluttered. With a whoop that carried across the plain, they raced towards Marric in a display of horsemanship that brought grunts of astonishment from his cavalry escort.

They rode with their bows unstrung. But remembering archery he had seen in Cherson, Marric knew that in seconds, if the Huns chose, his friends, his soldiers, and he himself, might resemble archery targets. He breathed deeply and prayed Stephana would not detect his fear.

Now the Huns were so close that Marric could see the gold on their ponies' harness. They rode in a circle about Marric's companions.

'Don't draw!' Marric ordered.

Closer and closer circled the Huns. Now their arrows were nocked, ready to fire. Then a rider whose armour gleamed as richly as his horse-trappings broke from the ring. He whooped and pounded towards Marric, a spear pointed at his heart. Nicephorus gasped and Stephana muffled a cry.

Have I miscalculated? Marric would die too quickly to regret it if he had.

The Hun reined his pony aside so sharply that it screamed and reared.

'Ha!' the man bellowed. 'Fighting Hawk!'

'Uldin!' Marric caught the khagan of the Kutrigur around the shoulders in a kinsman's embrace.

They lounged on sheepskins in Uldin's tent, trying to ignore the Huns' characteristic odour of horses, sweat and soured milk. Marric sat between the khagans, while his soldiers and Nicephorus ate and drank among the warriors of note. Since Stephana was Marric's seer, she, too, sat at Marric's side, waiting for her services to be needed.

In the smoky lamplight the Huns' flat faces gleamed and their narrow eyes glittered. Marric tried to read them. He saw no anger, at least none directed at him. But he sensed an alertness.

They waited for some sign.

Then he must provide them with one.

When the food trays had been removed, he rubbed his hands politely on his arms to clean them, and leaned forward.

'So, khagans,' he asked ironically, 'what brings you from the steppes? Surely not since the days of Atli have so many ventured forth.'

A snort of laughter greeted his words.

'We missed our brother, the Hawk, and came to seek him in his nest. Yours is a soft nest, brother, and rich. You should share it.'

Despite Ellac's implied threat, Marric chuckled. 'The Hawk does not rest safely in that nest.'

'That we already know,' said Uldin. 'She whom your father took as lesser wife—'

The banter of only moments before was gone. Marric remembered Stephana's vision of how Ellac and Uldin agreed to ride against Byzantium.

'I was . . . sent away . . .'

'You should not have allowed that,' Ellac answered. 'The Witch Queen, in your absence, sent armies against the Hordes. Women, children, horses – all slaughtered and our tents burnt.'

They were calling Irene 'Khazaroctona' in the city: Irene, Killer of Huns. She had brought their vengeance down upon her own head.

'Do you wish vengeance?' Marric asked the khagans. 'I do. Shall we have an alliance, as we had in the North?'

'We would examine your home, Prince of the Hawk,' said a dark-robed shaman as he entered. 'We would examine it very closely; perhaps even dwell in it.'

'My city is not for your plunder!'

'Not true,' said the shaman. Extending skinny arms, he gestured at the Byzantines. 'It has been revealed to me that the city shall fall.'

Chapter Eighteen

Marric forced himself to drink from a skin of mares' milk. Its sourness and the shaman's words made him want to gag. He laid the skin aside calmly, though, and asked, 'What of our alliance, men of the steppes?'

'We made alliance with *you*. Not with this woman who murders our families and herds.'

'I made our treaty for the city,' Marric said.

'It sent you away.'

'Irene sent me away.'

'Does she not speak for the city now?' Ellac asked craftily. More than Uldin, he coveted the gold, the silks, all the wealth he could loot from Byzantium, and Marric knew it. But even more than he wanted treasure, Ellac wanted to break the myth of the imperial city's invulnerability.

'She is an usurper!' Marric's dekarch cried. The Huns glared at him.

'There is an order to things as we reckon them in the city,' Marric chose his words with care. 'The gods rule through chosen leaders. My father was one such. But if Irene serves aught beside her own ambition, it is the Dark.'

'If we took the city,' Uldin said, 'we could stop her. Then you could rule—'

The screams of dying citizens and horses, children impaled on lances, arrows feathering the markets and, rising over all the ruin, fire, as the Huns looted. They rode their ponies up the steps of the very temples themselves and into the palace. There they sat Marric down as their puppet on his father's throne, awash on a tide of his people's blood.

'NO!' He would not live to see his home such a waste, nor pretend he ruled thereafter.

'Do you doubt the shaman?' Ellac's voice was silken.

Warriors shifted position. Marric's guard exchanged wary looks.

'How can I doubt his visions?' Marric asked. 'But I would ask my own seeress to confirm their truth.' He rested a hand on Stephana's shoulder. She looked over the men without fear.

'I need a bowl,' she said. 'And fresh water.'

The things were brought. The shaman gestured, and singers raised their voices. He was preparing himself for *yryq*, the rites of divination. From a beltpouch he poured the scapular bones he would use to foretell. They had been polished from many years of use. Light flashed off their yellowed surfaces and Marric glanced quickly away. He had seen this rite once before. That time, he had sat through it, watching the way men watch jugglers during a lull in the feast.

Now he couldn't take his eyes off the bones. They glistened with a power he could feel, and wanted to avoid. Somehow, Stephana's visions seemed gentler and more natural. She touched his hand, even as she leaned forward to study the shaman's actions.

'He is *kam-quam*,' Uldin said to her. 'Touched by the gods. Will you truly set your power against his?'

'I will witness,' she said. 'And then I will call upon the Goddess for a vision of my own – and he will witness that.'

The shaman raised his face up to the light. Flawed by cataracts as his eyes were, he could barely see this world. But that would not hinder his sight in the one he sought now to enter. In a harsh, eerie voice he began to chant. Stephana stiffened, her hand closing upon Marric's.

– *He descends into his vision*, – she bespoke him.

– *I must see this.* –

A hint of fear. Stephana needn't remind him that the other world was perilous for him, but he would trust her with his soul.

He felt darkness and a sense of great cold. Then he was travelling in the form of a mote of light. At terrible speed he raced over a landscape that the Sight revealed to him: a steppe, barren of all life, covered with deep snow. They were heading north. There, in the fabled lands, shining lights drifted between ground and sky. The beasts themselves there were fierce, few, and very strange. Ahead of the lights that were Marric and Stephana, gleamed the track of the shaman.

Now, mountains reared up in the dream landscape. Their path suddenly lay between awesome ranges of tremendous height and stillness. With a suddenness that almost snapped Marric free of Stephana's protection and into disaster (– *Steady, beloved!* –) the shaman descended, dropped into a crevasse, and swooped down for a landing in shadowed snow.

There stood a structure all of ice. A reddish bird was trapped in its heart. As they watched, animals – a horse, a great white bear – approached and battered at the ice palace. It broke into a glistening maze. The scarlet bird shrieked and beat at the other animals with beak, wings and talons. A blow crumpled it. The bird lay dead on the frozen ground. Blood seeped from its broken body and stained the whiteness of the snow.

– *Do you see?* – That was the shaman's voice.

Then they found themselves fleeing after him, struggling as their energy waned, to fly back over the mountains of that other world and to reclaim the bodies they had abandoned.

Marric opened his eyes. *Well, I always longed to see World's End,* was his first, wry thought. He glanced over at Stephana, who looked pale, but smiled at him.

As the shaman's apprentices struggled to revive him, the man shuddered. Slowly he rose and looked at the scapular bones.

Cast at the height of his vision trance, they lay in the same pattern that the ice shards had formed.

'Behold,' the shaman said. 'Your walls lie riven!'

'Are you convinced?' asked Ellac.

Marric glanced at Stephana again for direction. She leaned forward to look at the bones, then at the shaman.

'One thing more,' said the shaman. 'On my journey within, I had company.'

'The seeress from the city?' Uldin asked.

'Not only her. The Hawk himself,' the shaman whispered, pointing a finger, almost as withered as his own prophetic tools, at Marric. 'The Hawk journeyed with us between the mountains and saw the city of ice shatter. Let him speak.'

'I saw a white bear and a horse,' Marric said. 'Indeed they struck walls made of ice, and the walls broke. And the red bird died.' He paused. 'But the bird was not a hawk, and certainly not the Great Hawk that I have seen, that greeted me before the walls of the city today.' It was impossible, thought Marric, that that hawk could ever die.

'Is the city prince *Tängr* – a half god – that he sees with a shaman's sight?'

'The Prince is a warrior,' said Uldin.

'A khagan—'

'And a great one,' Uldin said. 'Were he of our blood, he would be fit to be called khagan of khagans.'

'But he is a man of the city!' Ellac shouted.

Stephana touched the hand of the Huns' shaman. She freed her hair from its scarf, then turned to the bowl and pitcher of gem-crusted gold that the shaman's apprentices had brought her.

She held up a hand for silence and waited until everyone's attention was fixed upon her. The fire crackled once. Men jumped, but Stephana remained as serene as she had been when the beggars clutched at her stirrups.

'The bird died,' she said. 'At the blows of Stallion and Bear, the ice walls shattered. Your shaman saw truth. Shall I complete his vision?'

She raised her eyes to Marric's, a look more intimate and more reassuring than a caress, then poured water into the bowl. She

171

cupped her hands over it. Her lips moved soundlessly in an invocation of the powers she served.

Shadows began to move in the water. Marric leaned over the bowl, trying to give Stephana his strength.

'The bird – dead. Blood in the snow, far too much blood, but look, above it! The Hawk, the Hawk flies free and perches on the greatest tower of the city—' she whispered. Another shadow formed: a woman in a fair room, twisting in pain from the dagger in her breast. Marric leaned closer. Did Stephana foresee Irene's assassination?

The sorceress breathed on the water and broke the vision.

'So much is true: the bird's death means victory,' she said. 'But the bird is Irene – red, not golden: certainly not the Hawk of my lord's house. Dying, she stabs with her beak and wounds the city, as we have all seen. Then it turns for healing to its new ruler and his allies – but without conquest.

'Seize the city as you now plan, Lords of the Steppes, and can you truly promise you will not destroy what you hope to rule?'

A muttering came from the Huns. Stephana fell silent. Ellac himself poured her a cup of water. When Marric moved a saddle into place behind her back, she leaned against gratefully.

'I cannot rule the city as a puppet.' Marric took over Stephana's line of reasoning. 'Stallion and Bear aid the Hawk; they do not destroy. The Empire needs its rightful lord or – you have seen what Irene has become. Her ambition has destroyed her, and her evil reaches out to touch the whole world. Once you gave me clan-right. Give me help now, or, at the least, give me leave to depart unharmed.'

Deliberately exploiting the length of limb that made him tower over the Huns, Marric rose.

'Uldin, when we raced our ponies to Cherson, neither losing to the other, you called me brother. There are no losers nor victors between us. As brother to the clans, I shall deliver the Stallion's blow to the bird the shaman saw die. Will that content you?'

The torches guttered while the khagans thought.

'Let him go, great lords,' cackled the shaman. 'Let him bear your burden for you.'

Uldin nodded, then leaned over to speak to Ellac. The other khagan still scowled, unconvinced. 'Let him shed his own men's blood, not ours. Why should we care?' At that, Ellac nodded assent too.

Uldin clapped his hands, ushering in a procession of slaves bearing gifts. Apparently, he had waited to present them until after it was decided that Marric and his people were guests, not captives.

Marric received a spear with a blue horsetail dangling from it, the insignia of the Hordes, and a gold-hilted blade. Stephana received bracelets of heavy gold. Nicephorus received a jade statue that had come from the Lands of Gold. Each of the soldiers took up daggers with finely chased hilts.

Marric saluted the khagans and began farewell courtesies.

'Where now, lord?' asked the dekarch.

'To the Bearmaster.'

He reached out to pull Stephana to her feet. She brushed free of his hand and stood poised, listening to some inner voice. Her face was very pale, and her eyes gleamed the mad blue that dances at a flame's core.

'Say you so, Prince?' The voice was not her own. 'You will have your trip for nothing.' Robust laughter burst from her, and she rushed, in a tangle of skirts, cloak and glistening hair, out into the camp. The shaman chuckled and whispered to the khagans.

All the men followed Stephana outside. She walked down the long aisle that divided the Huns' tents. Her earlier, febrile energy was gone, but she raised arms in greeting to a party of twelve riders, whose horses' bits and bridles gleamed with silver.

Riding in the van was a man Marric had not seen for years. By now, he thought, Audun Bearmaster must be vastly old. That last year of his father's life, when Audun had come to court, his hair had been grey and gold. Now, the beard that swept his byrnie, the braided long hair that shone in the light, was the white of northern snows: fit match for the bears that he alone of the Aescir nobles could master. He glistened with jewellery – belt-pouch, bracelets, a torque and, hanging far down his chest, a magnificent braided rope of heavy gold.

Marric turned to the khagans. 'Are you such friends with the Aescir that so small a party dares enter your camp?'

'There is no great friendship, brother, but no feud either. We thought perhaps that they might join us in an attack. But that whitebeard who rides the red steed told us that the Bearmaster wears no man's collar.'

Stephana walked towards the Bearmaster. Bowmen stood with arrows ready to fire. Marric tried to go to her, but found his path blocked by the men of his command. They would not allow him to risk himself, swear as he might.

Audun Bearmaster swung off his horse and let his reins fall to the ground. He walked over to Stephana. Composed as a queen receiving guests in her own hall, she drew herself up to meet him.

'He will not harm her,' Marric told the soldiers. 'Let me go. By all the gods,' he cried, angered by their protectiveness, 'will you have my curse?'

Reluctantly they allowed him to go to the Bearmaster.

'So you heard us,' Stephana asked, unsurprised. She spoke to him, a man she had never before met, as if to a long-time friend.

'I heard the bear invoked,' Audun answered, 'so I came. I knew it travelled over-mountain in company with the stallion and the hawk. So I came here. But I know other things, too: chief among them the fact that a grain ship from Alexandria landed rich cargo: food for the city and a man who calls himself a merchant. He is no merchant, but a princeling I once knew.'

'And still do, by Horus!' Marric cried. 'Audun Bearmaster, well met! Have you brought me my white bear?'

'A bear!' Audun roared. 'A bear for a man of the city that demands tribute of us, then raids our waystations at Birka and Staraja Ladoga when we refuse – as we have a right to do? A bear for a man of the city that wounds its Princess—'

'Before all the gods,' Marric interrupted, 'how fares my sister? Alexa fell before I could help.' To his horror, he heard his voice roughen. Let Audun understand that even if Alexa and he had fought, he would have died trying to save her.

'Her wounds are healed,' Audun said, 'and she is well settled in the Isles of the Mists.'

The golden king and queen that Stephana had revealed to him in the water of vision, that night in Taran's hut, would preserve her safe until Marric came to claim her.

'If you seek her there at all, seek her soon,' the Bearmaster said. 'But you ask me if I have a bear for you. Have *you* a crown to show me, eh? You are ruler by blood: become ruler in deed, and I shall bring you a bear that will not bite the hand into which I give it.

'Let me look at you, Prince,' Audun ordered, the way he had done ever since Marric was a child. He nodded approvingly, then reached out a hand to Stephana. 'We're among friends here,' he bellowed at his men, to the astonishment of Marric's soldiers, the bemused Huns, and – possibly – the horses. 'Dis-*mount*!'

Stephana took Audun's outstretched hand. He smiled at her, his face gentling. Taking off one of the chains he wore, from which hung an agate medallion carved like a woman's face, he flung it over her neck.

'Daughter of fate – that is what you are.' He spoke softly to her. 'Wife perhaps, but not queen; heart's solace and heart's breaking. Am I right, lady?'

Stephana raised her hand to touch Audun's gift. It was so heavy that her neck almost bent beneath it. 'Have you a bear for my lord?' she asked.

'Yes, but he must earn it! And he will, he will. Are you content, little seeress?'

How could he know so much about her?

'I am content.'

'When we next meet, you shall guide me,' Audun declared. His words rang with a significance Marric could not understand.

'Your name, lady?'

'She is Stephana,' said Marric. 'In Alexandria, she and Nicephorus saved my life several times.'

'They are welcome to me for your sake, then, as well as their own,' Audun said ceremoniously. Nicephorus greeted him in his own tongue, and he grinned at the courtesy.

Now, Ellac and Uldin came up with offers of hospitality. Audun would accept only water for the horses and – to avert ill feeling – a drink taken out under the stars.

175

'You would have ridden in search of me,' he told Marric. 'I thought the time had come when I should search for you. Some of my men are kin to those in Miklagard.'

'Do they inform on their city?' Marric raised his eyebrows.

'Why should our aims conflict?' asked Audun.

That was true, and in a healthy Empire they would not.

'Only imagine how ill it could have gone in our river cities if we had had no warning of Irene's attacks. We evacuated all we could. But now is no place to speak of that. You would ride to my camp, I understand. I come to bear you company – my bears and I.' He roared with appreciation of his own pun. Enchanted, Nicephorus joined in. After an instant, so did Marric.

The soldiers murmured in surprise at a majesty so little like the hieratic dignities to which imperial service had accustomed them. What was Audun? Marric wondered, not for the first time. No one knew what his source of authority was, nor where he found the white bears which his whim – or some destiny – made him give to ruling kings. But he could not doubt that Audun, in some way, did have the loyalty of most Aescir.

It was almost dawn when they finally left the Huns' camp. One of the soldiers had to lead Stephana's horse; she was too weary to ride alone. Audun himself lifted her into Marric's arms.

'Try to sleep,' he urged her. 'Aescir hospitality can be about as overpowering as Audun.'

'I have noticed,' she said. She nestled against him with a contented sigh. What had Audun meant by his description of her, anyway? *Daughter of fate. Heart's solace and heart's breaking.* Like many Aescir nobles, Audun was a poet. Given Aescir poetry, he was also a master of riddles. Marric could not decipher these. Still, if Stephana accepted them he, too, might as well call himself satisfied.

The dawn wind tugged at Marric's hair and he brought his cloak around to wrap Stephana more warmly. Violet and scarlet banners flamed at the horizon, heralds of dawn and of victory.

Chapter Nineteen

Hostile looks and more hostile mutters attended their entry into the Bearmaster's camp at mid-morning. Beyond it, the sun dashed sparks from the water of the harbour and picked out the bright trimmings on the high-prowed ships beached nearby.

'Red Empress' men.'

'Does she think us such nothings that she sends such a tiny force against us?'

Marric loosened his sword in his sheath. He was glad that Stephana had insisted she could ride her own horse at the last rest stop. Audun shook his head briefly, reproving his caution.

'Have you brought us here to betray us?' Marric asked.

'You know better than that,' Audun snorted.

They rode past a high-fenced pen. Within, white bears weaved about or napped. As they passed, one rose to its mammoth haunches and roared at the Byzantines. One of the guards watching the bears bristled and reached for his axe.

'They killed Ivar at the ford! Who will provide for my sister Ingebjorg now, and her far gone with a third child?' he yelled. Brandishing his axe, he rushed towards the dekarch.

'Hold!' Marric grabbed his officer's bridle and grappled him for his sword as Audun leapt from his horse. The smack of a fist against a stubborn jaw ended that scuffle, and Audun faced Marric, holding the man's axe and rubbing his knuckles against his scarlet cloak.

'He has a hard head,' observed the Bearmaster. 'One grain of sense remains in it. His sister's man was killed by Imperials, and Ingvi here isn't wealthy. You're too hotheaded to be a rich man, Ingvi. Attack guests of mine again and, so help me, I'll put the greater outlawry on you. Understand?' He faced the man down. 'Well, do you?'

Ingvi shook his head, spat out blood and several broken teeth, and nodded sullen assent.

Audun swung back easily into the saddle. 'If these were Jomsborgers, I doubt I could bring you into my camp and expect to see you ride out alive. The Reaver of Jomsborg doesn't answer to me, you see, but these men do. What do you say, Prince, about Ingvi's brother-in-law?'

Marric had been giving urgent orders to his men. The Bearmaster's question turned him around. 'I say your discipline is worthy of the imperial regiments themselves.'

'Aye, but are your regiments worthy of *me*? Consider Ingvi's family, Prince. The Jomsborgers would swear you bloodfeuds on their account and they'd be enough to make the Huns look like puppydogs.'

Marric looked over the Aescir. Many had assembled in a flat space before the Bearmaster's shelter. Two men walked the unfortunate Ingvi up and down. Aescir could be commanded only after they had been convinced, Marric remembered his father saying. These Aescir, many still bandaged or limping, would take a lot of convincing.

'Why did you stop him?' he asked Audun.

'You are my guests. I came to the city not for vengeance but for law. Your father, Alexander, always dealt fairly.'

'And so shall I,' Marric promised. 'Warriors' oath on it. Will you share blood with me?' He walked over to Audun. 'Then, even if I might withhold compensation from your men as Emperor – Horus forbid I do such a thing! – I could not deny them their rightful weregild as a fellow warrior.'

He walked out into the clearing. 'Men and lawspeakers of the Aescir, witness that I, Marric Antonius Alexander, acknowledge all debts of the Empire incurred in my service or out of it.'

'Will that content you?' he asked Audun.

The Bearmaster threw a burly arm around Marric's shoulder, then stripped off his tunic. 'Draw,' he ordered, 'and make the first cut.'

Aescir surrounded them as Marric's knife slashed first the Bearmaster's arm, then his own. They clasped forearms and let their blood mingle and drip on the earth.

'When may we expect our weregild?' asked a lawspeaker.

'When I have my throne,' Marric said bluntly. 'Help me gain what is mine, and you'll have it that much sooner.'

'Fellow trader!' Audun bellowed his huge laugh.

He led them all within his shelter. A woman almost as old and large as the Bearmaster served them ale, boiled grain, meat, bread and honey.

Marric tore at the food with gusto and matched Audun horn for horn of the strong ale. Finally, both men leaned back and grinned.

'You will be wanting to know about your sister, won't you?' Audun asked. He set his horn down and wiped his lips with the gold-furred back of his hand. 'Her wounds were messy, not deep, and she healed rapidly. Except—' he looked closely at Marric.

The Prince felt his food turn to lead in his belly. Was Alexa disfigured, or so damaged in mind that she had less wit than a child?

'I last saw that look – conscience-stricken, I suppose you'd call it – on the Princess herself,' said Audun. 'Oh, never fear, Prince, the lady is well enough now. In our first days out of the city, she had some fever. She tossed and wept in her blankets, and cried out that she had turned on you when you'd meant her only good. I left a much daunted lady with Queen Olwen, that let me tell you.'

'But she is well!' Marric raised glowing eyes to the Bearmaster. 'Stephana said so, but to have actual word of her – that is all that matters.' Tears scalded down his face, and he was unashamed of them. Imhotep's rebuke, 'Master of no man, least of yourself,' could not apply at such a moment.

'We will get her back,' he said, his face lighting up. Then he turned to Stephana and took her hand. 'You and she,' he said. 'I know how it is when women live too closely together, but she will come to love you.'

The seeress raised Marric's hand to her cheek.

Audun's face was sombre as he looked at them.

'Time to think of this later.' Marric regained his composure. 'Were Alexa here, she would share my counsel. I have a throne to win, Audun. Let me ask you once more: do you come here for compensation?'

'No,' said the Bearmaster. 'Though I shall be glad of it. I came here, as I said, for law. One land, one lord.' His voice took on

179

the chanting tone of an Aescir harpist. 'Otherwise the land fails, as even now the Empire wanes.

'Irene stretches her nets wide, Prince. About the East you have heard from Ellac and Uldin. The news from the West is graver. Irene has proposed to the Reaver-jarl in his island fortress that they ally, and offers him marriage.'

If the Jomsborgers entered Byzantium, the Varangian guard would never declare for Marric against distant kin. 'And the Reaver's answer?'

'Grettir can return no answer yet. The northern seas are full of fogs. Winter approaches. Irene can expect no word for months.'

'Jomsborg has attempted the city before,' Marric said. 'But they have no high opinion of women there. By spring, then, I will wear the Horus crown or my grave wrappings.'

Audun watched Marric, the older man's candid blue eyes turning deep and thoughtful. Once again, Marric thought of Imhotep, of all the other priests who examined him, who demanded things of him, and who so often found him deficient. Finally Audun nodded. 'What would you have of me, Prince?'

'Your vow not to move against the city. Let Irene fear attack, but receive none. Once I rule, though, I shall bargain for shipwrights. I must teach the pirates a strong lesson. Will you aid me?'

'Many of my folk will,' said the Bearmaster, 'but I am old. I will stay at home and nourish my bears. Would you see the one I have reared for you?'

Loving his bears, Audun would not make this offer if he still had doubts of Marric. Nicephorus caught his eye and made a small victory sign.

Audun rose. Out of respect, the others rose with him.

'What does this mean, lord?' the dekarch asked.

'It means acceptance,' said Marric. 'You heard the Bearmaster: one land, one lord. Audun only gives bears to such men or women. Irene failed his test, but I will not.'

'Don't misjudge Audun Bearmaster,' warned Nicephorus. 'That bluff manner of his is largely a mask. Stephana, do you read aught of him?'

'He called me "Daughter of fate,"' she said, 'but he himself is one of its agents.' She huddled into her cloak and drew nearer the fire.

She is a priestess, not a warrior, Marric thought. *This life taxes her strength too greatly. But because she loves me, she will continue long after her strength is gone. I must protect her even from her love – and I will!*

Scrabblings broke in upon his thoughts.

'Now then, brother mine, no need, no need. You go to greet a prince. Remember your manners.' A coughing bark answered Audun. He entered, followed by the bear.

It was a male in magnificent condition: large, but without the massiveness characterizing a fully grown beast. Its fur was white, of course, and incredibly thick. About its neck shone a necklace of ancient gold coins. This Audun flipped off, his hand inches from the bear's gleaming muzzle and sharp fangs. He tossed the necklace over Marric's head. It clattered against his armour.

'My guest gift to you, Prince. When you have housing for your bear, summon me, and I shall bring him to you.'

Intelligence gleamed in the bear's eyes. Fascinated by the beast, Marric rose to his feet. As a child he had always imagined that his father's white bear understood human speech.

Knowing that the Aescir watched him, Marric moved slowly towards the bear. He extended one hand to touch jaws that could easily bite it off. The beast's head wagged as it surveyed Marric with equal curiosity.

'Friend?' Marric asked tentatively.

With a joyous bellow, the bear knocked Marric's hand aside. He exclaimed in shock at the coldness of its nose before he was engulfed in the most powerful hug of his life. It was like being awash in white fur, or wrestling with the tide. The bear's great paws rested on his shoulders.

He found himself doing an absurd dance merely to keep his balance, so he flung both arms about the bear and hung on for support.

Audun calls this creature my *bear? As well say that I am its* man! Marric laughed. The sound of his laughter, with slightly

181

wild overtones as if tension had snapped too suddenly, made him laugh even harder.

'Back, brother,' commanded Audun. 'Back! You will join your master soon enough.'

With immense strength he pried the bear away from Marric. The Prince stood laughing and trying to regain his breath. Groaning mournfully at being deprived, the bear shambled outside. 'Quiet, brother, quiet,' they heard its keepers say.

'Love at first sight, my Prince?' Nicephorus asked.

'Something like that.' Marric shook himself. Bears that size could snap spines, crush flesh, hurl grown men across clearings. This bear had merely – merely! – hugged him until his ribs had almost cracked. *As well for me that I wear armour*, thought Marric.

Stephana turned to him when he sat down once more. 'Would you like me to hold you that tightly?'

'I wish you could.' She looked better than she had, but he knew how tired she was. She seemed to like the Bearmaster – and he, her. Good. By the time Audun returned, Marric had made his plans.

'Was my father's bear as fine a fellow?'

'Almost,' said Audun. 'What was it you really wished to say?'

'About Stephana, here.' Marric touched her hair. 'This life of mine – hiding, plotting, riding into danger – is no good for her. Could you give her safe haven here?'

'Marric, no!'

'But yes,' Marric told her, and clasped her hands. 'You are exhausted. How often you will have to endure this . . . It is only for a while, Stephana. I will return for you.'

She shook her head. 'I want to stay with you.'

'But I want you safe. Audun, will you grant my lady hospitality?'

'The lady has a voice, remember?' said Audun. 'She can well judge for herself. Let her.'

'You know what I am,' Stephana said to Audun, 'and you know that I do what I must do. I will stay with my lord.'

Audun bent his head in acquiescence and deep respect. 'You are answered, Prince.'

'I would have you safe, cherished,' Marric pleaded with her. 'How can I make you reconsider?'

'You cannot,' Stephana said. She stood close to him, her hands enfolded in his against his chest. 'But ask me anything else. Please. I *am* cherished. And I don't want to be safe if it means leaving you!' Her voice rose. Then she calmed herself, and went on: 'You trust my visions now, don't you? Trust them one more time, my heart. I have seen you enthroned, and I know – *I know* – that my presence has helped place you there.'

'The thing is fated,' Nicephorus broke in softly.

Who asked you? Marric all but turned on his friend.

'If I thought I could, I would leave you among allies, too,' he told Nicephorus. 'You protect your own family by staying away from them.'

'As you well know, the priests guard them for me better than I can. And my wife is a woman of sense, like Stephana. You do not suggest I skulk here because I am a man. And I would not consent to.' Nicephorus walked over to Marric. 'Let me call you Mor right now, my friend. You must permit your friends to choose to follow you. Taran warned you: you have the gift of drawing hearts and minds. Accept it, Mor. What must be, will be.'

Finally, the tears coursing down Stephana's face persuaded Marric. He brushed them away with a tender hand. 'Isis protect you, Stephana, if you will not yield to me on this.'

'Ask me something else,' she said again, beginning to smile. 'Anything except this.'

'I am answered,' Marric told Audun. 'Bearmaster, I thank you, not least of all for your understanding and friendship. I only regret I have no gifts to bestow in return for yours – except for my friendship. You possess that already.'

'Send me word as you can,' said Audun. 'We are allies under law.'

Marric embraced the older man and met a strength almost as great as that of his bear. For one precious moment he was a boy again, impulsively flinging his arms around his father. Even for so brief a time, it felt good to be a child again. But even such a short return to boyhood was too long an indulgence for a would-be emperor.

Marric broke away. Without looking back he walked towards the horses. The necklace of gold coins clinked against his harness and he raised a hand to touch it. In the coins lingered some of the incredible vitality of their last wearer.

What was Audun? he wondered. He had rescued Alexa, recognized Stephana immediately for what she was – and then, those bears . . . Marric decided he was too tired to search for answers. He had a long ride back.

They reached Byzantium at dusk. Drizzle had begun to fall and the sky turned sombre, foggy, heavy with a smell of rotting shellfish. The gates, closed behind them, seemed to shut them away from the freedom of the plains. The whole city seemed to be one great snare. Marric felt as heavily burdened as Mor the slave. The necklace he wore might as well read 'Property of Empire'.

In the safe house a welcome had been prepared. Fires scented with delicate incenses burned in finely chased braziers. The polycandela reflected their torches. No one besides servants awaited them. That was just as well. Marric knew that he and his friends were too near exhaustion to do more than rest. Daphne set out wine and food. When Marric thanked her, she flushed and fled.

Typical Daphne behaviour, Marric thought. She was really at ease only around Stephana and, to some degree, around Nicephorus. A message awaited the latter, reporting on his young son's recovery from a broken collarbone. His relief cut Marric off further from that cozy world of children, small ailments and shy servants. He wanted only to sleep. Then Merikare, muffled in a cloak, was admitted by the guards. He brought Marric word that several of the prefects of the city wanted to meet with him.

Stephana withdrew. The prefects and priests came, then left. Marric and Nicephorus coughed over dusty records in poor light until Marric took pity on his friend's jaw-stretching yawns, and ordered him to go and sleep. Sighing heavily, Marric drew out old maps and his grandfather's *Strategikon*. No more wine for tonight, he decided. He sorted through his welter of documents once again, found the ones he wanted, and rubbed his temples where a headache was beginning. He had a night's work to do.

Chapter Twenty

Wearing the plain wool garments of merchants (with army swords concealed beneath their cloaks), Marric and two of the house guards strode from the Mangana at sunset. As quickly as they might, without attracting attention, they turned from the main streets to the safer back ways.

As they rounded a corner, a noblewoman's litter swung towards them. Just in time, Marric remembered to give place to it on the crowded sidestreet and not to look at its occupant. Noting that the woman was guarded, he pulled up his hood. There had been far too many hired swords about recently. Nervous at the presence of enemies outside the city, and of rumours within it, Irene had tightened security until – as the market gossip pungently remarked – cataphracts outnumbered catamites in the brothels.

Market gossip was also buzzing about the Dionysia to be held early in the spring.

In the crowded market Nicephorus intercepted Marric and his escort. He had been watching the children who raced among the stalls and, Marric suspected, wishing he could see his own children. Marric had offered to have them brought to join him in the safe house – as safe as any place in the city could be for him – but Nico had refused. A pity – his wife, Ariadne, would have been company for Stephana. Recently, Marric had become concerned for her safety, given the increased security and a new outbreak of robberies and stabbings in the city. Even though Stephana had threatened the overseer with a lance, Marric privately believed that she could never have killed him. She rarely even wore a dagger.

Men loitering in the streets nodded as they passed: more temple guards. As they entered the safe house, Marric flung off his cape and looked around. Usually Stephana was waiting for him, but he saw only the two guards he had told to protect her.

They rose and faced him uneasily.

'Your lady is upstairs,' one said.

'What's wrong?'

'No, lord, she is not ill,' said the second. 'This is what happened: at noon, she told us that she wished to go to the Temple of Isis to meditate. Preferably, accompanied only by her maid.'

Marric's face gave no sign of the relief he felt. But the Temple of Isis was too near the palace for him to like her going there at all, let alone without protection: he himself rarely went to the Temple of Osiris opposite it.

'That's a nest of court ladies,' Marric said. 'To be sure, Stephana is a priestess and has every right to be there, but they've never seen her before. With that hair of hers, she is too easily recognized. Anyone might track her here.'

'I told her you would say that, my Prince,' said the second guard. 'She asked if we kept the birds from singing or deprived the hungry of food. She said she was about that desperate to be allowed out.'

'We offered to send for a priest or priestess, but she turned on us. "You morons," she said, quiet, but so you could tell how angry she was, "don't you see that that would bring the disclosure you fear too? I'm no one, nothing; no one will even notice me." And she walked past us and started for the door.'

Marric could imagine the scene: Stephana, anxious at being deprived of her freedom, stalking past the guards; Daphne skittering in her – indubitably – regal wake.

'I stopped her, Prince. I am very sorry, but I took the lady by the wrist and turned her around.' The man looked down and flushed uncomfortably. In addition to Marric's reaction, which the man probably dreaded, he was also remembering what Stephana had said. The slaveblock made slaves the masters of invective, if not of themselves.

'After the lady . . . finished her say, she ran up to her rooms. And there she's stayed.'

Marric clapped the man on the shoulder. He could not let him worry because he had had to deny something to the woman whom they knew that Marric cherished.

He strode through the garden and up the stairs. If only Stephana could understand that the restrictions on her were not permanent. Certainly, Byzantine women moved as they wished in the city. But Stephana, despite her harsh schooling as a slave and the victim of many men, was innocent of this city and must be protected for the good of all of them. Once he ruled, she would have whatever she wished: anything, to help her forget what her life had been until they escaped Alexandria.

Her door was shut. He knocked on it.

'Go away,' Stephana called. 'Spare me your company. My lord set you as my guards, not my jailers.'

'I'm not the guards,' Marric said. He pushed the carved door open. Stephana lay face down on their bed – the very picture, he thought with an incongruous twinge of tender mirth, of a spoiled favourite sulking in the women's quarters of the palace.

So long a slave, Stephana must fear any restrictions on her movements as a return to bondage. He might think of her as a priestess and as his wife in all but name, but how did she think of herself? As his captive?

Perhaps he had been wrong to keep her pent in so closely. The Goddess' service was as necessary to Stephana as song to the nightingale that fluttered outside, or food to a starving child.

The perfumes that Daphne had opened to soothe her mistress were cloying in the air. Marric flung open the violet hangings to let in the night breeze. Emboldened by her mistress' tears, Daphne began a reproach which turned into a squeak.

'Out!' Marric jerked his chin at her. After he heard her sandals clattering away down the corridor, he shut the door and sat down beside his lover. Gently, he raised her. He turned her face up and stroked her hair back from it.

Saying none of the things he wanted to, Marric simply held her until he felt her grief and anger abate. Her head dropped on to his shoulder. He supported her with one arm while he reached for wine and a goblet.

'I needed to speak to the Goddess,' she whispered. 'In her

187

own home. To see her image beyond the curtains of the temenos, the inmost shrine. And I needed just to get free – only for a little space, Marric, but they would not let me.' Her hands rubbed her throat as if they felt the collar he had broken from her neck.

'Be still,' he told her. 'Drink this. All of it. No, now the rest.' She shook her head. But as she tasted the wine, the thirst her long weeping had brought on made her take the cup from him and drain it.

'Now, another one,' he urged her.

She laughed shakily. 'You know I cannot. Adepts are terrible drinkers, Marric: no endurance at all.'

'Don't endure for now. Give in,' he whispered. Eyes meeting his, she drank, then settled back in his arms.

When he held her thus, there was no real need of words. But as the night deepened, Marric spoke for a long time, aware only that Stephana was watching him, had not refused to listen to him.

'—If you hate being held captive here, remember that it is only for a short time that you must take care. No later than spring, I promise you. By then—'

Perhaps Stephana feared removal to the palace, where she might become one of the many women there without family or protection. 'Do you worry what the future will bring you, my heart?' he asked. 'Even after I have promised you that you will never have to fear again?'

He felt her shake her head 'no' against his shoulder and held her even more tightly. 'Listen to what I plan for you.'

He heard a muffled 'no need', but continued anyway.

'You shall have your own place, your own wealth, to go or to stay with me as you choose. Please, Stephana, stay with me. Do you know you will be a great lady – my wife, in all but title? When we have children, as I hope we will, I shall acknowledge them. And their future will be as bright as any mother could hope. You are important, love. What if Alexa gives me no son or daughter, and you do? A child of ours might wear the crown. Does that mean nothing to you?'

'Don't talk of it!' she begged in a soft wail. 'We cannot think that far.' Terror quivered in her voice.

'Ill luck from aiming too high?' Marric asked. 'Where is my

brave love? I will have Merikare or Theophilus pray to avert it, I promise you. And when this is over, we will go to a place in the country that will be your own—' He wanted to make her smile again.

'Would it please you,' he suggested, 'if I went to the priests and asked for initiation? You have long wished that I—'

The words, spoken on impulse, resonated in the silent room, stirring the shadows, and turned Marric's thoughts back on himself. He had long rejected the idea, telling Imhotep that he was not prepared, or that he was Emperor, not magician – anything to avoid the burden he knew he feared and did not want. It, not the crown, would represent the ultimate symbol of his enslavement to his Empire.

Then he remembered what Audun had said. 'One land, one lord.' An adept-emperor would strengthen the mystic bond between ruler and realm. In that case, did he really have the right to refuse the burden of magic? Stephana's powers wore on her. Still, they had kept her sane in slavery. How could what was so great a part of her life possibly harm him? And if he wished to hold her, he could not prove less worthy than she.

Let his land or his love require initiation of him and he would submit. Somehow, he would find the strength to keep himself clean of the lust for power that had brought Alexa to grief and corrupted Irene. Somehow.

Stephana pulled herself upright, hands on his shoulders. She touched his cheek as he stared into the dusk, returning his attention to her.

'Seek initiation only if it is what you must have,' she whispered. 'Not to please me, but only out of your own need.'

'What else?' he asked, and put away his doubts.

Stephana's lips moved up his throat to his mouth, robbing him simultaneously of speech and thought. He eased her down on the silken covers of the bed, caught up by the dizzying speed with which her passion rushed to meet his and to sweep them both out beyond their senses into a place where the stars, the roses and the nightingale's song held them embraced, as if they floated peacefully in some primordial, light-filled sea.

* * *

Soft hair pulling free from under his head, a warm body moving apart from his own, brought Marric back from deep sleep to instant, silent watchfulness. Keeping his eyelids all but closed, he saw Stephana, seated at the foot of the bed, shake her hair back and wrap a loose gown, interwoven with threads of silver, about her. She knotted it and gazed down at him, her face unreadable. Marric feigned the rhythmic breathing of sleep. She stood and walked over to the window, the white silk of her robe drifting about her.

The moon had risen, its white light cool, but Stephana did not shiver as she stood in the pillared embrasure that overlooked the garden. She extended her arms, and even the nightingale fell silent, drowsing under some unheard spell. Stephana bowed her head and stood praying for a long while. The soft silk of her robe slipped out of the loose knot on to the floor, leaving her naked to the night air and the chill caress of the moonlight.

It tangled in her hair the way he had watched it so many times, and turned the long, lovely lines of her back and legs to silver.

He heard her whisper, so faint that it teased at his understanding. 'Let me keep free. For his sake, though, I could wish . . . Mother, watch over him.' Marric's eyes dazzled, and he blamed it on the moon's brightness.

'But I have so little courage!' Her voice broke on the last word, and she hid her face in her hands, away from the all-seeing eye of the moon. Even that gesture acquired an exquisite, hieratic significance: if Stephana could not go to pray in the Goddess' shrine, here she prayed with all her heart. The light seemed to grow about her, enveloping her in brightness.

Such a moment was too private even for a lover's eyes. Marric willed himself to sleep again, and to dream of silver light . . .

'Marric?'

The low, sweet voice calling his name awoke him. As he heard it call him a second time, he propped himself on his elbows and raised his face.

The lamps had gone out. The woman who called his name was tall and slim, light gleaming from the curves of her breasts and sides as she stood beside him. That was all the figure had in common with the woman Marric had watched praying. This woman was taller than Stephana. She carried herself with such grace that an emperor's pride seemed but the louting of a slave before his master in comparison.

Godlike, Marric breathed to himself. Then he saw the crown that the figure wore – a gleaming disc set between silver horns. It was the Goddess herself. Isis stood before Marric, and her white light soothed his heart.

'Marric?'

'Here I am,' he breathed. What title could he give one so high?

'Brother, husband, son: in some ways you are all of these to me, triply dear. But the time for you to intrude upon the women's mysteries is not yet, beloved. Leave my daughter to her freedom. She loves you dearly. Being part of myself, how should she not? But before she is yours, she is her own – and mine. You are both in my hands, sheltered under my wings against your enemies. Remember that, and let my daughter go her own way.'

The Goddess-form bent over Marric. He smelled the fragrance of her breath, the perfume – an ecstatic, ineffable blend of roses and myrrh that might make a dying man rise from his bed and walk again, restored to health and unimpaired youth. Almost fainting from that scent, Marric fell back. As her face bent towards his, he watched her eyes, fascinated. At one moment, Isis seemed to look down at him with his mother's calm gaze; at the next, he thought she had Alexa's vivid, dark eyes. But at the instant her lips touched his, Marric closed his eyes on a vision of Stephana's blue eyes suddenly deepening, becoming the Goddess' all-seeing stare which engulfed whole stars, the world itself, and Marric's awareness.

The rising sun restored Marric to his senses. There was a sweet scent lingering in the room, more than he could ascribe to the flowers arranged within it. Stephana lay in his arms, her head on his shoulder. Her breasts were warm against his side, and one of her hands rested lightly against his heart. The dawnlight made her hair look more silvery than ever before. Her face wore a look of transcendent peace.

The white robe lay pooled on the floor where it had fallen from her the night before.

That was no dream, Marric thought with a prickle of awe. *The Goddess herself stood before me.*

He even had proof. The night before, the hangings that drifted between the room's window-pillars had been delicately tinted violet gauze, banded with darker taffeta strips. Now, the bands gleamed silver, and the hangings themselves were pure white.

Chapter Twenty-one

Marric leaned against one of the columns of the portico of the Temple of Isis and looked across the square. The day was warm for spring. Across the way, the priests were coming and going on errands Marric could not fathom. Somewhere in that building was Merikare. Somewhere, deeper within, past the high-walled shrine where all might come and worship, there had to be some mysterious maze of corridors where the High Priest presided over whatever it was they called initiation.

As he waited for Stephana and her maid, with his man pretending to loiter nearby, Marric forced himself to contemplate the promise he had made his lover. He would present himself for initiation. At the time he had promised, his intention had been real, as sincere as his concern for her the night she had shown him how enslaved his protectiveness was making her feel. In the intervening months, Marric had taken care to see that she no longer felt so much bound.

As for his promise, there was always something – a staff meeting with Marcellinus, an urgent whisper of messages smuggled inside the walls, a conference with the priests on other subjects – to forestall him.

Twice, he himself, choosing times when Thutmosis guarded

the gate, had ridden out to speak with the khagans. They were putting on a fine imitation of a siege.

Lately, conversations with Merikare and Theophilus had turned on Irene's revival of the Dionysia. Merikare saw it as a desperate attempt to establish some legitimacy for her reign. Marric thought of it as an ideal opportunity for him to demonstrate his support. He knew the plays to be performed, knew them well. There was one in particular, the *Ion*, that offered tempting possibilities for political statements.

He was dodging his promise, he realized. Why? Nicephorus had survived initiation. Stephana had passed so far beyond it that the priestesses called her sister – and one of no junior standing – on her first visit to the temple. He sighed and shook his head.

Women's voices grew louder as they approached where he stood. He heard Stephana's voice and listened harder. Then, hearing the urgency in it, he slipped behind one of the enormous pillars to allow her some privacy.

'You would willingly resume a place on the Wheel, daughter?'

'Say that I have not enough courage to escape it,' Stephana said. 'I need more time . . . another life . . .'

'You are lying to yourself!' The priestess' voice was sharper than Marric had ever heard it.

'Very well. Here is the truth. I do not wish to lose—'

'What can you lose?'

'Please be still,' Stephana whispered. 'He might overhear.'

Hushed words, then a blessing followed. Finally, Stephana came in search of him.

'You were not bored?' she asked, raising her voice slightly as she walked towards Marric. Her hands adjusted a white veil about her hair.

'Not severely.' Marric smiled at her and nodded to Daphne, who flushed and looked away. 'Assuming that you're not tired—' Stephana laughed at him – 'we might look in at the Hippodrome. One of the plays rehearses there. Would you like that?'

Her eyes sparkled. 'You, too, Daphne? Come then. I assume that for such a short journey I need not be carried like an image in a procession?'

'Not if you would prefer to walk.' The streets were well-scrubbed this close to the palace.

Marric knew the Hippodrome well – from the kathisma, or royal box, down to the ring he had driven in during the chariot races all the young nobles loved. But the women with him had never before seen it. Their admiration of the rows of tiers, the elaborate spina and the stage erected on the sands, was unfeigned.

With Nicephorus at his elbow, Marric watched the performance carefully. The actors were testing machinery by lowering on to it, first a heavy sack, then a performer.

'*To pass name and sceptre to his true-born son*—' recited the Chorus.

The actor swung aloft in the concealed harness of the machine as the chorus mimed awe first, then adoration of the god. In this part of the old play, the god descended before the Temple of Apollo at Delphi, to tell the hero:

'*You are Ion, who will conquer Asia.*'

'There,' said Nicephorus. 'If we could only exchange the mask that the God will wear for one bearing your features . . .'

A hiss distracted Marric. His guards tensed, hands darting to weapons concealed about them. One of Audun Bearmaster's men beckoned.

'How did you get in here?' Marric whispered.

'No time, lord. Listen to me. Word has come from Jomsborg: the Reaver refuses the Red Empress.'

Irene will be enraged, Marric thought.

'My lord bids you look to our kinsmen in the Guard,' whispered the Bearmaster's man.

With Jomsborg hostile and Audun camped outside, the Aescir among the Varangians might well be considered suspicious by a queen whose fears and ambitions outweighed her reason and right to rule.

'You cannot stay here,' Marric said. 'Get away now!' That very evening he would have to speak to the officers sworn to him.

The Aescir vanished into the shadows.

Playing indolent escort, Marric sauntered over to Stephana. 'I am quite bored now,' he told her, and laid a hand on her shoulder. His touch and gaze alerted her, and he cocked his head to indicate that they should leave.

Stephana brought Daphne back to the here-and-now. Casually, they made their way outside.

'Quickly!' Marric whispered. He waved Nicephorus away. He would return Daphne to the house by a back route.

Outside the Hippodrome a party of Irene's special security officers rode up and down. From time to time they cut someone out of the crowd of passers-by, detained him, and then either released him or had him marched off – usually the latter.

'My lord,' Stephana smiled brightly at Marric. As she intended, her voice carried. 'May we go to the perfumers' stalls?' They would provide one way of getting through. Isis certainly had answered his love's prayers for courage.

'Let us simply ease through this crowd. I hope you do not fear the press of such a rabble?'

'With you with me?' But the hand Stephana laid on his arm trembled from her efforts not to clutch at him.

They inched their way along the Mese. A hand suddenly fell on Marric's shoulder. Stephana stifled a gasp.

'I will just be detaining these people,' announced an under-officer.

A little too quickly, Marric turned. He thrust Stephana behind him. For once, he hoped, she went armed, but he doubted it. His hand dropped by the hilt of his dagger.

Sunlight sparkled on the carved stone of the buildings and danced on the blue waters of the Horn. *Is this the last time I will see that?*

'I thought I should stop you, my Prince,' whispered the officer.

'Marcellinus sent you?'

'Aye. Thank all the gods I was on duty.'

'I will also thank you. Rest assured, I do not forget my friends. What news do you bring me?'

'From Jomsborg, my lord. The Reaver returned Irene's ambassadors in very damaged condition. He says that – save his granddam – he will permit no woman on his island. Least of all the Red Empress.'

'Why this cordon?' Marric gestured at the line of cavalry, which was an effective blockade.

'The Empress has decided that the Varangians are disloyal. She wants them taken into custody.' The officer's voice was flat, expressionless. Not for him to criticize where he might be overheard: his service to Marric showed what he really thought.

'You will never take them unless they consent to their arrest. Osiris' death, they are *loyal*, man!' Marric thought of a battle between the axe-wielding Northerners and imperial cataphracts, and felt sick.

'We hope that they will.' Understandably enough, the man looked uneasy. Like the Jomsborgers, the Varangians had a reputation for ferocity. 'Now, lord, I have to appear to release you, then go arrest my brothers-in-arms, Horus aid me.' He shouted at another officer. 'This one's safe; the lady went to the temple to pray for a son!'

'Irene has gone beyond love of power,' Stephana whispered. 'Now she craves destruction. If the Varangians resist—'

'They could tear the city apart.'

As if led there by a perverse fate, several Varangians sauntered by. At first they reacted to their arrest with disbelief, then with bellowed outrage. Two, indeed, handed over their weapons to Irene's officers. But the others shouted defiance and reached for their axes.

Blood stained the scrubbed stone of steps, buildings and columns.

'They're mine,' Marric groaned, 'and they're killing one another.'

Stephana flung her arms about him. 'You cannot help it yet, beloved. *You cannot!*' Her touch restrained him as well as gave comfort, yet she seemed the very picture of a woman long protected and suddenly thrust into violence.

'They have broken through – ah! stolen the men's horses, have they? They will ride for the gates and join Audun, I would wager. I hope they make it. But wait! One man is down – he waves the others on . . .'

Imperial troops secured the wounded mercenary and stripped him of his weapons. Blood from his scalp clotted on his braids and ran down his armour. He staggered as he walked, but they propped him up before their commander. Marric remembered that man from their days as recruits together. He liked pain, liked it altogether too much for Marric's taste.

'Kill this one,' he ordered.

'In the temple precincts?' one of his men protested. 'That's sacrilege.'

'Do it or die with him!' shouted the officer. 'Then one of you can cut – what do they call that trick of the Jomsborgers? – the bloodeagle on him. We will prop him before the walls.'

Marric tightened his arms about Stephana. He could feel her power radiating out to the condemned man: *faith, compassion, strength*. As long as she thought she could help, she would not move. The Varangian stood frozen in shock. His eyes scanned the crowded forum absently, as if he did not see the people who stared and whispered.

'Stephana, can you give him an easy death?' Marric asked. He ached at the man's pain and confusion. And just when the Bearmaster had asked him to look to his kinsmen!

'He fights to live. I cannot interfere with that,' she said. 'You can help him, though. Let him *see* you, watch you, know that his death matters to you.' She looked up at him earnestly. 'You have the power to do it, love. I promise.'

Marric summoned the undervoice and sent his message as strongly as he could – *trust, respect, sorrow* – at the Varangian. – *You are seen, guardsman!* –

The man straightened almost to attention. He glanced over at Marric, then quickly looked away. – *Watch how I can die, Prince* – his expression seemed to say. With a yell as ghastly as any Jomsborg berserker's warcry, he hurled himself at the commander and seized his sword.

'For the Prince!' he shouted. '*Marric!*' He drove the blade into his own heart. The shock of his death hit Stephana, and she screamed. The commander turned to look at her. Then he saw Marric and gasped in amazement.

'Run!' Marric ordered. The compulsion upon him to watch, to watch carefully this latest of Irene's atrocities, vanished. He had been recognized.

Her white veil trailing from her hair, Stephana ran. She lifted her skirts with both hands so she could run faster. The veil fluttered free.

'This way!' Marric pulled her into a cross-street where they stopped, panting for breath. This part of the city, near the stalls of the perfumers, was sweet-smelling, tranquil . . . but blood stained it too.

Marric knew he had just run out of time.

He tightened his arms about Stephana. 'Can you walk now?' he asked. Seeing them huddled in the shadows, anyone would have taken them for lovers stealing a moment together, not plotters who must gamble their lives on their schemes.

Stephana raised a hand to her hair and discovered that her veil was missing. She began to laugh. 'So much for defying one's fate, beloved! Come, let us go home.'

Chapter Twenty-two

When Marric rose, slightly before dawn, Stephana kissed him sleepily. The familiar, beloved touch conveyed no awareness that she knew where he was going.

He walked to the Temple of Osiris. During the night the pavement before it had been sanded clean of blood. Still, Marric found himself avoiding certain places. Here, a foot soldier had fallen, his throat cut. Here, an officer had stabbed his own horse to prevent a Varangian's stealing it. And here – Marric recoiled from the memory – was the place where the Varangian had met his eyes, saluted him, and killed himself.

Rest easy, brother. Marric glanced at the horizon. The sun was rising.

By now, Audun would have received word of the man's death and would honour him. When Marric won back his throne, he would attempt to find and compensate the man's family. He would never forget his sacrifice.

Marric thought that his unwillingness to walk over the blood-polluted stones augured well for his purpose. Today he would seek initiation from the priest of Osiris. Once he received whatever power it might confer, he could be about the Empire's business again.

He walked up the shallow stairs between the porphyry lions that a long-ago Emperor had brought back from Egypt and given to the temple.

One land, one lord. If Marric's land required him to take initiation, he would. What was it? Nicephorus and Stephana had never disclosed any details of their own ceremonies, yet they had power they could draw from. That shaman in the Huns' tents – he had a different sort of power. So, too, did Audun Bearmaster. It was past time for Marric to acquire power, too.

He strode more boldly than he felt within the temple. Incense prickled at his nostrils and woke strange sensations and stranger memories of a life . . . lives . . . Priests, underpriests and acolytes, preparing for the dawn service, observed him in silence and without surprise. His entire life might have been spent in arriving at this place.

An ancient priest, even his bald scalp wrinkled, pointed out a corridor painted with symbols that were old when the stone was first laid in the ancient Temple of Osiris at Heliopolis.

'The High Priest will see you.'

Marric's footsteps echoed as he walked down the corridor. Hieroglyphics were painted on the sloping walls; they made the place look like a tomb. His mastery of the old tongue did not allow him to read the signs.

The corridor angled sharply and ended in a tiny chamber. In it sat the High Priest on an ivory stool. He did not rise or otherwise greet Marric. The gold serpent crown of his priesthood glittered on his shaven skull. Arched brows framed narrow, deep-set eyes as dark as Marric's own, eyes that pierced him. And, above them, the gemmed eyes of the serpent stared at him, too.

As Marric stood there, the centuries seemed to roll back. No longer was he a prince of Alexander's line, uniting Egypt, Greece and Persia. No longer did he live within a Byzantium that sickened under the rule of a madwoman they called witch and Red Empress. He was not a prince who had been a governor, slave and, now, an insurgent. He was not Stephana's lover, nor Nicephorus' friend. Very simply, Marric was just one in an age-old procession of supplicants. And the High Priest was what he had always been since the first temples rose by the Nile: the intermediary between mankind and the gods who dwelt at the Horizon.

Both men studied one another. Marric shook off his awe and remembered his boyhood, fidgeting at his father's side during endless rituals. This same priest had always glared him into silence and stillness, overmastering him when even his father could not.

He didn't seem any older now than he had then: he still looked like the oldest man in the world – and one of the strongest. What was his name? Marric should have known. It troubled him that he could not remember. The priest had always been just that – the High Priest.

Since he was evidently prepared to sit silently forever, Marric spoke. 'I have come to take initiation.'

'Many seek initiation. Few are found worthy. Why do *you* seek it?'

Marric shrugged. He looked into the High Priest's dark eyes and made a plea of the Empire's need, his own dawning awareness that he might serve it better if he were more than a warrior-king. Under the man's unrelenting gaze, even his love lay revealed. Would the priest understand that too?

Priests. They had failed to save his mother. They had not warned his father of Irene. And they had let him be sold in Alexandria. If Marric took initiation, he would *be* a priest. And what did he feel about that? Love, or loathing?

He looked away from the High Priest to a mural of Osiris calling on the elder gods for aid. He remembered the scream, '*Ha-k ir-i!*' that was torn from his throat as nameless, incomprehensible power manifested itself through him, a violation of his deepest self.

'You do not seek initiation for yourself,' the priest stated.

'For the Empire.' Marric was content as he was. But whatever the Empire required of him was his duty to perform, even this sacrifice of his inner peace. Though priests were always preaching sacrifice and unselfishness, Marric's answer seemed not to please this one. He had never succeeded in doing that.

'Just like that?' asked the priest. 'Do you know what it is?'

'A discipline,' Marric answered. 'I understand . . . it is hard. Very hard. That I wish it *now* . . . will make it harder. But I am a soldier, I have been a slave. I can endure it.'

The priest waved him towards a mat, and he sank down on it gratefully. He was not cold, not tired, hungry, or even greatly afraid. Still the tension within the tiny cell made him tremble.

'Hardship?' repeated the priest. 'You say you can endure it?'

The man was pale-skinned, unscarred: what could he know of the lashings of sun, of shame, of metal-tipped whips that had all but torn the fighting life out of Marric? Massage and oils had drawn the last of the stiffness from his back and sides, but he would always bear scars – only some of them physical.

The priest held up one hand for attention. 'Initiation is not a hardship of the body, but of the spirit. I do not doubt your physical strength. You have discipline, stamina, and I respect your dedication to a goal. But is that goal the goal of this Temple?'

'Ever since I returned from Cherson,' Marric burst out, 'priests have jabbered initiation – some wonderful, mystical thing – at me, then refused to explain it!' Even Stephana. But anger would not win the priest's cooperation, Marric thought. He continued more quietly. 'Will you tell me?'

'You subordinate your entire being to the powers of which you become a part. But that is only the beginning.

'Prince . . . my son, you do not wish these powers for yourself. But it is for yourself you must wish them. Without that desire, they will consume you.'

'If you could save your child from starving by working in the sewers, wouldn't you do it?' Marric asked. 'Can I let the Empire die because I will not give it what it needs? It is father and child to me: so if it requires me to take initiation, then, yes, I do ask it for myself!'

Marric rose from the mat and started to pace. Five steps up, five steps back across the cell. He suspected that the priest might have stopped him with a glance, but he did not. Instead, he watched Marric, making the Prince aware of himself as a physical being: tall, tanned, muscled, enjoying even this tiny release from iron self-control. He was healthy and welcomed what his health brought him, even to the slight sweat that had broken out on his brow and upper lip.

'Yes,' said the priest. 'Look at yourself. The initiation you seek will take you out of body—'

'One night I lay dying,' Marric interrupted. 'My friends could not bring me back. My spirit rose . . . there were pillars, and I saw the gods, my father, my mother . . .'

'But you chose to return to your flesh.'

'How could I leave my work here undone?'

'Prince, Prince, I am not accusing you. But never seek to deny how much you love living or the world you live in. It is your greatest genius.'

The textures of fine cloth, of Stephana's soft skin, or of sun and dust on a drill field, the test and play of weapons, the savour of dark, red wine – Marric smiled. His senses served him well.

'Do you understand now, my son? You have travelled out of your body. You have used powers latent within you, set your feet on the way. This is well done. All of these things are lesser initiations that will prepare you for the great one you claim to seek.'

'I do indeed seek it.'

'Are you ready to survive it?' the priest asked. 'Tell me, how long did it take you to decide to come here?'

Marric lowered his head, feeling a humiliation as keen as the time he had stood, naked and feverish, in the slave market.

'The Empire dies,' he whispered. 'If I were initiate, I might heal it.' He hid his face from the cruel wisdom of the High Priest. Where the city had shone would be a ruin. Barbarians would graze their herds among the tumbled stones of palaces. The Empire's treasures would be stolen, to gleam unloved in squalid huts, one paste earring, perhaps, cherished while great statues crumbled. If the Empire died, Marric might as well die, too. He could not restrain his tears.

The priest let him grieve silently for a time before embracing him with a father's touch. The gentleness in his hands surprised Marric. He was tempted simply to yield to it, to accept the priest's counsel and comfort.

'You will be ready one day,' the priest spoke in his ear. 'But not yet. You have power enough to rule right now.'

What power? The power that watched a soldier slay himself, that skulked in passageways, plotted, and talked, talked, talked, while all around the Middle Sea, enemies converged?

'Right now, your desire for life is your greatest power. Trust to it,' said the priest.

Marric freed himself from the man's clasp. Dull heat began to burn within him: when he would let himself identify it, he would call it relief and shame. 'Why am I not fit?' he asked.

'Very well, my Prince. I will show you.'

The High Priest touched one of the stone blocks the height of a man that made up the cell walls. It slid aside, revealing a staircase. His face graver, more deeply lined than usual, the priest beckoned Marric forward. 'This . . . all but violates an oath I swore long before your birth,' he said. 'But I accept the consequences. One day you will be one of us. Then you will understand the risk I am taking. I only hope I hasten the day by showing you why I must refuse you now.'

The High Priest led Marric through a maze of stairways and connecting rooms. Some of the rooms were bare of anything but wall paintings. Other cells held acolytes seated on thin pallets, so deep in meditative trance that their own High Priest's passing did not cause them even to stir. Marric saw more and more of these as they walked further down the labyrinth of corridors. They must have left the Temple of Osiris, must be walking underneath the forum itself, he thought.

What awaited him? Even the priest seemed ill at ease. He had spoken of breaking faith. Matters must stand very ill with the Empire if its High Priest felt drawn to such actions.

'The people you see have studied for years to control their minds and bodies. For the past seven days they have subsisted only on herbs and water, to prepare their bodies to undergo initiation. Try it and fail, and your spirit burns itself out. Then you must start all over again in your next life, at a much lower level.' The priest's voice sounded very sad. 'Marric, your mind and spirit are very strong, but they are strong in this world alone.'

'I can see lights,' Marric whispered. 'Over that man's head, and that woman's. Hers is green.'

'One day she will be a powerful priestess of Isis,' said the priest. 'Green magic, the power which burgeons, fails and is reborn. What will your power be, Marric? When you know, you will come back to us. Then we will not turn you away.'

Again, the High Priest touched the wall, and the great blocks of dressed stone slid aside. They entered a tiny chamber. No torches illumined it. Light shone from the stone itself: not the phosphorescence of decay, but a white light that Marric somehow knew was the blending of all colours. The only thing that did not glow was the sarcophagus of basalt and porphyry that occupied most of the room.

'Look into it,' said the High Priest. '*Lie* in it, if you wish. Imagine yourself lying in it, every fibre of your body straining towards your ordeal. The lid lowers over your face, shutting out sound, light, air.

'Do you wish to live, Prince? Your body convulses and gasps for breath – then escapes from its shackles—'

Marric would not refuse the challenge. He swung a leg over the sarcophagus, lay down, and shut his eyes. He heard the priest's voice soften, dimming as if it came from a greater and greater distance. His hands went to his throat, he was choking.

And then he felt himself freed, floating . . .

'Once you have left your body and begun to wander the planes of light,' droned the far away voice, 'you will encounter tests, dangers . . .'

Visions of slavery, of death, of grief drawn from Marric's past confronted him. *These are not real. These are in my past, not my future. Get away.*

Amazingly, the visions did.

I can take this! Marric felt a surge of exultation. He pressed onwards eagerly, towards the unimaginable frontiers that surely lay ahead. The voice was soon left far behind, whispering its warnings.

Merciful Isis, what was that?

A circle of blackness materialized, with red lights glistening wetly within. It was immensely powerful, it was moving his way, and it was ravenous. The red lights extruded into sharp claws that shot out beams of fire. Even in his spirit-form, they burned him. He felt pain, rage, panic – where to escape, nowhere, flee anywhere at all from the thing that now bore such a face—

'Come you back!' The High Priest clapped his hands together sharply.

Sweating heavily, Marric reeled from the immense sarcophagus. He steadied himself against its side, then recoiled from it in loathing. How could anyone enter that thing, knowing—

'They do not know. But now you do. So you pay the price of your own rashness.'

The priest grasped Marric's shoulders, sustaining him. Marric forced himself to look into the older man's eyes. Their minds were still lightly joined and Marric flinched under the impact of sorrow he had not imagined . . . – *Guard him, His Majesty ordered. I obey. He has the right to try. I shall give him every chance, including what I might not give my own flesh, my son, my son . . . he had to try, too, but when they brought him forth, the heart died within me, too. You, Prince, you will succeed where my son failed. I will see to it.* –

His son? Marric hadn't known the High Priest had ever had one. *What makes him think I can succeed where a priest's son fails?*

'You didn't see it?' Marric was still shuddering. 'Black, horrible, crouching . . . it would have devoured me.' Wherever it was, that was a place Marric knew he had no courage to go back to.

'You saw the Watcher at the Gate. Initiates see it, master it, and return. Some do not return; we have our failures. When you are ready, Prince, you too will pass the Watcher unharmed. But not now.'

The priest supported Marric, as if he were a man old or enfeebled by illness, back to the main part of the temple. The stone slabs closed quietly behind them and hid that perilous sarcophagus. So that was initiation! Courage wasn't enough to survive it. He only hoped he would not pollute the sanctity of the temple by vomiting like a boy after his first battle.

With his sickness and shame mingled envy. Nicephorus had passed this test. So had Stephana, his love, whom he could never, never marry because her blood was not fit to ally with his. That was the finest joke of all. He was the one who was not fit.

Stephana . . . if she could pass that Watcher, she was worth a dozen such as he. How would she bear to look at him, to touch him, lie with him in love, now that he had demonstrated how unworthy he was?

'Right here. No, lie down,' the priest ordered. 'Don't try to talk yet.' He was assisted to lie on the mats in the priest's austere chamber. A soft wool blanket was spread over him. 'The trembling will stop in a moment.' He heard sandals pad into the doorway, a murmur of thanks, and then the same sandals walking away. At least the priest had not admitted anyone to look upon him in his shame. And to think he hoped to rule as adept and as Emperor!

'Drink this,' ordered the High Priest. 'We give it to adepts to prepare them for the Great Workings. It will restore you.'

Whatever vile potion he was handed, he didn't want, but the priest made him swallow it. Bitterness poured down Marric's throat. He coughed, then rose up on one elbow.

'It seems I cannot even bear an initiate's diet,' he said wryly. The potion sent heat through his body, battling the chill of terror that had not left him since he panicked before the Watcher.

'I will let you rest for now.' The priest's gentle, inexorable hands compelled Marric to lie down again. How had he ever thought the old man weak? Gods, Marric was as tired as if he'd fought all day. The priest laid one of those cool hands on Marric's brow for a moment. Then the light in the cell dimmed, and he was alone.

The cordial he had drunk bereft him of his senses.

Marric awoke without the languorous awareness of moving from sleep to consciousness that he usually enjoyed. His mind was clearer than he had ever known it.

So initiation – the way of the priest – was not his way. He had been right when he feared to reach for those powers. Though Marric blessed the High Priest's kindness in saying that he was unready, the truth was he was simply unworthy. Marric smiled cynically. He might be a flawed instrument, but he was all the weapon the priest had to turn against Irene.

He lay motionless, staring at the ceiling. If he could not unite with the powers beyond the Horizon and use them, what could he do?

Besides initiate priests, other people dealt with the gods. Healers tended those who were sick or in labour, embalmers prepared the dead for their last journey . . . and then there were the actors, whose masks symbolized that they enacted divine rôles.

Could we but get at that one's mask . . . Nicephorus had wished the day before, in the Hippodrome. Yes. Let Marric don that mask, assume that actor's role as the God who descends to mankind during the play. It would answer well. In fact, there were lines that could be added to the God's speech, so that the people who watched knew that their true ruler lived, aye, and stood before them.

As the High Priest entered the room again, Marric sprang to his feet. Ignoring a brief dizziness, he stalked past him down the corridor. At this very moment, the actors would be rehearsing.

Marric might not have gained the powers he sought, but he was still a fine strategist. So Irene had revived the Dionysia as a way of reaffirming the old ties binding the Empire to the gods? Two could play that game: Marric knew how easily *Ion*, the last play scheduled for tomorrow's festivities, could be manipulated into serving as a way of announcing himself to the city.

Attempting to push defeat, anger and shame to the back of his mind, Marric strode towards the Hippodrome. He would persuade the actors to fall in with his plans. He had to.

The scheme was dangerous. All the better. He would show the Osiris priest that there were other ways he could cope besides long study and entrance, alive, into the tomb.

Then Marric shivered, despite the hot sun. Certainly, the Hippodrome had made men emperors before. But it had also served as their death place.

Chapter Twenty-three

'Too many things could go wrong if my lord plays Apollo tonight,' Stephana repeated.

'But I tell you, we cannot afford to wait!' Caius Marcellinus stood up so fast that his chair fell crashing onto the floor behind him. 'The Prince – well enough for you both, lady, that the man who detained you at the Hippodrome was loyal to me – can't you understand? The Prince was *seen*! That puts all of us at risk!'

Stephana's face was very white. Her hands, which had been clasped tightly in her lap, came up to her throat, then dropped. She didn't take her eyes from Marric.

'Look you,' Marcellinus said. 'The actors are willing. Nicephorus has altered the speech and there isn't a false word in it!' Stephana looked at him briefly, then dropped her eyes. Marcellinus had always treated her with the grave courtesy he would accord a woman of his own rank, at first for his Prince's sake, and then for her own.

'Is it Prince Marric's safety that troubles you, lady?' He asked her that in a much gentler voice. 'The ropes are sound. And I will have guards stationed throughout the Hippodrome.'

'We will have no better opportunity,' said another man. 'All the people we must influence will be there. And the mob: we give them a show, the appearance of risk, and they'll adore it. But there will really be no risk at all.'

Stephana rose from her chair and folded her slender arms about herself, as if chilled by something other than the breeze from the courtyard.

'I *am* worried for my lord's safety,' she said, almost in an undertone, 'but not that way.' She was silent for a long time. Finally, she burst out, 'You see this as a calculated act, an act of desperation. I say, simply, that I fear acts of desperation. You tell me, "You are a woman, and so your fear is understandable . . . for you." But I have fought, and I have lived . . . very hard. And I tell you, I fear what consequences this show of yours may create.'

She took Marric's hands. 'Irene is desperate. Look what desperation has done to her – forced her into madness and mad pride. The way she had the Varangians arrested and butchered proves that. Now, this travesty of a festival – Marric, can't you see? Assume the mask of the God, put words into his mouth, and you share Irene's hubris. Have you forgotten everything you have learned? This time, your penalty may be harsher.'

'It's the ends and the means again,' Nicephorus spoke up. 'If you assume the God's mask, you become the God. That will mean a price to pay—'

'Then I will pay it!'

Stephana drew her hands from Marric's. 'I fear that you will.'

Marric began to pace. Up and down the carpet and the stone floor he walked restlessly. He had seized on this plan as something he could *do*, some useful action that could salve his inadequacy. Stephana might be able to wait for Isis to descend and crown him: he could not.

'The choice is mine,' said Marric. 'I will go through with tonight's spectacle.'

'I will stay here,' Stephana said suddenly. 'Not because I refuse to watch, but because you must not be distracted—'

'I think that is wise,' said Marcellinus.

Marric was surprised by his own ambivalence. Yes, he wanted Stephana there to witness his triumph. But he also wanted her safe. Her misgivings unsettled him; he had never gone against her judgement before.

'I understand,' Stephana said. 'Marric, I do understand. You feel that the tide turns against you, that Irene will either attack and win, or be deposed, but that it must be *now*. But—' she made a gesture of rejection, of shutting herself off from the discussion – 'I am only what I am: a former bondsmaid with some faint gift for interpreting the Goddess' will. If you say that I do not understand statecraft and strategy, you are quite right. But in that case, why ask my advice at all?'

She left the room quickly. Marric watched her as she walked through the garden, her head held a trifle too high.

'Do you wish to alter plans, my Prince?' asked Marcellinus.

Marric shook his head. 'Caius, I will need you in the Hippodrome. And you, Nicephorus. Be certain that you have a weapon ready for me, too. I have no wish to precede Irene to the Horizon.'

Marcellinus and his men saluted. Nicephorus contrived his own disappearance. Marric went to find Stephana. He discovered her searching through chests of clothing with such determination that he knew that she was still far from calm.

'At least,' she said, trying to laugh, 'I shall see you dressed as an emperor tonight. I have long wished to.'

'Sit down, Stephana,' Marric said. Slowly he knelt before her and cupped her shoulders in his hands. 'You,' he said. 'My very dearest. Why were you not my kinswoman? You should have been Empress, far worthier to rule than I.' The day's humiliation bowed his head. He was glad to lay it in her lap. Stephana's hands stroked his hair, traced over his ears, and began to ease the tension from the knotted muscles of neck and shoulders. Marric sighed.

'So the Temple refused to receive you,' she said finally.

'The priest took me down to see the sarcophagus. I suddenly . . . I was falling, falling out of my body. I panicked.' He pressed his face against her legs, glad she could not see his face. He could feel her reach out to soothe him, the touch of the priestess as well as the lover. He shook his head. Unfit, unworthy.

Stephana slid cool fingers inside the neck of his tunic.

'You saw the Watcher, did you, and feared it? How not? Marric, would you set a boy still unable to lift a shield in the forefront of a cavalry charge? I tell you, in facing such creatures as the Watcher, you are just such a boy, and not the Prince or the General. There is no need for this shame . . .' she tugged at Marric's hair and he raised his face.

'Do you believe me?' Marric admired the hollows and curves of her face, drawn fine with concern. He had trusted her unreservedly from the moment when her voice had drawn him back from death.

He nodded, and she kissed his forehead.

'Must you do this thing tonight?'

'Yes. Not for pride, love, but because I can truly see no other way.' He stood and pulled her up against him. 'You will be safe here.'

'Do not fear for me,' she said. 'I no longer do.'

'After tonight, there will be no reason to fear,' he promised.

'I know.' Her hands cupped his face and drew it towards hers. Urgently, she kissed him. As he embraced her, she melted against him even more closely.

'I love your touch,' she said against his mouth. 'Have we time now?' She caressed him with an abandon new to Marric. She was tense: had she chosen this as a way of easing her anxiety? It didn't matter. Her desire would be his joy to assuage. Marric lost himself in the rose scent of her hair, the softness of her lips, and the instinctive movements of her body as it received him.

'I do not want to leave you,' he whispered much later, then kissed the valley between her breasts. Lazily, he fondled them and laughed softly as her nipples stiffened again. He slid his hands down over her belly, between her thighs for the pleasure of watching her react, then of responding to the demands her body made. Abandoning herself, she cried his name and fell back almost unconscious.

Finally Marric drew apart from her and raised himself on his side. He kissed her eyes, heavy lidded from ecstasy.

'When I return tonight, we will finish what we have begun.'

'I will wait for you,' she promised. Languorously, she watched him wash and dress, smiling sleepily at the splendour of the violet silk he wore.

When he knelt by her side to kiss her again, she seemed to have drifted into sleep. Marric touched her face, wishing they had a child, then turned away. Swinging a dark cape over his shoulders, he left for the Hippodrome.

I have led armies in the field! Again Marric reminded himself. His palms were sweaty, and he twisted in the harness which stagehands adjusted about his body; they concealed it under the robes of the god he was to represent, and left him alone. He forced himself not to move. If the harness were not perfectly adjusted, he might fall.

To fall, in front of the whole city . . . Marric preferred an honest battle. At least if you took a swordthrust or an arrow, you died fast among men who understood what was happening. You didn't have to think of the long drop to the spina – or the arena floor itself – to lie broken, possibly screaming in pain as Irene looked on, highly entertained.

The actor playing Xuthus, the foreigner who adopts Ion, stalked by, tall in the high boots of ritual drama. He held his mask like a helmet in the crook of his arm. Incredibly, he reached out to touch Marric's shoulder.

'We've all felt what you feel now, Prince. I imagine it's like before a battle. The ropes are sound, and our stagehands know their business. Just remember: before you begin the god's speech, breathe deeply.'

Prince or no prince, in that moment Marric loved the actor like a brother. Ion walked past him and nodded. He was followed by an actor masked as a priestess, and the file of the Chorus.

'*Born of a mortal father or of Apollo Loxias,*' a man in a rumpled tunic hissed at Marric for the fifth time that hour. 'That's your cue. Prince, Prince, will you hold yourself like a god and not a tyro! Remember, you begin your speech *after* Ion finishes his. Do *not* look down or at the audience, or you will forget your lines.' The man turned away, muttering something about amateurs.

At least Marric's voice was trained on the parade ground. And there was a speaking trumpet built into the mask of Apollo, which fitted his head far less comfortably than his helmet. Marric held the mask in his hands and looked at it: a handsome thing, richly polychromed, its features chillingly, inhumanly regular.

It was almost time for the God to speak.

Marric put on the mask and waited for his cue.

'—*born of a mortal father or of Apollo Loxias*—'

The machine swung him into the air and the harness tightened on his body. When the God in the machine appeared, the audience always hushed in awe. But this time the mood spread even to the actors. The Chorus' disciplined line broke, Creusa recoiled before the God who had been her lover, and Ion made as if to run. The actors knew that Marric's speech was more than

212

a ritual representation of the God to mortals. And they were frightened: Irene's vengeance was swift and terrible.

Why had they helped him? Conviction? The delight of achieving a spectacular effect on stage? There was no time to think. High in the air, Marric kept his body immobile, held his masked head high, and began to speak.

Nicephorus had adapted the words from the *Ion* of Agathon, sweetest of the ancient Athenian playwrights. Strain roughed Marric's voice; he had none of the melodious diction of the actors. But the horn in the mask carried his words even to the uppermost rows, and thrust it into the ears of Irene. She sat in the royal box across from him. They were almost on a level. Red-gowned and glittering, she twisted some kind of gauzy white fabric in her hands. Naturally, she wouldn't believe in this sham, but her subjects must be impressed.

'Do not look at the audience,' Marric had been told. But as he spoke his first line, something made him gaze out over the crowd. *'I am no enemy that you should flee from me, but gracious towards you—'*

The audience seemed like some pain-ridden beast, crouching as a newcomer approaches it, not certain if it will be a hunter to kill it, or its keeper, to bandage its hurt and reassure it before taking it to a safe home.

'Hear you the will of the gods—'

As the audience gasped, the receptivity to mood for which all actors pray fell upon Marric. Just so, he remembered, had the combined will of the priests on board ship channelled through him to call down lightnings against his enemies. The audience wanted to believe him, wanted truly to witness the God's descent to announce his will. And it wanted to end the torment of blood and doubt that the Red Empress inflicted – even for an hour.

They wanted, they wanted – Marric's voice became more resonant and took on the reassuring overtones he had used to hearten recruits, or comfort Stephana.

'Take this youth and go to the city of Empire. Set him on the throne,' proclaimed the God.

In a play, the God could restore order so easily. The audience sighed in wonder. They wanted more. Their need made Marric draw on reserves of strength and spirit. These were his people, his Empire – and he would save them. Who needed the priests? These actors had a magic all their own.

Now his speech told not of Ion's misfortunes, of how he had been left swaddled on a hillside to die, and been rescued by a prophetess, but of Marric's own story: captured, enslaved, sent far from home, but returning.

In the royal box, Irene stiffened, her ringed hands tearing at the white gauze they clasped. Around her whispered the patricians, forming into small groups which dispersed and reformed into new sources of new whispers. Among them, Marric knew, were aristocrats whose favour he had to have. Throughout the Hippodrome, Marcellinus' men would be reaching for their weapons in case Irene set her own troops on the crowd.

But still the audience leaned forward, enthralled and unsatisfied. More still? What else could Marric give them? His speech was ending, and they were still not satisfied. Their longing tore at him.

Going down to hell to rescue Osiris, Isis had had to strip herself as the price of entry, and before Osiris could be restored to life. Could Marric do less?

'Cherish your blessings. Ion shall lift his sceptre over Asia in splendour. I decree for the city a happy fate.'

As the echoes of Marric's final lines died, he reached up and removed the mask of the God. For a heartbeat, for several heartbeats, there was silence. Then the actor playing the prophetess ran forward waving a serpent-tipped wand.

'Marric!'

From all over the Hippodrome, Marric's supporters took up the cry.

'Marric, Marric!'

Below Marric, on stage, even the actors were shouting. The audience, sensing the answer to their needs, joined in.

'Mar-ric, Mar-ric!'

They made his name into a chant. The paired syllables rang out deafeningly. Marric forced his chin higher, seeking to look like the palace sculptures of the gods, his face proud and immobile, his eyes staring past these mortals into infinity.

'*Mar-ric, Mar-ric!*'

Now they were stamping their feet. From the boxes of the aristocrats, from the doors into the arena itself, ran soldiers. Just as Marcellinus had planned, here was Marric's guard.

Irene's eyes locked with his. He saw rage there, a burning, almost mindless malevolence which a pyramid of skulls could not satisfy; a thirst for blood which she could not slake even by turning the Golden Horn red.

She stood and screamed something, bird-shrill. Red light spurted from her palms. Marric smelled hemp burning, felt the ropes supporting him high above the ground begin to tremble and slacken. Where were the stagehands? Let them lower him before he fell! As the ropes yielded to the fire, he felt himself swaying. Then they were lowering him. His feet touched ground, and he threw off the robes and harness of his role to stand free before the crowd in the purple silk of a prince of the city.

Irene shrieked words – a spell? – and threw the fragments of the white veil down. Then, in a storm of crimson silk, she rushed from the royal box.

Where had she gone?

Marcellinus ran up to Marric and embraced him, pounding his shoulders in a joyous victory dance completely unlike anything Marric had ever dreamt that the man might do. They were surrounded by all the men who had schemed with them: soldiers from the Mangana or the Fleet, nobles who had visited him in the safe house, even a few priests.

The chant of Marric's name and thunderous cheering washed over him. Nicephorus, Marric noted absently, was weeping.

Caius Marcellinus released him and gestured the others to fall back. Now those nearest him wore the white of the Candidatoi, the aristocrats among the city's soldiers. Marcellinus saluted, then himself stood aside as a much older man, his stern face a fined-down version of Marcellinus' own, came up beside his grandson. This was Valerius Marcellinus, Treasurer of the city, confidant to princes, his father's trusted minister – and now his.

Splendour gleamed, draped over the old patrician's out-stretched arms. He shook out the gleaming folds of a *paludamentum*, the triumphal cloak of the emperors. It shone white and silver and purple in the light of a thousand torches. Gems crusted it at throat and hem, and formed a blinding surface on the tablion at the cloak's right side. Slowly, he approached Marric and wrapped him in the ceremonial cloak of his heritage. It was much heavier than he expected.

The treasurer backed away from Marric, as if they were both at court. He bowed deeply, then bent his body in the full prostration accorded only to reigning emperors.

And the cheering continued as the Candidatoi and the nobles surrounded their lord and brought him out from the arena of his victory into the square.

Chapter Twenty-four

Carried from the Hippodrome on the shoulders of men shouting his name, with torches swooping and waving about him, Marric felt, not like the emperor they acclaimed, but like the god whose part he had taken. Why had he feared to take up this power? He had forgotten. It was exhilarating; he could see how people came to crave it like some rare drug.

Out of the gates of the Hippodrome the crowd of worshippers poured, heading for the palace. Only the Varangians might have withstood them, and Irene had ordered them imprisoned. The heavy folds of the cloak Valerius Marcellinus had laid upon Marric's shoulders were all that prevented him from feeling he could fly there like the hawk.

As the procession surged past the Temple of Isis, something small and fast shrieked his name and hurled itself down the steps and into the path of the mob. A woman! As dancing people shoved her, sending her sprawling, she screamed in panic. She would be trampled, Marric thought. This night of his triumph, no one should die – except Irene.

He held up a hand and the procession stopped.

'Lord Marric, please, my lord, please come!'

He signalled for his bearers to set him down. The paving felt oddly insubstantial. Part of him was still floating above the crowd and contemplating his own invulnerability. He walked forward to where the girl cowered in the midst of men with drawn swords, her face hidden in her hands. Then she turned to face him.

'Daphne! Why aren't you with your lady?'

She ran to him and fell at his feet. He lifted her and sensed how her slight body quivered under his hands. What was the child doing out alone? She clung to him, fearing him less than the crowd.

Marric placed her firmly on her feet and gave her a little shake. It would be hard to reassure her in this tumult of men whose eyes, teeth and weapons glittered in the torchlight.

'Why are you here, Daphne?'

'My lady . . . she sent me . . .'

'Alone at night through the streets?'

'Yes, yes, she sent me to beg you; come quickly, oh do come!'

'What's wrong, Daphne?' Marric lifted her off her feet.

'She sent me, said she had to send me away before . . .'

'What is it, Prince?' Marcellinus had come up beside Marric. His eyes widened as he recognized the girl.

'Get Nicephorus. Stephana sent her maid after me. Daphne, she sent you away before *what happened*?'

Except for the tears that poured down her face, Daphne had herself under control. 'My lady said . . . she said I should not be sacrificed to her fate.'

Stephana's cryptic remarks, her melancholy, even her passionate response to him that very evening: these were the actions of a woman who saw her fate reach out to seize her and dared not – would not – stand aside.

'NO!' Marric screamed that denial, and flung Daphne aside, so that the soldier nearest had to catch her. He ran out of the square, down the twisting streets. Sweat poured down his ribs; the heavy imperial cloak hindered his stride. But its weight was not as great a burden as the sudden, appalling fear of years of power, a desolate lifetime of royalty without Stephana close beside him.

Men followed him, but he outran them and came up gasping, one hand against his side, in the doorway of the little house. Just where a torch usually lit the way inside, the body of a man in a rusty tunic, rustier now with blood, sprawled. Even before Marric turned it over, he recognized one of the temple servants.

He pushed the heavy door open. The house felt vacant. Overturned chairs, polycandela lying askew, their lights snuffed, told a grim story. In the garden he found another of his men, dying from a throat wound, lying atop a man wearing the crimson livery of Irene's personal guard.

'No.' This time he whispered it. He forced himself to go on. The garden was trampled over. He saw more dead men, one lying headdown in the tiny fountain Stephana had loved. Did she foresee this? He had accounted for all but one of the house staff when that man staggered into his path. Marric caught him as he fell, and knelt beside him.

'Tell me!' he cried.

'Queen's men . . . the Red Empress with them . . . too many,' the man gasped. Bright blood streamed from his mouth and nose as well as from the sucking chest wound that would kill him in a moment or so. 'We . . . we fought, lord.'

'None better,' Marric assured him. The armsman coughed, a hideous, bubbling sound, and died.

He took the stairs to the upper floor three at a time and shouldered the door open. Stephana had summoned him, and he dreaded what he knew he would find.

A bloody dagger lay on the floor. It was the one he had given her. Had she fought at the end, knowing that her guards were dead? These outer rooms stank of power and evil magic that Marric could put an evil name to. Irene! He pushed on to the inner room.

The curtains, silvered one night by Isis' touch, were charred now. Tremendous energies had deflected against them to score the walls and trace black burns across toppled furniture. Shards of fragile glass crunched underfoot; the scents of ointments and perfumes mixed sickeningly with the remnants of Irene's magic.

'Stephana?'

He heard a faint whisper. She lay on their bed, looking almost as she had when he left her there. Now she wore a white shift. It was bloodstained from the dagger buried between her breasts.

She held the knife clasped in both reddening hands, as if she could hold her life within her by force of will.

Marric screamed and dropped to his knees beside her. He gathered her close, as if his touch could ward off her death. While he had been playing the god, exalted as ever any fool could dream of, imagining that everything he had ever wanted lay within his grasp, Irene had moved fast. Stephana – she must have sensed her death coming for her.

'Daphne found you,' Stephana's voice rose weakly. 'I am so glad.' She sighed. Her eyes lit at the sight of him. One of her hands fell limp against the dragging magnificence of his cloak. He pressed his lips against it and embraced her tightly. She cried out in pain.

'Forgive me!'

'It was my . . . veil,' Stephana whispered. 'I dropped it . . . the riot that day . . . she traced me.'

'You knew this!' he accused. Stephana nodded, then winced as even that slight movement brought pain.

'Knew . . . I told you . . . my fate. I was to help and not fear . . . you, my Marric. You. I did not know . . . it would be so fearful, or so sweet.'

It all came clear now. Stephana's pleas for courage, her grief when he tried to plan her future – that damned place in the country! – and the future of the children she knew she would never have: she knew, she knew. Dying at her feet in Alexandria, Marric had claimed her pity, demanded her help, then her love. Now, at the moment of his triumph, he had cost her her life, too.

Stephana's hand against his cheek was wet with more than her blood. Then Marric's tears dried.

'Tell me,' he begged.

For the last time their minds united and he relived that final evening:

Stephana woke from sleep as if roused by some long-awaited summons. She rose, threw on a shift, and summoned Daphne. Taking the child's hands in hers, she looked deep into her eyes and ordered, 'Fetch Prince Marric. Do not fear to seek him out wherever he may be. Once you leave this house, no harm will come to you: I swear it! Tell him . . .' Then the love that had weakened her in her quest for freedom from the Wheel surged up for the last time and made her rebel. Yes, she would accept release, but she would see him one last time. She had promised she would wait for him. 'Tell him I beg that he come to me with all haste. *Now run!*'

Daphne fled, and Stephana prepared herself. Marric was a warrior, a fighter born. He would expect her to defend herself. And she would not, she realized, lack for courage at the end. Not this time.

She spared a thought for the body she must cast aside tonight – lithe, well cared for now, and still tingling from her lover's embrace. It wanted to go on living, to enjoy the promises Marric had made. But Stephana had disciplined herself well. Though she knew it was futile, she picked up the jewelled dagger Marric had insisted she keep by her. Briefly, she cradled it against her cheek as if some essence of the giver remained in it.

From the moment she had lost her white veil in the riot, she had known to await this moment. The Goddess was merciful: Stephana would escape rebirth, there would be very little time to fear or to hurt, and she had even known love, coming at the end of a wretched life to transmute it into triumph. She fell into a trance to prepare herself.

Almost before she heard the death screams outside, she sensed her enemy's presence: female, savagely vengeful, filled with a malice more than human. Irene burst into the suite.

Stephana rose to face her. For a long moment, the women examined one another. Irene had power, great power that wreathed itself about her in a red-tinged aura. Stephana summoned her own defences in time to deflect bolts of crimson flame that charred the hangings, fused bright mosaics into black glass, and wrecked the peaceful rooms where, briefly, she had known such happiness.

'Why?' she asked the Red Empress.

'Ask him of my son. For one of mine, one of his,' Irene said. Her dark eyes shone like the gems on her garment. Again, fire erupted, and Stephana surrounded herself with a nimbus of white light. If Marric came, even now, he might stop Irene and she could live just a little longer. She wanted to. The force of that desire weakened her. Then fear surged up sickeningly, but not for herself. If Marric came now, he would die, crisped by fire he could not protect himself against. Stephana's heart went out to him: proud, so very proud, and unaware of what fate had in store for him.

Irene's next attack caught her by surprise. She screamed and lunged at Stephana with her dagger. More by chance than by skill, Stephana parried it, and her blade slipped off Irene's to score the Red Queen's arm. The sight of the blood she had drawn appalled Stephana for an instant. Her defences wavered . . . *hideous agony in her breast, and she fell back across her bed . . . heard Irene's laughter trailing away down the hall . . .*

'I fought,' she whispered.

'My brave one,' Marric wiped blood from her lips.

'No pain . . . now.' She had accepted her pain long enough to see Marric again. Now she could seek release. As Marric's mind slipped from contact with hers, he realized that though she saw her death as grief for him, she welcomed it as her own triumph.

'I cannot bear to lose you,' Marric said.

'You will not. But . . . let me go . . . for now.'

Marric stroked her long hair and brushed it back from her face. Stephana's eyes were filling with light, her lips parting as if she spoke to people he could not see. The unconsciousness that blessed men dying of wounds was not for her: if he wanted to help her, he must find some other way of easing her passage. He must accept it. Though he would have traded Empire and all at that moment to have her whole again, he bent and kissed her brow. 'Be free, Stephana.'

Feebly, she attempted to cast light around herself. He backed her with strength he didn't know he had. Into that light flowed other energies. Marric saw wraithlike faces he could not name.

221

Then Stephana tried to pull the dagger from her breast, to pass from life to the Horizon more swiftly. Her hands slipped on the hilt, too weak for the task.

'Pull the blade out,' Marric's master-of-arms had always said, 'and the man dies mercifully.'

'You will indeed be the death of me,' Stephana had told him. He did not want to be responsible for her death. But he was. And he couldn't deny her easy passage.

Kissing her again, he gathered her close. 'Don't look, beloved,' he whispered, and laid his hands over hers on the hilt. He used all his strength to draw it quickly from the wound. As the hilt, unshielded by contact with her flesh, blistered his palm with the residuum of Irene's power, he hurled it from him. The blade skidded over the floor, and he heard other people in the room recoiling from it.

Stephana's head fell against his shoulder, and her eyes closed. She sighed, and he caught her last breath in his lips.

Marric bent his head over hers and fell forward on to the bed. He could hear Daphne weeping, but his own grief dried his eyes and clutched at his throat so that he could make no sound. The gemmed cloak he had been so proud of lay over him and his dead lover, enclosing them in a darkness that he wished were forever.

Chapter Twenty-five

When Marric raised his head, he knew precisely what he had to do and where he needed to go before he could squeeze the life from Irene with his own bloodstained hands. He rose. Very tenderly, he straightened Stephana's body. Then he stripped off the oppressive splendour of his cloak and draped it over her. There was a crimson splotch of her blood on the pearls, moonstones and woven silver. He thought that that was fitting. If the Empire were bought at the price of Stephana's blood, it were bought too dearly.

He had been a fool again. He had been a fool to fear Stephana's powers, a fool to think he could manage without them. If he had only been a magician, his love might be alive now. But, he vowed, he wouldn't tarnish his memories of Stephana with guilt and regret.

Stephana belonged with her own. The priestesses would care for her. So he would take her to the Temple of Isis. Surely the Goddess would give him a sign, a way to use the rage that surged up in him like fire through drought-parched fields. That rage, he knew, was dangerous. It would devour him – as could the magic. But he would not allow that to happen.

Marric gathered his dead love up in his arms. Her hair cascaded down on to the cloak, and the pure line of her throat had a pathetic beauty that tore at him.

Why can I not weep? Marric thought. It seemed impious. But if he could not mourn for her, there must be someone gentler than he, someone innocent of blood.

'Where do you go, my lord?' Daphne gasped.

'To the Temple of Isis, Daphne.' Here was a mourner for Stephana. 'Will you accompany your mistress there one last time?'

The Goddess would protect Stephana's poor body now that he, try as he might, had failed to keep life within it. He would leave her in Isis' care. And then he would go and kill Irene. And if he had to use magic or be used by it, so be it. It couldn't hurt him worse than he had already been hurt.

His men crowded into the battered house and murmured at the slaughter. As he walked past them, they fell silent. Nicephorus held out a hand to him. 'Mor?'

There would be time later to hear everyone's lamentations. Now Marric must take Stephana home. Outside, soldiers swarmed in the street, holding back passers-by and the adoring mob that had screamed his name in triumph while the Empress cut out his heart.

Like a sleepwalker, Marric moved past them, taking the turns and twists to the Temple of Isis without thinking of his way. The simple actions of carrying the cloak-swathed body in his arms, of placing one foot before the other, of not crying out in rage and dashing to the palace, kept his thoughts at bay.

Daphne walked behind him. Despite her fear, she was determined not to abandon her mistress. As he walked up the steps into the portico, she followed. The square was filled. The folk who had chanted his name whispered it now as the story passed from one person to the next.

The ancient High Priestess barred his entry into the temple.

'You have blood on you,' she pointed out, her voice distant.

Marric knew that Isis' deepest mysteries were not for men. But overriding knowledge, overriding sense was the command of his instincts: Stephana must be returned home.

'In the rituals,' Marric said hesitantly, 'Isis succours Osiris. She does not die. But look! Here is one of her priestesses slain. Mother priestess, Stephana's spirit flees to the Horizon without honour. Is that right? And can you honestly say that there is no blood – ever – in what you do? Or deny any of your daughters entrance here? Go on, Daphne.' Stephana's maid slipped past him into the shadowy entrance of the temple, and the High Priestess allowed it.

'She is the maiden,' Marric said. 'You are the sibyl, and Stephana – she should have been the bride.'

The priestess' eyes softened, and she held out her arms. 'The Goddess will welcome her. I shall call my daughters to bear her within.'

'No. I had a vision once. The Goddess appeared to me and told me, "The time has not come for you to invade the women's mysteries." But that time has come now. Let me pass, lady.'

The High Priestess stood aside. With Daphne guiding him along the way that no man had walked since the temple was consecrated, Marric entered the innermost shrine. Sweet incense burnt in copper braziers. The fires cast shadows on to the walls and stroked the mosaics and paintings into vivid life. Dominating the room was a monumental statue of the Goddess, her wings outspread, sheltering an altar carved of the same unpainted marble as itself. Statue and altar glistened in the radiance of the giant silver polycandelon hanging high above. Marric's eyes blurred as he laid Stephana down on the altar. He touched her face, thinking to mould the motionless features into some sort of calm, but Stephana had died in triumph. Her bloodless lips were parted in a smile he still could not understand.

Daphne helped him smooth the gemmed cloak into ordered folds. Except where Stephana's blood had darkened them, the jewels on the tablion glistened moon white. The girl crept to the foot of the altar and crouched there.

Marric backed away from the image of the Goddess, richly adorned in gemmed necklaces and fine silks. Then he prostrated himself before it.

The Goddess' face blurred in the light. Now she looked like a maid even younger than Daphne, innocent and joyous. The light playing on her perfectly carved features shifted, and she looked like a stately woman of middle years, her beauty enriched with experience and a mother's love. He had seen this aspect of the Goddess before, when he had journeyed, sorely wounded, into that other world and chosen to return. He had known it as a child, had had it to warm him for too brief a time.

'Take care of her for me, Mother,' he entreated.

From aspect to aspect, the face shifted. Marric contemplated it in awe. Finally, the Goddess' face became incredibly venerable, wise with visions like those by which Stephana had shaped her life and, at the last, transcended it.

Above him, the polycandelon swayed. Was it only the flickering of its lights that made the statue change its appearance?

A priestess slipped into the shrine. She filled several of the braziers, then walked over to inspect the chains that suspended the polycandelon. Marric found himself observing her movements, not because of their grace but because she appeared to favour one arm. As she struggled to lift that arm towards the chains, hissing under her breath at the pain, Marric saw that her arm had been bound up hastily with a silk veil, the way a man might bandage a knife-scratch after despatching his enemy.

Irene!

Just as the polycandelon crashed down from the ceiling, Marric flung himself to one side. Silver branches buckled and tore free of the heavy base that would have crushed his skull. Sweet-scented oil puddled on to the floor, then burst into flames that spread to the dry, ancient wood within the shrine, and licked towards the trappings of the Goddess' statue.

The wounded priestess laughed, a shrill, evil sound. He had last heard it in Stephana's memories.

'Damn you!' Marric shouted, and started after her. He could survive a few burns. All the while he was healing, he would remember how his hands had felt as they closed around her neck and snapped it. The leaping flames cast a red light over Irene, who looked as if she stood bathed in blood. Soon he would have her in his hands, he exulted. Irene ran to one of the walls. A touch released a block of dressed masonry, and she slipped within the doorway thus formed.

Marric hurled himself at the opening. Sooner or later the passages had to lead to the palace itself, didn't they? In the days of the adept-rulers, what had such passages been used for?

The secret door was sliding shut, but in three . . . two . . . more steps Marric would—

Daphne shrieked.

Marric spun round. The block slammed shut behind Irene. Daphne screamed again, then started laughing the panicky high laughter of hysteria. She still crouched at Stephana's feet. But gradually she was inching along on her knees to put the altar and her mistress' body between herself and the fire which twisted up the beams to the roof. The way to the door was blocked and the flames were out of control.

They cast furious lights on the cloak, on the ruined polycandelon, and the great statue, wrapped now in burning silks. Daphne wore light cotton garments. In another instant she would lose the rest of her nerve and run screaming into the flames. Marric had freed her. He was responsible for her. And he had brought her here.

'Daphne, hold!' he commanded.

Flames rushed up between them. They might die in the shrine, burnt offerings to Stephana's spirit, which neither needed nor wanted such sacrifices.

Some suicidal fragment of himself – the last surviving bit that the Empire had not claimed as its own – cried that the burning could be no worse than his guilt at Stephana's death, or the lust for vengeance which throbbed in his veins. Let him simply throw himself down beside Stephana and lie there until the fire devoured them both.

Daphne screamed again, a high-pitched, mindless keening, and Marric put aside fantasies of suicide. Daphne had loved Stephana and deserved better of Marric than for him to abandon her.

In all the rituals in which Marric had ever participated, the strength of his body and spirit had been something to be used by others. Now he must summon and harness it himself. He had sworn by Stephana's death not to fear her powers – and to try to make them his. He had not expected to be forced to fulfil that vow quite so soon. But it was right that he do so in her presence.

Marric stared into the flames. Fire could be doused. The ground could smother it, or water could drown it.

There was no earth, no water here. That left air – a gust of wind to blow the flames aside.

He reached out and stripped the ceremonial cloak from Stephana's body. Let the fire free her quickly. The heavy fabric of the cloak would shelter him and Daphne. He swung it about his shoulders. Then he extended his hands sharply downward and out. Energy radiated from them up around his body. He shut his eyes against the leaping, deadly flames that danced nearer and nearer. They cast ghastly crimson shadows on Daphne's contorted face. But now she was rising to her knees, biting her hand to stifle her screams. Wonder drove the insane fear from her eyes. Closer yet: the fire cast a cruel illusion of rosy life on to Stephana's pallid features.

No. The flames must part. Marric did not ask that they go out, for such was not the nature of fire. But he did ask them to divide as if wind brushed them. That much the fire could do. And that much it must do.

The effort of concentrating on moving the blaze forced a moan

227

from him. His eyes squeezed so tightly shut that red and orange patterns leapt before him. Sweat scalded down his sides.

Flames, part! he commanded silently. He visualized his desire and focused all his will upon it. The flames must part so that he could rescue a child and an empire.

Again Marric's hands moved. He looked up and saw the flames bow down on either side of a narrow path, to form an aisle twice his height. He would have just enough time to reach Daphne and escape, assuming his will or the beams of the shrine did not crumble first.

'Daphne!' He ran to her and swathed her in his cloak.

'My lady—'

'She is at peace. Now it is our turn. Be brave a little longer, child.' Panic would bring the fires down upon them. Already that path of safety to the door had narrowed. Tiny runnels of fire danced on the scorched stone. Marric lifted the girl, hid her face against him, and started for the door. Fire licked at him. He smelled his hair scorching. But the heavy cloak protected them both.

Out of the sanctuary he walked, as carefully as if he led some procession. Behind him, the fires of Irene's malice roared into new life, engulfing the room. A crash as the ceiling caved in broke Marric out of his trance. He turned just in time to see the great statue of Isis, unstained by fire or smoke, appear to nod at him before the fire and debris hid it. Then he was running out into the portico and down the steps, into the safety and the heavenly coolness of the night air.

The priestesses stood watching their temple burn. Tears poured unheeded down their faces and glinted in the firelight. Nicephorus and Marcellinus ran up to him. Marric set Daphne on her feet.

'Irene started the fire,' he told the men. 'But this time, I almost had her.'

'Storm the palace?' suggested Marcellinus. 'With the Varangians under arrest, we can take anything she throws at us.'

'Except magic. And for the second time in one night, my home will be turned into a slaughterhouse!' Marric snapped. 'I will not have my name be a symbol for bloodbath. Caius, Irene would make living torches of your men. Truly, she exists only to destroy now.'

Marric thought rapidly. 'But if Irene learned the inner ways, I can too. If . . . yes. A small force might move fast and strike within the palace. To the temple!'

Above the roar of flame and the clamour of excited people in the forum, over the deep-voiced orders of soldiers trying to keep them away and unharmed, came the thunder of drums and sharp music of horns and sistrums. Out from the Temple of Osiris came its priests. The High Priest, wearing full regalia, led them. He extended his hands in a gesture much like the one Marric had used to control the fire.

Above his head appeared light which formed into the manifestation of a giant hawk, sigil of Horus and the Emperors. It rose and circled the forum three times. Then, after it had captured everyone's attention, it hovered over Marric's head and cast brilliant golden light upon him to reveal him to the crowd: weary, his face streaked with soot, his mantle scorched and smeared with ash and blood.

'Marric! Emperor!' The voices were joined by a rhythmic clatter of swords against shields as soldiers acclaimed him too. In a minute, they would escape from his control and attack the palace, bringing upon themselves the magical holocaust Marric dreaded.

'Let the crowd go to the palace, but restrain them!' he ordered Marcellinus. He heard his orders being relayed. 'Then I want you, Nico, you men, too – come with me!'

They ran up the stairs to the High Priest.

'Irene used the inner ways to slip in and fire the shrine,' Marric spoke fast. 'She tried to kill me, damned near did, too. The inner ways . . . open them to us!'

Against the blasphemy of destroying one of the great centres of Isis worship, what was the lesser hubris of donning the mask of a god? The Osiris priest nodded assent. Marric thought he saw tears in the old man's eyes, then blamed it on the smoke from the ruined temple. There was no time for mourning: the old priest kept secrets Marric needed, and was agreeing to reveal them.

'I shall lead you as far as I can,' he said. 'Prince, may the gods favour you in this, as in all else.'

Marric passed again within the Temple of Osiris. This time the walls themselves opened to receive him.

Chapter Twenty-six

The High Priest led them through the temple and down winding, shallow stairs into the passages. At his urgent command, they pressed against the righthand wall. To their left, the way dropped into the echoing darkness of a pit. At another turning, the priest counted the stone blocks, counted them again, and then carefully pressed the beak of a hawk carved in high relief.

As his companions passed that place, he gestured upward. High overhead, sharp-pointed spears lay ready to fall on anyone passing by without intimate knowledge of the ways.

These passages reminded Marric of Alexandria – which was to say, of a particularly large and lethal trap.

How many snares were there? Marric did not dare to ask. He had heard old tales of such places, and of traps which men too foolish to know when to keep silent might spring upon themselves.

– *Many such* – said the priest in his mind. – *Order your people to keep close; blood should not be shed in here by accident.* –

Marric waved Marcellinus to move in closer. His two – no, three – guards followed. There was something strange about the third man-at-arms, whose mantle almost dragged along the ground. It was Daphne. What was she doing here?

Marric caught Nicephorus' arm and pointed.

– *You were so intent on following the priest that she escaped your eye* – Nicephorus spoke mind to mind. – *Would you have left her alone in that mob?* –

Irritation at the girl – *she will slow us; one of the men will have to look after her* – nettled Marric, but he dared not speak. Finally, the priest stopped before a carved wall. When he touched various parts of the ideographs that covered it, a block slid aside.

'From here on, you may speak in safety,' he whispered. 'Through this passage lies the second level of the ways.'

'You knew about her!' Marric accused.

'Thea has a right to be in at the kill,' said Nicephorus.

'This is not a hunt!'

'But it is,' said the High Priest. 'You hunt along these tracks to punish the woman who has used unlawful sorcery. She has injured this child, too. Let her decide now whether to go on or to turn back.'

Marric beckoned to her. 'Why, Daphne?' he asked.

Daphne pushed back her tangled hair. For the first time in Marric's acquaintance with her, she dared to meet his eyes. 'Prince, you come because you must. These loyal men come with you. Nicephorus comes because he is wise and will never leave you. I am not wise, nor very brave – but, oh, master, I loved her too.'

Marric nodded, acknowledging Daphne's claim. When he closed in final challenge with Irene, there should be one witness who was motivated by love, and by love alone.

Caius Marcellinus hissed in impatience. 'This is a ridiculous strike force!'

'As the priest says,' Marric answered, 'we are not a strike force. We are a hunt.'

'I will keep up,' Daphne promised.

The High Priest beckoned them on.

Here the stonework shone with that same light that Marric had seen in the chamber that held the sarcophagus of his aborted attempt at initiation. The light unmarred by shadow daunted him.

'We are nowhere near,' the priest reassured him in an undertone.

'Does Irene know these ways?'

'I would be surprised if she did. Many of our walls can be changed. How she learned the inner ways leading to the Temple of Isis – the Dark Goddess must have revealed them to her. We have all become too slack. Who would ever have thought that the temples must defend themselves against the palace?'

Marric thought of the ages-dead Greek who ruled long before the Empire was ever formed. Old Draco had made no laws against the slaying of parents because he thought it a crime too hideous for humans to perform. Like the priests, he had been overtrusting.

'This place is warded,' Nicephorus whispered. 'Feel the power!'

They descended flight after flight of stairs and passed through chambers lined with stores. These levels might be places of study and access to the palace. They were also an efficient line of defence. Marcellinus nodded appreciatively.

'This is a labyrinth,' he noted. 'I think we have walked a distance much greater than that from the temple to the palace.' He waved at his men and at Daphne. 'Stay together. Fall behind, and you may wander forever.' Fear roughened his voice. Marric could well understand it. What would Caius do against the Watcher? Probably no better than he. Marric would be very glad, he decided, to exchange these light-filled passages for honest stone.

By now the regiments and the crowd would have followed the hawk-sigil to the palace. Marric could visualize the scene: night paling towards dawn, the golden hawk swooping over the walls and, far below, subjects held barely in check by soldiers loyal to him.

Fierce gladness filled him as he thought of Irene's execution. Both Nicephorus and the priest winced; Daphne looked up in sudden alarm. Some quality in the air or the light down here must intensify thoughts and emotions for those sensitive to them, Marric decided. His emotions burned hotter here; the violence of his feelings caused the adepts pain. Then Daphne must have some marginal sensitivities, too! He could not consider that.

Power, Marric concluded, created its own backlash. An important lesson for him to learn. He would himself be the backlash for Irene.

They had reached the end of the light-filled corridors and come up against a wall of roughly hewn grey stone.

'Here our defences end,' said the priest. 'You will find torches on the other side of this slab. Keep to the right, always to the right, and walk carefully. When faced with a turning, take every third right upward. Nicephorus, do not summon light. Instead, use a torch.'

The soldiers, followed by Nicephorus and Daphne, knelt for the priest's blessing. Before he realized, Marric was kneeling too. Thin hands clasped his temples in a gesture more fierce than the conventional laying on of hands in benediction. Knowledge of the path ahead entered Marric's mind. He could guide his people into the palace – assuming nothing blocked their way.

The High Priest activated the wall-mechanism. The stone ground aside slowly, as if long unused. The narrow opening revealed only blackness.

'Daphne, do you come with us?'

Daphne stepped forward into the darkness before the others. She lifted a torch down from the rack she found, and lit it with the flint lying nearby.

When six torches bobbed in the corridor, the priest raised his hands to bless them again. His face, serene against the white light, was the last thing they saw before the stone slab moved back into place. They turned towards the palace.

'What a spot for a fight!' Marcellinus commented. 'Ten men at the head of this stair could hold off a regimental wing for hours.'

'I do not think Irene has the regiment to throw at us,' Marric said. He started up the first of the many stairways ahead. Three landings, then a turn to the right. Three more flights upward, then right again. It was like climbing through a shell, Marric thought. He halted abruptly. Here the air seemed thicker and fouler. The torch he carried flared, then guttered close to extinction. Now it gave off a graveside glow that drew an answering light from moss on the rotten wood that shored up the walls. *Like that dungeon*, Marric thought.

'Careful of the air here,' said Marric.

'I have patrolled the mines, lord,' one of the men spoke up. 'This is not—' he screamed, a sound that exploded into a gurgle as he clutched his throat and staggered around the curve of the stair. Then he fell. His torch dropped with him, like a pale meteor, into the pit beside the stairs.

'What made him fall?'

Nicephorus paused beside Marric and extended his own torch. It burnt on, unchanged. So did Daphne's. The light, extending out to several feet, showed that only one side of the passageway was walled. They walked a winding shelf along a high cliff, it seemed. Daphne dropped her too-long cloak and kilted up her skirts.

Keeping close to Nicephorus, Marric ventured up the last few stairs to stand on a narrow walk. A frail bridge arched across that unfathomable gap.

'Quickly.' If they stopped to think what might have turned the air foul, what had killed the armsman, they might fall themselves. Marcellinus coughed rackingly. The air was getting worse.

Marric crossed first, followed by Nicephorus. Marric turned and held out a hand to Daphne. He found himself aiding a soldier, who was then followed by Marcellinus.

Had Daphne panicked again?

She shook her head. Neither the foul air nor vertigo affected her as they had the men. Her torch still burned bravely. Stepping out on to the narrow walkway, she balanced as easily as a bazaar urchin walking an orchard wall that separates her from the fruit she wants to steal.

Good girl! Having lit the men's ways, she waited to cross until she was sure of their safety.

Then Marric heard a cracking, as of stone giving way.

'Daphne, quick!' His hand dug into her arm just as the bridge collapsed in on itself. The light from Daphne's torch cast long shadows as it fell.

'Cloaks over your heads,' gasped Marcellinus.

Marric gagged at the smell of something dead and long-decaying. He steadied Daphne and considered. She was motivated only by love – and did not suffer from the foul air. Nicephorus, too, appeared untroubled. Whatever this was, it attacked selectively. It was not *real* in the same way that the soldier it killed had been real: it was a lethal and highly effective sorcery.

Around Marric the air grew fouler and fouler until he collapsed, gasping, on his knees. He grew angry, and his mind whitened almost to unconsciousness. He could not breathe, he was falling, falling into a pit like the man they had lost on the stairs . . .

Nicephorus caught him and held him hard.

234

'Don't fight it, Mor. Think!'

Think . . . of what? A stinking hold where slaves lay tangled together and a prince had been thrown in among them . . . had struggled then, too, until Nicephorus had befriended him. A comforting thing to think of. Nico was no warrior, yet he had survived initiation when one bout with the Watcher left Marric sick. Strength . . . Nico had strength enough to adapt and to accept. Stephana, too, had possessed that sort of strength.

He, too – had he not vowed over her body to cease challenging the Powers?

Marric drew a deep, shuddering breath. For one moment – sheer indulgence before the real fighting started – he let his head rest against Nicephorus' shoulder. He could hear Daphne's breathy, tremulous voice urging Marcellinus and his men 'Easy . . . steady now . . .' The priest had been right to refer to this chase through the secret ways as a hunt: as with most hunts, the most patient, not the strongest, were frequently the most successful.

Marric rose gingerly to his feet. To his surprise, he still held a torch, had apparently tightened his grip on it as he fell, in the same way that any man, falling from a height, will claw loose pebbles and stalks of weeds. He raised the torch over his head and it woke into rich, golden flame.

'Come on,' he urged.

The stair turned several more times before walls rose. At the end of a long, straight flight there loomed a door. Nicephorus reached it first and pushed. The door opened only enough to admit a narrow beam of light. Marric saw his companions' faces: Nicephorus, as keen as if he hunted his quarry over a sunlit field; Daphne, the timidity in her expression gone forever; Marcellinus and his surviving man, haggard with the strain that he, too, felt.

'Stand back, Nico, Daphne. If we put our shoulders to that door, we should be able to move it.'

The great door creaked open into a wide hall bare of all furniture, deadfalls or men-at-arms.

'This is too easy,' Marcellinus whispered. 'We enter, the door locks behind us, and the Red Empress sends in her killers.'

'The door only locks from this side,' said Nicephorus.

'I think it was *left* unbarred,' Marric concluded. 'If people win

235

through to the palace, there has to be one last line of defence . . . nothing to harm friends, but something effective enough to take out some very stubborn enemies. I don't think we're going to face human adversaries here.'

'What shall we face, my lord?' the soldier asked fearfully.

The man reminded Marric of himself, resenting the powers of the unseen world, fearing them, and finally beginning to adapt, to accept them and use them to protect himself.

'In the ways, when I almost fell,' Marric said, 'I felt rage. At that moment I would have traded my birthright for Irene's neck between my hands.'

'Feelings,' Daphne spoke up. 'They will – she will send emotions, our own emotions back at us.' She snuffed her torch and joined Marric in the wide passage.

'Get back!' The place needed to be tested, and Marcellinus knew it.

'We haven't the time,' said Marric. 'How long do you think the mob will be held back?'

He strode down the hall. Waves of emotion battered at him. First came lust, seeking to tantalize him, then to drain him, but he had known love and could not mistake one for the other. Ambition: but Marric *was* rightfully the Emperor. He sought only to gain what was his. Rage came next, but his thirst for blood seemed to have fallen into the pit in his place. Grief followed, and it hit him hard. He had had no time to mourn Stephana's death. He slackened his pace. Tears he had thought himself unable to shed poured from his eyes. Uncertainty followed grief: his father's misgivings, the priest's concern, Alexa falling into the grip of dark magic. Who was Marric to think that *he* could prevail, or use the power in his blood without being corrupted by it? Hubris. Hadn't he felt like a god that evening in the Hippodrome? Look what it had cost him. Far better for someone like him to give up and mourn. That way he could do no harm. There was no hope.

No.

Marric would not let his grief destroy him. Stephana would not approve. And despair – the absence of hope – could not be trusted. If a slave, beaten, naked and dying, could be restored to life and acclaimed as the ruler of Byzantium, there was always hope.

And if he had not summoned whatever magic he could summon to burn, to rend, to torment after Stephana died in pain, then he would not.

The despair Irene sent at him washed through him. Then it ebbed, a catharsis that reassured even as it purified. He would survive all the stronger for his doubts and errors. He reached the end of the hall and turned to the people who watched him.

'Accept and master anything you feel,' he called to them. 'Just keep moving.'

As Marric's companions crossed, the hall erupted into mass hallucinations. Its dark walls spurted imaginary Greek fire. Huns with arrows on their bowstrings galloped from side to side. Three pirates with scimitars tore a shrieking girl-child from her grandfather, then despatched him with one blow. The roughly paved floor seemed awash with blood. But the fire did not sizzle flesh, the child screamed soundlessly, and the arrows never whizzed out to pierce bodies.

Now Nicephorus extended his hands and summoned a pale, golden light which wrapped about him and sent out tendrils to the others.

Do not run!

Marric wanted to shout that. If they panicked, they would slip in that imaginary blood; the arrows and flames would turn real and consume them. Already the fire licked nearer. Nicephorus was weakening from his efforts to protect their party.

Marric took a deep breath, attempting to visualize energy flowing from himself to the scholar. He concentrated on an image of Nicephorus standing firm, arms outstretched to protect his friends. With a glad cry, as if she woke from a nightmare, Daphne freed herself from the barrage in the hall. She walked up to the pirates as they tore the child from the old man again.

'That was years ago,' she said. 'I have done my grieving. Now I am free. I will pass here.' She walked through the illusion and came to stand beside Marric. Taking his hand, she helped him aid Nicephorus as he guided Marcellinus and the soldier through the hallucinations. As they neared, the task became easier. Then the floor seemed suddenly to drop away, as the men relived how their comrade had clutched his throat and fallen into nothingness.

'Steady,' Nicephorus murmured. Strength flowed out of Marric into him as Nico tensed for one last effort. Leading the others, he stepped out over the pit that seemed to yawn beneath his feet.

Marric demanded silently that he see paving stones there again instead of emptiness. Gradually the stones solidified. And they were across. Nicephorus slumped against the wall.

'I am sorry, Nico, that there is no time for you to rest,' Marric said. 'Daphne, help him along. Caius, the gates—'

Ahead lay another corridor and a flight of stairs. Daphne flung her arm about Nicephorus' waist and started towards it. Marric looked at the stairs. The instincts that had saved him tonight told him that they were clear, that all the killer illusions, all the traps lay behind them, not before them.

'I would prefer a human foe,' said Marcellinus. 'I shall rejoin my regiment at the gates.'

'No killing!' Marric ordered. 'Not unless you have no other choice.' They were coming into the central parts of the palace now. The cut stone of the foundations was overlaid by marble and travertine. Soon they would approach the royal suites. 'Get moving,' Marric ordered the commander.

'I'll send you reinforcements, my Prince.'

Marcellinus saluted, then left quickly. Now they hastened past an arcade that opened on to a garden. The east began to glow. After the stink of the underground ways, the air was very sweet. Overhead hovered the giant hawk. As the rising sun struck it, the hawk shimmered and altered shape. It became a phoenix, symbol of rebirth and a new age.

Now the doors through which they passed were silver. Lamps hung from jewelled chains, and the floors they crossed were gem-bright mosaics or Parian marble. Marric knew these halls well. How not? He had spent his childhood in them. Near this shrine on the left, close to that throne room down the hall (where as a boy, Marric had particularly liked to go, because of its mechanical lions), was the suite his parents had shared. At least his father had never brought Irene to those rooms: her quarters, which were even more lavish, lay further on. They were nearing them.

Slaves stationed nearby fled as the small company approached and they recognized Marric. They came to the doors of Irene's suite. A soldier flung them open and Marric walked past him into the audience chamber.

Chapter Twenty-seven

The silver doors were balanced so delicately that Daphne could shut them, and did, before Marric had had time to think of barring her entrance. This was no place for the child.

In arrogant declaration of Irene's usurped title, she had had the walls of her presence chamber newly faced with porphyry. It glowed crimson in the light of a tarnished polycandelon. On a massive table lay implements – a curiously shaped knife, its hilt wound with black and scarlet cords, candles wrought in forms Marric refused to do more than glance at, a goblet, and several books bound in yellowing ivory and old leather. He hoped it was simply leather. Behind him, Nicephorus hissed in distaste and made warding-off gestures.

Turning from that sinister table, Marric faced the woman who sat in an immense porphyry throne cushioned with scarlet. As he had seen her the night that men dragged him from his dungeon, Irene was garbed with imperial splendour. She wore an unbelted silk robe. Her long, lustrous hair hung down her back like a lavish cloak. On it rested the imperial crown, a gemmed circlet with fillets hanging from it. Marric longed to seize it from that unworthy head.

Irene's face was very pale. She sat immobile, as if the force of her tremendous will alone held some terrible shock in check. If she was countering the backlash of her deflected necromancies,

239

she concealed her struggle superbly. Her eyes, intense and far too bright, gazed out into vacancy like the icon of some fallen goddess. Only her hands moved. They twisted a ruined collar of rubies and gold. The last time Marric had been in the same room as Irene, she had lashed him across the face with it.

Her immobility stripped the moment of anger or of triumph. Marric stopped at some distance from her.

'Irene.'

Gradually, awareness returned to the usurper's dark eyes. She withdrew from the trance she had entered to block their passage through the underground ways. She had been very beautiful once, Marric remembered. Now her olive skin was ashen, the full red mouth too dark, too bitter, and twisted from her night's failures.

'So you have come for revenge. Emperor, you call yourself,' her voice was pure vitriol, 'and don't you just look like one.'

Marric's silken garments were marked with sweat and blood, and with grime from the passages. His cloak, too, was blood-stained and scorched by the fires through which he had run.

'Not for vengeance,' he said, remembering Audun Bearmaster. 'I come for law.'

Marric stood straight, almost at attention. When he had last been in this room, men had forced him to his knees before Irene. She had stood so close to him that he could smell the musk of her perfumes. As she had intended, he had trembled in hateful, involuntary response. Now as he looked at her, he felt nothing. He had passed through bloodshed, heartbreak, flame, and even triumph. Now remained only what must be done.

He was Emperor. He must pronounce judgement.

'So righteous, are you not, with the blood on your hands?' Irene taunted him. 'Or do you think that simply because you're a competent general, you can hold on to the Empire? That takes more than strength of arms. Its enemies—'

'*Your* enemies.' Marric cut through her words. 'My father – whose memory you betray – held our neighbours in check. You outraged them and turned allies into enemies. You cannot hold what you stole, Irene. Give it up!'

'Before you snatch it from me? The Empire needs far more

than armies. It needs magic, which I possess. Test my strength, Marric. Come here and take the crown from me. If you dare.'

Marric took a step forward, then paused. Irene looked drained of power. But that might be a supreme act to make him approach her, touch her, and be blasted by the fires she could summon. He had diverted death by fire or falling in the arena, death by treachery or open attack tonight, and then run a magical barrage.

And I am no priest, he thought.

'Take off the crown,' he ordered.

Irene laughed.

'Stand up!' ordered the armsman who had come with Marric, angered at hearing her defy his lord.

'No!' Marric shouted. 'Don't touch her. She is dangerous – and once she was my father's consort.'

Defying both men, Irene rose and came towards them. Worn and defeated she might be, but her body still possessed a sinuous grace she could use as a weapon.

'I should have an axe,' she taunted Marric. 'Or perhaps I could merely open my robe and lay claims of parentage upon you like some vulgar Clytaemnestra. But I think it as well that *you* remain the only actor in the family. Such cheap theatrics, playing Apollo before the screaming mob. Will you shed my blood now? Beware, lest I summon Furies of my own to strike you down!'

'You are not Clytaemnestra. And I am not Orestes,' said Marric. 'Take off the crown.'

'And then what? There is a mob outside. Of your rousing, no doubt. Will you give me to them?'

In some way Irene would accept that, would welcome a savage death as a sign of his failure to control himself. There were punishments for lack of control. He had felt them. If he failed now, he would pay later.

'Always destruction,' he answered. 'That is *your* way. The Varangians who might have held loyal to you and the crown you still wear are imprisoned by your orders. Now you have nothing beyond the choices I make for you.'

He turned to Nicephorus. 'Find physicians. This will not be a murder, but an execution. For all the gods' sakes, Irene, you have been a queen. Die like one!'

'As your father died? How *did* your father die, Prince? Do you know?'

'Did you contrive his death, too?' Marric had often tortured himself with that very question. *This is for you, too, my father.*

Irene seemed to grow in stature. Then, as if the effort were too great, she dwindled. 'I never came first with him, not I nor my son. There was always the Empire, or his love for you and that sister of yours. Even the memory of your dull mother.'

Alexander had married her to keep watch on a treacherous minor sept of the imperial line. He had been right. He had paid for his rightness with his life. Then, maddened by her son's death, Irene had become like the tiger who kills a man once and then craves more and more blood. And, at the last, she had sought not love, but worship. Her passions had destroyed her as surely as some venom or other had slain his father. And the worship she gained was the terror men accord beings whose ways are incomprehensible, swift and terrible.

'I killed your wench myself, you know,' she said. 'That mewling piece of sanctity tried to fight. She lacked the courage to kill.'

His Stephana, dying in his arms. For an instant, anger rose in Marric's blood. Irene smiled, white teeth shining.

'That hurt you, didn't it? But you and Alexa murdered my son, didn't you? A life for a life.'

Behind them, the doors swung open. Nicephorus entered with two palace physicians. They hesitated, not knowing whether to acknowledge Marric or prostrate themselves before Irene. A guard gestured at them with a sheathed dagger.

'Poison,' Marric ordered. 'See that it is quick-acting and painless.' A physician bowed, then started towards Irene's ritual vessels. 'Stay clear! Those are hers. You cannot trust them.'

'Get me a cup of wine,' the man ordered Daphne. As she obeyed, they all stood waiting silently, except Irene.

'Another slavegirl, Marric?' she goaded him again. 'Whatever do you see in them? And when you could have had—'

'Alexa lives,' he said. 'As our father and mother intended, we shall rule together and heal this land.'

Daphne brought cup and wine to Marric for approval, then presented them to the physicians. Stephana had taught her that courtesy. Even as the physicians unstopped tiny phials and poured their contents into the dark wine, Marcellinus entered, a troop of soldiers at his back.

'The crowd disperses, my Emperor,' he reported, saluting. 'I detached some of my regiment to free the Varangians.'

Nicephorus walked about the audience chamber, pushing aside heavy draperies. Dawn flooded the room, and Irene winced at the bright light. She seemed to age and diminish before Marric's eyes. She had failed with his father, with Marric and his sister, even with her son. She had failed with the Empire. Her magic had only served to drain her. Now she was weary of life and magic both: her defences were only the struggles of a demonic spirit in its final moment before the priest exorcises it.

'Give her the cup,' Marric ordered the physicians.

The men brought it to her carefully. They feared that she might dash its contents in their faces. Two of Marcellinus' officers moved in.

'These men will conduct you to your bedchamber,' said Marric. 'I assume you wish to meet your death with dignity. Lady, take up the cup.'

Irene lifted the goblet. It was a plain silver thing. As her hands folded around it, the metal began to tarnish. She raised the cup in an ironic salute.

'I will not drink to your health, *Emperor*. So you will wear my crown after my death: what of it? With it, take my curse: as long as you wear that crown, you will never know peace.'

Several of the soldiers clutched amulets or made the sign against evil.

Irene turned on her heel and walked into the inner room. Her robes swayed with a desolate grace.

'If you only knew,' Marric whispered to the doors as they shut behind her, 'your curse comes too late.'

There had remained little enough of Irene to execute. He adjusted the soiled grandeur of the imperial cloak about his shoulders to protect him against the chill of dawn or of some premonition.

Then the doors of Irene's chamber opened. The physicians

emerged. Draped over one man's hands was a purple cloth. On it rested the imperial crown.

At a sign from Marric, he laid it on the porphyry throne. Then the physicians left.

'Guard the crown, Caius,' Marric ordered. 'Let no one touch it until the High Priest comes from the temple to purify it.'

Soon the embalmers would come, and Marric had no desire to linger here.

He left the audience chamber, ignoring the fact that everyone in the room had bowed. More soldiers and innumerable priests thronged the hall. They, too, bowed – except for the High Priest himself. He came to Marric and placed an arm about his shoulders, offering him support he had not realized he needed.

The enormous strain of his performance in the Hippodrome, of Stephana's death, and the long night of struggle, purgation and execution made him stagger. The priest guided him back down the hall towards the Emperor's suite. That had always been his father's place. Now it was his.

But duties still remained before he could collapse into the sleep that mind and body demanded.

'If the Varangian officers are fit for duty, let them be briefed. You should also send an embassy out to Audun. Tell him—' Marric smiled – 'tell him I want my bear. He can deliver it himself. I want messengers sent to Ellac and Uldin: perhaps they will attend my coronation. There is a captain at the West Gate . . . an Alexandrian, very reliable. Send him.'

In years to come, stories would be made, he supposed, of Marric, the Emperor who had been a slave. He might as well give the historians material to work with, or the singers would invent some for him. In his fashion, Thutmosis had tried to be kind. And the youth was loyal and capable, worthy of preferment.

When he came to the last obligation he could think of, his voice was only a hoarse whisper. 'Daphne,' he called.

Marric brought Daphne to kneel before him. She regarded him trustfully. For her, he supposed, he was still a man, not some half-divine representation of order. *Empire will be lonely*, Marric thought, looking down at Daphne's pretty, weary face. *It would be so simple, so simple* . . . the girl already idolized him. But a man who had been loved by Stephana could not mistake worship for love. That had been Irene's fatal error.

'What would you do now, Daphne?' he asked, raising her. 'No,' he shook his head gently. 'The palace is no place for you. Not without *her*.

'You have several choices, Daphne. When I bring Princess Alexa back, you may serve her. Or, after it is rebuilt, you may enter the Temple of Isis. Do you wish to marry? I will see you have a good dowry, and Nicephorus will help you choose a husband who can take care of you.'

'As if she were my own daughter or sister,' Nicephorus promised. 'You will live with my family, won't you, Daphne? My wife, Ariadne, will be glad of you.'

'That family of yours, Nico,' said Marric. 'I want to meet them.'

'After you have rested,' Nicephorus said. He grinned apologetically at the idea of commanding his Emperor.

'Daphne?'

'Sire, I wish . . . I wish to live quietly,' Daphne said. 'I do not want power, not like this. Not as a priestess either. I would always remind you of—' her eyes filled and she turned away for a minute. 'But a house, children . . . please, I would like the dowry.'

'You shall have it.' Marric bent and kissed her forehead. 'Take her home with you, Nico. When you have rested, come back. I need you with me.'

Nicephorus bowed, then left. The distance between Marric and the rest of the world increased.

I must find Alexa soon, soon. They had shared their childhood; Alexa was as royal as he, would not impose that hurtful distance upon him.

The High Priest guided him into his father's room. At his orders, servants produced hot water, a silken robe, and food and wine. Marric waved it aside.

'You should eat.'

'I should also see the Varangians, quiet the city, and tend to the Huns. And I need rest, as Nicephorus pointed out. But there is not time for me to do all of that now. So I will trust Marcellinus to keep awake just a little longer, and I will go to sleep. Someone get these lights out of here!'

The bed looked very soft, very rich. Heavy curtains – *I am going to become mortally weary of Tyrian purple* – turned the light of dawn into a comforting dusk. Marric waved the servants away. Still, the High Priest lingered. Marric wondered why he didn't withdraw. Surely he had duties which called him: a crown to purify, ceremonies of acclamation and coronation to arrange, so that people might know that their ruler had returned to guide them out of turmoil and dark sorceries.

'Your father, my Prince,' said the Priest. 'He would have been . . . most gratified.' He, too, bowed and left the room.

Marric glanced up at his retreating form, startled. He knew that Alexander had always loved him, that he had even – in a way – taken pride in him. But to satisfy his father, to please him – ah, he had never dreamed he would do that.

He lay down. He had no one to share this bed with. No empress yet occupied Antonia's apartments. *I must bring Alexa home.* Probably he had already had as much of companionship, of love, as any man deserved in one lifetime. But it would be good to have Alexa near as a sister, a companion, a lover.

Gods, he was tired. And lonely. Still, Alexander was gratified. The priest had said so. Marric sighed.

Then his memories of Stephana rose up to engulf him. The acerbic voice that had taunted him back to life in Alexandria, the frightened woman of whom he had demanded not only love but the conquest of fear. Now that Marric had a moment to himself, it would be good if he could weep.

His eyes started to burn. He lay on his back, hoping for the relief of tears, but none came. After a time, he gave up. He had been right when he said he could either rest or grieve. Sleep hit him like an undertow and dragged him down.

Chapter Twenty-eight

'The Emperor sleeps! Save your stories of what the barbarians said, or that ten thousand loaves are waiting to be filled with coins, until he rises. Get out!' That was old Valerius Marcellinus' voice. It woke Marric to the awareness that Irene was dead and he was Emperor. He felt no exultation. Since he conquered his emotions in the underground ways, he had felt nothing at all.

Food was brought in and he ate far more than he thought he could. The imperial servants said little to him about the coming Triumph, or about anything else. Despite his feeling of isolation, he was thankful for their silence. When they finally bowed themselves out backwards towards the door, Marric went to the window. The gardens were heavy with the odours of jasmine, iris and roses. He would never again be able to see a rose without recalling how Stephana had loved them. The scent of the roses mingled with the salt of the sea, borne to him on the evening winds, and made him melancholy. His weariness returned and he went back to bed. He could count on the Marcellini, father and grandson, to manage.

Marric slept. He had a strange and wonderful dream. He was walking in the gardens below his windows, when suddenly the gardens of the palace shifted, and fused with the tiny, exquisite garden of the safe house. The nightingale sang and water splashed into the white basin.

Towards him, over a pleasant lawn, Stephana walked. Marric's heart almost burst with joy as he ran to her, arms outstretched. Then he noticed the strangeness. No wind rustled her garments. Her feet did not quite rest on the ground. And when he flung his arms about her, they closed on nothing.

Stephana floated back what would have been a step or two, and looked at him. Her silvered hair hung loose down her back, the way he had loved to see it. Her eyes seemed larger and more shadowy than he remembered. In her hands, she held a red rose, the blossom resting between her breasts.

Slowly, Marric's arms fell to his sides. 'Have . . . have you really come back to me?' he asked. 'Why can I not hold you?'

Stephana moved closer to him. He was aware of her presence only by a faint sensation of mist which brushed his face as she raised her hand to stroke his cheek. And the scent of roses . . . even in this wraith-form it lingered about her. She gazed up at him, and though he could see her face clearly, he could not read her expression.

'What becomes of me now, love?' he asked. 'Do you come to tell me?'

Stephana laughed very softly. 'I am so new here, I can scarcely know what will befall *me*. The Powers say I am to guide people—'

'Can you be *my* guide?' Marric broke in eagerly.

'Oh my dearest, I wish I could! But yours is such a powerful fate that you will need a wiser guide than I, one long used to such a task. I . . . I but returned this one time to thank you.' Her face blazed with such love and joy that Marric gasped. This was Stephana as she really was, untrammelled by the bonds of her flesh and the memories of her last life, free to express the joy in her heart fully.

'To thank me?'

'For freeing me! I told you: it was destined that I direct all this final life towards helping one person. If my courage held, I would bring about his triumph and my own release. At first, I feared you. Mor – when you were Mor you needed so much from me – love, pity, even cruelty, so you would live on. You wanted *me*, and I could not refuse you.' Once again Marric felt mist brush his face. 'So we have our victories now, you and I.'

She started to drift away.

'Do you still love me?' he called after her.

'More than ever.'

'But is this all for us? Will you never come to me again?' Marric asked. His hands went out towards her. Again he touched nothing.

'I should be grieved, beloved, if you did not remember me. But I should be even more grieved if you remembered nothing else. Such as this—'

Marric followed her over to the fountain. Stephana raised her hands above it. The water splashed down, then clouded into a vision of a man and a woman whose hair was golden, almost brighter than the circlets they wore. And standing between them, Alexa.

'*There* lies your future!' Stephana exclaimed. 'When you feel most lonely, think of it. The gods bless you and cherish you, Marric, as I do.'

Then she was gone. 'Wait!' he cried. That woke him to the light of day.

The peacock mosaic on the floor shone as blindingly as the sunlight on the faint edge of the sea.

At the heavy door the captain of the Watch knocked three times. Marric's servants entered to prepare him for his Triumph. Caius Marcellinus entered with them. So did Nicephorus. Marcellinus wore the white and gold of the Candidatoi, Nicephorus a blue robe. *I will have Nico take the belt of civil service before long. I want him nearby.* Marric would tell him later.

'Your family, Nico?'

'They await your pleasure outside,' Nicephorus smiled. 'There has been a short delay. The Bearmaster is insisting that he inspect the quarters assigned to your bear before he takes his place in the procession.'

Marric drank wine and indicated that the other men join him, despite the shock of the cubiculars in attendance. Then they dressed him in a long, tight-sleeved tunic of white silk that rested easily on his scarred back. The marks of the lash on their ruler also shocked his attendants. Marric listened to details of his Triumph. He would descend to the harbour and sail towards the Golden Gate. Through it, as befitted a conqueror, he would enter his city.

'As if I had not already been living here for months,' he remarked. Nicephorus laughed. Even Marcellinus managed a faint smile. The servants were affronted. Marric assumed they would grow used to it.

Absurd, this ceremony – or was it? The people needed public affirmation that the land was back in the keeping of its rightful lord . . . or of law, as old Audun might say. In one sense, Marric could not *be* Emperor until he submitted to the ritual. Call it

249

another form of the initiation he had been denied, one that he was competent to handle now.

He waved away the hovering servants and put on gold-embroidered scarlet shoes himself. Then he stood and allowed them to drape the mantle of Empire over his shoulders. It had been almost miraculously cleansed of the grime and smoke of his passage through the inner ways. Only a faint trace of blood on the breast showed that it had ever been used to wrap a dead seeress.

The garments, Marric realized, were similar to a priest's robes. The thought amused him. But that was proper. A ruler consented to be the channel on earth between his realm and the gods.

He was to be crowned today! Why was he so calm? Surely he might expect to feel something more. If only Alexa stood beside him, arrayed as Empress in the robes of Isis, while they received the homage of the crowd and the ambassadors, he might not feel so lonely.

'Parade armour is on board ship, sire,' Marcellinus reminded him.

Respecting Marric's mood, Nicephorus followed him out silently. He presented his family: two daughters, a young son, and Ariadne, his wife. She was not pretty, but her face was gentle and kind. Daphne stood beside her and held the younger girl's hand.

A vindictive whisper distracted Marric's attention from his friend's family.

'No! Even if Irene did seize power, she is to be buried honourably,' he ordered. '*I* will not begin my reign with an outrage.' The minister bowed and fled to see to it.

The archons of the Fleet saluted Marric. They brought him on board a great gilded dromond with purple sails and trappings. It glided softly in the waters of the Bosphorus, ahead of many other ships. All along the seawall, soldiers cheered. The townspeople rang bells and wooden semantrons until the air echoed with their welcome.

They landed at Hebdomon. Marric changed into a purple tunic, the gold-washed parade armour, and a helmet on to which a crown sparkling with amethysts had been fitted. The Varangians awaited him. They were clad in dress scarlet. Their lancepoints and axes had been touched up with gold leaf. The Candidatoi stood nearby with swords drawn for the triumphal entry. Marric ordered them sheathed: no naked weapons would be allowed into the city today.

They brought him a white horse to ride, an Arab, all prance and fiery nostrils. A heavy necklet of pearls encircled its arched neck. Marric mounted and the parade formed up behind him – the Varangians and Candidatoi nearest, followed by a train of other soldiers, officers of the civil service, and patricians. Riding among the foreign nobles, on a horse that almost bent beneath his great weight, was Audun Bearmaster. The men nearest him kept a respectful distance from the white bear that danced behind Audun's horse at the end of a gold chain. Sometimes the bear walked upright. At other times it scrambled about on all fours, scattering people to right and left. Ellac and Uldin led a troop of riders who wore their bows unstrung in token of peace. Even the dusty coats of the steppe ponies had been brushed into something approaching a shine.

The procession entered the city. Along the line of march, people had hung their choicest tapestries: embroideries and rugs from Persia, silks from Babylon. Every balcony held men and women dressed in their finest. Children tossed flowers and perfumes at the men below.

Outside the Golden Gate, Marric dismounted before the Temple of Horus. Before entering the temple, he removed his sword and prostrated himself humbly. He could not believe that he had ever scoffed at these ceremonies. Now priests, bearing the emblem of the hawk, joined the procession. Marric mounted and rode towards the Golden Gate. Before entering, he bowed to his city as if saluting an overlord. The priestesses of Isis draped him and his men with garlands. Children nearby scattered roses and sweet herbs.

There had been a time not long since when the scent of roses had meant things more quiet, less glorious, but infinitely more to be cherished. For the people cheering, Marric was the gods' representative on earth, not a man. He would almost have traded it for the sight of one slender, silver-haired women. But she had died to bring him to this moment. He must not cheapen her gift.

Past obelisks and fountains, beneath the huge triumphal arch of the Golden Gate, Marric rode. Finally, the procession reached the main square.

A booth had been built near the Temple of Osiris. The High Priest advanced. He bore in outstretched hands the diadem that had last rested on an empty throne. He looked fierce, satisfied, as he laid the crown on Marric's brow.

Accept my life, Marric prayed. There would be no journey to World's End, no gentle-voiced lover, nothing beyond his duties for him now. And he must be content. He hoped the priest was satisfied. They had both waited for this moment.

One of the protonotaries handed him a lance and he climbed up the steps to the temple. One by one, the captives from Irene's reign were brought before him. Protocol called for Marric to remain motionless, unseeing, while soldiers cast the prisoners down beneath his foot. Marric stood motionless as his man moved the lance he held until its gilded point touched the captives' throats in token of the Empire's power to take their lives. The crowd cheered. Marric awoke slightly from the trance in which he had ridden and received the adulation of the city. He smiled as mechanically as the metal lions he had admired as a boy, and laid the lance aside. The High Priest nodded in approval. Judgement there would be, and retribution, but on captives he had taken by himself, like the pirates he had vowed to sweep from his seas.

The foreign ambassadors were pleased, too. Audun's laugh bellowed out. Finally, when the protonotaries finished handing out the ten thousand loaves that Marric had woken to news of, he was free to ride towards the Hippodrome in a four-horse chariot. He shocked a few dignitaries by driving it himself.

Snapping the reins over the backs of the four white stallions, Marric drove out into the arena. Faster and faster the horses ran around the spina, while the crowd roared approval. The wind against his face refreshed him. For the first time that day his smile was unforced. Then he left his chariot, almost regretfully, for the royal box.

Into the tiers below crowded the rest of the procession, even the captives. Now the Hippodrome was dazzling with the bright clothing of racing factions, tumblers, jugglers and dancers. The actors filed by. One of them caught Marric's glance and waved at him. It was the man who had played Xuthus. Good work, he seemed to say, one artist's approval of another.

Marric flung back his head and laughed, his detachment gone. Indubitably historians would call this the supreme achievement of his life. He would wager that Nicephorus was already honing phrases for the inevitable biography. In it, he would have to be the Emperor, not the man – even though Nico knew better.

He rose from his throne, went to the front of the kathisma, and held up his arms for silence.

'Emperor you hail me, and Emperor I am!' he shouted to his people. 'I am Marric Antonius Alexander, son of Alexander and Antonia, who rule beyond the Horizon while I, as Horus-on-Earth, am viceregent here. But where is my Empress?'

He paused to let tension build in the waiting crowd. Of course they had heard the rumours which Irene's creatures had spread. They must be wondering. For if the Emperor were necessary to this land, equally so was the Empress.

'Listen to a vision revealed to me this very night. Alexa, rightful Isis, still lives!'

The crowd's frenzied cheers silenced Marric, but only for a brief while.

'Guided by Audun, Bearmaster of the Aescir and a great friend of our House, she passed into the Kingdom of the West, into the Misty Isles, where the rulers honour her as the favoured daughter of the Goddess. I' – he would not use the 'we' of imperial propriety; 'we' would wait for Alexa's return – 'swear to you that I shall not rest until I have gone into the West and, just as Isis restored Osiris to his people, brought back the Princess to rule at my side.'

Just as on the night he played Apollo in this very arena, Marric felt himself united to his audience by groundswells of emotion; deep, tidal surges of rightness. They channelled from his people into him, and from him out again to nourish them.

What if Irene had cursed him never again to know peace? This union was enough for him – almost.

'So I swear to you, this first day of my reign!'

Julian May
The Many-Coloured Land £2.95
Book One in the Saga of the Exiles

The year 2034 was when a French physicist discovered a one-way fixed-focus timewarp into the Rhône valley of six million years ago. By the start of the 22nd century, there are those who seek to escape a world of technological perfection – the misfits and mavericks of the future, who pass through the doors of time and enter a battleground of two warring races from a distant planet.

'Grips the reader and doesn't let go' VONDA McINTYRE

The Golden Torc £2.95
Book Two in the Saga of the Exiles

Exiled beyond the time-portal, six million years in the past, the misfits of the 22nd century become enmeshed in the age-old war between two alien races. In this strange world, each year brings the ritual Grand Combat between the tribal Firvulag and the decadent city-dwelling Tanu, possessors of the mind-armouring necklet, the golden torc.

'Altogether enchanting and engrossing . . . I was captivated by its glamorous, sinister movement through the misty forests of Earth's true past' FRITZ LEIBER

The Nonborn King £2.95
Book Three in the Saga of the Exiles

The dominion of the Tanu has been broken, and in the aftermath of cataclysm Aiken Drum seizes his hour to grasp control of the Pliocene world. Some, human and Tanu, rally to him – and others fear and hate him. The Grand Master, Elizabeth, the mad Felice, the goblin hordes of the Firvulag – all are thrust into a violent and stormy struggle for irresistible power.

Julian May
The Adversary £2.95

Aiken Drum is king of the Many-Coloured Land . . . the last chapter in the Saga of the Exiles has begun. The Firvulag are rising, and the children of the metapsychic rebels are racing to reopen the time-gate back to the Galactic Milieu. Marc Romillard, defeated leader of the rebellion, takes up his destined role in the power play, determined to keep the gate sealed and to create the new race of Mental Man. Which side will he aid when Tanu meet Firvulag in the last great contest of the exile world?

A Pliocene Companion   £2.50

The Saga of the Exiles, the critically acclaimed science fiction quartet, has become an international bestseller. *A Pliocene Companion* now follows, and it is essential reading for all followers of the Saga. It contains a descriptive listing of all the characters, a chronology, the author's original maps, two interviews with Julian May herself, and much more. The book offers the reader a chance to explore further the surroundings of a world six million years in the past.

All these books are available at your local bookshop or newsagent, or can be ordered direct from the publisher. Indicate the number of copies required and fill in the form below.

Send to: **CS Department, Pan Books Ltd., P.O. Box 40, Basingstoke, Hants.   RG21 2YT.**

or phone: 0256 469551 (Ansaphone), quoting title, author and Credit Card number.

Please enclose a remittance* to the value of the cover price plus: 60p for the first book plus 30p per copy for each additional book ordered to a maximum charge of £2.40 to cover postage and packing.

*Payment may be made in sterling by UK personal cheque, postal order, sterling draft or international money order, made payable to Pan Books Ltd.

Alternatively by Barclaycard/Access:

Card No.

Signature:

Applicable only in the UK and Republic of Ireland.

While every effort is made to keep prices low, it is sometimes necessary to increase prices at short notice. Pan Books reserve the right to show on covers and charge new retail prices which may differ from those advertised in the text or elsewhere.

NAME AND ADDRESS IN BLOCK LETTERS PLEASE:

....

Name —————————————————————————

Address —————————————————————————

—————————————————————————

—————————————————————————

—————————————————————————

3/87